POST
STORIES
1948

THE SATURDAY EVENING POST STORIES

1948

RANDOM HOUSE · NEW YORK

FIRST PRINTING

CONTENTS

POST
STORIES

1948

THE STOLEN BELT

By WILLIAM B. MAHONEY

KYRL'S QUAY looked down at the River Lee, and across it at Pope's Quay, and above that, at the hill that was Shandon. The houses along Kyrl's Quay were five-story tenements, and one morning in late autumn a boy stood in the front room of a flat on that street as his mother adjusted a leather belt around his waist.

"There now; stand back," she said.

He moved three steps, until his back came up against the table.

"There," she said. "That's a real present from your Aunt Mary." She gazed admiringly at the belt. The boy looked down at it and put his hands on it to feel the way the leather was worked.

"No, Tommy, you'll be smudging it up now," his mother said. "Don't you know how to take care of anything?" She nodded and put her head to one side. "'T is a fine family you were born into," she went on. "A credit to the countryside. A distinguished family. Never forget that, Tommy. On your mother's side you come from the best blood in Ireland. No drunkards. No rakehells. 'T is like your Aunt Mary to be sending you a present like that, all the way from America. 'T is like my own dear family, God bless them, to be thinking of others."

The mother sat then and put rough hands to straightening the boy's shirt and smoothing his hair. Her eyes watched him closely as she talked.

"'T is you I can read like a book," she said. "You don't believe me now. You think your old mother is blathering about her family again. Someday you'll be proud of it. The best blood in holy old Ireland."

The boy wanted to finger the intricate working of the leather. The mother, watching him, read the perplexed wanting on his face.

"'T is a fine owl fool you'll turn out to be, I'm afraid," she

3

said. "A dreamer, an owl fool like your father, maybe." She paused and looked intently into his face. "Maybe someday you'll be making me ashamed of you. I wouldn't be surprised. 'T is a dreaming fool you'd be indeed if I didn't watch over you like a mother hen." She pressed a sharp finger against his chest. "You just love your mother and everything will be all right," she said. "Hear that? No matter what kind of a thing you are. If you do that ——"

She gave him a playful slap, not knowing her own strength and the shock of it to the boy.

"Go on now," she said. "You'll be late for school if you don't hurry. Get on with ye."

He nodded mutely, pressing his back against the sharp edge of the table and hearing it creak behind him. The mother moved forward suddenly and threw her arms around him. She kissed him, nearly smothering him in the huge motherly embrace. Then she seized his shoulders and shook him.

"Are you going to stand around all day now?" she asked. "You'll be late for school again. Ah, the trouble you are to me, the worst of my sons. Hurry up now and get to school, and make sure you learn something today. Mind you, you'll have to stop that owl-foolish dreaming before it gets you into trouble." She turned away and stopped again. "And mind you take care of that belt," she said. She picked up the papers from the packaging and crumpled them in her hands as she went into the kitchen.

The boy looked around the room, gloomy in the November morning. His eyes caught the brooding lithograph of the crucified Christ on the wall, looking down at him with foreboding, as ever. Suddenly he put his hands on the belt and felt it. It was rich and smooth and soft and ridged. It was a cowboy belt. It was his belt. He would take care of it.

All morning in school he was conscious of it. It was around him like a warmth. It made him feel good all over, because it was such a wonderful belt and it was his. It would be his always. He would wear it when he grew up, and still it would be the best belt in the world. It would be fine to be grown up and to have had that belt always, ever since he was a boyen in the fourth class, like he was now.

The belt made him see things differently too. He noticed how shabby most of the other boys were, and how their trousers drooped, and the ways they kept them up. Joe Buckley, there, in the front row, he had a belt too. But it was just a belt. Marty Grogan kept his pants up with a piece of string, but everyone knew that his people were poor and that his father drank. Dinny Keefe had a belt that pretended to be a cowboy's, but you could see it was a five-and-ten imitation. Maybe he stole it. A lot of the Cork boys would steal from the five-and-ten. Kevin McCarthy had a set of paints he got that way.

The boy noticed how pale most of the others were. They were thin and pale. It was queer that his new belt made him notice those things as he never had before. It was different today, and all because of it. He ran his fingers across it again, under his jacket, and smiled to himself.

"Tommy," the teacher, Brother Flynn, said, "Tommy, are you listening to the class and all? Or are you dreaming again? Come up now to the front of the class, Tommy, and we'll have a word on it."

Tommy saw suddenly that the class was watching him. They were laughing a little, partly at him and partly to please Brother Flynn. Tommy got up and walked up front, past the rows of desks, and as he went he realized that Brother Flynn had probably been speaking to him and he had not heard at first. Brother Flynn was drawing the leather strap slowly through his hands, looking mildly regretful.

"Hold your hand out now, Tommy," Brother Flynn said. "You'll get six for that."

He brought the leather down, high on Tommy's hands, up near the wrist, and Tommy felt silence fall on the room and the smiles going away. Then he stopped noticing, because the pain came in a moment.

The boy sat in a sunny corner of the yard to eat his lunch. The jacket was still held tight about him. He thought of the belt and smiled to himself, and listened to Marty Grogan talk and the others laughing together.

"Tommy took six this morning," said Grogan. He laughed

again. "There's hardly a day passes that Tommy doesn't get in some kind of trouble. He always gets caught."

They were laughing at him quietly, Tommy saw, except for Paddy Kelly, whose huge, mournful eyes in a thin white face stared at him with the unspoken sympathy that Paddy felt for everybody.

"It didn't hurt," Tommy said foolishly.

They laughed again at his lie.

"Naw," Dinny Keefe said. "It don't hurt at all."

"You get used to it," Marty Grogan said. "After a bit, you even get to like it."

Tommy watched the other classes playing in the yard. The third class was at the usual game of taking prisoners and putting them in the great wire wastebaskets, which were big enough to hold four boys at one time. Tommy watched them and finished his lunch, which consisted of three slices of bread and margarine. Somebody nudged him, and it was Paddy Kelly, silently sneaking him a piece of toffee. "Go ahead," Paddy said. "Take it." He was whispering. Tommy shook his head. Paddy was trying to cheer him for the laughter and the beating in school. But Paddy couldn't have more than that one piece. Tommy couldn't take it. He was conscious of the belt under his coat, and that Paddy's sympathy was unearned.

"Look," he said to Paddy. He opened his jacket and showed the belt.

Paddy Kelly whistled. Marty Grogan's eyes widened, and Dinny Keefe fell silent. The belt stood out, raw and new and beautiful. For a moment Tommy felt that it could not possibly be his. He loved the belt, but it made him uneasy. Their silence flawed his possession of it, somehow. It was as if he had stolen it.

"Holy Mike!" Grogan said. He was studying it close up, his head down, and Tommy saw that Marty's ear was running again. "Holy Mike!" Grogan said again. "Where did you get it, Tommy?"

"My Aunt Mary in America," Tommy said. "She's in a big business there. I think she's very rich."

They were silent again, staring at the belt. Tommy felt of the belt uneasily. He knew he was repeating his mother's statements of the morning. The boasting had shamed him then, and it shamed him now, but he couldn't stop.

"My mother's family is a famous family," he said. "Some of them are in America. They are all kinds of things—priests and writers and businessmen. They have lashings of money."

"Is it a cowboy belt?" Paddy Kelly asked, in awe.

"Yes," Tommy said. "It's the same kind of belt Tom Mix wears in the movies."

Grogan whistled a tune flatly through his teeth. It was The Mountains of Mourne, which Grogan whistled whenever his mind was working fast.

"Come on; we're all finished eating," Grogan said. "We'll play a game of kick-the-can. Tommy will be on my side."

Before he knew it, Tommy was lined up with Grogan and Keefe, and facing Paddy Kelly on the other team. Paddy smiled at him, and when it came to catching Tommy, he just couldn't seem to do it.

"That's a very wonderful belt you have there," Grogan said to Tommy as they walked back toward the classroom. He was close and intimate beside Tommy. "I'd give half of my life to have a belt like that," Grogan said.

Tommy touched the belt gingerly again, and his unease came out in the same upended way as before.

"Hell," he said to Grogan, "I might get another next year. Maybe even sooner. My Aunt Mary or Uncle Jim in America might be sending on another, or one of those special guns. It might even be a real gun," he said. "But if I get another belt, Grogan, you can have this maybe."

Grogan shook his head sadly. "No, I suppose they won't be doing that," he said. "I suppose I'll never have a belt like that. My people," Grogan said, "are just poor people. Our owl house up there by the Cattle Market will fall down any day, my father thinks."

They were silent, weighing the misery of Grogan's life, its dark hopelessness, as compared with the galaxy of Tommy's relatives in America.

"My ear has been giving me hell today," Grogan said. "You know, Tommy, you were the best player in the yard. You're getting better every day."

This, Tommy realized, was gross flattery. Yet it found a weakness and a shame to thrive on within him. He felt behind it in Grogan a weight of hatred and envy, but the flattery warmed him and brought for the moment a feeling of comradeship and pity, and an elation that he was accepted in the company of Grogan and the Cattle Market toughs. He thought of Grogan's ear and Paddy Kelly's cough.

"Lend me the belt for a minute, Tommy," Grogan said. "Let me put it around my waist just this once."

"I'd like to do that, Grogan," Tommy said. "But I couldn't. My mother ——" he started to say, and stopped. How could he tell Grogan that his mother had warned him? How state in cold daylight the weight of childishness this meant, this weakness and fear of his mother? "I can't," he said. "You know I'd like to."

Grogan looked at him with surprise. "You can't let me wear it for a minute?" he asked. "Would I get it dirty, do you think? It isn't good enough for the likes of me, I suppose, and you with all your rich relatives in America."

"I didn't mean that at all," Tommy said. "You know that, Grogan."

"I don't know it," Grogan said. "Here, let me put it on for a minute. It won't hurt, will it? I'll give it back to you the next second, man."

Tommy opened the belt and took it off slowly, fumbling, with a weakness in his fingers. He wanted to say no, no, no, but his tongue was silent. He handed the belt slowly to Grogan. Grogan handed him the piece of string that he used as a belt, and Tommy held it, watching the other boy put the belt on, watching him tighten it, watching him look up slowly at Tommy again.

"The class is waiting, Tommy," Grogan said. "We'll have to hurry in there or you'll be in trouble with Brother Flynn again."

"Give me back the belt and we'll go in," Tommy said.

"I'll do it inside; I'll sneak it to you," Grogan said. "Come on; we have to hurry in now."

"Give me back the belt," Tommy said.

There was a laugh in Grogan's eyes now. They said plainly, slyly, with jeering, that now the belt was on his, Grogan's, waist and it would not be coming back so quick. For Tommy now there came a coldness into the watery air of Cork. He saw that they were still standing on the iron stairs outside the classroom, alone, and he knew that Brother Flynn would be out to look for them any moment. Grogan stood there, not answering the demand, and now the door behind Tommy swung slowly open.

A hand took Tommy and spun him into the classroom. "What's the matter with you today, Tommy man?" Brother Flynn asked. "Don't you like our school? Would you like me to send you home to your mother with a little note? Would you like to talk to the head?"

Tommy stood mute, and felt Grogan sidle past him quietly, aiming for his seat.

"Hold up there, Grogan," Brother Flynn said. "I see you too. You'll both come to the front of the class now, and we'll have a little example on promptness for the others to remember."

His small, frosty blue eyes regarded them for a moment. They stood in front of the silent class.

"I'll have to give you ten, Tommy," Brother Flynn said. "It's the second time today, you know. You can take them on the left hand if you want." He turned to Grogan. "You'll get three, Martin Grogan," he said. "And I hope you have a better memory than Tommy here."

"I'm sorry," Grogan said. "I was trying my best to get in. I didn't want to be late."

"All right," Brother Flynn said. "Go to your seat, boy. . . .
"Hold out your hand, Tommy."

Injustice and confusion flamed in the boy. He stood there, his tongue twisted, and tears very near his eyes. And because the utmost humiliation would be for him to cry in front of the class, he clenched his teeth. He couldn't speak about the belt. It was too complicated. He'd get it back, somehow, at once. He held out his hand again. He'd get the belt back, he said to himself, if he had to kill Grogan for it.

It was nearing the end of the school day when Grogan held his hand up, two fingers out. Brother Flynn nodded, and

Tommy saw, with shocked terror, that Grogan was getting up and leaving the room.

He might not come back. Tommy held his hand up too.

"You'll have to wait for Grogan to come back," Brother Flynn said. "Sit down, Tommy. You can wait a minute."

Tommy sat down. He waited in torment. He heard the last bell ring. Grogan didn't come back.

Tommy was sitting in the yard by himself, watching the other boys go out. Paddy Kelly came along and sat beside him.

"What's the matter with you, Tomeen?" asked Paddy.

"Grogan got my belt," Tommy said. "I can't go home and face my mother without it."

Paddy was silent, thinking this over. "Did he knock you down and take it off of you?" Paddy asked after a while. It was the kindest thing he could ask, knowing as well as Tommy that it was not the truth.

"No," Tommy said. "He wanted it for a second. But then he wouldn't give it back to me."

"Oh," Paddy said. "You gave it to him."

"Only for a second," Tommy said.

"I'm afraid Grogan won't say that," Paddy said. They were both from the Cattle Market area, and he knew Grogan and his kind like his own brothers. "Even if you prove he has it, Grogan will say he gave you something for it."

"But I didn't get anything," Tommy said.

Paddy shook his head. "I have to go now, Tommy. I have to do some things for my mother. She's sick again. Don't wait for Grogan to bring it back. Take it off him. And do it today, if you can find him. That's the only chance you have at all."

Paddy left, and Tommy felt his eyes filling with tears as he watched the thin figure go across the yard and down the steps and out of sight. He wasn't crying about Paddy Kelly's mother, who, it was said, had consumption. He was crying because he felt so lonely and his belt was gone and somehow he would have to get it back from Grogan. That would be bitter.

Tommy circled the long way around toward the Cattle Market. He started up Fair Hill, and changed his mind and went down Blackpool and up past Shandon and the long way down to the river. He went along Pope's Quay and then up the steps toward Blarney Street. Terror drove him into the circling. He couldn't go home and he couldn't go straight to Grogan's house.

The Cattle Market was on the rise of ground above Blarney Street. There in the center was the slaughterhouse and the stench. Around it were some of the wretched slums in Cork City, in the dead time we are writing of, after the First World War.

Going up through the slums, Tommy saw the shawlies in their doorways, and cringed from them. He had seen them battling in the public squares, drunk, on Saturdays. A shawlie was a woman too poor or too ravaged or too branded to wear anything but the black shawl over her head and shoulders when she went out.

The gray old buildings leaned into the street, along the littered alleys in the dark corners of the slums. He found Grogan's street and went slowly along it, looking at the warped doors and the mold and crumbling of the houses.

He knocked at the door of Grogan's house and waited. After a while he heard slow steps coming down, and an old man went past him, unseeing, tapping his slow cane and staring ahead out of rheumy and fading eyes.

"Could I see Marty Grogan here?" Tommy asked, stepping along backwards to keep in front of the old man.

The old man walked on silently and sightlessly. Tommy gave it up and went into the dark hallway. The damp walls pressed around him, and the blind faces of doors stared at him. The stairs going up had gaps in them where the wood had rotted away.

He knocked on the first door to the right and waited without result. He knocked on the other door and heard slow steps answer. The door creaked open. A gaunt face looked out at Tommy. He saw the body draped in a black shawl, and with a start it came to him that Grogan's mother was a shawlie. The woman made a hissing sigh and waited for him to speak. Tommy fumbled with a stiff tongue and finally found words.

"Is Marty Grogan there?" Tommy asked.

"Who wants to know?" The woman stared at him with icy eyes in her haggard face.

"I go to school with him," Tommy said. "My name is Tommy Connolly."

The woman was silent for a moment, staring at him, weighing his clothes and background.

"Is my boy in trouble?" she asked.

Tommy shook his head rapidly before he could speak. "The brothers didn't ask me to come here," he said. "I want to see him myself."

"He's not in," the woman said. She slammed the door.

Tommy stood in the dark hallway, feeling like an alien, an enemy in the house. He waited. He heard people go past outside, and noises in the house. In the Grogan flat he heard a crash and a curse. He started and moved deeper into the shadow of the door, to be out of sight. He waited. Time crawled past, dark and unseen, and felt only in misery. Time went past, and Tommy weighed it, weighed himself, and twisted inside himself.

Then there was a spatter of steps outside, steps racing up to the door, and he heard Grogan's voice shouting, "Farewell, me laddies!" to unseen friends outside, and Grogan had burst in the door and was facing Tommy, laughing with wildness. The laughter went out of his face and the wildness went after it, and cunning came onto it—cunning and alertness and savagery.

He turned his back on Tommy without a word, and went to go in his door. Tommy caught him by the shoulder.

"I've been waiting here for you, Grogan," Tommy said.

Grogan said nothing. His shoulder quivered, trembling under Tommy's hand. There was violence repressed in the tremble, fear pounding with hate in his heart.

"What d'ye want?"

"You know what I want."

"I don't know you. Who are ye, bothering me here in my own house?"

Tommy put his other hand on Grogan's shoulder and shook. "Come off it, Grogan," he said. "Give me back my belt."

"Your belt?" Grogan said. "I don't know what you mean. I don't have your rotten old belt."

Tommy pushed the other boy up against the door and thrust against him. "Give me back my belt," he said again.

"Take your hands off me," Grogan said. "Let go of me. Let me alone."

The door swung slowly open behind Grogan, and his mother was standing there, still wrapped in the shawl.

"What is it, Marty boy?" she asked. Her eyes swung and fastened, glittering, on Tommy. "What is it now, my son?"

"This fellow is bothering me, ma," Grogan said. "He won't let me alone. He was going to hit me."

The shawled woman limped out into the hall and put a gray, horned hand on Tommy's shoulder.

"You let my boy alone," she said. "You go back to your own house and stay away from us. Leave us to our own troubles." Her voice rose. "Maybe you'd like a box on your little pink ears?" she asked.

"He has my belt," Tommy said. "He took my belt off of me today, and he won't give it back. I want it back or I'll tell the police."

"The peelers indeed," the woman said. "You'd be going to the dirty old peelers, would you? How would you like to end up in the river on a dark night?" she asked in a fierce whisper.

Grogan stepped forward now and threw open his jacket. His trousers were tied with string again.

"I don't have any belt on," Grogan said. "I don't know what he's talking about, ma."

The woman's hand cuffed Tommy smartly and sent him back against the outer door. "Get out of here now," she said. "Let my poor boyeen alone. Go on. Go on with ye."

Tears came to Tommy's eyes again, and he turned and went out the door and down the steps. He walked along the alley toward a street, and suddenly something struck him on the back. It was a piece of cinder. When he looked around, Grogan was hunting around for another missile, and there were boys running toward him from farther up the alley. They were yelling, and they would be Grogan's friends.

Tommy began to run. He couldn't stop running, after a while. He got down to Kyrl's Quay and up the stairs and into their flat before he stopped. And then he stood still, facing his mother, seeing his other brothers sitting, staring, and on them all the knowledge that Tommy had been running from something and that there was terror and despair on his face.

He stood there panting, and before him there was this tableau of people sitting and watching him, and his mother standing before the stove, the kettle in her hand, staring at him, weighing him. And Tommy knew, too, that unerringly she was probing for the truth, and that the belt and what he had done were slowly coming into her mind.

Tommy lay in the darkened bedroom and listened, still sobbing to himself convulsively. He stifled the sobs and fought them and tried to hear, because in the other room they were talking about him. He lay on his face. His back and hind quarters were sore and blistered from the beating.

He had told the truth, and that was his mistake. He knew it. If he had said Grogan had beaten him and taken the belt, like Paddy Kelly had hinted he should say, they would have understood, and blamed Grogan. This way they blamed him, Tommy, as a fool.

"He'll have to get it back himself. The boy will have to grow up and fight his own battles," his brother Terence said.

"Maybe we ought to talk to this Grogan woman," said his brother Mike.

"That wouldn't do," Terence said. "He has to learn this is a jungle, this world. There's wild beasts in the streets, and he has to stand up himself and be ready for them, or he'll go to ruin."

"No, boys, not now," his mother said. "You'll be at one of your arguments again."

"If it wasn't for the English, we'd have something in this land," Mike said. "If it wasn't for the Free State sellout of our hopes, we wouldn't be living in this bitter, beaten country. It isn't Tommy's fault, in a way. We're not all the same. It isn't a world of beasts, now. It's a world of hunger and misery."

Terence's voice was angry. "Don't be bringing in the IRA again," he said. "It's not the fault of the Free State. It's the way things are, all over. What do you think the other boys saw when they looked at that belt on Tommy? Who wouldn't want it?"

"They only want it because they have nothing. Nothing, do you hear?" Mike said. "Misery, wretchedness and defeat. A bitter brew," and Mike's hand thumped the table, as it always did in an argument.

The mother groaned. "Will you let me alone with this arguing now?" she said. "I'm tired of this ranting. Let me think about it myself. I'll give Tommy another day to get it back, that's all. Let him get it tomorrow, and get it himself, if he wants a quiet life. That's enough of it now."

If he could only forget about the belt, Tommy thought. He'd be glad Grogan had it. But he couldn't stand it when Grogan started wearing it and the others laughed at him. And nobody would let him forget it. He would be disgraced and a fool forever if he didn't get it back.

He fell asleep into a trouble of dreams and woke crying during the night, shouting from his sleep. His brother Mike moved angrily next to him in the bed. "Shut up now, Tommy boy," he said. "Shut up and go back to sleep. I'll help you out if I get a chance." But Mike was only talking in his sleep, Tommy knew. This was his own problem, and Mike couldn't do anything about it. Mike didn't even go to the monastery, but to the trade school. Tommy wished he were as old as Mike, and listened now for a second, half asleep, to the noises in the house, and watched shapes in the darkness before his closed lids, and fell down a wall into sleep again. Something peaceful came to him briefly out of the terror, just at the poised, balanced moment when sleep took over, and then was lost in dark tides, like the River Lee outside, and an evil like the dead body that Saturday twilight and the women yelling along the quays as it went down, the face twisted and bloated and disappearing into the shadows and the tides and death. In sleep, Tommy did not know the body or sense that it stood for something slain, maimed, a part that went out of life with youth, and had to be banned and forgotten, and that was left floating forever down the tides of sleep.

He went out the next day with his mother's warning ringing in his ears all the way up across the North Gate Bridge and then up Shandon Street and so along to the monastery school, which is where he was being trained to be a citizen.

She had told him, "Don't come back without it, boy."

He was early, and he waited beside the gate and watched

the boys come in. Paddy Kelly came along and stopped beside him. "Did you get it?" Paddy asked without needing to.

"No," Tommy said, "but I'll get it today. I'll get it some way, Paddy." He kept his voice straight, though a surge of pity for himself threatened it.

Paddy waited beside him with his small cough, smiling at the others going in, turning worried eyes on Tommy in between. After a while, Grogan came along with three other boys, and he was laughing and wild-looking again.

Tommy stepped in front of him, and silently now Grogan regarded him. "I want it back," Tommy said.

Grogan smiled. Without a word he opened his jacket. There was a string holding up his pants. The other boys burst out laughing. Tommy watched Grogan and the others go past, and on up through the gates into the school yard, and was still standing there when Paddy shook his arm.

"Come on, Tommy," Paddy said. "You'll be late for class and in trouble again."

Tommy went with him, up to the classroom. Where could Grogan have put the belt, he asked himself, and found no answer. He was certain of one thing: Grogan would have hid it. He wouldn't trust another of the boys with it.

Tommy sat dazed in class through the morning, and Brother Flynn let him alone. Tommy felt him watching with puzzlement, sensing the trouble Tommy had on him. During arithmetic time, when they were busy with a test, he put his pencil down and went up to Brother Flynn.

"Could I speak to you for a moment, sir?" he asked.

"Go ahead, go ahead," Brother Flynn said, "if it's important."

"Marty Grogan took a belt off of me yesterday," Tommy said. "He won't give it back, and it was a new present from America. I have to get it back, my mother says."

Brother Flynn nodded. "We'll speak to Grogan about it."

He called, and Grogan got up slowly from his seat and came up to them, doing his best to look innocent, Tommy saw, and doing it well.

"Did you get a belt off Tommy here?" Brother Flynn asked without any preamble.

Grogan shook his head. "I did not, sir," he said.

"Are you sure of that?"

"Yes, sir. I don't know anything about his belt."

"He does know," Tommy said. The class was watching now. "Dinny Keefe knows I had it yesterday, and Paddy Kelly knows Grogan got it."

Brother Flynn called again. Kelly and Keefe came up. "Did Grogan take this boy's belt?" Brother Flynn asked.

They turned blank faces on him.

Keefe shrugged. "I don't know anything about a belt, sir," he said.

"I showed it to you yesterday lunch," Tommy said.

Keefe looked puzzled. "Maybe I heard something about a belt," he said. "But I don't remember. I was busy playing kick-the-can." The brothers frowned on this game. It was clever of Keefe, Tommy knew, as it changed the subject neatly.

"If I catch you at that game again, you'll hear about it," Brother Flynn said. "You can go back."

Keefe went back and sat down.

"Tommy says you know about the belt," Brother Flynn said to Paddy Kelly. "Now speak up with the truth, boy."

Paddy shook his head. His eyes touched Tommy's with sadness for a moment, and then turned away, back to Brother Flynn. "It's the same as Dinny Keefe," he said. "I think maybe I heard somebody mention a belt sometime, but yesterday I was playing that game. I don't remember anything, sir. I was minding my own business."

Brother Flynn shrugged. "Sit down," he said to Paddy, who went slowly back to his desk. The teacher stared at the two boys. "Maybe Grogan took it," he told Tommy. "There's no proof of it, though. Your witnesses didn't stand up. Are you sure there just wasn't a fight between you when you were late yesterday?"

His eyes watched Tommy, and Tommy could see in them, dimly, a pleasure in the situation. Brother Flynn was enjoying it. Another time he would give Grogan the strap for this. But not now. He was leaving it up to Tommy, because Tommy was a dreamer in class. That was clear.

"Thank you, sir," Tommy said. He went back to his desk and sat down. He felt Grogan go past him, sidling and quiet and mouselike, and knew that the other was laughing inside.

Tommy waited. Time crawled and he felt the others watching. When he would look up, he would see the smiling eyes of Grogan's friends on him, laughing secretly. They knew; it would get all around the playground this lunchtime. It would unless Tommy did something about it.

Slowly his anger at Paddy went away. Paddy was minding his own business, like he said. He was Tommy's friend, but his people were as poor as Grogan's. He couldn't tell on Grogan and get him into trouble. That was different from siding with Tommy in a fight. Brother Flynn was authority, and you didn't go to that kind of authority. Not in a fight like this. You had to settle it yourself, and your mother and Paddy and Brother Flynn would only make it worse if you tried to make them do it for you. You couldn't talk to Grogan, because Grogan would talk for a year and say something different every day. You would have to take it away from Grogan, and that was all, no matter how you did it.

Time went by, and then there was the lunch bell. Tommy went out quietly. He left his sandwiches behind, lacking an appetite for them. He went past the secret smile of Brother Flynn. He went out into the yard and sought out Grogan and faced him, with the other boys, Grogan's friends, around, and Paddy Kelly showing up at his side like a shadow.

"Grogan," Tommy said, "we're going to fight. Come on now."

Grogan laughed. This was what he wanted. He was sure of himself in this. Tommy, the soft dreamer, could never beat him. He nodded.

"Leave one of your friends," Tommy said. "One is enough. Paddy will come with me." Paddy did.

Grogan beckoned to one of the boys, and the four went quietly along to the hedge at the inner side of the yard, and along its shadow to the path near the Blackpool boundary. They found the bald spot in the bushes, and Grogan took off his jacket and squared off, the smile creasing his face. Tommy kept his jacket on. He went in fast, striking at Grogan's face, and felt blows come back. He drove through them and crashed into Grogan as desperation and strength flooded into him.

Everything came all together, with a smell like the River Lee and a dead body drifting out on the tides. In an access of rage, the humiliation and defeats came back to Tommy now, the tones of his brothers' voices talking about him, the whip-lash of his mother's tongue, the terror in the dark hallway that was Grogan's home, and the panting, frantic race back to his own house.

Hands hauled at him, and he twisted out of them. He was on top of Grogan, and he was beating Grogan's head steadily and remorselessly into the dirt, lifting it and driving it down. He felt them pulling at him, and he twisted with savage strength out of their hands and lifted Grogan's head and pounded it down again into the dirt, and, holding the hair, he took a scraping fistful of dirt and rubbed it into the other's face. Again he pounded it, and Grogan's white, smeared face was there before him, hateful and terrified and alone and ravaged.

"Give me the belt," Tommy said. He held the head and waited for a moment. The hands hauling at him let go.

"I don't know what you mean," Grogan said bitterly. "If I had a belt, you could kill me for it. You'd never get it."

In a frenzy now, Tommy tore at the other's clothes. He ripped the shirt open, as knowledge came to him, and there on the thin waist, along the bony juttings of ribs, he saw the belt. Grogan had no undershirt on. His body was emaciated. The belt was tied there, hidden under the shirt. It had been there all the time.

He opened the belt as Grogan's writhing stopped. He opened the belt and took it off and stood, and he looked at it. It was new and raw and wonderful and ugly.

Tommy stood, and, standing, he gazed around now, and he saw that half the class had followed them, sneaking in to see the fight. The space in the bushes was packed with bodies and thronged with silence. The eyes watched Tommy. He took the string out of his pocket and dropped it on Grogan, who still lay there.

"There's your string back," Tommy said. He looked around at the silent class, at the eyes watching him. He looked at Paddy Kelly and saw his wide, sad eyes turned down now on Grogan and all the beaten and dispirited of the world, at his own dying mother, at the death from consumption that would be on himself soon.

Tommy stood there like that for a moment. He began to

push through the crowd. He got through and he began to run. As he ran, there were tears in his eyes and a sobbing on his lips. He ran out of the yard and down the lane, and passing Shandon he was still running. He was crying too—crying for the part of himself left back there, wrenched out of him, torn in poverty and misery and hate out of his life. He was crying for the body floating down the tides of sleep and gone forever from the world of the day.

I AM NOT A STRANGER

By JAMES STREET

A DRIZZLING rain was falling and I had driven about a mile beyond the village before I realized that something was strange about the place and I slowed down, debating whether to turn back and satisfy my curiosity. The debate merely was to appease a sense of logic that taunts me, but seldom influences my behavior.

My curiosity was responsible for the trip, my first to the South. I teach history in upstate New York and was doing my thesis on American Myths, a subject so broad that I broke it down to one myth as an example. My intent was to explore the fable and show how it affected its believers with such social phenomena as tradition, honor and chauvinism.

I had chosen North Carolina's Mecklenburg Declaration as my possible myth. Mind you now, before I am pilloried, I do not plead that the Mecklenburg Declaration of May 20, 1775, is a fable. I do not know, and I no longer care.

I wrote to the University of North Carolina, and that venerable bulwark of free thought, and sometimes athletics, graciously offered me its facilities. So I got into my car, christened Rozinante in honor of Don Quixote's horse, and sallied forth.

Soon after I left Richmond, Virginia, the towns began to look alike; a town square, a Confederate monument, a Post Office Café. It began raining and twilight was nigh, so I hastened through the North Carolina hamlets and, as I reported previously, was beyond the last village when it came to me that something there was different. So I turned around.

There was a sign on the outskirts which announced:

LYSTRA.
PLEASE DRIVE CAREFULLY.
WE LOVE OUR CHILDREN.

The rain changed to a fine mist and as I approached the town square I pulled over to a curb. A girl was sitting on a bench under a spreading live oak. She had no umbrella and

21

was just sitting there, protected somewhat by the tree, although the rain was blowing against her in a spray.

She glanced up and smiled as though we were old friends. I am a young man and have black hair and, although I wear glasses, young women, particularly students who face examinations without preparation, sometimes smile at me. However, no girl ever had smiled at me as this girl did; a warm challenge, a drama, a book. I considered her smile flirtatious, even amorous, and then I was ashamed of myself for thinking so. She was only being friendly. I smiled at her and she tilted her head and laughed. I instinctively thought of the Irish myth of the rain nymph.

Then she called out to me, "Hey! What do you do up in New York when it rains?"

"We get in out of the wet," I called back. "Those of us who are sane."

She folded her hands across her knee and leaned against the tree, as though there was nothing left in all the world except her and the rain and the joy of sitting there. She gave me no more attention.

I started my car and rode around the square. There was the Post Office Café, the movie advertising a Western, and the Lystra Hotel. A fat man was rocking on the porch of the hotel. It was like all the other little Southern towns I had passed, so I glanced over at the girl under the tree and headed away again.

Then it came to me, and I gasped and turned around quickly. There was no Confederate monument in Lystra!

The fat man on the hotel porch didn't stop rocking as I parked and stepped hurriedly from Rozinante to shelter. There I removed my hat and rubbed away the moisture, then I opened the screen door and saw that the lobby was empty. "I need a room for the night," I said to the fat man.

"Most folks do." He stopped rocking. "Tell me, son, what do you folks do when it rains?"

It was the same question the girl had asked. I could see her from the porch, still sitting in the mist and twilight. I decided to answer the question in the Yankee fashion of asking one. "What do you do here when it rains?"

The man got slowly to his feet. "Oh, we just let it rain." He opened the screen door and walked to the desk and I followed and signed my name to the registry. Laren W. McCall. Malone, N. Y.

The hotelkeeper studied my name, then put on his glasses and peered at it and up at me. "Scotch, huh?"

"Probably," I said impatiently. "Way back. I don't know."

"What's the W for?"

"Winton," I said brusquely. "Is it important?"

He closed the registry and handed me a key. "My middle initial is W for Worth. Last name is Culpepper. We don't get many folks from New York."

I was bursting to ask him why Lystra had no Confederate monument, but I felt the question might be impudent at that time. So I said, "What time is dinner served? I mean supper."

"Six-thirty," said Mr. Culpepper. "But I wouldn't eat supper here if I was you."

That was too much for my patience and I asked an explanation. Mr. Culpepper reached into his shirt pocket and took out a partly smoked cigar.

"Well, I tell you, Mr. McCall," he said. "I set the best dinner table in North Carolina. Been doing it for forty-three years. Always the same price. Four bits." He chewed down on his cigar. "But stuff is so high now that to make out on my four-bit dinner I have to scrimp on supper. So I don't brag about my suppers."

I suddenly liked Mr. Culpepper. "Do you eat supper here?"

"No. I gen'ly eats up at the Morgan place. Mrs. Morgan sets the best supper table in North Carolina. Four bits. She lays it on for supper, but scrimps on dinner."

I started up the stairs to see my room and he waited until I reached the landing, then called up, "Ever been in a country hotel before?"

I said I had.

"Well, it ain't no use of climbing them steps just to see your room. It is eighteen by fourteen feet with two windows. One stuck. There's an inkwell and no ink, and a Gideon Bible. Bathroom is down the hall. Tub drips."

Despite my usual reserve, I laughed and I am glad I did. My mirth seemed to prime Mr. Culpepper and he began chuckling in even strokes like a steam piston on a merry engine. His chuckles swelled into laughter and he shook and swayed. Laughter was an art with Mr. Culpepper.

I knew then that I could ask him about Lystra without offending his pride, so I followed him to the front porch and sat in a rocker. The rain was passing, but the girl still was under the tree.

"I noticed," I said, "that Lystra is not like other Southern towns. There's no Confederate monument."

He cut his eyes over at me, then looked down at his cigar. "The whole town is a monument, son."

Just the way he said it, proudly and sadly, caused me to change the subject quickly, and I nodded toward the girl under the tree. "Is that a custom here? To sit out in the rain?"

"It's her custom," he said.

"I wonder why she does it." I was watching the girl. She put her arms above her head and stretched. Then she got up and started toward the hotel.

Mr. Culpepper's cigar was out, so he threw it away. "She's Leah Beth Morgan. I've known her all her life and I never asked her why she sits in the mist. Maybe she just likes to sit under a tree and it araining."

"She's a very beautiful girl."

Again he looked over at me. "Uh huh. She has her mother's looks and her daddy's soul. Her daddy is dead." He put his hands behind his head and rocked, watching Leah Beth Morgan. "Some folks say her daddy drank himself to death." I was sizing Mr. Culpepper up as a garrulous old gossip and then he said, "But here in Lystra we know he was mommicked."

My ears began tingling. "Mommicked." I happened to know that the word is archaic English, meaning destroy, and had heard that it still was used in sections of the South.

I was thinking of my thesis and said, "So he was mommicked?"

"That's right. Married Bernice Conner. Prettiest darlin' in the county. She didn't kill him. She just wrung his spirit dry and he withered." He stopped rocking. "She's a mommick, all right, but she still sets the best supper table in North Carolina."

As Leah Beth Morgan approached, she called to him, "What'll we do if it rains, Mr. Cul?"

"We'll just let it rain, honey. Come on over and meet a friend of mine."

The girl scarcely was damp. A few drops of moisture were on her hair. Again I had the feeling that she was a rain nymph. One good look at her brown hair and bare legs dispelled that myth. Mr. Culpepper presented me without getting up. I stood.

He said, "This is Mr. McCall. Laren W. McCall. The W is for Winton."

Miss Morgan looked at me for two or three seconds before she spoke and when she acknowledged the introduction her voice was as calm and gentle as the twilight now that the rain had gone away.

"He's from Malone, N. Y.," Mr. Culpepper said. "Aims to eat at your house."

"That is, of course," I said quickly, "if you take paying guests."

She sort of cocked her head to one side and smiled. "This is not Natchez or Charleston, Mr. McCall. We take boarders. We'll be glad to have you."

"He's curious why we ain't got a secesh monument," Mr. Culpepper said and resumed his rocking.

Miss Morgan put one foot on the hotel steps and leaned against the banister, looking away.

"I just happened to notice that none is here." I wished she would sit there and rock with us. "I am a schoolteacher and am making a study of the South."

She glanced over her shoulder at me. "You're a schoolteacher and never heard of Lystra?"

I didn't know, and still do not know, if she was teasing me. "Am I supposed to have heard of Lystra? Is it famous for something besides beauty and hospitality?"

Mr. Culpepper yawned and stretched. "You two walk on up to the house and she can tell you about this town. I'll be along t'reckly."

I was grateful for the suggestion and joined Miss Morgan on the steps. We walked across the square and I commented that nobody would believe that she had been sitting in the rain.

"The tree kept me dry," she said. "Even in a heavy rain only a fine mist seeps through a live oak."

We were walking along a gravel sidewalk. The earth smelled fresh after the shower. "Do you sit there for any reason?" I asked.

"I like to sit in the rain. Don't you?"

"I've never tried it, but when it rains I want an umbrella."

There was a trace of mockery in her laughter. "That takes all the fun out of it. Like swimming in your clothes or sleeping with the windows down. I'll bet you even think the rainbow is just a spectrum instead of the hem of heaven's gown."

"Well, isn't it?"

"Here in Lystra we call it the hem of heaven's gown. We like it that way."

And suddenly so did I. The stars were coming out, scouting for the moon which hung back timidly, over on the rim of the world. "Now tell me about Lystra," I said.

She took my arm. Yes, I had known her only a few minutes, but she took my arm. "Lystra," she said softly, "is where none came back. All the young men volunteered and formed Lystra Company and joined the Confederate Army. They rode away one night and none came back."

"None!"

"Not a one. They all were killed. So you see, we don't need a monument. Lystra herself is monument enough."

I was musing her words. She made it all sound as though it were yesterday and I glanced up the street, rather expecting to see them helling down the pike on white horses. They'd be laughing and singing and wearing yellow sashes. They always did in such stories.

My sanity returned quickly. Here was what I was seeking; a myth that had influenced an entire community. I forgot about the Mecklenburg Declaration. Lystra Company and its dead demigods were what I wanted.

So far as records go, no company in the Civil War suffered obliteration. Therefore, I was willing to stake my doctorate that Lystra Company was not mommicked. It smacked too much of the mansion-and-white-column myths, the moonlight-and-magnolia fables, the white horses and yellow sashes.

"I never heard that story," I said. "Didn't a prisoner come back? Or some wounded men?"

"They all were killed," she said slowly. "They all rode away together one night and vanished. Every young man in town."

We turned a corner and I was glancing down at her face. Then I looked up and gasped. There was a lawn, a spreading green apron for a white mansion. And it had columns. The moon tried the sky and, finding it safe, began soaring. Magnolias were on the lawn. I gulped and felt sheepish and I knew, without asking, that it was the Morgan place.

There were several boarders on the wide porch. Leah Beth introduced them to me and then showed me to the living room and her mother.

"Mother," she said, "this is Mr. McCall."

It was hard to believe that Mrs. Morgan, an old lady with white hair and a gentle, sad face, was a mommick. On second thought, however, I realized I was in the presence of despotism, the tyranny of sweetness and long-suffering.

"What brings you to Lystra?" Mrs. Morgan asked.

She was the first person to ask me why I was there, and on hearing my explanation she leaned forward and stared at me. "Who are your people?"

Leah Beth was embarrassed. I had anticipated the question and was glad she asked it, because it confirmed one of my opinions about the South, the Shintoism of the fading families.

My mother died when I was a baby, and my father, a heating engineer in Buffalo, married again. I was reared by my father's sister because he wanted me to grow up in a small town. My mother came from Watertown, New York. And despite all the odes to motherhood, I felt closer to my aunt than to my mother because I never knew my mother. There was nothing unusual about that.

I was telling about myself when Mr. Culpepper came in. He listened for a second, then turned to Mrs. Morgan. "Bernice, for Lord's sake spare the bones. Besides, I'm hungry."

We went in to supper and it was all Mr. Culpepper had promised. I was dawdling over my coffee when Mrs. Morgan, watching me, said, "Leah Beth, since Mr. McCall is interested in Southern history, why not show him the sword in the tree?"

Mr. Culpepper excused himself and waddled out of the

room. Leah Beth loked down at her plate, then said, "If he wants to see it."

"Of course he wants to see it," Mrs. Morgan said.

Leah Beth motioned for me to follow her into the long hall and we walked to the back porch. She called it the back gallery, and we stood there above an old rose garden. I felt like an unbeliever in a shrine and was about to say so when I noticed the big tree at the far end of the garden and saw the steel blade in its trunk. I knew it must be years old and rusted, but it seemed to gleam in the moonlight with a strange, eerie brightness.

"That's it," she whispered. "That's the sword in the tree."

"Who put it there?" I whispered too.

"One of those who rode away and never came back."

Her hands were resting on the banister of the gallery and the moon was in her eyes. I touched her hand and she didn't move it. I did it because she was a beautiful girl and because I wanted to feel something alive. "Do you care to tell me about it?" I asked.

She shrugged and took her hand away and looked up at the moon. "My aunt was living here. She was my great-great-aunt, really. She was twenty-two. My age." Then she smiled wistfully. "They called her a maiden lady. The night they rode away her lover came by to tell her good-by. He came up that path yonder."

I looked and there was the path. "Was he riding a white horse?" I asked.

"Yes. A white horse. He was wearing a yellow sash. They met here in the garden. That tree was just a little sapling and he stuck his sword in the tree and told her that as long as his sword remained there the honor of this house would be without blemish. The tree grew up around the sword, but there it is; still there."

I was entranced. Eventually, however, my senses returned. I said, "May I come back by daylight and see it?"

She looked at me. "If you want to."

I walked slowly back to the hotel, and Mr. Culpepper was rocking on the porch. "Did you see it?" He didn't look up; his eyes were closed.

"Yes. And I'm going back tomorrow and look at it. What happened to the aunt? The maiden lady? Pine away?"

"Uh huh. That's right, son. Her baby lived on a few weeks."

"Oh!" I said.

"Uh huh. We had a mighty fine rector here, so the story goes. He wasn't too good to fib a bit for the Lord. He said he'd married 'em, but there was no license record. Records in them days were pretty skimpy, though. She waited and waited for him to come back, then punied and died of a broken heart."

The same old fable. I went to my room and fell asleep thinking about my thesis.

Bright and early the next morning I sauntered up to the Morgan place. Just as I expected, it wasn't the same by day. There were bare spots on the lawn, and paint on the house was peeling.

I walked around to the rose garden. The bushes needed trimming and the verbena was rank. I went straight to the tree and examined the sword. Then I almost laughed.

It was not a sword at all. It was the blade of an old scythe. Obviously, a worker had hung his implement over a branch of the tree and forgotten about it, and the tree had grown around it, and the handle had rotted away.

The story was clear to me then. A lost lover is the usual alibi for an old maid.

I turned to leave, and Leah Beth was standing by the gate, an impish smile on her lips and the devil in her eyes. I did laugh then. "It's an old scythe," I said.

"Is it?" she said. "We thought it was a sword."

"Why, it's plainly a scythe."

Leah Beth still was smiling. "You are a mommick, aren't you? Knowledge must be a wonderful thing. It must be great to know the difference between a sword and a scythe, between bitter truth and beautiful illusion."

I couldn't take my eyes off her for a minute, and when I did I turned back to the tree and peered at the blade. "Amazing," I said. "The first curved Highland broadsword I ever saw. Some might erroneously call it a claymore."

She came to me and stood there by the tree, looking up at me. "You are sweet, Laren. You are a gentleman, a darling."

I bent my neck and kissed her cheek without embarrassment or explanation. It seemed the right thing to do. Besides, I wanted to do it.

My heart was light and gay as I ate Mr. Culpepper's famous four-bit dinner, and then I got drowsy and went with him to the front porch and we took rockers.

I said casually, "That's a broadsword in that tree up at the Morgan place."

"Uh huh." He was nodding.

"Any of your people in the Lystra Company that didn't come back?"

"Uh huh. A great-uncle." His head slipped to his chest.

A cloud rolled in from the east, bringing a breeze and threats of another summer shower. The breeze rustled the hedge around the hotel and Mr. Cul opened one eye and cocked it over at me. "It's gonna rain."

I studied the sky and said, "Uh huh. Let's just let it rain."

A warmth came into Mr. Cul's face and suddenly I felt an affinity for the old man, as though I had supplied the code words to his affections and had slipped into his heart and found it large enough to accept a stranger who wanted to be liked in Lystra.

I was happier than I ever remembered being before. The rain started gently and I walked out into it without my hat. Across the square Leah Beth was under the live oak. I dashed for the tree and sat beside her.

No word was spoken. The shower brushed the tree and sprayed us with a fine warm mist. I felt for her hand and we sat there until the late sun drove the rain away. The rainbow whipped across the sky and I whispered, "It's the hem of heaven's gown."

"You are a darling," she said.

In my rhapsody, I told her I loved her, trying to hide my haste behind my fervor. I had known her only a day.

She rested her head on my shoulder for a few minutes, then stood and smoothed her dress. "Let's go home to supper. You stay in Lystra awhile and if you still think you love me, then I am yours."

"You can never doubt that I love you, Leah Beth. I'll even come after you on a white horse if you want it that way."

"Wearing a yellow sash?" The devil was back in her eyes.

"No. I draw the line on that."

We held hands all the way home.

The weeks that followed were an idyl, a séance with serenity, and I asked her to marry me.

She said simply, "I was beginning to worry."

"I'll get a job here," I said. "I'll not ask you to go North with me."

She rubbed her nose against my ear. "I believe it is customary for the woman to go with her man. But what will your folks say if you come back with a provincial girl who sits bare-legged in the rain?"

"I have no family except my father. And we never see each other. I haven't even written him in a year."

"That's a long time," she said. "And what about your work? Your thesis?"

That was the rub. We were sitting on the back gallery of her home, over the rose garden, and there, dull in the moonlight, was the scythe in the tree, evidence of the very myths I sought. I broached the subject carefully. "I'd like to do my thesis on Lystra," I said.

"That would be fun," she said. "Maybe I could help."

I took the next step. "I'd like to explore the legends of Lystra. No monument. None came back. The sword in the tree, and all that. It's exactly what I need."

I felt her looking at me and I dreaded to face her way. But when I did she said calmly, "Why not?"

"I might hurt the people here. They might not like me any more."

Leah Beth laughed. "Why, you conceited darling. Lystra doesn't care what a Yankee Ph.D. says." She lifted my hand and rubbed it across her cheek. "You and all the others will never learn that, will you? You'll never learn that Lystra and all her poor little Southern sisters do not prize your ideas as highly as you do."

That got under my skin a bit. "All right," I said. "Then I have my thesis. I'll write the fables, then the facts."

"Have you got the facts?"

"I can get them quickly," I said. "Even if I can't get the

name of the worker who left that scythe in the tree I can
furnish a preponderance of evidence to explode the myth."

"Is that a fact?" she said. "Well, now, I do declare."

In that brief minute I was more student than lover, and I
asked, "What was the name of your great-great-aunt? The
maiden lady."

"Leah Beth," she said quietly.

"No cheating now," I admonished her. "No kidding."

"Her name was Leah Beth."

I wasn't surprised. Mrs. Morgan was the kind of woman
who would name her daughter after a martyr, after a lonely,
hallowed relative. "Very well," I said. "The man's name?"

She began smiling and I had a premonition. "Now don't
try to tell me his name was McCall."

"His name wasn't McCall," she said. "It was Culpepper.
Laren Winton Culpepper."

I almost laughed, but I knew she was serious; that she was
telling me the truth. "How did he spell Laren?" I demanded. It
usually is spelled "Loren."

"With an 'a,'" she replied.

I looked at the scythe in the tree and then I did laugh. "No
wonder you looked at me strangely when I first came here."

"We didn't look strangely at you," she insisted. "That's your
imagination. We understand coincidence." There was neither
shame nor sadness in her tone when she said, "Of course you
heard that my maiden aunt had a son. There is no doubt that
her baby died, Laren. In case you care."

"Oh, for goodness' sakes," I said. "I wasn't thinking about
that. I was thinking how coincidence can play the devil with
research."

That wasn't exactly the truth. I glanced at the path he rode
up and at the tree, and at the sword in the tree, and remembered the pledge of honor to this house. I kissed her good
night.

Mr. Cul was sitting in the lobby, and I asked for ink. I
wanted to write my father about Leah Beth. Then I changed
my mind. "Don't bother," I said. "I'll use the phone." So I went
to my room and put in a call to Buffalo.

Dad was as cheerful as ever. I told him quickly what I was
doing in the South so he wouldn't think I needed anything. "I

just wanted to tell you I'm going to marry a girl down here," I said.

"What kind of girl is she?" he demanded. I scarcely heard him. The connection was bad.

"She sits barelegged in the rain," I replied.

"Good for her," dad said. His voice trailed off and I asked him to repeat his words.

He raised his voice. "Connection's bad up here. It's raining and storming."

"Well, let it rain," I said.

He was silent a second, then, "What did you say?"

"I said just let it rain."

"That's funny," he said. "I haven't heard that expression in a long time. Your mother used to say it."

It was my turn to be silent and I felt a sudden catch in my stomach. "Listen, dad, some of the people here go in pretty heavy for family stuff." I was blaming a whole community for Mrs. Morgan's curiosity, but I needed a reason for my questions. "I was named for mother's father, wasn't I?"

"That's right. Laren Winton. Lawyer in Watertown. Born, bred and died there. And a mighty fine citizen, son, in case those people down there start any family stuff."

"Where did he get his name?" I gripped the telephone until my knuckles were white.

The connection began to clear up and dad said, "Your great-grandfather also was Laren Winton. We never knew much about him."

He would have dropped the Culpepper. That's the first thing he'd do.

Dad's voice was very clear. "He became sort of a legend, told over and over until the family believed it."

"Yes," I said. "Go on."

"Your mother used to laugh and tell the tale with all the trimmings. He said he was from Missouri. Must have been South Missouri, the way he talked, your mother used to say." Dad's chuckle made me lonesome to see him again. "He was a strange man and kept to himself. It was during the Civil War and some said he was a deserter." Dad began laughing. "I used to tease your mother and call him a horse thief. He was poor as Job's turkey when he first came to Watertown, but he had a fine white horse."

I didn't hear much more. His words seemed jumbled. I kept saying to myself that it could be. I promised to bring Leah Beth to see him, and hung up.

I wanted to be with my beloved and tell her that Laren Winton had come back for Leah Beth. I wanted to pull that sword out of the tree and tell her that her family's honor was redeemed. Such sentiment is a lover's privilege.

I walked rapidly down to the lobby and Mr. Cul was sitting at the switchboard, staring at the gadgets.

"How is your dad?" he asked, turning his head a bit to look at me.

"How did you know I was talking to my father?" I demanded.

"Shucks, son, I had to get the call through."

I didn't know and I never want to know if he listened. It came to me then, as clear as a church bell on a frosty night, that I must never tell Leah Beth or anyone else. And if Mr. Cul knew, he would never tell.

For it might be true, and if it was true, then one lived and Lystra no longer could be the place where none came back. The fabric would fall apart. It would be just like any other Southern town. They might even erect a Confederate monument, might cut down the live oak on the square and put one there.

I was in such a hurry to see my darling that I ground old Rozinante's innards. It was just an old coupé, but I could make believe it was a white horse. The door to the realm of playlike is closed to no man, not even a professor.

So let the scythe be a sword. And when it rains, let it rain. I am no mommick.

THE RANSOM OF
PETER DRAKE

By JACLAND MARMUR

IT'S GETTING on daylight along the Coast, but away out here it's the middle watch. I can see stars swinging past my hooked-back door when the ship rolls down, and the smell of the trade is sweet. It's quiet in the radio shack. The noisy wash of the ocean doesn't bother the stillness at all. Not in a liner. Not in the middle watch. And in just three minutes I got a traffic schedule with KPH. It'll be Joe Pagini over there, and Joe's an old-timer. The minute I open up, he'll know what kind of a transmitting key I use. He don't know why I use it, but he'll know right away it's me. Even before I give my sign, I'll hear him through the break-in relay, bustin' in from Frisco two thousand miles away.

"Good morning, MP," he'll say. "Got nine for you. Go ahead."

Then all the while I'm rapping out the code with the earphones tucked at my temples, I'll be thinking of Peter Drake. Till my message hook is clean. I wish it was Pete Drake's sideswiper I was using. But it couldn't be. So I did the next best thing. I made me one of my own, and I swore I'd learn to use it right. I hope I did. Because if it wasn't for him, I wouldn't be here.

He didn't belong to the afterguard. He didn't belong in the fo'c'sle, either. The devil only knows where he belonged. Not in the cargo steamer Trintipal, that's sure. But that's where he was, signed on as ordinary seaman for the voyage home to Seattle by way of Shanghai and Tsugaru Strait in the winter right after the end of the war. The Old Man picked him up in ruined Manila because we'd sent two men ashore to hospital and the bos'n's crowd was short. You know how bos'ns are.

Me, I didn't even know he was on board. Not till the following day. The Trintipal was nosing the cobalt water of Manila Bay, and the third mate, Tony Fuller, was spilling tobacco ash on the settee of my boat-deck shack when we heard this voice.

"Give us a drink!" it said. I looked up. All I could clearly see was a face in the doorway's frame. The whisky sweat was beading out on it. His eyes were haggard, and his hair was a dusty gray. "Sparks," he whined, "for God's sake ——"

He poured half a tumbler of my Scotch and he drank it neat. Then he went away. He never even said thank you or be damned, and I don't know yet why I did it. Except he needed that drink. He needed it worse than medicine. Tony Fuller laughed.

"That'll teach you," the third mate said. "Offering the bottle to one of those wrecks! Y'oughta know better, Sparks." Mr. Fuller snorted and stood up. "That's Pete Drake," he informed me, "and the mate is welcome to him. He says he don't know anything about ships. He's a liar. He knows his way around."

"Where the blazes did he come from?"

"Who ever knows where they come from—them shoreside bums? Or, for that matter, where they go?" Tony Fuller stepped over the weatherboard. "They live in a middle world all their own, halfway between the ocean and the land." He started aft for the ladderway, lean out there in the brilliant sun. "You better lock that bottle up!" he warned. "What's left of it, I mean." And the third mate laughed again.

Well, all right. They take you off your guard when their eyes peer out at you from the unlit caverns of their private agony. But I didn't intend it should happen again. All the way across the China Sea, whenever he shuffled along the boat deck with his narrow shoulders hunched and his head bowed down, he threw a quick sidewise glance toward the radio shack. I looked the other way. But you could tell from how he walked a tipping deck that he'd walked it once before. He was on the deck with the chief mate's crowd when the Trintipal hunted Steep Island Pass at the Yangtze River mouth in a cold, gray, drizzling mist. From the bridge he looked small and withered in his shabby reefer coat down there, peering against a windy distance with his gray head bare and his feet spread wide. Tony Fuller was right. He had a seaman's stance. They always stand like that. And while we lay moored off the Shanghai Bund I saw Peter Drake again. I saw him clearly enough that time. He was drunk. He was drunk as a cockeyed lord. But I couldn't throw him out.

He came into the radio shack. I had a small dry battery and a sounding buzzer hooked across my transmission key. A straight conventional key, it was. Same as most of the telegraph monkeys use ashore. I was beating out some five-letter cipher, practicing to get my ticket upgraded when the Trintipal got home. I didn't pay much attention when the door pulled open and slammed again. I thought it was Tony Fuller. He was always barging in. But it wasn't. It was Peter Drake.

"It's lousy, Sparks." He was standing over me, swaying a little, his head cocked over on one side, half a crooked smile on his lips. "It's lousy stuff," he said.

"What did you expect in Blood Alley? Fancy liqueurs? It was whisky, wasn't it?"

He uttered a bitter little snort at the hard, dry irony of my tone, and the crooked smile slipped the rest of the way across his lips. Then he looked around with a drunk's exaggerated care, his watery blue eyes taking all my equipment in.

"It sure has changed," he whispered.

Right then something clicked in my mind. He was turning away. I reached over and flipped my receiver switch on. A babble of code came pouring from the speaker. Peter Drake stopped short at once. He stopped swaying too. I was right. He was reading the stuff. All them old brass-pounders are alike. They never forget it. They can't. It gets into the blood. They never forget it to the day they die. It made Peter Drake spin savagely around. His eyes were ablaze.

"Turn that off! Turn it off, I say!"

I grinned at him. "Sure. So you think my fist is lousy, do you?"

He was breathing hard. It took him a while to quiet down. A fist is a radio operator's own peculiar characteristic of sending, like a man's handwriting and his signature. Drake knew what I meant, all right.

"I never liked a straight key," he mumbled. "Got no class to it. No class at all."

"Oh." I grinned again. I was having fun. "One of them old-time speed burners. A fancy bug man, hey?"

He shook his head. "No." Something seemed to be warning him he ought to get away from where he didn't belong any more. But the whisky kept churning his memory. He was doing fierce combat with both. A big soiled hand passed across his face, and he sagged suddenly down on my leather settee. "Got no use for a bug," his thick voice growled. "No use at all." He wagged his head and brushed shadows aside with the same big-fingered hand. "What is a bug? It works sideways, all right, instead of up an' down like a common key. One contact is solid, and the one opposite works against a vibrator rod y' can adjust for speed by moving the little controlling weight back or forward. All right. Y' hold the lever on one side an' y' got a dash. Y' thumb it the other way an' the weight on the spring rod rattles the dots off for you. No skill. No personal skill at all. Just a damn mechanical contraption! Now y' take a ——"

"You must be one of them old-time sideswipe crackers!"

"One of the best!" The old buzzard's watery eyes began to glow. "We used to build our own." He leaned forward. "Y' make two contacts on solid vertical mounts about an inch apart. Your sending lever swings between. That's got to be good spring steel. Not too loose. Not too tight. Just right. Y' use your thumb an' forefinger on it. Side to side. Y' make your own dots an' dashes with a sideswiper. Y' space 'em the way y' want. Y' give the stuff your own personality. It's got class! It's you! It's no one else! A key like that is an artist's tool! In my day ——"

"Hell!" I said, wanting to keep him wound up. "All you old-timers are alike. Just the same as windbag men. You think that broken-down gear you used to operate is still the only thing."

He looked around at all my modern tube equipment with a deep and drunken scorn. "You call this operatin'?" He snorted. "Short wave!" The crooked smile began to show again. "I suppose y' can work the Coast the minute you get outside. Copy your press around the world. Nuts!" he said. "Y' don't know what seafarin' is. I remember comin' home from the China Coast them days we used to get up in the middle watch, hungry to hear the first voice from home. Just before daylight was the best. The static dies down. Y' can hear things then. Maybe the old Matsonia, nosing round Diamond Head for Honolulu harbor an' clearin' KHK. Paul Snagg was chief in her. Snaggy used a bug."

Peter Drake wasn't looking at me any more. He was looking somewhere else, off where the shades of his old profession lived. He called them up for me, one by one.

"Next night you'd sit there all of a sweat, tuning the six-hundred-meter dials by a hair, hunting KPH. He used a rotary spark gap for his traffic calls. That old rock crusher had a deep, rich tone. The minute you heard it, you began to grin. You were coming home! Boy, it sounded sweet! Then KFS with his bubbling arc. It used to break every now and then, like a kid's voice when it's changing. An' maybe KSE from Wilmington, coming in with that fluting, quenched-gap note, like a young girl gettin' angry. That was Freddy Cugle, standing the graveyard watch, draggin' his dashes long. Freddy was a straight-key man. You'd hear 'em for maybe a minute just before daylight came, working the coasters, faint an' far away. You felt pretty fine that day. 'Heard Frisco this morning!' you'd tell the crowd at breakfast in the saloon. An' they'd all grin back at you. Even the engineers."

I grinned myself. But I let him rave. I just kept wondering when he'd stop. He didn't. He couldn't. Not yet.

"I used to run two days behind a tanker called Segundo," his voice growled on. "Rod Gibley was in her then. We used to clear half the Pacific traffic, Rod an' me, on a relay schedule with old PH. Y' talk about sideswipers!" His eyes began to glow again. "I never had to give my call. Not me. The minute I opened up, the whole damn ocean knew who it was. It was Drake! Pete Drake! It couldn't be no one else! They'd all come bustin' in right away. Better than if they heard my voice. That's what I mean. Y' take a key like that an' y' learn to use it right an' ——" He broke off at last. He tried to get up. "Nuts!" he snarled. "What am I doin' here anyway?"

"I was going to ask you the same."

"Who? Me?" He made it to his feet this time, swaying. "Goin' home. Heard Helen died. Gotta see the kids."

"Kids? You mean you ——"

"Hell, no!" He gave that drunken snort. "They ain't mine."

"Well, then what ——"

"We was gonna get married, Helen an' me. She married someone else, though, an' I guess they're all grown up by now. But the way I figger it, kids is kids. They could 'a' been mine."

"Drake, you're nuts! I know that yarn myself. Any woman who won't marry a man just because he goes to sea has got no right to ——"

"Who said she wouldn't? That's a lie! She begged me! It didn't make no difference to Helen. I told her I lost my ticket, an' still she ——" He broke it off there, sharply. His eyes were suddenly wild. He thought it was me who'd betrayed him. "You!" he spat. "You ——" He turned blindly away, groping for the door. But something savage took him by the throat, spinning him around. It wasn't the whisky, either. Whisky couldn't make a man's eyes burn like that. Not all the whisky in the world. "Yeah!" he said. "I lost my ticket. No inspector took it away from me. I took it away from myself! I was in the tanker Placenta when the gas exploded in her a thousand miles off the Flattery Cape. So I sent out the SOS. Sure! On my hot-shot sideswiper! Then I ran like hell for the boats."

"Look here, Drake; take it easy. What else could you do?"

He didn't hear me. He heard a voice, all right. But it wasn't mine. He'd been hearing it for twenty years. "I never cleared the hook!" he told it. "I just sent the SOS an' ran like hell for the boats. The position was off. Why wouldn't it be? No sun or star fix on the bridge for days with the North Pacific weather we'd had! Thirteen hours it took the liner Redondo to find us in the sleety fog. She was sixty miles away. She did fourteen knots! And it took her thirteen hours. I saw five men die in the boats in that time. I can hear them yet. Johnny, the little oiler—he's the worst. Johnny doesn't scream. Johnny only moans. No one blamed me. They never said a word. Why should they? I got the SOS off, didn't I? What else could I do? . . . I could have stayed where I belonged! I could have stayed till the hook was clean! Maybe I could have raised a couple of ships with direction finders. I could have sent them v's till they took cross bearings on my spark. They could have laid the Placenta's position down to a pin point on the chart! I never even froze the key! I just sent the SOS an' ran like hell for the boats. That's how quick it happened. Just like that. The first time Johnny moaned, I knew I'd lost my ticket. He took it away from me. Right there in an open boat. He was right! I never sailed on it again. But he keeps on moaning anyhow. He won't never stop!"

It poured out of him. Then he swayed there, panting. I never again want to see such a tortured fever in the eyes of any man.

"Drake!" When he turned half around in the doorway and saw the bottle I was offering, the crooked smile came back. "Why don't you build me a sideswiper?" What else could I say? "I'd like to give it a try."

"Sure!" He emptied what was left of the Scotch. He took it quick and neat. "Sure, I will," he said. "First thing when we get to sea."

Then he stepped to the boat deck over the weather coaming, into the darkness and the cold. He left the empty bottle where he'd tossed it on my settee. He left the smell of stale whisky and the echo of his voice. Funny. It wasn't bitter. It was full of a hollow scorn. And next morning the Trintipal sailed for home.

All right. I was only talking. You've got to talk the most when nothing you can say is any good. But Pete Drake kept his word. I guess he cadged what he needed from the first assistant and used the engine-room machine shop on his watch below. The first I knew about it, the Trintipal was pushing through the Japan Sea on the run to Hakodate. I came into the radio shack after supper for the usual evening watch, and there it was. He left it on my log table, this sideswiper he'd made, this precision transmitting key. He had good sense. He just left it while I wasn't there, and went away. The two polished vertical contacts glistened in the down-flung light. The sending lever between kept trembling gently from side to side with the vibration of the ship. It was good spring steel, all right. I knew he built it out of a whole lot more than good spring steel and polished contacts, though. So I didn't grin. I reached down. I let the small wooden finger piece come between my thumb and forefinger, and I gave it a careless whirl. That made me frown. I hooked on a dry cell and a sounding buzzer. I tried it again. It was awful. Like a fellow mumbling with mush in his mouth. Was I really as lousy as that?

"Now what the blazes have you got there, Sparks?" It was

Tony Fuller, barging in for a smoke on his way to the bridge, with half his mind on the weather. "Smells like it might be pretty dusty outside the Strait," he said. "What kind of a crazy gadget is that?"

"Sideswiper. A very fancy transmitting key. I never used one before. I was giving it a try."

"Sparks, all you birds are nuts. Always fiddling around. No wonder you can't sleep nights."

"Yeah." I grinned. "Takes lots of practice, Tony, to use one of these and use it right. The damn thing's got my goat."

That's all I told him. The rest belonged only to those of us who wore a different cut of the cloth. Then I put Pete Drake's precision key away. I thought maybe he'd come up there some-time, curious if nothing else, and give me a hint or two. He never did.

Meanwhile the Trintipal came snoring out of Tsugaru Strait, climbing the great Pacific circle toward the lightship on the Swiftsure Bank four thousand miles away. Tony Fuller was right. It was dusty enough. The westerlies were roaring up there. The ocean hills ran long and steep under lightless tatters of lower cloud. The Trintipal angularly climbed the white-veined flanks of the combers, hung there all of a shudder for a moment, and then plunged down, smashing green water all around her into acre-wide fields of foam. White cataracts gushed off the break of her fo'c'sle head, snarling across the forward well where the life lines were, and flinging icy sheets of spray as high as the weather cloth on the bridge. She was good in a seaway, though. She lifted clean and nice. She made you feel she was doing all right and knew all about this stuff. She had weathered gales before, tipping her funnel lip over whenever the sleet squalls came. I tried that sideswiper once or twice again. Then I gave it up in disgust. I just couldn't make the thing talk. The minute I touched it, it blubbered, that's all. I knew I'd have to get someone to show me the knack of it. In the end, it was Peter Drake who did.

We were four days out of the Strait and the gale was nearly spent. I was catching a little shut-eye on the bunk, wedged between the battery panel and the main transmitter stand. That much I know for sure. Then something exploded some-where. I remember that too. Something was roaring. Concussion took hold of the ship, hurling her aloft and then dropping her all at once. There was only a violent instant of consciousness between one dark sleep and another. Then the blackness closed again. But this one wasn't natural. It had to be struggled against. It was wrong. And the roaring went on. I don't know how long it went on. Then all of a sudden I recognized it. It was steam. And the ship was still. She was rocking in the water, but she was still. The engines weren't turning down there and the wheel was dead. The minute I knew that, the darkness began to shred away and a face was floating somewhere in the middle space. It kept getting closer all the time. Then the steam roar stopped. Abruptly. Suddenly the face belonged to Mr. Fuller, the Trintipal's third mate. And I wasn't in the bunk at all. I was on the deck, halfway across the shack. Pain stabbed my shoulder.

"I don't think it's broken. I got the bleeding stopped." He was strapping my arm against my side. "Hold still," Tony Fuller said.

That's how the nightmare began. It began up there near the fiftieth parallel toward the end of a heavy gale. It began with a floating mine. Some of it's blurred and fuzzy, like it happened to someone else. But things stand out, like things you see in a lightning flash, captured like that forever against surrounding blackness, frozen, immobile and crystal-clear. Pete Drake was a thing like that. All of a sudden, there he was, withered and small in the doorway's frame, peering in at the wreckage while Tony Fuller helped me stagger to my feet.

"Half an hour, Sparks," Fuller was saying. "An hour at the most. If we're lucky, the Old Man says. We're overhauling the starboard boats. She's filling up fast. Here's the position. You do what you can!" He turned and saw Drake. How would Tony Fuller know why Peter Drake was there? "You!" he ordered sharply. "You stay here! Give Sparks a hand! You do what he says!"

Drake didn't even look at him. "The antenna's okay," he told me. "I just checked."

He did what I told him. Something funny was in his eyes. Half the forward bulkhead was stove. You could see the ocean through the splintered hole. You could see it lifting under ragged clouds in the weird half-light of a sunless dawn, the long hills ribbed with foam and glinting bottle-green, hurrying away. Underfoot, the Trintipal rocked soddenly. She didn't rise. The voices of men at the boats and the creak of gear sounded far away. There was very little time.

He did what I told him. We heaved the wreckage aside. The power tubes and the generator looked all right, but you never can tell till you wind her up. It was broken leads I was worried about. We did a bailing-wire job of splicing. My strapped-up arm wasn't numb any more. Pain kept knifing through it and across my chest. My right-hand fingers were thumbs, all thumbs. They wouldn't do what I wanted them to.

"All right, Sparks. Come along now." That was the Old Man, large in the doorway, blocking the ocean and the light. His voice was grave. "We are ready to launch," he said.

Ready to launch? That was nonsense. I had to get out on the air first. How long could men last in open boats in these latitudes? They could float around for days on that freezing wilderness of water if no one knew they were there. They wouldn't have a chance. I had to have more time. How did I know how long? Look at the wreck. I must have bellowed something like that at Captain Blandon. I was pretty groggy.

"I can't hold the boats any longer," he told me. I remember his voice. It was quiet and slow. "If the ship falls over any farther, we'll never get them away. There are badly hurt men to think about."

"Then launch them! I'll jump, sir! I'll jump as soon as I get an SOS out!"

"Very well. But you haven't got much time." And before Captain Blandon turned away, he added, "I'll stay too."

Sure he would! I knew damn well he would. It startled me to see Peter Drake still there, calmly finishing a cold splice on the leaded cable from the emergency-battery bank. Then he stood up. I'd forgotten all about him. Suddenly the shouted orders from the boat falls came very loud and clear. That and the deep overtone of moaning wind, the slapping noise and wash of the running seas. I started pulling the litter off the operating table.

"Clear out!" I remember barking that at Drake. "Get the blazes out of here now!"

"Sure," he said in the gentlest voice I ever heard. "Sure, I will. Right away." All in a moment it slashed across the back of my brain. My head snapped round quickly. And I heard him say, "It was just like this. It was almost exactly like this."

I suppose it was. But I didn't have any time for his miserable pangs of rum-soaked memory. Not now. I picked up what was left of my typewriter and heaved the broken mill aside. Then I groaned. The transmission key was smashed. I looked at the other one, and I groaned again. Then I flung open the tool chest—and there it was. The sideswiper. The precision key that Drake had built.

"Hook this up!" I sent it sliding on its base across the table to him. If he didn't have sense enough to get out of there, he might as well be useful. He didn't stir. He was in a daze. "Hook that damn thing up!"

He did. His fingers were trembling. They were trembling fearfully. I closed the main power line and the antenna circuit. I flipped the generator-starting switch, holding my breath. It was all right. It began its quick ascending whine. I reached over, pressing my thumb to the finger piece of that brand-new key, closing the contact on that side. But my eye was on the instrument panel. The needle on the radiation ammeter moved. The set was putting out.

"All right, Drake. Here's the position. The call is KPTS. Sit down. You're on the air."

He looked at me. He just stood there and looked at me, pleading. He half raised his trembling hands. "Me?" he said. "Me? With these?"

Then he sat down. I don't know what went through his mind. For an instant he looked around. The crooked smile slipped past his lips. In that wrecked place he saw the changes time and a war had wrought to a once-familiar trade. Through a jagged bulkhead hole he saw empty davits and the boat falls dangling. He saw the ocean, the long, wild-running hills, the tumbling hurry of the lower cloud rack, and maybe he heard the wind. Maybe he heard a whole lot else. Who knows what he heard? He was flexing his right-hand fingers.

"Twenty years," I heard him mumble. I heard him as plain as day. "Twenty years."

He reached out slowly. He touched the key. He tapped it again. Then his thumb came up to the finger piece and he sent off a trickle of v's. His eyes weren't pleading any more. His eyes were beginning to burn. Twenty years? What's twenty years to a man who ever pounded brass? What damage or harm can twenty years do to the language of your youth? They're all the same. They never forget it. It gets into the blood. They never forget it to the day they die. Drake's fingers stumbled a little. Then all at once the trembling stopped. They took hold. When they did, that sideswiper began to talk.

That's the clearest thing of all. That's the thing I remember best. It isn't blurred or fuzzy. It's sharp and shadowless. He had the earphones at his temples. He was braced against the sharp angle of the listing ship. And in that wrecked place, with a foundering deck beneath him, he didn't look old any more. I watched him, fascinated. And I listened. You think he was sending an SOS? Sure. But only with his fingers. This was Drake again. He was clearing Pacific traffic with a hot-shot sideswiper and a crummy old quenched gap. He was picking up relay stuff for KPH. Drake. Pete Drake! He never had to give his sign. The minute he opened up, the whole damn ocean knew who it was.

Maybe they did. Maybe even now they did. Maybe the restless shades of all the old brass-pounders heard him. If they did, then they knew. They knew right away who it was. Snaggy, somewhere off Diamond Head. Freddy Cugle, the straight-key man. They'd know. The instant they heard this fluting note, their heads would all come round and a wrinkling smile of recognition would suddenly touch their eyes. The stuff rolled off his fingers like a flowing song. I never saw fingers work a key like that. I never heard stuff like that before. Then the Trintipal lunged over. She teetered and hung there. She didn't rise. I looked up. Captain Blandon was back. His face was drawn. He was frowning severely at Drake. And at me.

"It's all right, sir." Speech sounded hollow. The ship was dead. It sounded like speech in an empty cave. "He knows his stuff," I said, giving Peter Drake the simple accolade.

"Well, come along! At once!" The Old Man's voice was brittle. "The boats are afloat. They're standing by. I've kept lines from them to the boat-deck rail. They'll haul us aboard when we jump. Can you manage, Sparks?"

"I'll manage, sir. We're ——"

"Then I'll signal the mate."

"Yes, sir. We're coming right away."

"Hurry! She is on her beam ends now."

Then we were all alone again. Me and Drake. But not for long. "You listen to me! The Old Man won't leave till the last! I know!" I spat the words out at him. I knew what I had to do. "You tell him you can't swim. You're scared. Tell him anything you want. I can't help you in the water with this arm. He can. Get him over the side first. I'm coming back. You understand?"

"Sure. Sure, Sparks. I understand."

"I can use one side of that sideswiper. Good enough to be read. That position you sent don't mean a thing. We need compass bearings for a fix. Those boats will be floating around in a gale or a freezing pea-soup fog. You think I want to hear the things you hear? You think I want to wind up a damn drunken sousehead like you? Not on your life! Not me! I'm coming back!"

"Sure." He was moving ahead of me on the steeply slanted deck, his narrow shoulders and his gray head bent. "Sure, you are," he said. "And you're dead right, Sparks."

Then all in an instant he spun around. There was the funny look in his eyes. I saw it. That's all I saw. His fist smashed out at me. He had gathered up all his strength, leaping. My head rocked back with shock. I knew it. That's all I knew. I found the rest out later. I found out, huddled under a greatcoat in the stern sheets of Tony Fuller's boat.

He told the Old Man I fainted. I was cold, all right, out cold. That's how he got Captain Blandon to jump first. Then he lowered me into the water, a bowline under my arms, and waved all clear to the mate. They started to haul us across. And he stayed. He went back. He went back where he belonged.

That's how it was in the Trintipal. I saw her go down. We watched her from across a narrow space of ocean in that freezing, sunless dawn. The boats kept climbing to the white-flecked crests, rushing down to where the valleys glinted, ominous and green. I kept my eyes on the boat deck, on what was left up there of the radio shack. That's where Peter Drake was. I never saw him again, but I knew that's where he was.

I knew what he was doing there. He was working the tool of his trade. The artist's tool. He was getting us plotted down to a pin point on the charts.

We saw the Trintipal shudder suddenly. Her leeside decks were awash. . . . *Whoever knows where they come from— them shoreside bums? Or, for that matter, where they go?* Stuff like that kept bubbling, without rhyme or reason, across the back of my brain. *I never even froze the key. I just sent the SOS and ran like hell for the boats.* There she was. She was going now. *The first time Johnny moaned, I knew I'd lost my ticket. He took it away from me. Right there in an open boat.* Steam gushed from the Trintipal's engine-room skylights. We heard the bulkheads inside her explode. The concussion was muffled. *Hell, no. They ain't mine. But the way I figger it, kids is kids. They could 'a' been mine.*

The Trintipal's wheel flung clear, the blades shining and motionless. Her head was sliding under already, dragging the rest of her down. There was nothing left but one great whirl-pool on the ocean's face, and the broken debris swirling. She was gone. He went with her. But first he cleared his hook. He went back after twenty years and cleared his hook at last. He never expected a chance like that. It doesn't often come. He had an enormous good fortune. He saw his chance and he took it. I don't know yet where he came from, but I can tell Tony Fuller for certain where he went. He went back where he belonged. His smile isn't crooked any more. I know that for sure. And I know Johnny, the little oiler, doesn't moan. He's got his ticket back. He deserves it. I know that in all the ships who listened to him doing the Trintipal's last work, they tapped their keys for single dots when they heard Drake's set whine out and die. They were sending him their 73's—a brass-pounder's way of giving farewell. Farewell and godspeed. In my mind I sent him my own. He deserved that too. . . . We were picked up three hours later. We only lost one other man.

I told Dorothy all about it. I never would have seen her again if it wasn't for Peter Drake. Dorothy didn't think a girl ought to marry a man who went to sea. She had decided we ought to sign off for good. But I went back anyhow, and I told her. I told her all about it. She listened till I was done, the funny little wrinkles gathering between her eyes. Then she nodded.

Dot's gonna have a kid now. It's our first. I sure hope it's a boy. I'll get a deadhead message when it happens. Maybe I'll get it tonight. Because here I am in the middle watch with the earphones tucked at my temples. I'm waiting to meet a traffic schedule with KPH. It's Joe Pagini over there, and Joe's an old-timer. The minute I open up, he'll know what kind of a key I use. He don't know why I use it, but he'll know right away it's me. Then all the time I'm rapping out the code I'll be thinking of Peter Drake. Till my message hook is clean. I wish it was Pete Drake's sideswiper I was using. But it couldn't be. So I did the next best thing. I made me one of my own, and I swore I'd learn to use it right. I hope I did. Because if it wasn't for him, I wouldn't be here.

It's schedule time right now. I got my fingers on the key. I'm rolling the stuff off sweet. I'm calling for KPH. There he is. What did I tell you? I never even gave my sign. But here he comes through the break-in relay, bustin' in from Frisco two thousand miles away.

"Good morning, MP," he's saying. "Got nine for you. It's a girl. *K*—go ahead."

THE HAUNTED MEADOW

By W. A. POWERS

MANY Americans who were stationed in that part of England during the war will remember the village of Little Waddlingford, in Cambridgeshire. Some may even recall William Packard's pub, the Running Pheasant, which stands across the main street from the post office. In most ways the Running Pheasant is a completely average English public house with low eaves, a high sloping roof, and low, oak-beamed ceilings. No one—except perhaps some of its most devoted regulars from the village—would call it the best example of a late-eighteenth-century pub, and yet no one would term it the poorest. From its polished, brass-topped, walnut-handled beer pulls to its serried bottles, dart board, and the fox's mask that hangs above the main door, it is everything you imagine an English country pub to be and is typical of dozens of its sort throughout England.

Some distinction, it is true, is contributed by the row of carefully executed sailing-ship models that lines the top shelf behind the bar, and the colored, gilt-framed engraving of Nelson as a midshipman that hangs as a centerpiece beneath them. In an inland village in the heart of the East Anglia farming region you don't normally expect to find such nautical embellishments. Yet they are easily explained once you learn that Mr. Packard, the publican, is a pensioned petty officer who spent over forty years in the Royal Navy. What isn't so easy to explain is one of the items, propped against the lacquered hull of the ship Victory, that forms a part of the Running Pheasant's collection of war mementos.

As with all public houses that were located near a military establishment during the war, the Running Pheasant was often given souvenirs by the troops who stopped there on their leaves and on week-end passes. Whenever he received one, Mr. Packard always proudly fastened it with a shoemaker's brad either to the bottle shelves or to the low-hanging oak beams above the bar. In time he had an impressive array

50

of British, American, French and Polish regimental badges and emblems of rank, and many a postwar visitor has been regaled with the stories behind a commando knife that was carried in the attack on Dieppe, a German Iron Cross taken from a prisoner at Arnhem, and a hunting horn which was found hanging from the turret of a knocked-out British tank at Knightsbridge, in the western desert. Mr. Packard is as proud of each one of them as he is of his collection of ship models, and never tires of pointing them out to newcomers or telling how he came to receive them.

The souvenir that stands against the hull of Nelson's Victory, however, is never mentioned. Strangers who notice it and happen to call attention to it are probably struck by Mr. Packard's sudden lack of expansiveness and by his intense preoccupation with some glasses he has just finished polishing at the opposite end of the bar. Even most of the villagers are uncertain of its origin or significance. They know it first appeared after an illness with which Mr. Packard came down on Halloween, of 1947, and which Doctor Dalrymple described as a recurrence of a fever he had contracted years before while serving in the Far East; but that is all. The few who know more can scarcely look on the Running Pheasant as just an ordinary public house.

When the news first came, early in 1942, that the airfield four miles outside the village was to be taken over by an American bomber group, everyone wondered what it was going to be like to have the village overrun by swarms of strange soldiers. Mr. Packard, who had never seen any Americans except occasional prewar tourists, had his doubts about how they would mix with his regular customers, or, more particularly, how his regular customers would mix with them. Secretly he rather hoped that the Americans would overlook the village and be drawn to the market town, which was eight miles in the opposite direction from the field and boasted three movie houses and a dance hall.

With most of the Americans this turned out to be the case, but the crew of the Lambsie Divey, as they called their bomber, had found the Running Pheasant during their first pass from the field and soon became regular visitors. Mr.

Packard remembered well the night they first appeared and took their seats at the corner table, talking and joking among themselves in their strange and strident jargon. Often he recalled how noisy and young they had sounded that night. Later he had grown more used to it, or perhaps they actually had become more subdued and lost some of their brashness as they began to see more experience. When he first saw them, though, he couldn't help but think what a strange lot they were, completely alien in dress, speech and manner to anything that had ever been seen in the village. His regular customers, too, he noticed, looked a bit askance and glanced with all-too-evident misgiving at the table in the corner, and talked even more quietly among themselves than they usually did.

That the regulars should feel resentment over the intrusion of the Americans was only natural. For years they had looked on the Running Pheasant as something of their own, a place where they could meet, gossip, quietly reminisce, and casually carry on their bitter feuds at darts. These began every night with the arrival of Mr. Halloran, the butcher, and continued until closing time. Every evening the tourney began in the same way; it had become almost a ritual. Mr. Halloran would arrive shortly after eight o'clock, say his good evenings, and order a pint of bitter. No mention of darts was ever made until he had slowly drained his glass. "Well, boys," he would say then, wiping and smoothing his mustache with the inside of his thumb, "who's ready for a go at the board?" That was the signal for Mr. Packard to snap on the corner light above the dart board and for all the regulars to retire to the end of the room to be either spectators or competitors in the evening's match.

The first night the crew of the Lambsie Divey came in, young Moe, from Brooklyn, broke the tradition of years by exclaiming, even before the top foam on Mr. Halloran's beer had settled, "Hey, what do you know? They've got a dart board in the joint!" Then, turning toward the bar, he asked, "Any of you guys ever play this game? I used to be champion of the Greenpoint Police Athletic League."

The regulars, all of whom were expert darts players, received the remark in silence. All eyes unconsciously sought out Mr. Halloran in the same manner that lesser prelates might

turn toward an archbishop as being best fitted to reply to the
attack of an infidel. Mr. Halloran was recognized not only as
dean of all dart-playing matters but also as general spokesman
for the village on all subjects from the right of way in certain
fields to its choice of representatives for the county council.
While everyone watched him, Mr. Halloran slowly drained his
pint and deliberately smoothed his mustache. Then he turned
to the others at the bar and said, "Come on, boys, let's give
the Yanks a game. Two of them and two of us to a side."

That was the start of a friendship that sprang up between
the regulars of the Running Pheasant and the Americans. Had
Mr. Halloran reacted in any other way, they might never have
got along at all, but by giving his benediction to it the ac-
quaintanceship became rapid and sure. Every evening they
were free, the five Americans—Moe, Hank, Lanny, Tex and
Pete—came either together or separately to the pub, and soon
everyone came to know and accept them as if they had lived
in Little Waddlingford all their lives. They were invited to
Sunday dinners; afternoons they taught the children softball
or tried to master the intricacies of cricket, and on Saturday
nights they practically took over the dance at the community
hall. Bit by bit the strangeness of their speech and manner
became more imperceptible. The village itself, especially the
children, came to pick up some of their slang and customs, and
nights when they couldn't get away from the field or were off
on a mission both Mr. Packard and the regulars missed their
youthful gaiety and high spirits.

The last visit the crew of the Lambsie Divey paid the Running Pheasant was two nights before Halloween in 1943. That
night and Halloween itself were dates that Mr. Packard could
never forget, even though his memory had become hazy about
many more widely known events of the war. It was bitterly
cold, and the boys had arrived late, after all the regulars had
said an early good night. When they came in, Mr. Packard
served them in the small private bar, where a fire still was
burning. He remembered clearly the excited spirits they were
in as a result of a successful mission to Düsseldorf that
morning.

As they took their places at the table near the fire, Tex
started the banter which had become almost their trade-mark.

"Barman," he said in his slow voice, "what have you got that's fit for the best tail gunner in the Air Force?" And Lanny, who came from Wisconsin, replied, "Give him some beer from Milwaukee, Packy. We're not proud about these Texas foreigners drinking it."

"Would you settle for a pint of mild and bitter?" asked Mr. Packard.

"That swill!" said Hank. "Why, in Kansas we wash our hogs in better brew than that."

"Yeah, Packy," added Moe. "When are you guys going to learn to make something a civilized man can drink? Three or four hundred years old, this burg must be, and still you don't know what good beer is."

"Make it five, Packy," said Pete, who was the quietest of the lot, and while Mr. Packard went behind the bar to draw the pints the raillery continued.

"When in Rome," Lanny said, "I guess we got to do what the Romans do, but maybe I won't be glad to get back to the States and a good cold glass of beer!"

"Me," added Hank, "come the peace, I'm going to start exporting ice to England. I'll get a big, seagoing tugboat from Navy surplus and drag whole icebergs over from Greenland."

"And I'll put juke boxes on them," said Moe. "Thousands of juke boxes and pinball machines. If the boys back in Greenpoint only knew what I'm going through!"

It was the same pattern that their talk took every night, and Mr. Packard was always amused by its pace and lightness. The secret, he knew, was never to take them seriously. After he had served the five pints of mild and bitter, he drew another for himself and joined them at the table.

"Hey, sarge!" exclaimed Lanny, as soon as Mr. Packard was seated. "What about throwing a Halloween party for all the kids—the same as we used to have at home? They've probably never seen a real Halloween in their lives."

"Sounds like a good idea," replied Pete. "When does it happen?"

"Night after tomorrow," said Lanny. "We're sure to have a pass that night. We can get apples and pumpkins from the field, there's plenty of candy in the PX, and we can get one of the cooks to whip us up a half dozen pies."

The idea caught on at once, and they all joined immediately in the planning. Lanny promised to put on a ghost act with a sheet and some phosphorescent paint, Tex said he would bring his guitar and sing cowboy songs, and Hank vowed he would tell some stories that would keep them all awake for a week. Mr. Packard, for his part, offered to turn over his back store-room for the occasion and to have old Luke, the thatcher, decorate it with cornstalks and pumpkins.

It was long past closing time when all their plans were finally made. The boys were determined to make it the biggest treat the kids had ever seen and promised to come in from the field as soon as their passes were granted. As they piled into their jeep, which was parked in front of the door, they called back their familiar good nights. "So long, Packy! Thanks for the beer." . . . "Don't forget that juke box!" . . . "For a limey, you're an O.K. guy!" . . . "Don't take any wooden nickels!" . . . "We'll be seeing you, Packy!"

Then they started off into the night, and that was the last time that Mr. Packard or any of the village saw them.

Two mornings later, while the frost was still thick on the frozen October ground, everyone in Little Waddlingford knew that a big American raid was about to come off. At four in the morning Mr. Packard, along with the rest of the village, was awakened by the coughing and roar of the giant engines as the planes warmed up and taxied from one end of the field to the other. By five-thirty he had counted one hundred and forty-four separate take-offs—more than had ever left the field on a single mission. Something special was on, he knew, and the Lambsie Divey was almost certain to be taking part.

Nearly all that day the American planes were away and the air was heavy and still with their absence. Everyone was conscious that a raid of exceptional proportions was on, yet no one ventured to speak of it. A hush hung over the village, as though it were a house where a patient lay dangerously ill. Mr. Packard busied himself quietly with preparations for the party, trying his best to keep his mind off the prime preoccupation of his mind. He saw the schoolmaster about gathering the children, had Mrs. Beecher clear out the back storeroom, and arranged with old Luke to have him and his helper decorate it with cornstalks and pumpkins.

It was almost midafternoon when the first of the planes began to return. First, four orderly flights of twelve arrived, then groups of eight and ten, and during the next half hour broken flights of six, four and three. Without speaking of the figures, the village kept tally of the arrivals as surely as they did the runs at a county cricket match. By four-thirty Mr. Packard had counted a hundred and twenty-nine. Some of the planes, he knew, might have made emergency landings at fields somewhere in the south. If the Lambsie Divey was among them, he hoped the field wouldn't be too distant for the boys to be driven up to Little Waddlingford in time for the party. He knew they were looking forward to it and would have as much fun at it as the children themselves.

Complete darkness came at five, and with it a light autumn fog and rain. As he approached the Running Pheasant from his last errand, Mr. Packard saw an American jeep parked close to the door. His first thought was that the boys hadn't been included in the mission or had arrived back early, but then he recognized the driver as a soldier to whom they had once introduced him.

"Evening, Mr. Packard," the boy called out. "Great weather for ducks and owls."

"Good evening," replied Mr. Packard. "Seems as though you lads have been having a day of it."

"One of the biggest yet. Bremerhaven caught it this time."

"How has the Lambsie Divey made out?"

"A wireless message came just as I was leaving the control room saying she'd crossed the coast. They're expecting her in any minute now. She's only flying on three engines, but she waved off landing at the emergency field in Suffolk. Said she had enough gas to make it home O.K."

"Rather a bad night for landing, isn't it?" asked Mr. Packard.

"Their skipper can put that crate down anywhere. This is duck soup. Wait a minute . . . that sounds like them now!"

Although the fog by now was so thick overhead that it was scarcely possible to see the treetops, Mr. Packard unconsciously looked upward. At first he could hear nothing. Then, all at once, he caught the muffled but unmistakable sound of engines that seemed to be approaching the village from the direction of the Channel. As the noise grew stronger he became aware that, instead of being a steady, even roar, it had a rising and falling pulsation which he knew meant a plane flying on three engines.

"That's them all right," said the soldier at his side. "There's no mistaking that knocked-out engine."

For a while the noise maintained a steady intensity and it was impossible to tell how far off it was, or even whether it was getting stronger or fainter. Then, without warning, the sound leaped to a crescendo of thunder and the plane seemed to rush directly over their heads, becoming lost to the north almost as suddenly as it had approached. When they next picked up the sound of the engines it seemed to be off to the west in the direction of the field.

"He's probably circling"—explained the soldier—"waiting for them to talk him in. They've got these fog landings down to a science now."

But during the next fifteen minutes the big plane continued to circle tantalizingly and unseen overhead, presenting to those listening on the ground only a huge and varying orb of sound. One segment of its course brought it directly over the village, where the roar of the laboring engines seemed to transfer itself into a trembling of the ground. Then the noise would soften and become lost in the night as the plane traveled off to the north and the west for another approach. Even though the quietly spoken reassurances of the soldier beside him kept Mr. Packard's spirits up, he couldn't help worrying a bit about the aimless, merry-go-round monotony and suspense of the giant machine thundering through the darkness.

When it happened, it came as suddenly and stingingly as the crack of a bull whip.

"Oh, oh!" said the figure at Mr. Packard's side. "Something's up. One of the other engines is coughing."

A break in the set cadence of the plane's engines could plainly be heard, and the next moment the bomber, with fire shooting from one exhaust, seemed to hurtle over their heads at almost roof-top height. Even before the noise of the explosion reached them, the great flash from the direction of Four Acre Meadow reflected itself in every window on the north side of the village. Mr. Packard remembered later that he had been able to read the inn sign over his head by it, and saw the sign quiver, as though from a sudden gust of wind, when the sound of the blast itself came. In scarcely more than a minute it was all over save for the crackling fire on the horizon, and the darkness that followed seemed deeper and blacker than anything the village had ever known. There was a personalness to the loss, as though some part of the village had been destroyed as well.

The next day a small white In Memoriam cross with the boys' names on it was put up to one side of the bomber's charred and twisted remains. A piece of the nose with the plane's name on it had been hurled clear of the wreckage, and someone propped it against the foot of the cross—a torn piece of aluminum with the words Lambsie Divey and the figure of a small gamboling lamb still discernible across its face.

Often during the months that followed, Mr. Packard walked by the spot and thought how much better it would have been if, rather than listing the boys by their official ranks, names and initials, the marker merely said: "This is for Hank, Moe, Lanny, Tex and Pete—five Yanks who gave their lives for their country and the world." It was by those names that the village had known them and would always remember them. On his walks he would stop a few minutes at the cross, either to pluck weeds from the grass around it or to readjust the aluminum nose covering, which no one had ever removed. Having known the boys better than anyone else in the village, Mr. Packard looked on the cross as his own responsibility. Scarcely a week went by that he didn't pay at least one visit to the scene of the crash, but after Halloween of 1947 the village noticed that his visits suddenly stopped and that, when he did take a walk, it was always in a direction other than Four Acre Meadow.

In most ways Halloween of 1947 had been a normal night at the Running Pheasant. No one who saw Mr. Packard noticed any sign of illness or a trace of the fever that had him closeted under Doctor Dalrymple's care for the next three weeks. There were a few customers in before supper, then a lull, and at seven-thirty most of the regulars turned up, as they usually did. Mr. Halloran came at his usual time, had his usual pint of bitter, and in his usual manner suggested a game of darts. While the match was in progress Doctor Dalrymple, who was only a rare visitor, came in, and Mr. Packard joined him in a tot of whisky. For a time they talked of the children's party four years before and of the plane crash which happened the same evening. It was the first time in a long while that the loss of the Lambsie Divey had been mentioned, and while they were talking about it the night came back to Mr. Packard in all its detail. During the course of their conversation he had two or three whiskies with the doctor, but there was really nothing in that which could be held responsible for what occurred later on.

When the dart game was finished, all the regulars retired to the small room with the fire, and the conversation, because it was Halloween, worked its way around to the subject of spirits, ghosts and apparitions. Among the farmers of the region there was a great deal of superstition and folklore, and for most of them the spirit world was a very real thing. Mr. Packard was always interested and amused by their stories of sights they claimed to have seen in the fields outside the village, but, even with his seagoing background, he never put the slightest stock in what they said. "If there were such things as spirits," he often remarked, "surely a man would have seen one in sixty-three years of living and traveling."

For a long while Doctor Dalrymple kept them all interested by recounting some of the more historic fantasies—of ghosts that were reported generation after generation in certain castles and houses, of the white horse that in one night galloped from Land's End to John o'Groat's with his actual hoof marks being discovered the next day at several points along the route, and of the several separate witnesses who had reported hearing Drake's drum being beaten on the Channel during the evacuation from Dunkirk. The supernatural was one of the doctor's favorite studies, but, while Mr. Packard listened with interest to all he said, it didn't lessen his disbelief in the slightest. He had never seen a ghost or anything that passed beyond the realm of reality in all his sixty-three years and, until he did, he would continue to think of the whole subject as being nothing but the sheerest fiction.

At ten o'clock Mr. Packard called out his customary, "Time, please, gentlemen! Time!" and the men finished their drinks, said their good nights, and in small groups or separately started for home. The usual routine at this hour was for Mr.

Packard to close up the bar, bolt the door, and then retire to his bedroom upstairs. Tonight, however, when the last table was cleared and the last glass shined, he didn't feel in the mood for sleep. Whisky, when he had more than his customary one or two of an evening, always tended to leave him a bit sleepless. Instead of bolting the door, he took his old navy greatcoat from the peg on the hall wall and set out for half an hour's walk.

The night outside was cold and clear, with the full moon just rising in the sky. Despite the briskness of the air, it was a good night for walking, and Mr. Packard puffed contentedly on his pipe as he strode out toward the end of the village. When he started, he had no preconceived plan or notion of where or even in what direction he would walk, but after ten minutes he noticed he was crossing Four Acre Meadow and heading toward the copse at the far side. Doctor Dalrymple, he thought, would probably say that what led him there was some sort of reflex action of the unconscious, evolving from their conversation earlier in the evening. Whatever it was, he could see no harm in taking another look at the cross and paying his respects to the Yanks on the anniversary of their crash.

It was while he was still in the middle of Four Acre Meadow that the first irregularity of the evening occurred. With the copse still a hundred yards away, Mr. Packard suddenly began to hear the unmistakable rising and falling sound of voices in the distance. That in itself was odd enough, as the people of the village and the neighboring farms were early retirers and few were ever abroad at that time of night. At first he thought that possibly a gypsy caravan was camped in the copse for the night. Several had passed through the village during the previous two weeks on their way south for the winter. But, as he approached closer and the voices became clearer, Mr. Packard knew definitely that they were not gypsies. The accents were indisputably American, yet there hadn't been an American in the district since the airfield closed down shortly after the end of the war.

If Mr. Packard had been a superstitious man, he no doubt would have turned back right then and there, and spread the news that the copse was haunted. That was the way, he told himself, all those daft tales of the supernatural got their start.

The only thing to do was to investigate the matter to its fullest and find the logical answer and explanation—which probably would be a simple one. It wasn't at all impossible that the voices came from some Americans on a camping trip. Of course, it was hardly the season to be camping, but Americans, especially American tourists, were always doing odd and unreasonable things. Or it might be a group of deserters. Some Canadians, who had been missing over a year, had been found in a Gloucestershire wood only four or five months before.

As he approached closer, he thought he heard something that rattled—not at all an eerie rattle, but something quite familiar which at the moment he couldn't quite identify. Then a voice called, "Come on, you sixey! Baby needs new shoes! Oh, you eighty from Dakatie!" This was answered by another voice, which remarked, "Five bucks says you don't!" Then the first replied, "You're covered. Come on now, you sixey!" It was four years—four years and two days—since they had said good-by to him outside the Running Pheasant, but there was no mistaking the voices of Tex and Moe.

By this time Mr. Packard was at the edge of the copse, scarcely thirty feet from where the plane had crashed and where the single white cross shone in the moonlight. Even at that distance, he could make out five figures in sheepskin boots, leather flying jackets, and long peaked caps. They were all there—Tex and Moe playing craps, Hank and Lanny lounging on their backs, and Pete sitting with his arms on his knees.

Hank spied him first. "There's old Packy!" he cried. Immediately they all jumped to their feet and ran toward him, all trying to clap him on the back and shake his hand at once.

"Hi, Packy!" shouted Tex. "It sure is good to see you."

"We were beginning to think you were never coming," said Lanny.

"Sorry we couldn't make the party," added Pete. "For a while there I thought we were going to crack right into the Running Pheasant."

"That really would have been the pay-off," said Hank. "Especially when it was just because of the kids that we didn't put down at that field in Suffolk."

"Hey, Packy!" asked Moe. "What ever happened to that

Scotch Land Army Girl that used to come to the dances? What a number she was!"

For a time the overwhelming surprise of the scene and the shock of hearing the familiar voices again left Mr. Packard without power to reply. It was all too far beyond anything that had ever happened to him, too much against all he had ever believed. Instead of answering their questions, or asking any of his own, he could only stand and gape at them in silence. In the moonlight he could make out every detail of their uniforms and their facial expressions. They looked in every way just as they had the dozens of times he had seen them before.

"I guess you're wondering what the hell we're doing here," said Pete.

"That's putting it mild," added Tex. "Poor Packy probably thinks he's gone completely nuts."

"What it is," explained Pete, "is that Halloween is a special sort of day up where we've been. They call it All Saints' Eve, and anyone who wants one can get a pass to midnight to come back to the last place they were on earth."

"The only catch to it," said Hank, "is that you can't move from that place unless someone sees you. This is the fourth year now that we've come down and sat twiddling our thumbs on this bank."

"Yeah," said Moe. "They've as many rules and regulations and as much brass up there as we had in Squadron 217, and everything's just as fouled up. Me—I always land in the wrong outfit!"

"Hey, Packy!" asked Tex suddenly. "How about giving us a beer? They'd have a pretty tough job pinching you for serving us after hours."

"That's an idea," said Hank. "Even that warm English beer of yours would taste good right now. How about it, sarge?"

"It's O.K. with me," answered Pete, "but we better get started. We haven't much time."

The next thing Mr. Packard realized, he was heading back across Four Acre Meadow, arm in arm with Hank and Moe, and the others were following behind. Hundreds of questions and protests rushed to his mind, but there wasn't one he could manage to put into words. Later he could only remember the walk back to the village as something that had happened in a dream, the details being dimmed by the haze of unreality. He knew that the boys had bombarded him with questions of their own about the village, the airfield and various people they knew, but what he said to them in reply, or whether he replied at all, he couldn't for the life of him recall.

When they arrived at the Running Pheasant, he threw open the door, turned on the lights, and led the boys into the small private parlor. Almost automatically he put another peat block on the fire and went behind the bar to draw five pints of mild and bitter. Then he poured a whisky for himself.

"Still the same old joint," said Moe, when they were seated. "And still no juke box!"

"I like things to stay the same," said Lanny. "You go back to the States after four years and everything has been torn down or changed into something different. This makes you feel at home, no matter how long you have been away."

"I bet," added Hank, "we could come back here a hundred years from now and still find it just the same."

"By then," said Moe, "it would probably be the only bar in the whole world that didn't have a juke box."

"Tell us about the party, Packy," asked Pete, after the beers had been set on the table. "Did it go off O.K.?"

"Yes, the party went fine," said Mr. Packard. "Mr. Halloran took charge of everything, and almost all the children in the village came. The back storeroom was all done in cornstalks and pumpkins, we had two big tubs for apple ducking, and in front of the fire we had Doctor Dalrymple's skeleton."

"What about the ghost?" asked Lanny. "That was what I was going to be."

"Doctor Dalrymple played the ghost," answered Mr. Packard. "We had all the lights go out and he came in through the side window. A lot of the children were frightened, but they loved it all the same. Then he told them stories and ended up by doing a dance with the skeleton in his arms. I guess they liked that best of all."

"We didn't spoil things," asked Pete, "by—well, by not turning up?"

"They all missed you," said Mr. Packard, "but we told them you were kept at the field and couldn't get leave. It wasn't until the next day that they found out it was your plane that crashed in the woods."

Hearing his own voice and summoning up the details of the party four years before made Mr. Packard feel more confident and gave the only reality there was to what was taking place. His whirling mind needed something solid to rest on, and this supplied it. All the while he talked, they listened attentively, smiling and nodding their heads in approval. It was almost as though they had worried all this time that their crashing and failing to show up had spoiled the party for the children.

When Mr. Packard finished describing the night of the party, Pete stood up and said, "Well, Packy, I'm afraid we've got to be going. It's almost twelve."

"Things are tough up there," added Moe. "They picked up a lot of MP's at Normandy and now the whole place is lousy with them."

As they rose from their chairs and started for the door, Mr. Packard walked along with them, just as he had done all the nights they had come before. After opening the front door for them, he stood and watched them put on their caps and button up the collars of their leather flying jackets.

"It's been great fun seeing you, Packy," said Pete. "Wish we could do it more often."

With the first booming stroke of twelve from the clock in the village square they all shook hands with him and went out into the street. He was still standing in the doorway when they turned and waved to him from the crossroad that led out to Four Acre Meadow. Their parting voices blew back, as though through the years. "So long, Packy! Thanks for the beer." . . . "Don't forget that juke box!" . . . "For a limey, you're an O.K. guy!" . . . "Don't take any wooden nickels!" . . . "We'll be seeing you, Packy!"

Mr. Packard watched their retreating figures blend and become enveloped in the ground mist that rolled in from the meadow. Even after they were lost from sight, he stood motionless in the open doorway, trying to piece together all that had happened since he started on his walk less than two hours ago. To none of it could he find any sense or explanation. All he could think was that the whole thing was some sort of hallucination, possibly brought on by the doctor's tales earlier in the evening and aided by the few extra whiskies. It might even be, he told himself, that he had fallen asleep by the fire and only dreamed that he had been out for a walk to Four Acre Meadow.

As for the fact that he, Horatio Packard, had actually seen and talked to a ghost—five of them, no less—he would have none of it. The proof, he suddenly saw, was simple. All that was necessary was for him to go back into the small private bar and see that it was the same as he had left it at closing time, with all the tables cleared and the glasses shined and lined at one end of the bar. That it would be that way, with no traces of any visitors, human or supernatural, he was prepared to stake his entire Admiralty pension.

This thought strengthened his confidence more than anything that had happened since the queer business began—or he imagined it began—at Four Acre Meadow. Moving with a sudden deliberation, Mr. Packard closed the front door of the Running Pheasant and bolted it securely. The warmth of the room felt good after the cold of the night, and he was cheered by its brightness. As he put out the light in the hall, he laughed, thinking of the tricks a man's mind could play on him. Had the same series of hallucinations happened to any of the farmers of the district, he imagined how hesitant they would have been to face the proof that was sure to be in the next room.

"The only way to beat superstition," he told himself, "is to follow the facts to the end." He even had a mind to telephone Doctor Dalrymple and cite the case in full to him as evidence of how superstitions start. Then he opened the door to the private bar and saw that the table in front of the fire was bare and clean. There was only one chair that was pushed out of place—the one he himself had been sitting in, and no doubt sleeping in too. Yes, he would call the doctor, despite the hour!

The telephone was in the front hallway, and before going to it he decided to put out the lights in the private parlor. The switch was beside the bar itself and, as he went toward it, his eyes looked up at his row of ship models along the top shelf. There, propped against the hull of the Victory, was a toy lamb, scarcely bigger than a man's outspanned hand, which he remembered well, even though he hadn't seen or thought of it in years. It stood there with its woolly legs apart and its head cocked to one side. It was the mascot which the boys had always carried in the plane with them and sometimes brought to the pub. They had bought it at the toy shop in the village just before their first bombing mission and had promised to give it to the Running Pheasant when their tour of operations was over. With difficulty Mr. Packard made his way to the telephone in the hall and his voice, when he gave the doctor's number to the operator, was uncertain and barely audible. The lamb, he knew from talking with others at the field, had gone with the boys on the day of their fatal flight to Bremerhaven.

THE SENATOR'S SHADOW

By DANA BURNET

THE first time the senator's shadow came loose was at the end of a momentous day in his life. At one o'clock that afternoon he'd been informed by the National Committee that he'd been chosen to make the keynote speech at the party convention in June. At approximately eight o'clock that evening he'd asked Mrs. Weatherly to marry him. Then at eleven-thirty P.M., alone in his Washington bachelor's apartment, his shadow had come loose, with unsettling results.

After all, even in these chaotic times, a man ought to be able to rely on his own shadow. Especially a man like United States Senator Thaddeus Ward Dowell, who was the soul of reliability. His career had been based on loyalty to the established order. His very physique was orderly.

He was a tall, virile, robustly handsome ex-lawyer of fifty, with a fine profile and a thick shock of grayish-black hair that, no matter how he tossed his head in debate, never became disheveled. This was due not to any restraining lotion, but to nature. He was as solid and changeless as a statue, which someday no doubt he would be.

A veteran Washington newspaperman once wrote of him: "When you see Senator Dowell rise to his feet on the floor of the Senate, you know you are looking at Status Quo in person."

This same newspaperman—a middle-aged chap named Digges—called the senator shortly before eleven-thirty on the night in question. The phone was ringing as Thaddeus Ward Dowell entered his apartment. He went directly into the living room, picked up the receiver and released his famous baritone, "Senator Dowell speaking."

"This is Pete Digges."

"Ah, yes, Pete. What can I do for you?"

"Senator, there's a rumor going around Washington that you're engaged to be married. Is it true?"

"No comment, Pete."

67

"Okay. So much for the record. Now, for my private information, when do you expect to announce it?"

"If and when any such announcement is made, it will come from the proper source and be released through the proper channels."

"Senator, no one would ever accuse you of impropriety! But you're an important figure today, and Mrs. Madelaine Weatherly happens to be the most glamorous woman in Washington ——"

"Pete, are you on your private phone?"

"Yeah."

"Well, you've never yet betrayed a confidence, so I'll tell you—I have a rather irrelevant impulse to tell someone—that I've asked Mrs. Weatherly to be my wife."

"And she said she'd have to think it over."

"How did you—ah ——"

"Senator, Mrs. Weatherly is known and respected, even among newspapermen, as a woman of conviction. She's not only the widow of the late Judge Weatherly—a great Jeffersonian Democrat—but she's a true liberal on her own account. A sincere liberal. You, on the other hand, for all your personal integrity and impenetrable virtues ——"

"I thank you."

"—— are a conservative of conservatives. A standpatter from here to where the dog caught the rabbit. It stands to reason, therefore, that the lady—regardless of her feelings in the matter—will have to do some thinking before she consents to marry you. How's that for summing up the case?"

"Shall we," the senator said in sonorous tones, "change the subject?"

"Okay. How do you feel about being the keynoter at the convention?"

"I answered that question at my press conference this afternoon."

"Yeah, I know," Digges said. "You're pleased and honored, and so forth. I just wondered whether there was any chance ——" The slightly raucous voice broke off with a laugh. "No! I'm too old a hand to ask that one."

"What is it, Pete?"

"Well, you can put it down to advancing senility, but I

wondered whether you might be tempted, at Philadelphia in June, to speak to the American people as Churchill spoke to the British in 1940 or as Lincoln spoke at Springfield in 1858. I believe you could do it—and what a spot for it!—if you dared let yourself go."

"If I dared —— I don't think I quite understand."

"I withdraw the question. It's a cub reporter's pipe dream. Good night, senator. Don't forget to send me a wedding announcement, if and when."

"Wait a minute, Pete. What was your question again?" But there was only a click at the other end of the wire.

The senator walked to his favorite armchair, sat down, filled and lighted his pipe. To the left of the chair was a standing lamp with an extra-strong bulb for reading. He reached up and switched on the light, but he didn't want to read. He sat erect, leaning forward slightly, one hand on his knee, the other clutching his pipe.

Which speech of Churchill's had Pete referred to? Probably the greatest, the one that had saved England, perhaps the world: "We shall fight on the beaches . . . in the streets . . . on the hills. We shall never surrender." And Lincoln at Springfield in '58. Wasn't that the famous "House Divided" speech?

Well, well. No use thinking along those lines. Great men at great moments spoke with the tongues of angels, but he was not among the angels. He was only a humble worker in the vote-bearing vineyard, and his own big moment, waiting to be born of a June night still weeks away, was not a rendezvous with destiny. It was or would be a date with political discretion.

The speech that he, Thaddeus Ward Dowell, would make at Philadelphia would be precisely what the party leaders decided it must be to win the election. It would be the classic clarion call to turn the rascals out. There was nothing wrong with that; it was in the American tradition and was what the American people expected.

Or did they? Or was there abroad in the land the same thought that Pete Digges had half expressed, the same wish, unconsciously formed, to hear greatness speak? To hear the greatness of a people speaking through the lips and from the heart of some man lifted up, seeing clearly the truth of his time and saying it simply, strongly, as the heroes of history had been inspired to say it?

"Here, here, stop this!" the senator said aloud. "Come out of it!" Feeling, as always, the need of an audience, he addressed his shadow lying on the floor. The strong light sharply outlined the shadow and he spoke to it while sternly exhorting himself. "You're a party regular, Thad Dowell! A member of the old guard, a private in the ranks . . . or at most a top sergeant. Don't get too big for your breeches. Don't step out of line or try to stand alone or ——"

He stopped short. His shadow no longer lay at his feet. It was moving, with a sort of flowing motion, toward the opposite wall. It reached the baseboard, glided up the wall to its full height and came to rest against the plaster.

The thing was so smoothly done, so natural, in a queer sort of way, that the senator's first reaction was one of mere annoyance. He said gruffly, "Come back here. I'm talking to you."

The shadow shook its head.

"Good Lord!" said the senator. "You're loose!" He closed his eyes. When he opened them again the shadow—his shadow—was still standing there.

"All right," the senator muttered. "All right, I'm having a hallucination. Might as well make the best of it." Controlling himself, he reflected that a man can learn something from any experience, so long as he doesn't flee from it in panic.

"I trust ——" he began, but his voice squeaked, and he paused to strengthen it. "I trust that we are still friends?"

The dark figure nodded, and Thaddeus wiped his brow. "Well! I must say that's a relief! You can hear me when I speak?"

Another nod.

"But you can't speak to me?" queried the senator, and when the shadow shook its head, he added hastily, "No, no, of course not. You wouldn't have the wind. The ability to speak is certainly a windy function. So, as I'm rather good at it, I'll do the talking and you —— But what shall I call you?"

The shadow shrugged. The senator said, "When I was a boy, I had an imaginary companion—as so many children have—named Brother. Being an only child, I suppose I wanted one. Anyway, he seemed as close as my own shad —— that is, as a real brother. How does the name strike you?"

The figure not only nodded but bowed.

"Splendid!" the senator said. "How are you, Brother?" Then he waved his pipe as though erasing the question. "No, don't try to answer that. I must learn to keep our conversation on a two-dimensional level. But I'd like to know the purpose of your present action. I take it you have a purpose?"

Brother nodded decisively. It made the senator nervous, and he said, "You're not going to haunt me, are you?"

Another nod, followed by a headshake.

"Yes and no," translated the senator. "From which I gather that you do mean to haunt me, but not to any unbearable extent. In short, your intentions are honorable. Or may I say benevolent?"

This time Brother's nod was a great comfort to Thaddeus.

"You're doing this for my own good? . . . Yes, I see. Thank you. Though I don't know what I'm thanking you for. Can you give me some hint?"

Brother seemed to be meditating.

"Look," pleaded the senator. "I've played charades. If you have a message for me, just act it out and I'll try to guess it."

Immediately, Brother went into action. He began to make gestures, flinging out one arm, then the other; lifting both in air, clenching his fists, pounding his chest—if a shadow can be said to have a chest—pointing upward, pointing at Thaddeus and finally spreading out his hands in dramatic appeal.

"I don't get it," the senator said.

Brother's head drooped. He seemed chagrined and dejected.

"I'm sorry," the senator said. "Do you want to go through your act again?"

Brother perked up and repeated his pantomime. The senator blew a lopsided smoke ring. "I still don't get it. Could be a man making a speech, but —— Oh! You nod your head! So I've guessed it. But such an extravagant performance can't possibly refer to me. . . . What? You nod again? My dear Brother, I assure you that you're mistaken. Ridiculously mistaken. No offense meant!" he added, as the shadow began to quiver ominously. "But I'm noted in Washington for the reticence of my delivery. I never wave my hands, and my most expansive gesture is to hook my hands in the armholes of my vest or, in warm weather, under my suspenders."

Brother turned his back on the senator.

"Oh, come now!" Thaddeus said uneasily. "Don't be annoyed. This thing is complicated enough without adding ill feeling to it. Why don't we just call it all off? Come join me again, won't you?"

It was no use. Brother didn't budge from the wall, and suddenly Thaddeus had an awful thought.

"Good heavens! Suppose this should happen in public? Suppose I were addressing the Senate, and you, with every eye upon us, decided to walk out on me? What would my colleagues say? What would Mrs. Weatherly say? What would the newspapers make of it? I can see the headlines now! SENATOR DOWELL DIVORCED BY HIS OWN SHADOW! It would be a national disgrace and a party disaster. It might even cost us the election!"

This outburst had its effect. Brother turned back and shook his head at the distraught senator.

"You mean you won't abandon me in public?"

Brother nodded reassuringly, and Thaddeus was moved to press his advantage. "Look here. I'm a very busy man. I'd be extremely grateful if you'd refrain altogether from haunting me by day."

Brother appeared to hesitate; then he gave another nod.

"Oh, thanks," breathed the senator. "I'll do as much for you sometime. And now . . . I seem to be exhausted. What say we go to bed? I have a meeting in the morning and —— Oh, no! Not that again!"

The shadow was going through its oratorical routine for the third time. Thaddeus could stand no more. He reached up and switched off the light. That wiped out Brother.

Feeling strangely guilty, Senator Dowell crept into his bedroom and undressed in the dark. He was safe in the darkness but as he lay wrestling with insomnia—he counted constituents instead of sheep—he feared that he had not seen the last of Brother.

Yet so elastic is the mind of man, especially of political man, that in the morning the senator bounced back to normal.

His face, as he shaved, was as ruddy and cheerful as ever—he had always secretly liked his face—and he laughed at himself in the mirror. "Fell asleep in my chair last night," he told himself, "and had a nightmare. Must have been that angel pie I ate at Mrs. Weatherly's."

He wouldn't see Mrs. Weatherly again for a week. At the outset of his courtship he had decided to ration his calls, to indulge his ardor only at regular intervals. "In that way," he had told her, "no one can accuse me of impetuosity."

"I'm sure of that," Madelaine Weatherly had said, and then she had smiled peculiarly, in a way that both charmed and puzzled him.

Thinking about her now, he burst into song. He sang When the Roll is Called up Yonder I'll be There!, which led him to think not of heaven but of Philadelphia.

He spent most of that day conferring with party bigwigs about the speech he was to make at the convention. A rough draft of the speech had already been prepared by experts of the platform committee. It was a masterpiece of platitudes, ringing denunciations of the opposition and cautious promises that would not bind too closely the party nominee for President.

In sum, it was exactly what Senator Dowell had expected—a typical keynote speech, to which he would add only his lion's voice, his distinguished presence and his capacious diaphragm. No word or thought would be his own. Yet he would utter his lines with the conviction of an actor who believes in the play to which Providence or some lesser agency has assigned him.

Thaddeus Ward Dowell, dining out that night with a fellow senator, expressed himself as well content with his role. He was, he said, an instrument—a wind instrument, he might have added, if he'd been in a lighter mood.

He had not thought of his shadow since morning. But as he entered his apartment about ten P.M. he suddenly remembered Brother. His hand on the hall switch hovered uncertainly, then dropped to his side. In the broad light of day, he had convinced himself that last night's experience was a dream. Now he was not so sure.

He thought: *If I don't turn on any lights, there can't be any shadow.* Perhaps it was cowardly not to try it and see, but again he thought of his duty. If he saw Brother again he might develop a neurosis, embarrass the party high command and possibly end his own career.

He went to bed in the dark. The next night he did the same thing. By the third night it had become a habit. The week passed. It was time to call on Mrs. Weatherly, but then she telephoned and said that she had to go to New York on business. Would he forgive her, and come to dinner a week from tonight?

Thaddeus was disappointed and upset by this break in his routine. Also he wondered what business Mrs. Weatherly had in New York. He used the intervening days to memorize his speech, and there were times when he wished that Brother could see how restrained were his gestures.

Ultimately the note on his memo pad read: "Dinner, Mrs. W. Seven sharp. Black tie." The night had come, it was now June, and as he drove himself to Georgetown the senator thrilled—or at least tingled—with anticipation. Perhaps tonight, with the marriage month at hand, Madelaine would say yes to him.

Her eighteenth-century, white brick home on N Street was a perfect setting for Mrs. Weatherly's serene, somewhat old-fashioned beauty. Nature had given her the hourglass figure that lately has returned to favor, and she had preserved it—as she once told Thaddeus—with fasting, prayer and the help of a good foundation garment. Her eyes were large and limpid with a friendly light in them, and her mouth was a pink bow drawn for laughter. Even when she was serious, there was usually a hint of laughter about her lips. She was forty-five, and quite frank about it. With her looks, other women said, she could afford to be.

"Now, Thad, I'll tell you why I went to New York," she said, when they were having after-dinner coffee in the drawing room. "I went to meet the head of the Atlas Newspaper Syndicate, who wired me last week, offering me a job."

"A job?"

"Yes. You know people are always after me to write on political subjects. They seem to think I'm in a position to know what goes on—especially in Washington."

"Which you are," said the senator.

"So I've signed a contract to cover both major conventions for the syndicate. I'll be in Philadelphia, Thad, to hear you deliver your keynote speech."

"Well!" said Thaddeus. "I hadn't figured on that."

"I hope my being there won't upset you."

"Madelaine, you won't approve of my speech!" The senator sighed. "Oh, why couldn't you have been born a member of my party?"

She gave him her faintest smile. "I wasn't born a member of any party. My father was a Republican, Tom Weatherly was a Democrat. I've voted both tickets. In the coming election I have no particular choice. I only hope and pray it won't be a dyed-in-the-wool party man, but a real, honest-to-God, bigger-than-life American."

Thaddeus said rather stiffly, "I see nothing wrong with electing a party man, if he belongs to the right party."

"And that," she said, "will be the burden of your speech!"

"I can't discuss my speech, Madelaine, even with you."

"I know that. You don't have to. I can guess what it will be. The party—first, last and always! The party, right or —— Why, what's the matter, Thad?"

"Nothing," the senator said, but his voice was weak, for he had seen his shadow on the floor. A lamp at his shoulder cast it strongly at his feet, and though it seemed quiescent, he was alarmed.

"What are you staring at?" Madelaine persisted.

"I—ah—I thought I'd spilled coffee on your rug."

"But, Thad! You look so pale! Are you ill?"

"No," he said, "it's simply—it's my eyes. I've been having trouble with my eyes lately. Do you mind if I turn out this light?"

"Of course not, though the room will be quite dark, I'm afraid."

"I'm not," said Thaddeus. He quickly turned out the light, got up and walked to the Queen Anne sofa on which she was sitting. He sat down beside her. "Madelaine," he said, shaken both by love and by his narrow escape from Brother, "have you made up your mind about me?"

She leaned forward to put down her coffee cup on the table before her. "I can't," she said.

"Can't decide, you mean?"

"Yes. I like you very much, but —— Oh, how cold that sounds!"

"But you don't like my politics!"

"It's more than politics, Thad, and it's more than liking or disliking. I can't marry you till I'm sure ——"

"That you love me?"

"Till I'm sure," she said, "what kind of man you really are."

"But, my dear Madelaine, there's no mystery about that! I'm just what I seem to be. I always have been."

"I wonder!" she said. "It's so easy to deceive oneself."

"You think I haven't been true to myself?"

"I don't know. . . . Yes, that's just what I do think! I think there's something in you, Thad—at times I seem to have glimpses of it—that comes close to greatness. It's not what you say or think; it's what you are. You must have shown it as a sergeant in France during the first World War, when you swam a river under shellfire to take command of a company whose officers had all been killed ——"

"But I never told you that!"

"No. I heard it from a friend of mine, a general in the War Department. He was one of the men you commanded."

"Well," said Thaddeus helplessly, "that was a long time ago."

Her laugh was gentle. "You were twenty then. I figured it out." She turned her face toward him. "What were you like before that, Thad? What were you like as a boy?"

"Why," he said, "I guess I was just an ordinary boy. If I rose at all above the average, it was because I had to work for everything I got. I was always hungry."

"Oh, poor Thad!" Madelaine said; and then, "But maybe hunger is what greatness comes out of. Some kind of hunger ——"

"You keep talking about greatness! I'm not a great man!"

"You were great in France. There must have been something that made you so. Some inner compulsion, some vision ——"

"No, no," he said impatiently. "I obeyed my superiors, that's all. I was a soldier, and I still am. When I deliver that speech ten days from now, I'll still be obeying my superiors. I have faith in discipline, in organization ——"

"But not in yourself!" she cried. Her voice was strangely uncontrolled. "That's why I can't decide to marry you! Oh, I know I'm all mixed up and I suppose I'm unfair, but I want for myself what everyone wants in these dreadful times—the great heart, the clear mind, the spirit not afraid to speak out!"

It was what Pete Digges, the newspaperman, had said to him in other words, and suddenly it made Thaddeus angry. "I don't understand you! I'd better go."

He got up, and she rose with him and put her hand impulsively on his arm. "We haven't quarreled, have we?" she asked, and her lips smiled at him.

"No, we haven't quarreled. I'll see you again, I hope, after Philadelphia."

"Perhaps we'll meet there."

He said, "Perhaps," and so the evening ended on an indefinite, unfinished note. He drove home in a turmoil of conflicting emotions.

He went to bed in darkness as usual—he wanted no encounter with Brother tonight!—and dreamed that he was hungry. He was young and thin and all hollow inside, and yet he had to make a speech in the auditorium of the high school back home. A big American flag hung over the platform and there was bunting around the walls; they were holding the Graduation Day exercises and he was Senior Class Orator, and he could see all the faces turned toward him, waiting for him to begin. He raised his right arm in a futile gesture.

He woke with a horrified start. Still dazed by his dream, he sat up and switched on his bed lamp. And instantly—there on the wall beside his old mission-oak dresser—was Brother.

"Oh, no!" gasped Thaddeus. He reached for the light. But the shadow struck a pose that stopped him. It raised its right arm; and suddenly it became the thin, tense, nervous figure of a young man in a high collar.

"Me!" said the senator hoarsely. "You're me, as I was on that day in the auditorium long ago. It was June, 1916, I was eighteen years old and I had to deliver the valedictory address."

Brother gave an emphatic nod, and then launched furiously into his familiar oratorical routine.

"Oh, yes, I see! You needn't go on; I've got it," Thaddeus said; and added, "I suppose I did wave my hands in those days, but at least I made that speech. I'd written it myself, and I was scared to death, but I didn't fail, so you needn't keep reminding me of it."

The shadow pointed to the mission-oak dresser.

"What is it? What do you want now?"

Brother held his point and Thaddeus stared at the dresser. It was the first piece of property he'd ever owned. His mother had given it to him for his eighteenth birthday and he'd treasured it ever since. He got up now and walked over to it. Brother began to quiver excitedly.

"Am I getting warmer?" asked Thaddeus.

Yes, nodded the shadow. Its finger was aimed downward, and the senator stooped toward the bottom drawer.

"Warmer?" he asked again, and the response was more encouraging.

He pulled out the drawer. Brother went into a kind of jig, and from that moment on, Thaddeus was guided by dawning remembrance as well as by the shadow's promptings. The drawer was full of dusty mementos—old papers, notebooks, schoolbooks, class photographs, and so on. Then Brother's shadowy finger, greatly elongated, crept past the senator's nose and came to rest on a faded denim schoolbag.

"Ah!" said Thaddeus. "How many years I carried that! But there's nothing in it."

There was, though. Opening the bag, he took out a single copy of The Oracle, his old high-school magazine. "All right," he said to Brother, "stop pointing. I see the date: June, 1916."

With fingers that trembled slightly, he turned the pages. And there it was:

THE AMERICAN DREAM
VALEDICTORY ADDRESS
BY THADDEUS WARD DOWELL, '16

The senator walked back to his bed, sat down on the edge of it and groped for the reading glasses he kept on his bedside table. As he put them on, he was astonished to see that Brother had rejoined him. With the light behind Thaddeus, the shadow was now where it ought to be, lying on the floor and firmly attached to his feet.

"Oh, so we're friends again!" said the senator.

He began to read the address:

Fellow Students, Members of the Faculty, Assembled Guests: This is a solemn hour, not only for us who are gathered here but for the nation to which we owe allegiance above all other allegiances, with whose great life all our little lives are bound. Today our country stands, and we stand with her, at the crossroads of destiny. Beyond the shrinking sea, hatred and death and tyranny have ravaged and are ravaging a continent. The threat of war hangs over our own beloved land, and so it is well for us all, old and young alike, as we face the troubled future, to search for a faith that will not fail us in our time of trial.

Where shall we find that faith? Does it lie in our riches of gold and steel? In the shrewd brain, the busy hand that puts such treasures to use? Does it lie in our fields, our factories, our turning wheels, our deep wells, our iron mountains? These are blessings which only fools would deny. So, too, are the customs and institutions which even now, in these days of grave danger, have plunged us into the midst of a national political campaign.

Thaddeus thought, *Why, that's so. It was Wilson and Hughes that year.* He continued to read:

But in all humility I say that our faith does not lie in material wealth or industrial genius, or even in those inspired documents, the Declaration of Independence and the Constitution of the United States. The faith I speak of lies rather in the spirit that moved our fathers to create those instruments of freedom. It lies in the American dream.

The senator stopped reading. He took off his glasses, blurred with sudden tears. He looked down at Brother. "I know you now," he said. "You are my secret conscience. You are the ghost of my youth."

Then he wiped off his glasses and went on reading the speech he'd delivered so many, many Junes ago.

Ten nights later, on the stage of the huge auditorium in Philadelphia, Sen. Thaddeus Ward Dowell rose to expound the party gospel to the faithful, gathered in a pale, perspiring mass before him. The preliminary pandemonium had ceased, the convention had come to order. On the platform behind the rostrum sat the members of the party hierarchy and their guests; in the boxes and at other vantage points swarmed the newsreel men, the radio men, the television magicians, the legions of the press. Among them, Thaddeus knew, was Mrs. Weatherly. He had seen her once briefly in the lobby of the hotel where they both were staying. Her face was lost now in the pale haze that filled the hall. Above the stage a spotlight made a pool of light in which the speaker stood.

Silence, that rarest of political phenomena, had fallen on the house. The flags, the long-handled placards, the state standards were still. The delegates sat waiting for the ritual to begin. Their compelling business was to nominate a President. But the keynote speech was indispensable. The man who would sound it was known to them as a famous orator, renowned for his infallible memory.

They had no way of knowing that the senator's memory had failed him completely. He stood there in the spotlight, in enormous loneliness, seemingly lost in thought. Actually he was staring down at Brother, who lay in peace and propriety at his feet. "You did this to me," Thaddeus muttered. "All right, I'll show you."

He lifted his head and began to speak, "Fellow Americans: This is a solemn hour, not only for us who are gathered here but for the nation to which we owe allegiance above all other allegiances, with whose great life all our little lives are bound. Today our country stands, and we stand with her, at the cross-roads of destiny."

Behind him there was a stir, a ripple of movement as the party leaders—especially those who had written the keynote speech—sat up in their chairs. In one of the boxes, Pete Digges, the Washington newspaperman, turned a pocket flashlight on the first page of the senator's manuscript, advance copies of which had been issued to the press. Other flashlights winked around the auditorium and there was a rustling of paper, like the sound of dry leaves in a gust of wind. A wave of wonder swept over the audience. It, too, stirred and sat up and was caught in an excitement it did not understand.

Then, as the senator's rich voice rolled on, an almost unnatural quiet replaced the restlessness. The excitement remained, it increased, but it did not burst forth. The whole vast gathering seemed to hold its breath, aware of some strange diversion from the norm.

Only Thaddeus, alone in his misery—which had also become a kind of exaltation—knew that he was making a speech based on the address he'd given in high school when he was a young man gripped by a hunger not altogether of the flesh. His oration had nothing to do with party issues or party politics. It wasn't patriotic spellbinding, but the speech of a prophet invoking the soul of his people. It poured from his lips in a living, thunderous torrent. On and on it went, until at last he paused, stepped back and lifted his head.

"Our fathers," he said in a tone that touched almost softly the ears of his listeners, "had a vision of Man triumphant over all the forces of enslavement, on guard against the evil within himself and forever resistant to tyranny from without. That is the American dream. Of Man victorious, dignified by freedom, master of his mortal fate. If this dream dies and we gain the whole world, yet shall it profit us nothing. But if all the fruits of it are destroyed and the dream itself endures, then we may say truly that America lives on.

"So let us measure ourselves, let us measure our leaders, let us measure the candidates who will come before us, by a standard of faithfulness to the American dream, and by that standard alone!

"I hold it to be our duty to the nation, and to those suffering millions in other lands who look to us for leadership, to choose here a man who will be not only the next President of the United States but who also will stand, with God's help, as champion of the civilized world. To this end, and to this man, we must pledge our loyalty and our labor, our uttermost treasure and, if need be, our lives, so that this dream of freedom will not vanish from the earth, or its light be withdrawn from the uplifted, sorrowing faces of mankind!"

The stillness, when he had finished, was like a mass hypnotic spell. It lasted for several seconds, and in those seconds Thaddeus Ward Dowell walked quickly off stage. By the time the storm broke he was out of the hall.

Behind him lay the ruin of his career. He had betrayed a political trust. His one idea was to escape, for the time being at least, the consequences of an act he could never explain.

He returned to his hotel. He was in his room, mechanically packing his suitcase, when someone knocked at the door. Inwardly shrinking, he went and opened it. "Madelaine!" he said.

She stepped quickly into the room, turned and faced him. There were tears in her eyes. "Thad, I had to come to you!"

He said stupidly, "How'd you know I'd be ——"

"I didn't. I just took a chance. I had to find you."

He stared at her. "All right, tell me. What happened? I mean, at the hall?"

"I don't know. I left when you did, as soon as I saw you start out."

He stood there with his big shoulders sagging. "I was going back to Washington . . . or somewhere. But I guess it's no good running away. I'll have to stay here and take whatever's coming."

"Thad, do you still want to marry me?"

He took a step toward her, and then he saw her tears. He shook his head. "You're sorry for me. I don't want that."

"Sorry for you? I love you . . . and worship you. I think I've loved you all along, but now I feel like kneeling down and ——"

"Madelaine! You don't understand! I made the wrong speech!"

"Yes, I know. I had a copy of the one they prepared for you. I read it. Then when I heard you speak —— Oh, don't you know what a great thing you've done?"

"But it means I'm through! After all these years!"

"Thad, I don't care! We've got forever."

"Forever?"

"Do I *have* to get down on my knees to you?"

"No," he said; and then she was in his arms and he knew that in his failure there was no shame and no dishonor. For her love honored him; her arms held him close, and her mouth, made for more than laughter, was satisfaction for all the long hunger of his youth.

After a while she said, "Now I've got to leave you. I hate to, but I've got a job to do. Besides, I want to know what's going on at the hall."

"So do I," he said. "But not just yet."

"I understand. But it doesn't matter now, does it? I mean, as far as we're concerned?"

He smiled and kissed her. "No, it doesn't matter now."

That wasn't quite true. After she'd gone, he discovered that he still had to face a certain confusion, a certain cleavage within himself. A man cannot break the habit of a lifetime without suffering some stress of soul.

The phone rang. It was on a table against the wall, and automatically he moved to answer it. Then he stopped and stood motionless, seeing his shadow on the wall. He'd completely forgotten Brother.

"You!" Thaddeus said bitterly. "You've done what you set out to do! I hope you're satisfied!"

The dark figure didn't move, but one arm was extended, pointing toward the telephone.

He pulled himself together and answered it. "Senator Dowell speaking."

"This is Pete Digges."

"Oh, yes, Pete. What can I do for you?"

The newspaperman spoke a single sentence; and the phone dropped from the senator's hand. The receiver spun crazily at the end of its cord. Thaddeus leaned against the wall for support. As he did so, he and Brother seemed to rush together, and vaguely he knew they would never part again.

For what Pete Digges had said over the phone was "Well, senator, how does it feel to be nominated for President of the United States?"

LONELY LADY

By MARTHA GELLHORN

I FIRST saw Fiona on a deserted deck of the Aquitania. As always, she looked too beautiful to be true. We were both eighteen then and the Aquitania was three days out of New York and I believed, in anguish, that we were caught in a typhoon and would sink and I did not mind. I remember thinking when I saw her that I was swarthy, dumpy and no one would ever love me, and then I crept down to my cabin and died the many deaths of seasickness. When the sea became reasonable again, I emerged and began to walk the deck. That was how I met Fiona. I stumbled over her deck chair, almost falling into her lap, blushed and told myself that she would never have been so awkward.

"It's a terrible sea," Fiona said. "It goes sideways. I'm having tea out here. Wouldn't you like some?"

"Oh, I'd love to!"

By asking questions, for I had not learned better, I found out that Fiona Farleigh was on her way to London to be presented at Court. I had heard of this, but never expected to know a girl who did anything so unlikely. Her mother and her maid were on board, but both still ailing. They lived in New York in the winters; no, father died some years ago. In the summers they always went abroad. Did she like it? It was very "agreeable"; the word puzzled me. I listened to that low, grave voice and felt myself to be not eighteen, but eight, and a hopeless babbler, and of course hideous.

All the time that I talked, for I talked much more than Fiona, I stared at her. She was my ideal and it made me feel dismal. Her hair was dark gold, something never to be copied, never in fact seen before: a great mane of color as warm as wood and overlaid with a gilt sheen. She wore it long.

"Oh, why, I thought, did I have this ridiculous stuff sticking out like a thatch on my head, for I was dark, yet no one would ever say "that raven-haired beauty, Miss Tilly Burke," and my hair was cut in a bob of no special length or style. On the day I missed falling into Fiona's lap, her hair was coiled at the back of her neck. Sometimes she wore it in braids like a crown.

If you said her nose was short and straight, and her skin so fine that, at the nostrils, it seemed transparent; or that her mouth was delectably carved; that her eyes were wide set, oval, large and of a blue like no other, having purple shadows in it; that her dark lashes were thick as brushes; and her brow and her chin and the tone of her skin, which was neither pink and white nor creamy nor gold, but all of these—then you had merely made a list of Fiona's face.

She was tall, too, and slender, and I never saw that she looked where she put her feet. She walked as if nothing could fail or fool her; there would not suddenly be a step where none was expected, or a slippery place or a hole or a bump.

Without much urging, I told Fiona the story of my life. I was going to France, to Paris, alone, to spend a year with Aunt Tilly, whose namesake I was. My family lived in Kansas City and I had four brothers and sisters and I was the eldest. Oh, said Fiona, and I guessed something like envy in her voice, so I made the most of it, though my brothers were young fiends who never stopped playing jokes on me, especially when I was dressed up to go to a party or when boys were calling, and my sisters borrowed my most desirable possessions and ruined or lost them.

Aunt Tilly Warner was my mother's sister, and had lived in Paris for seventeen years. She had a big house in the Rue de l'Université, which I pronounced roo de l'University, in an unabashed Kansas City accent, and she was rich. As soon as I said this, I felt ashamed, for I knew without being told that Fiona had much more money than Aunt Tilly and it was somehow wrong to talk about money with the rich. Aunt Tilly never came back to the United States because it depressed her, and Kansas City filled her with despair. She had written, not very graciously, to say that she didn't want her namesake to grow up without some of the benefits of civilization.

"What fun it will be for you," Fiona said.

We exchanged addresses, though Fiona announced with her usual sober honesty that she did not like writing letters and would be very busy, but if Aunt Tilly brought me to

London I must stay with them. Her mother had taken a house
for the season in Eaton Square. I did not dare offer Aunt
Tilly's hospitality. I had never met Aunt Tilly.

For almost a year in Paris, I cried myself to sleep with dripping regularity and wrote my family tragic letters, begging
to be returned to the bliss of Kansas City. Aunt Tilly had
looked at me as if I were not human, but a cross between a
tadpole and a wrecked automobile. She regarded me as almost
impossible raw material which might, with determination, be
changed into a presentable young girl. I studied French and
toured the museums with a tutor, until my feet felt like burning concrete. Mademoiselle de Neufchamp was fifty, of im-
poverished but excellent family, and was one of the most
narrow and snobbish human beings I have ever met. My diet
was supervised so that the comfortable puppy fat of eighteen
melted away; my skin was considered and though it seemed
beyond repair ("It's so brown, so peasant," Mademoiselle said)
many cures were applied. I was clothed in a way that seemed
idiotic to me; my little sister of fourteen would have refused
to look so infantile and modest.

My Aunt Tilly, poor woman, was trying to make an adoles-
cent from Kansas City into an aristocratic *jeune fille du monde,*
with the final idea of presenting me to a critical, clawing, but
superior world, where I would make an advantageous marriage. I longed for death. I used to watch men, especially
those of a marked criminal type, on the street, hoping one of
them would kidnap me. I poured out letters to my mother
and got in return troubled, sad, loving ones from her, begging
me to understand that Aunt Tilly was doing everything for
my own good. Then suddenly my life made me angry and I
decided I would show Aunt Tilly that I was twice as clever
as all the unseen but constantly vaunted young French girls. I
would become furiously presentable, which would teach Aunt
Tilly and also be an escape from this brocaded jail.

And I thought of Fiona, who had never suffered as I now
did, and probably never needed to. Fiona would be moving
with ease from triumph to triumph, from delight to delight.
For Fiona was beautiful; she knew exactly how to behave;
when she came into a room everyone must gasp with admiration.

Aunt Tilly was a great subscriber to fashionable periodicals. During the summer I saw Fiona's perfect face in the Tatler and the Sketch. The people around her never seemed to stand very close, and they had a way of looking at her with wonder that was almost doubt. The other women often appeared somewhat cross. Fiona was the same: grave, magnificent and serene. She was going to house parties, race meetings, balls. Her clothes were discussed with reverence. Her beauty was mentioned as if it were an act of God. In the spring, she was at Antibes, where her mother had a villa. ("Here on the Riviera, Miss Fiona Farleigh has chosen to wear only white.")

I wrote Fiona twice, and received no answer, and then I stopped. Mademoiselle had taught me the intricacies of good behavior: one does not thrust oneself on anyone.

Then, in June, more than a year after our crossing on the Aquitania, Fiona arrived in Paris. This fact was lengthily noted in the society columns of the Paris Herald. I disobeyed Mademoiselle's teachings, because I was like one dying for water in the desert, and telephoned Fiona's hotel. The remembered voice answered me charmingly, and I was invited to lunch. "We'll talk," Fiona promised. "I want to hear everything you've been doing. How lovely to hear from you, Tilly. I'm so bad at writing letters."

Aunt Tilly knew the Farleigh name, as she knew all names she considered worth knowing; and it was agreed that Mademoiselle would take me to the Crillon at one and call for me at three.

"I think you might begin to meet a few people, Tilly," my aunt said. "And we'll travel a bit, later in summer. You've grown into quite a nice young girl."

Fiona's sitting room could have been mistaken for a flower shop. There were roses everywhere, in such quantities as I had never seen. Fiona was friendly in her own way—very kind, but cool as the flowers. She looked like a lady, a real person, a grownup, in a soft beige dress while I looked like the Age of Innocence in French blue with a round collar and a matching straw hat trimmed in flowers. However, even the Age of Innocence, done by Paris dressmakers, is not to be despised.

"Tilly, you've changed. Let me look at you." She studied me. "You're perfectly sweet," she announced, and I felt like a baby

who has been admired in its pram, though Fiona did not
mean it unkindly. "What have you been doing all year, Tilly?"

So I told her, and from pride I tried to make it funny, pranc-
ing around the room as the dancing master ordered me to
walk, sitting on the edge of a chair and holding a conversation
in French, and Fiona watched and listened and smiled gently.
It didn't seem very funny, after all.

"What a tyrant your aunt sounds," Fiona said.

"Yes," I said, "and what use is all this going to be in Kansas
City?"

"You'll get married," Fiona said encouragingly, "and then
you can do what you like."

I did not see whom I could marry, unless it would be Aunt
Tilly's second footman, because I met no men. "Now please tell
me," I begged. "You're the one who has been doing things."

So, without emphasis, Fiona told me of the season in London
and her later travels.

"I saw pictures of you," I said; "with so many people."

People. Dear Lord, I thought, what I wouldn't give for
people. The people, it appeared, were "agreeable" and nothing
more. I did not dare inquire further. To a girl starved for talk,
Fiona was not very good value.

Then it was three o'clock and Mademoiselle telephoned
from below and I had to leave. Walking home, I felt a certain
bewilderment. Fiona was still my ideal, but there wasn't much
to do about her. I had come away lonely as I had gone. She
had no problems, and problems are what link people; and no
passions, and she did not laugh, and you felt as if you were
communicating from separate mountaintops. Wasn't she ever
unhappy, I thought; wasn't she ever anything—I could not
find the word, and searched, and thought *mixed-up*—like other
people?

I had hoped to go home in July, to the blazing heat of the
Midwest and my cluttered cheerful house and my adored
family. But Aunt Tilly offered to keep me, and mother urged
me to stay, though she wrote that she longed to see me every
minute of the day, and I wept and stayed. To make it up, Aunt
Tilly relaxed the prison regime. We went to Venice and the
Lido, and cruised on a yacht from Genoa to Cannes, and thence
to Villars in the Swiss Alps. In the fall, I was at last shown to

Paris, though with constant advice and instruction from both
Aunt Tilly and Mademoiselle.

That fall, Fiona went back to New York. She had written
me her plans from Scotland. It seems that on the ship there
was a gentleman named Mr. Charles Waldhaus, who was old,
bald and very ugly. He saw Fiona standing on a deserted deck
looking out to sea, and when they got to New York Fiona
became the star in his new Broadway production, a play
about a doomed young girl. How he persuaded Mrs. Farleigh
to permit this, no one knows. The critics remarked that Fiona
did nothing except be beautiful; on the other hand, she did
that surpassingly well. In the summer, she went to Hollywood,
and I saw her first picture. She was, as in life, dazzling to be-
hold, but on film as in life, you could not get close to her. She
stayed in Hollywood for nearly a year. Then, as casually as
she had begun, she quit the career of actress. She wanted to
go to the Orient, she said mildly, and she went, leaving behind
her the fame and the contracts for which other girls would
have sweated blood. I got a note from Peking saying that
China was very interesting, and she did enjoy the riding.

And meantime, I had married. I had three offers. My hand
was formally requested of Aunt Tilly by an aged marquis. As
I told Mademoiselle, he obviously wore corsets. The second
offer came from a gangling youth called the Honorable
Michael Fane. He was nice, if tongue-tied and dog-eyed, and
I almost took him except I felt I would always have the giggles
about his Adam's apple. I accepted Richard de Breuve, whose
mother, the old countess, was a friend of Aunt Tilly's. Rikki
was blond, which was unusual in a Frenchman, and tall,
another advantage, and he had a merry eye and he talked
to me as if I were actually in the room. He made me laugh
and I thought he was the best of the lot and I was in a terrible
hurry. So we were married, I propped up in billowing white
satin, and there was a wedding reception at the Rue de l'Université with the whole house lighted by candles. In the panic
which must precede all weddings, even ones more desired
and sincere than mine, I thought: *Fiona will marry because she
is head over heels in love, someone colossal, an aviator, maybe,
or an explorer, and not just a funny young man who provides
escape from an aunt.* I cried a great deal on my honeymoon

at the Breuve château in the Loire country, and Rikki seemed to understand. Then we returned, to live in a small airy apartment in Neuilly, and life looked brighter.

All this time, Fiona traveled. Her mother was not well, and took a house near Tucson; but Fiona, accompanied by a maid, saw the world. She did the Orient thoroughly and for a while climbed some perilous newsworthy mountains in Burma. Then she appeared in Cairo and then in Greece, where she plunged into archaeology. She went to Sweden and played tennis with the King. She bought a house near Perugia which became a center for artists. Her goings and comings were duly chronicled, and because Fiona had once been a movie star she had a sort of international interest as being one of the most beautiful women in the world, who had spurned a brilliant career.

About six months after my marriage, I fell in love with my husband and was furious with myself for having wasted six months, not knowing what a fine thing I'd got. In due course I produced an heir named Raoul and called Fatty. This child was bright red, screamed without ceasing and ate like a pig. I decided that if I had been able to go to a shop and buy a baby, Fatty was exactly what I would have picked. Fatty was perfect.

Rikki would return from his bank in the Place Vendôme, where he worked rather languidly, and together we gloated over Fatty. We did little, as I remember, except admire our offspring and laugh a great deal about nothing. I assured Rikki that with his frivolous ways he would never get ahead and be made president of the bank, and he assured me that he didn't want to be president of anything and he thought it ridiculous to throw away one's life working, anyhow. Aunt Tilly and the Countess de Breuve made many tactful donations to our home, and we both found this a most sensible system.

Then Fiona came back to Paris and one afternoon she appeared at our apartment, smelling deliciously of jasmine and dressed in moss green from top to toe. She was, still and in exactly the same way, too beautiful to be true. Fatty thrilled her, and she handled him as if he were made of thin crystal and she kept saying, "You're so lucky, Tilly." Finally—for by now I was a self-assured matron of twenty-two—I said, "Why don't you get married, Fiona, and have a Fatty yourself?"

"Because no one's asked me." As I was too amazed to answer, she remarked that in any case she had never seen a man she wanted. "I don't know anyone well enough," she said.

Rikki came home then, which was a relief because as usual I had lapsed into staring at Fiona and not finding much to say. But even Rikki was subdued by Fiona and nothing he said sounded very amusing. Fiona announced that she was leaving shortly for Afghanistan.

"Why?" I said.

"I've never been there." It seemed, to her, an adequate reason.

After Rikki had shut the front door, he said, "Whew!" It was the last way I expected a man to react to Fiona.

"Don't you think she's beautiful?" I asked.

"Oh, beautiful; she's too beautiful. I never saw anything so beautiful. Doesn't she ever laugh?"

"Not much, I think."

"Is it always such rough going?"

"Rikki, what is it?"

"I don't know. I bet Queen Mary is a lot cosier to talk to."

From time to time Fiona would come back, always alone. No one ever saw Fiona dining tête à tête with a man in a small restaurant, though everyone saw her at great dinner parties and balls and receptions. And I think people waited for some change in her looks, though she was still very young. But it seemed against nature to go on being so unremittingly beautiful. However, she did not change. She came to admire my daughter, who, though as fat as her brother, was respectfully called Marianne because, as Rikki said, it gave a girl a bad start to call her Fatty Second. And our little life went on, summers in the Loire, winters in Paris, a small, foolish, happy life which I would have been pleased to live forever.

In August, 1939, I received a letter that was completely unlike Fiona. In the first place it was jabbed full of exclamation marks. She announced that, next month, she was going to marry Ted Vanier. Ted was the most beautiful, the most adorable, the most kind, the most entertaining, the most gen-

erous, the most most man in the world and she could not believe that, after all these years—she was then twenty-five—
she could have such luck and she was divinely, madly, bliss-
fully happy. They were coming to Paris on their wedding
trip and I would see this miracle myself. Love and kisses.
There were x's at the bottom of the page, denoting kisses. If
Fiona had walked down the Champs Élysées, draped in a
bath towel, I wouldn't have been more startled than I was by
the style of this letter and the x kisses. But there was no wedding trip to Paris, because instead there was the war.

Rikki moved us to the family's château, south of the Loire,
in November. Only we lived now in the gatekeeper's lodge.
After the defeat, he came back to us, clearly in answer to
prayer; and he was changed. He wasn't frivolous at all. For
some time Rikki lived as we all did, patching and scraping
and combining, in order to eat and be clothed and warm.
Then he left for Paris, having given out the rumor that he had
escaped to England to join the Free French. But instead he
returned to Paris and adopted the curious and now incredible
routine of disguise: horn-rimmed spectacles, a mustache,
darkened hair, a false name. And there he worked in the
Resistance and I did not see him for years. I grew so old, in
my heart, in those years that age no longer means anything to
me.

In the last black winter of the war, we returned to Paris,
to the same apartment in Neuilly and to Rikki, who was very
thin and did not smile as easily as before. But we were together
and though I wished we had some coal and that the Germans
had left us a little more furniture and that there was glass
in every window, I could not complain of these things. Then, in
February, when it seemed there would never be sun again and
the war would never end, I heard from Fiona. The news was
brought by an apparition dressed in the American Red Cross
uniform who rang my doorbell one morning and stated that
she was Lorraine Morton, a friend of Fiona's. Lorraine could
honestly be described as "a raven-haired beauty" and she must
have found me as timid as a field mouse and pathetically
shabby, bundled up in sweaters, trying to clean my house
with limited soap.

Lorraine had only recently arrived from England, to work

in a Red Cross club in the center of Paris. Fiona was an old friend and she had asked Lorraine to look us up and see what we needed, so that Fiona could send packages which Lorraine would deliver to us. "It's very kind," I said, "but really we are managing all right."

This was my last attempt at self-respecting lies. For Lorraine, who was as competent as she was handsome, sat down and began to make lists with me, and I could scarcely believe that after all this time, plenty—in the form of soap and chocolate and sugar and rice and coffee and vitamin pills for the children—was about to return. I wanted to hear of Fiona, but Lorraine did not seem eager to speak of her.

"She married Ted Vanier. You knew that?"

"She wrote me," I said, "but then the war came. What's he like?"

"Ted? Oh, he's nothing much."

"No!"

"Well, you know, terrifically good looking, terrifically rich, terrifically sure of himself and bird-brained. Though with that amount of looks and money, I don't suppose it mattered."

I found this picture alarming and said, "But he loved her; she was happy?"

"I couldn't tell, Tilly. He seemed proud of her. As if she were twice as valuable as all his polo ponies put together."

But Fiona, following the tone of her letter to me, had swooned with love and floated on a cloud of joy. Her only sorrow was that she didn't have children, who would look exactly like Ted.

Then, after Pearl Harbor, Ted enlisted and was sent to the Pacific. Neither Lorraine nor I knew anything about this theater of operations, so Lorraine did not know at what island, in what landing, Ted was wounded. But he was seriously hurt, and sent back to hospital in Honolulu. Fiona had moved to San Francisco, which was the nearest she could get to Ted. For a while she worked in an airplane factory. When Ted was wounded, she tried to get to Honolulu and was firmly turned down by the authorities. She waited, counting the days and hoping and planning.

"There's a gruesome touch," Lorraine said. "Ted left a standing order for white roses, when he took off. They arrived every week, carloads of them. I don't like white roses, do you? They're like funerals. They kept on coming, even after he'd got home. He forgot to call the florist."

Lorraine knew most of this from a cousin who lived in San Francisco, and from scrappy notes Fiona had written. Ted returned. He had fallen in love with his nurse. He wanted a divorce. Fiona could not believe it, and pleaded with him, and blamed this change on the war, his wound. Wouldn't he give them both a chance, a little time? After all, Fiona reasoned, they had been so terribly happy. It appeared that Ted hadn't been as happy as all that, whereas the nurse was heart's desire.

Fiona gave in and went to Reno at Christmas time.

"She bought a ranch in Arizona. Her last letter said she had a perfectly wonderful foreman or overseer or head cowboy or whatever they're called, a returned veteran, who was marvelous with animals."

"Is she still beautiful?" I asked. Since so much had been destroyed, these last years, I was prepared to think that Fiona too ——

"Beautiful as the morning," Lorraine said. "Even in a smudgy newspaper picture. My cousin sent me one, from some awful Sunday magazine article about her divorce. I've got it at my billet; I'll mail it to you."

The packages started to arrive, and each one was a festival for the Breuve family. I wrote long letters of gratitude to Fiona and got back sometimes a half page saying there was no need to thank her and what else did I need. She never spoke of herself.

In June, when the war was over, Lorraine came to dinner bearing American cigarettes for Rikki and a bottle of authentic Scotch whisky. "I'm going to be married," she said, "the minute my angelic Mike gets out of the Army. Which will be soon. He's got quantities of points. Oh, what a lovely life we're going to have."

Mike was a doctor. Mike was brilliant. Mike was a saint. They would live in Albany, where he came from, and he would start his practice. "I'm going to be a little woman in an apron," Lorraine said with rapture.

For Lorraine, the raven-haired beauty who had been edu-

cated at a smart but not necessarily instructive school in
Florence, it seemed a rare project and Rikki mentioned this.

"Don't you believe it," Lorraine said. "I know exactly what
I want. Peace. Masses of peace. And making people well, not
fixing to butcher them. And a horde of brats, and neat little
dresses that I will cut out from a pattern. And, of course, Mike."

So we wished her joy, for she was leaving the next week, and
Rikki said that night, "Lorraine's all right. Nothing bad will
happen to Lorraine."

The packages continued to arrive. We battened on Fiona's
generosity. And we needed it. Aunt Tilly and my mother-in-
law had not survived the war and there were vast complica-
tions about inheritances in case, as Rikki pointed out, there
actually were any inheritances to receive. Naturally we neither
wanted nor expected help from my family. Rikki now took
his job at the bank very earnestly indeed. Fatty, who was no
longer fat, went to school in darned clothes, and Marianne, the
pet, had learned to wipe dishes practically before she could
talk. But the lavish packages came from different places, and
Lorraine's letters explained what Fiona's notes left unsaid.

Fiona had sold her ranch in Arizona and was building an
angularly modern house in Lake Forest, outside Chicago. A
talented young architect was doing the job for her. She sold
this house before it was finished and took on an orange grove
in Florida. Her neighbor, another orange magnate, was helping
her. The oranges stayed unpicked on the trees while Fiona
moved to a grand house in Washington, which was nightly
filled with important people. A young congressman had interested her in politics. Then she went to visit Lorraine in
Albany. Lorraine's letter said, "She is as kind and gentle and
remote as ever, but there's a strange glimmer in those ravish-
ing eyes. She looks hunted, or as if there were ghosts behind
the furniture. So beautiful, Tilly, and so lonely. All those beastly
men simply left her. Something shaming happened. She
turned those eyes on a young doctor here, a friend of Mike's.
With longing, really, but I don't suppose he knew that. Luckily,
he had to rush off to Wisconsin, where his mother was taken
ill, and Mike somehow bundled her out of Albany before he
got back. Still, in no time at all, Fiona had inundated Mike's
pal with gold trinkets, a cigarette case, cuff links, a lighter, a

penknife. Judging from this, I figure the previous gentlemen must have cost a lot."

I did not tell Rikki any of this, because it hurt and horrified me. And I conceived a great hatred for Ted Vanier, who had left Fiona with all that unused love.

The packages were now postmarked New York, and were more splendid than ever before. I also got a note from Fiona asking me not to thank her, but to tell her everything about the children. I wrote what would have seemed, to anyone else, the dullest mother-love sort of letters. In return, I asked Fiona to send me a photograph so that my children could know her too. She replied that she had no pictures, but would shortly have one made. This was in the autumn of 1946, and she was living in New York. The photograph followed soon after; it looked like Fiona at eighteen, at twenty-three, at twenty-six; always the same, flawless and unspoiled by time, and Marianne kissed it because it was so beautiful, and Fatty said, with awe, "Do you really know her, mummy?" We were both thirty-three, just lately thirty-three, and Fiona's beauty was as eternal as the spring and I felt myself a haggard old woman.

There was one package, more roughly made and full of plain things which might have been bought at a country store. It was obviously Fiona's own handiwork, and the postmark was Gladstone, Vermont. The postman brought it at the end of April. After that, there were no more. Presently I stopped writing Fiona because I was afraid she would think I was begging. And Lorraine did not answer my letters. I was sad and worried and kept asking Rikki what he thought had happened. "Probably Fiona's in Tibet and Lorraine's having another baby," he said. "Don't fret, Tilly."

One night in August, when we were in our living room pretending to be on a beach and making a fine conversation about imaginary fishes, mermaids and nonexistent sea shells, the doorbell rang. Marianne, wearing sunglasses she had found somewhere and a rag of cotton sun suit, opened the door. It was Lorraine.

We all shouted questions in pleasure and surprise, and the children rushed around like hysterical puppies. Then it developed that Lorraine had gone with her husband to Manchester, to some international medical convention, and they had decided to fly over to Paris for three days, as a second honeymoon. Mike was dining with some French colleagues, but we would all meet at the Deux Magots tomorrow night.

We put the children to bed and sat down to piece out the news of the last two years. We talked of Lorraine's daughter and life in Albany and life in Paris and then I asked about Fiona, though I was shy of this for fear—so delicate are the needy—that Fiona had tired of me and my family and our packages.

"I stopped writing you," Lorraine said, "because I couldn't say it in a letter and I couldn't write without mentioning Fiona and I knew I would see you this summer."

Rikki and I waited.

"I want to tell it all," Lorraine said. We still waited.

"Fiona went to New York, after she'd visited us. I couldn't warn her or advise her; and, besides, it was too desperate for that. She was hungry for love, Tilly; she couldn't live without it. So she took up with men, and poured presents on them, and gave them money, and buried herself in whatever interested them, and adored. And they left her. I'll never know why, because no one was more beautiful, and good, too, sweet, really. Anyhow, they left.

"In New York she found a young man who was starting out as an interior decorator. I thought him a ratlike creature when I met him there last winter. In a way, all Fiona's men were handsome, and that was odd too. It was as if she was afraid they'd resent her beauty, unless they had a fair share of looks of their own. This was a sleepy young man with enormous eyelashes and a purring manner, and Fiona told me that at last she was happy, at last she was safe, and had found a man who was not only a lover but a friend. 'We talk,' she told me, as if that was the most remarkable thing two people could possibly do. 'We sometimes talk all night. He understands everything.' So Fiona put money into his shop, became a partner, introduced him to everyone, helped him in every way, bought him presents until it was embarrassing, and adored. And then, one day in March, he sent her a note to say he was going to Bermuda for a vacation and when he came back he planned to marry a girl of nineteen he'd met while decorating her family's house.

"I don't know if Fiona expected to marry the others, but she certainly intended to marry this one. 'I'm not too old to have children,' she told me; 'maybe it was just something wrong with Ted and me; but Dicky dotes on children. We'll have two, anyhow, won't we, Lorraine?' And I said, 'Of course, you'll have ten, darling.' Not even to tell it to her, but just to send around a note and disappear. And there had been so many before, I guess, who disappeared; and this time she'd felt that she loved and was loved for life."

"Oh, I hate it all," I said, and Rikki put his arm around me.

"She went to Vermont to a farmhouse her mother owned there. I didn't know any of this. She stayed three weeks, entirely alone, thinking God knows what. Her maid told me later that Fiona looked in the mirror a great deal, and that she had never seen such a sad face. Then one night, when the maid was out, she did her hair in a crown of braids, and put on a diamond tiara and diamonds around her throat, and a sable cape over her pajamas and went to the garage and closed everything tight, and started the motor. She had brought a steamer rug to lie on, and at some moment she pulled the sable cape over her head."

"Lorraine!" I didn't recognize my voice.

"Mrs. Farleigh was too ill to travel; she lives in a sanatorium near Tucson. She sent me a heartbreaking telegram, and I got up to Vermont the same day. We buried Fiona there. She didn't have a home anywhere and it seemed as good a place as any. She was just as beautiful, Tilly, even when she was dead."

There was no sound in the room, except me, crying and trying not to make a noise about it and staring at our worn rug and not seeing it, but seeing only Fiona with diamonds in her hair. Lorraine kissed me and said, "I had to tell you." Then she turned to Rikki and said, "I'll be going home now. We'll meet tomorrow?"

Rikki took her to the door. I couldn't move, and sat by myself thinking: *How we failed her; why couldn't we have given her what she needed; why couldn't we have helped?* I didn't know how hard I was crying. It was Fiona's last three weeks, alone, looking in the mirror, which were unbearable.

I did not hear Rikki come back. "Tilly," he said gently.

"Darling." But I could not stop crying. He held me in his arms until I was quieter and then he gave me a handkerchief and said, "Wipe your funny nose. Darling. Darling. Wipe your funny face." We sat together for a long time, and finally Rikki said, to himself, "Thank God my daughter's going to be just an ordinary, homely girl."

THE LAST MAN ALIVE

By CONRAD RICHTER

IT'S JUST a relic today, a huge old box, plain and ugly as sin, with a heavy and unwieldy lid. The date, 1762, when probably it was made, is carved crudely in the dark-stained pine. Those who pass it in the museum scarcely give it a glance. *Of what use is such an ancient and monstrous thing in this modern world?* they think. For never in those early times did folks have such terrible problems to solve as today.

But if you wait till the guard has wandered into another room, you may, if you are strong enough, lift the heavy lid. And in the breath of vanished old quilts and early American life rising from the grain of wood you may catch the faint scent of hickory smoke and May apples that clung around the dress of Jess Galloway, the bound girl, as she stood that day of the mid-Revolution in the tiny settlement of Fisher Valley and faced what was ahead of them all.

Oh, she knew what awful thing was wrong with the world, and had known it for some time. Men in a hurry had been stopping off in the settlement on their way south. What they said was told only to the men behind closed doors, but you could let it to the women to find out. And when they had, they wished they hadn't, for this wasn't just an Indian scare. No, this was extinction, the end of the world for Central and Northern Pennsylvania, and perhaps much farther. The enemy was leading the savages to burn, scalp and exterminate. In all this great empire of forest, no white men or women were to be left alive.

Ever since spring, settler folk had been driven out, but now, with the terrible news from the Wyoming Valley of Pennsylvania, those still left were aclearing out their own selves. That was a sight to see, men, women and young ones in boats, arks, canoes, rafts—anything that would float, even hog troughs—arunning down the Susquehanna! Most of their farm and household stuff had to be left behind. And this was only the West Branch. It was the same on the North Branch. *Where*

100

did all the displaced settler folks come from? Jess wondered,
for these were just the lucky ones that got away. Behind them
in clearings for many a mile folks lay with woods flies abuz-
zing at their hacked heads and at the brains of their littlest
ones busted against trees.

But do you reckon the men in Fisher Valley would go? No,
not them. They said the Dunkards on the other side of Third
Gap in Limestone Valley weren't going at all, and Fisher Valley would wait till its crops were harvested. Even then it
would be hard enough to give up the good black land they
had cleared and the log buildings they had raised. Their flax
they would have to let unpulled, and their corn stand small
and green in the field. But their wheat and rye they could reap,
thresh, sack and tote along. It would give them bread this
coming winter wherever they might be.

Now today the last of the wheat was being flailed, and tomorrow they would go. Hardly could Jess believe that this
was their last day in the valley. Seldom had she seen a seem-
lier one. The air from the English Lakes blew clear and crystal
over Shade Mountain. The July sun lay golden on the long,
ragged wheat stubble. Blue dinner smoke rose from the small
cluster of clay chimneys, and the gray settlement walls looked
soft and homelike as guinea fowl.

But where was Ashael? All morning Jess had asked this of
herself. Here it was the last day and no sight of the stern young
Amishman who last spring had asked the elder to marry them.
The elder could have done it, too, for it was given him to
baptize and marry as well as preach. But he wouldn't set Jess
free till her contract was up. You might think Ashael would
get mad, so straight and small and doughty he stood, with a
blue eye like ice in his sightly face framed by his red hair and
beard. But the Amish were men of God, and more patient
than this one looked. All he said was he would wait, and went
back to his bachelor improvement over Shade Mountain.

This morning, threshing on the barn floor, Jess kept going
to the door. But never did she get a sight of his clean black
suit fastened with hooks and eyes, and his blacker hat with the
broad brim.

"If it's Ashael you look for, you needn't," the elder told her
at last. "He's not coming."

The bound girl felt the flail strike against her heart. "Didn't you send him word?" she cried.

"Oh, he's had plenty word. Not for anything but God would he leave his place, he said. You ought to remember how stubborn he is. Not a penny would he pay to buy off your contract. Not even to marry you."

"Why should he?" Jess stuck up for him. "He's just starting out, and poor."

"Not so poor. He has the Great Chest from the old country. But he wouldn't part with it."

"What would be the use? He can wait two years and get me for nothing."

"Yes, if you stay single for him. But how does he know some other man won't come along and buy you off from me? You're big and strong and a good worker. Some even say you're good to look at. Women don't grow on every bush in this country."

"Ashael don't need to worry. I'll wait for him," Jess said stolidly.

Just the same, hardly could she eat her early noon dinner. In the middle of it a Tioga man with long hair and a boy on the saddle in front of him rode out of the woods shouting terrible words. He halted by the elder's house and called that Dunkardtown in Limestone Valley had been burned. All were wiped out. Wasn't there some saved, Jake Bender asked. Not a Dunkard lifted his hand or complained, the stranger said, for that was against their belief. "It's God's will," was all they said as the tomahawk fell on themselves and their families. Of the whole settlement, only this boy he found hiding in the woods was left to tell him what happened.

Everybody in little Fisher Valley had crowded around to hear and sicken, everybody save Jess. All she could think of was Ashael alone over in his valley. None saw her, except it might be Mary, as she put the house between her and the people. By the run, her feet fell on the Indian path across the mountain.

Many a time when she went for the cows or on a Sabbath walk had she thought of her marriage day when she would take this path to Ashael's valley. First the path led through a wide hollow of noble pines and hemlocks. Even in winter the snow looked dark in here. Beyond was the spring where the great velvet bird's-foot violet and yellow lady's-slipper grew. Oh, this path would be a mortal sweet place to walk on your marriage day, but today she saw feathers in every bush and a spear in every sapling.

So thick stood the forest on the north side, she could get no look at the valley below. Not till she reached the bottom, had waded Ashael's creek and climbed around the limestone out- crop did she come out in the clearing. There stood the peace- ful scene like always, Ashael's log cabin, his round log barn, his stumpy fields in wheat, grass and corn, with a patch of potatoes by the house. From the woods came the lazy tank- tank-tank of a cowbell. The wheat stood uncut, for the season came a little later over here. In the hayfield loading his cart was Ashael.

His horse, lonesome over here in this valley, gave a little whinny at the sight of Jess. Until then, Ashael didn't see her. That was Ashael all over. The savages could crawl within a dozen yards of him and never would he believe they were there. He looked for good, not for evil. But, he was the man for her, Jess told herself, seeing him again standing there by his cart so straight and doughty for such a little fellow, and mighty brave to be living by himself over here in the wilderness.

His face hardly changed as she told him about Dunkard- town. His eyes kept looking around his little farm in the clear- ing. She hardly believed that he heard her. His strong cheeks kept warding off the bad words, so that it seemed even to Jess what she said couldn't be. The hay smelled tame and sweet like always over here in this peaceful valley. Wheat stood gold as a sovereign on the stalk. A bird sang mighty pretty in the forest, and over them stood the mountain like a sentry on guard. Only the ugly recollection of what the Tioga man had said kept coming back to plague her.

"Don't look at your crops, Ashael!" she begged him. "Just go before it's too late!"

"Run off, you mean?" He looked at her sharply. "Where can you go from the hand of the Lord? He can strike you down in Lancaster town as easy as up here."

"He kin," Jess agreed. "But most likely He won't want to. Now, I can't say that much for the Injuns."

"No red man would do me harm," Ashael promised. "Not a one ever left my door without something to eat or a place to sleep."

"That's what the Dunkards used to say, and look what happened to them!"

"It was the Lord's will," he said, very low, but Jess heard him.

"The Lord had nothin' to do with it," she declared warmly. "The Dunkards just wouldn't stand up and defend themselves."

"It's in our Bible. If your adversary strike you, turn the other cheek."

"You don't always git a chance to do that with an Injun," Jess observed. "Once his tomahawk hits you, you're a gone Josie. You got to hit him first."

"Our people," Ashael said, "don't take up arms against anybody."

"Wouldn't you lift a hand to save your own self . . . or me?"

"No, for to lose your life is to save it."

Jess looked at him. "Then it's true what Elder Kring said about you."

"What did he say?"

"That you were stubborn as a mule."

"I'm glad if I'm stubborn in my belief."

"Well, if you want to be stubborn, I kin too," she told him. "It says in the Bible it's not good for man to be alone. And if you won't come with us, I'm agoin' to stay up here with you."

The first alarm crossed the Amishman's face. "No, that you can't do."

"Why can't I? Who'll stop me?"

"I will," Ashael promised. "Never will I live with a woman in sin!"

"It would be only for a year or two," Jess explained. "When a parson comes through, we kin be married. If none comes, we could go down the river sometime . . . once our young ones are old enough."

"That's enough!" Ashael cried, and his face was dark with anger. "Till your time is up, you belong to the elder! If you won't go back yourself, I'll have to take you!"

Jess's mouth got a peculiar ropy look, and if Ashael had

known her better, he might have taken warning. But at that moment rumbling sounds rolled along the mountain, as of distant thunder.

"You ought to git your hay in first, Ashael," she said mildly. "I kin help you. Then you kin send me over."

"How do I know," he asked sternly, "that a girl who would live in sin will keep her word?"

"You're a man," Jess said, still meek as Moses. "And if I wouldn't, you could make me."

"Yes, well," Ashael agreed. "If you want to help a little, Jess, I won't say no. Afterwards, I'll walk with you over the mountain. I meant to go over anyway and give everybody good-by."

The rest of the day, scarcely speaking, they worked in the hayfield. Jess raked it into piles and stood on the cart to stamp down the forkloads from Ashael. Sometimes she took the fork her own self and swung up as heavy loads as he. She believed she could lift still heavier, but never would she shame Ashael in his own field. It took longer than they reckoned. When they finished, the sun was already down behind North Mountain. The valley felt cooler in shadow. But where was the storm whose thunder they had heard? The sky still hung without a cloud and blue as a gentian.

"Hadn't we better milk before we go?" Jess asked, still mild. And when the milking was done: "Ashael, I'm a mite hungry. I guess it's from the hay and crossing the mountain. If you feed every savage that comes this way, maybe you could spare me a bite of supper. It wouldn't hurt you to eat either."

He gave her a searching look, but did not refuse. Sitting there at the hewn table in Ashael's cabin, with Ashael's own bread and milk between them, with his fireplace on one side, his gun, that must be used only for game, in the corner behind the door, his bed on the floor, and near it the long chest that came from the old country, Jess felt almost like already she was Ashael's wife and mistress of his house and lands. Never, she told herself, would she give him up now. First she would put him off till tomorrow. Then the elder and the Fisher Valley folks would be gone.

So long did she keep sitting at the table after Ashael finished that he grew uneasy and restless. He got up and put away all save her bowl and spoon. Now with impatience, he watched her make what little she had left last a long time. Daylight faded from the cabin, so that already it seemed dark in here.

"I have seen many eat, but never a bird like you," he told her at last. "How do you get any work done?"

"I kin work with any woman!" Jess shot at him. "Or with a man either!"

"Then let's see how good you climb the mountain," he said, "or it will be dark on us before we get started."

She pushed back her bowl and spoon. "It's no use, Ashael," she said. "I'm not agoin' off without you."

She was not prepared for the terrible look that came on his face. "So the word of a girl that would live in sin is not worth anything after all?" he lashed her.

"I never said I'd go . . . only that you could make me," Jess reminded.

"So I could . . . if I wanted to," he rebuked her.

For a minute they faced each other, Jess with her black hair and slate-gray eyes, and Ashael with his red beard and hair and his eyes blue as limestone. He stood so straight and righteous for such a little fellow. Oh, he had muscles you could never pinch. He could give her a tussle, if he wanted to. But in her heart Jess knew that never could he throw her and drag her out. No, rather she could swing him off the floor and set him where she wanted.

"Only my belief stops me," he said, bleak as a plowed field in winter. "You needn't worry. I won't lift my hands against you any more than against an Indian."

He went to his long chest and began lifting out what lay inside. He made all into two piles and tied them up in the blankets from his bed. Then he went for the door.

"Where are you goin', Ashael?" she asked.

"Not with you, woman," he said. "If you won't go from here, then you can stay and I will go. The Indians can't drive me off. Only one like you can. If you come after me, I'll leave where I am and go up to Dunkardtown."

"Dunkardtown is burnt, Ashael."

"Not the land. A new house and barn I can build for myself."

Quietly she sat at the table. Presently she could hear him out at the barn, hitching up and throwing his farm things in the cart. He drove to the door and started to carry out his packs and kettles.

"You needn't do that, Ashael," she said, getting up. "I only reckoned to stay and help you with your work and cook your meals and sew your clothes. But I won't run you off your own place. If you won't stay, then I'll go my own self."

"You said that before."

"I'll go for sure now," she said. "Good-by, Ashael."

"Wait! I want to go along and see that you do what you say!" he said sternly.

"You needn't. I gave my word now."

"I'll go just the same," he told her. "You could hide in the woods and come back tonight or tomorrow. It has neither bar nor lock on my door."

Well, it was all over, Jess told herself as they tramped up the mountain. Likely this was the last time that ever she would see him or cross Shade Mountain. It was pitch dark when they reached the summit. The moon would soon be up, Ashael said, and then they could see, once they got out of the timber.

"You're sure they didn't leave this morning already?" he asked of a sudden, when they were halfway down.

Oh, she knew what made his suspicion. She had noticed it herself—the smell of smoke; not the good homelike scent of chimney smoke, but the rank stench of burning household logs, chinking and rubbish. It grew stronger as they went on by the dark spring, through the black pines and hemlocks and by the unseen swamp where the cows liked to get away from the flies. Then suddenly they came out of the woods and saw in the darkness before them great red eyes winking at them from where the settlement ought to be.

"Ashael, don't go any farther!" she warned him.

Ashael had stopped, but only for a moment. "I'm not scared," he told her. "Nobody will hurt an Amishman. But you better stay back. I can't answer for you."

It was true, Ashael feared nothing, she told herself as he went on, with her following close behind. Her eyes could barely make out the path in the meadow they followed. Halfway across, Ashael stumbled over something, and she thought she heard him take the Lord's name under his breath. When she reached down, her hand froze. Here in the path she could feel a dress and apron she thought she knew, but the body diked out in them lay stiff and cold.

"Ashael!" she cried, stifling a scream. "It's Mary!"

Ashael stood by with a man's clumsy sympathy. She could not see his face, but he did not take off his broad-brim hat.

"God's will be done," he muttered in the dialect.

Huddled there above the silent body of her friend, Jess waited while the story of this shocking thing worked like a deadly poison through her mind. The savages must have struck that afternoon not long after she had gone, and that had been the rattle of distant thunder that she and Ashael had heard. Likely Mary had run for the mountain, too, and here they had overtaken her. In her mind's eye Jess could see a savage with his uplifted tomahawk cutting her down.

For a while longer she and Ashael stood there, listening, watching. Not a shadow moved across the dying red beds of coals. No sound rose save the hoot of some big-eared owl up the valley. Where the settlement had stood and flourished with human life and household comforts, and with shelter and feed for the stock, now all was death and desolation.

When he started on, she came after. She remembered the saying of Jake Bender that seldom did the savages attack at night. No, they preferred to do their dirty work in the daytime and camp by evening in some hidden spot far from their bloody deeds. Just the same, she would have felt better with Ashael's gun in her hands. When they reached the ashes of the elder's barn, no rifle cracked or arrow sang, though they stood plain targets against the scarlet-orange embers. As they stayed on there, the moon came up, lately full, bulging a little on one side, as if misshapen with the evil of the night. Rather she would have had it down, for now they had to put their eyes on what there was to see.

One by one, they accounted for all of the settlement save three. Tilly Fegley they found lying on her face, scalped; and Mordecai with his wounded head in the spring that still flowed a little red, Jess fancied. Jake Bender was a mutilated sight and the reason plain to see, for his gun, with the barrel bent nearly double, lay by the ashes of his house. His wife and old mother were behind the wall of the barn, and Sairy lay in the garden, her sunbonnet hanging on a scorched bush of little dark brown blooms that the Pennsylvania Dutch call shrubs. The Tioga man and the boy on the front of his saddle must have gone before the attack. Not a trace of them could be found, or of the two small Fegley boys. Likely they were taken prisoner, for young whites make as good Indians as red ones. But where was the elder?

Then, as they came to the walnut by the run, a figure with gory head sat up and asked for a drink of water. He was a fearful sight to see, like somebody rising from the grave. His eyes already had the glaze of death, and when Jess ran with water in a broken pot, he had lain back again and barely could he swallow.

"Where are the others?" he whispered.

"They are here," Jess told him.

"Gone, all gone," he moaned.

"All save the Fegley young ones," Ashael said.

"And they are worse than dead," Jess added bitterly.

"Well, I am not long for this world either," the elder said, very low.

"You'll be better by morning, perhaps," Ashael promised.

"Don't fool yourself, Ashael," the elder whispered hoarsely. "Don't wait too long, like we did."

Ashael didn't say anything.

The elder went on. "One time you asked for Jess. Now I give her to you. She's no good to me any more."

Jess saw Ashael flinch.

"She must go down the river, elder," he said. "We are not married."

The elder lay a while breathing heavily, his pale eyes fixed on one and then on the other. "You want him in marriage, Jess?"

She turned slowly and looked at Ashael. "If he's awillin'," she said.

Together, she and Ashael waited. The elder lay for a while with closed eyes. They did not know if he was dead or dying, but then he looked at them.

"In the name of the Father, the Son and the Holy Ghost!" he began in a voice so strong it startled them. "We are gathered together for the purpose of holy matrimony ——"

That was the strangest wedding Jess Galloway ever knew,

with never a house or room to be married in, with nothing but the night air to stand in, with the holy words said by a preacher cut down like a tree on the ground, and with the moon for light while around them still glowed the evil embers. One time the voice of the dying elder rang out like that of God Himself, and then again it grew so faint that Jess had to bend her head to listen, for never would she miss hearing the words of her own marrying. But the worst was that Mary and Sairy couldn't be with her at her wedding.

She was Ashael's lawful wife now, she told herself when it was over. It put iron in her as she went around with him fetching the bodies in to be buried in the elder's root cellar. Never could they dig a separate grave for each this night. Here they could lay them all side by side, with the oldest at one end and the youngest at the other. Many times Jess went over their order in her mind, so she could tell where each lay. They had no box, but Ashael spread over them some bedclothes stiff with blood that had missed the fire. Then Ashael, with the pick, and Jess, with the shovel, caved in the earthen roof of the root cellar and covered them over with the dark, rich soil. Not till they were done did Jess come on freshly cut grass and leaves covering a spot of ground. When they bared it, they found a new grave. Ashael said it was an Indian grave, and if they dug, likely they would find the savages accounted for by Jake Bender.

It was late and the bulging moon half gone across the sky when they started back to their place in Ashael's valley. Rather would Jess have gone for the river, had Ashael been willing, but she was a married woman now, and where her man went she would have to follow. Oh, never, when she thought ahead of marrying Ashael someday, did she expect such a sober wedding journey as this over Shade Mountain in the dead of night, with the lonesome feeling that in this vast region they were the only white people left alive.

Her first word she spoke when they came to the summit. "Ashael, do you reckon you could do something for me and count it a weddin' present?"

"If I can, Jess, I'll do it," Ashael promised. Never had his voice sounded kinder.

"Will you put a bar on the door tonight when we git home?"

He was silent a while, and she knew she had displeased him. "I'll do it, like I said, if you want me," he agreed. "But it can do no good. Those who come by my house are always welcome, and I'd have to open the door anyhow."

Jess felt thunderstruck. "You mean you'd open to those red devils?"

"Their skins are red, but they have souls like we do," Ashael reproved her.

"Yes, souls black as the pots of hell!" Jess told him. "They'll never come in my house!"

"Then I'll have to go outside and talk to them."

"After what you saw tonight?"

"They did a bad thing, and I don't stand up for it," Ashael said. "But 'vengeance is mine; I will repay, saith the Lord.' Anyway, they would never do it to me."

"But what if they did?" Jess demanded.

"Then it would be God's will," Ashael said humbly.

Jess's face in the darkness was bitter. In her heart she prayed that Ashael's barn and house might be burned down when they got there. It would mean that the savages had come and gone. If the house and barn stood, it meant it was still to be. Oh, never for a minute did she expect that they would be overlooked. The savages knew every white place north of the mountains. Not an improvement but was marked in their minds for destruction.

Her prayer was not answered. When they came up the cartpath around the shale bank and into the clearing, there stood the house and barn in the moonlight exactly as they left them. The ax raised up undisturbed from the chopping block. From the barn came Gruzel's whinny, and from the woods the lazy tank-tank of Star's bell. The moon itself hung peaceful far up the valley, throwing long shadows over the fields. Only the black stumps made her think of savages abiding in the wheat. She picked up the ax from the chopping block and took it in with her. Inside the cabin, once they had lit a fire of hickory bark for light, all was tranquil and untouched.

Was it possible she had been wrong, she asked herself. Could it be that those red heathen would not bother Ashael, knowing his ways for peace? Then she forgot her fears, for this was her wedding night. . . .

It was getting daylight when she awoke. Now, what had wakened her, she wondered. Then she heard it again—an anxious whinny from the barn. Jess got up swiftly and went to the open window. A morning fog covered the valley, but it was not heavy enough to keep her from seeing a file of three figures coming, silent as the mist itself, from the woods. Almost she gave a cry of joy, for the first looked like a woman in a red-check gown. With a flash of warm feeling, it came to her that no longer was she the only white woman in these lonesome woods. Today she would have another of her kind for company. Then the joy died in her throat as she saw that the figure carried a rifle, like the others, and that all three had the same tufted and half-shaven heads. Suddenly she knew, with a wave of horror, where she had seen red checks like that before—in a tablecloth from some Pennsylvania Dutch settler's house, now likely in ashes and its mistress murdered close by.

"Ashael!" she tried to rouse him. As the file of men came closer, her eyes tried to make out what besides rifles they carried. Furry objects, they looked like, some short, some long and flowing, some black, brown and fair as tow. Now she recognized them for what they were—scalps stretched over hoops to dry, and perhaps the freshest was the long chestnut hair of Mary Bender.

"Ashael!" she begged, and touched him, but his breathing never changed from the long, deep snores that all night had seemed to suck up the air around her, so there was none left for her to breathe. Oh, she knew men were heavier sleepers than women. Mary used to say that her father would sleep through a thunder-and-lightning storm. But this man of hers must be the master sleeper of the lot. Or else his work of yesterday, the strain last evening and, on top of that, his wedding night, had been too much for him. In his red frame of beard, his sleeping face looked like a saint's, but one that even in his dreams knew his own will and would suffer none to change it.

She looked around. The great dower chest still stood open, its lid back against the wall as Ashael had left it last evening. She bent down and slipped her strong young arms under his back and knees. The rhythm of his breathing changed for a moment. Surely now he must get awake. Then, after a lick, his snores rang out stronger than ever, as if to drown out this interference. She lifted him quickly over the dower chest and let his body down inside. His knees had to stick up. His snoring had stopped now. She set a chip on the chest's edge for air and closed the lid. Then her fingers fastened the iron catch with the peg.

Now, God forgive her, but there Ashael would have to stay. In her bare feet she went to the door and braced it shut with a puncheon. As she straightened she saw a curious-looking stick moving beyond the window. It pushed higher and closer to the sill. Then she knew it for a bruised and splintered ramrod sticking out from its thimbles. A greasy rifle barrel and painted face followed, both turning this way and that, trying to find the Amishman in his bed.

Jess's hands were slowly fixed on Ashael's gun standing by her in the door corner. An ancient and heavy piece, the fore stock had been fastened to the barrel with bands of tow. Whether it was loaded or not, Jess did not know, only that Ashael's other gear he kept in working order. This gun might never be used save on game, but if she knew Ashael, it would be primed and ready. She cocked the hammer. At the click, the savage looked up and saw her in the dimness. Before he could turn his rifle, she drew a bead on that paint-streaked face and pressed the rusty old trigger.

The roar echoed through the cabin. Then, as the sound kept on, Jess realized it wasn't the shot any more, but a violent pounding inside the chest.

"Jess!" Ashael shouted. "Let me out!"

She paid him no attention. The savage was gone from the window, but now she heard them at the door. Oh, that was the savage way—to draw a white man's fire and then get at him with the tomahawk before he had time to reload. Jess threw down Ashael's gun, for it was no use to her now, and set her stout body against the door, with the ax beside her.

"Jess, live you yet?" Ashael called. "Let me free!"

"I live yet, Ashael, but I can't let you free!"

"Woman, open this chest!" he ordered in anger.

Oh, if Ashael wasn't a godly person, if only he had been one to quarrel and fight, like Jake Bender, she couldn't have opened the lid quick enough. If ever she needed a man by her side, she needed him now. But not a lover of peace to open

the door, hold out his hands, and then all he could say was,
"God's will," when a bullet fetched him down. Rather have
him stay where he was. That's why she had put him there.
And yet, how could she hold the door herself against three?
Already the puncheon was beginning to slip in the earthen
floor. She could hear the savages' fearful yells of exultation as
they felt the door give. In violent jerks and shovings, they
pressed it far enough for one with his hatchet to worm himself
a little way through, and another to put his head after.

With her strong foot and thigh wedged against the door,
Jess held them there. Ashael's ax hung clenched in her long,
powerful fingers. Now her face grew cruel and the memory
of what pitiful things she had seen last night steeled her arms
and heart. Sucking in her breath, she raised the heavy bit.

"That's for Mary!" she cried when she fetched it down. "And
that's for Sairy!" she cried louder, as she struck again and
kept on till both lay like butchered bullocks between hewn
door and log jamb. Then, taking a fresh hold, she waited for
the third. But, although she stood there a long time, none
came. She opened the door a little wider. The mist had
thinned. After a while the sun rose over Shade Mountain. The
clearing looked calm and peaceful in the light. She could hear
the sound of water running over stones in Ashael's creek. Over
and over again came the mortal sweet song of the woods
robin.

Not till then did she think of the window. It flashed through
her mind that the other savage could have reloaded and shot
her in the back while she stood there. But when she went to
the window, she saw him lying on the ground.

The loud rattling of the chest roused her. Well, she had
done what she could. She guessed she must leave Ashael out
now. Much rather she wouldn't, for it would take a braver
body to stand up to Ashael than to the savages. Making a sober
face, she pulled out the peg and laid back the lid. She knew
then she wasn't wrong, for his face was like the avenging
angel's when he came out. Not a word did he say to her, even
after he saw the savages at the door. In silence he took the
gun and ax, and carried them out to the barn. When he returned, it was with the shovel and grubbing hoe.

Long before he came in, she had breakfast ready, and he

ate his fill, but not a word could she get out of him. His face was grim as stone. Oh, she had time now to think over what she had done to him. She had lifted her hands in arms against those who came to his house. She had saved him, but she had disgraced him too. More than once had she heard of a Swiss or Dutch wife who bedeviled her man till he made a vow never to speak to her again. Not for a minute had she dreamed she would do such a thing to Ashael. She should have known better. Never need she expect him to open his mouth to her again.

That's the way it worked out. Corn ripened, was cut and husked. Snow fell and melted. Ice formed on the gats. Snow fell again, and this time it laid. Now, wasn't it too bad? They were two that had been spared from the heathen, maybe the only two for a hundred miles, and here they had to live together like dumb brutes in the stall! When he sat with her at their table, it was like he had no tongue. Even his prayers to his Maker were dumb. Only his lips moved.

Well, if he would say no word, neither would she, not even about the babe she carried. When the pains came on her one night in April, never did she let on. She got his breakfast like usual, though hardly could she wait to get rid of him from the house. The young one gave her a hard tussle before it was born. More than once that morning she would like to have called to Ashael for help, but she set her jaws tight. If he could take care of his business without talking, so could she. More than once she had helped with birthing. Now she tended to herself, crawling to the fire on her hands and knees for warm water to wash the babe, to smooth it down afterward with melted coon tallow, and for the child's long flannel gown she had long since sewed with Ashael's coarse thread and needle.

Back in her floor bed, Jess lay with her babe close by her. Well, Ashael could hold his tongue from this hour if he wanted. She had a man now she could talk to and listen to. Already he was telling her things at the top of his Tom Thumb lungs. If Ashael wasn't plowing in the far field, he couldn't help but hear him.

Toward noon, when the babe slept, she was startled to hear somebody talking. It must be Ashael talking to the horse, she reckoned. Then she heard voices she had never heard before—

white men's voices. They sounded from the barn. After while she could tell they were coming toward the house, for it was noon and time for dinner.

Not soon would she forget how strange and shy she felt when the soldier stepped into the cabin. Why, he was the first human, besides Ashael and the baby, she had laid eyes on since early last summer! Behind him came another. Both carried muskets.

"You didn't say you had a baby!" the first one called out.

Jess saw Ashael reach out his head at that. Oh, never a word did he say, but a look spread on his face that Jess never saw before and hardly ever after. He stood for a shake not knowing what to do, and this his own house and household goods. Then he came over to the bed, and Jess saw him watching the little old puckered red face sticking from the bedclothes beside her.

"It's a girl or boy, Jess?" he asked very low.

"It's a boy."

"You all right?"

"I'm real good."

"Can I get you anything?"

"No, but I reckon you'll have to git your own dinner," she told him.

That's all he said and that's all she said, but never would Jess have believed the good feeling that ran over her. Ashael had talked to her. Nerve strings she never reckoned she had in her body let go. The cabin took on a different look, like it had the first time she laid eyes on it. Through the window she could see the bright sunshine on the red flowers of the maples. Down in the gats peepers were calling.

Ashael got dinner, with the two soldiers helping. All the time they swapped news. Their talk sounded sweet as music in Jess's ear.

"We never expected to find somebody living up here," the first soldier said. "I still can't get it through my head. How was it the Indians didn't get you?"

Ashael thought for a minute. He looked over at Jess, and his face was sober as a dominie's on Sunday.

"It was the will of God," he said shortly.

CALL THIS LAND HOME

By ERNEST HAYCOX

ONE at a time, the emigrant families fell out where the land most pleased them, and at last only two wagons of the overland caravan moved southward along the great green valley of Oregon; then the Potters discovered their fair place and John Mercy drove on with his lone wagon, his wife in unhappy silence beside him, and Caroline and young Tom under the canvas cover behind. Through the puckered opening at the wagon's rear young Tom saw the Potters grow dim in the steaming haze of this wet day. Rain lightly drummed on the canvas; he listened to the talk of his people.

"Have we got to live so far from everybody?" his mother asked.

In his father's voice was that fixed mildness which young Tom knew so well. "The heart of a valley's always better than foot or head. I want two things—the falls of a creek for my mill and plenty of open land roundabout."

She said, "Rough riding won't do for me much longer."

"I know," he said, and drove on.

In middle afternoon two days later, the wagon stopped and his father said, "I believe we're here." Crawling over the tail gate, young Tom—Thomas Jackson Mercy, age eight—saw the place on which he was to spend the rest of his long life. In three directions the fall-cast green earth ran off in the gentle meadow vistas, here and there interrupted by low knobs and little islands of timber, and crosshatched by the brushy willow borders of creeks. On the fourth side a hill covered by fir and cedar ran down upon the wagon. A stream smaller than a river, but bigger than a branch, came across the meadows, dropped over a two-foot rock ledge like a bent sheet of glittering glass, and sharply curved to avoid the foot of the hill, running on toward some larger stream beyond view.

John Mercy turned toward the wagon to give his wife a hand, and young Tom noted that she came down with a careful awkwardness. Then his father stamped the spongy earth

117

with his feet and bent over and plunged his tough fingers into the soil and brought up a sample, squeezing and crumbling it and considering it closely. He was a very tall man, a very powerful man, and all his motions were governed by a willful regularity. A short curly beard covered his face as far as the cheekbones; a big nose, scarred white at the bridge, stood over a mouth held firm by constant habit. He seemed to be smiling, but it was less a smile than a moment of keen interest which forced little creases around mouth and eyes. To young Tom, his father, at twenty-eight, was an old man.

John Mercy said, "It will take a week of clear weather to dry this ground for plowing." He turned, looking at the timber close by, and at the rising slope of the hill; he put his hands on his hips, and young Tom knew his father was searching out a place for the cabin. A moment later Mercy swung to face his wife with a slightly changed expression. She had not moved since leaving the wagon; she stood round-shouldered and dejected in the soft rain, reflecting on her face the effect of the gray day, the dampness and the emptiness which lay all around them. Young Tom had never seen her so long idle, for she was brisk in everything she did, always moving from chore to chore.

Mercy said, "In another two years you'll see neighbors wherever you look."

"That's not now," she said.

"The Willamette's beyond this hill somewhere. There's settlers on it."

She said, "I long for back home," and turned from him and stood still again, facing the blind distance.

John Mercy stepped to the wagon and lifted the ax from its bracket. He said to young Tom, "Go cut a small saplin' for a pole, and some uprights," and handed over the ax. Then he got into the wagon and swung it around to drive it under the trees. When young Tom came out of the deeper timber with his saplings, the oxen were unyoked and a fire burned beneath the massive spread of a cedar. The tail gate was down and his father had reversed an empty tub to make a step from wagon to the ground. Between them, they made a frame for the extra tarpaulin to rest on, thereby creating a shelter. His mother stood by, still with her unusual helplessness on her, and he knew, from his father's silence, that there was trouble between them.

His father said, "Water, Tom," and went on working. When Tom came back with the big camp kettle filled, his father had driven uprights at either side of the fire, connected by a cross-piece on which the hook hung. He lifted the camp kettle to the hook and listened a moment to the fire hissing against the kettle's wet bottom. The grub box was let down from the wagon box, but his mother was idle at the fire, one arm around Caroline, who stood by her. His father was at the edge of the timber, facing the meadow; he went over.

"Now, then," his father said, "it's sickly weather and we've got to get up a cabin. It'll go here. We'll cut the small trees yonder, for that's where the good house will stand someday. So we'll be doing two things at the same time—making the cabin and clearing the yard." His eyes, gray to their bottom-most depths, swung around, and their effect was like heavy weight on young Tom. It was seldom that he gave young Tom this undivided attention. "We've got everything to do here, and nothing to do it with but our hands. Never waste a lick, and make every lick work twice for you if you can. No man lives long enough to get done all he wants to do, but if he works slipshod and has got to do it over, then he wastes his life. I'll start on that tree. You trim and cut."

The blows of the ax went through the woods in dull echo-ing, not hurried—for his father never hurried—but with the even tempo of a clock's ticking. His mother worked around the grub box with her disheartened slowness. First shadows were sooty in the timber and mist moved in from the meadows. He listened to the sounds of the empty land with tight fascina-tion; he watched the corridors of the timber for moving things, and he waited for the tree to fall.

The rains quit. Warmed by a mild winter sun, the meadows exhaled fleecy wisps of steam which in young Tom's imagina-tion became the smoke of underground fires breaking through. They dropped trees of matched size, cut and notched and fitted them. When the walls were waist high, Mercy rigged an incline and a block and tackle, but even with that aid his body took the weight of each log, his boots sank deep into the spongy soil and his teeth showed in white flashes when hard effort pulled back his lips.

After supper, with a fire blazing by the cabin, he adzed out the rough boards for window and doorframe and inner furniture, and late at night young Tom woke to hear his father's froe and mallet splitting the cedar roof shakes, and sometimes heard his mother fretfully calling, "Mercy, come now! It's late enough!" Lying awake, he listened to his father come into the wagon and settle down upon the mattress with a groaning sigh and fall at once asleep. The dying yellow of the firelight flickered against the wagon canvas; strange sounds rustled in the windy woods, and far off was the baying of timber wolves. Caroline, disturbed by that wild sound, stirred against him.

The rains held off and the meadows dried before the roof of the cabin was on. John Mercy said, "It might be the last clear spell all winter. I have got to stop the cabin and break that meadow and get the wheat in." He looked at his wife. "Maybe you won't mind living in the wagon a week longer."

"I mind nothing," she said, "except being here."

John Mercy turned to his son. "Go round up the animals."

The two brindle oxen were deep in the meadow. Driving them back to the cabin, young Tom saw his people at the campfire; they were saying things not meant for him, his mother with her arms tight across her breasts and her head flung up. Presently his father turned away to yoke the oxen, hitch on the breaking plow and go into the meadow.

The ancient turf became coiled, gloss-brown strips. John Mercy watched the sky as he plowed, and plowed until the furrows grew ragged in the fading day; and ate and built his fire and hewed out the cabin rafters, and by morning's first twilight shadows he was at work again, harrowing the meadow into its rough clods, into its pebbled smoothness. The gray clouds thickened in the southwest and the wind broke and whirled them on. With the wheat sack strapped before him like an apron, John Mercy sowed his grain, reaching for the seed, casting with an even sweep, pacing on, and reaching and casting again. Young Tom sawed out the top logs, shortening and angling each cut meant for the cabin's peak; and at night, by the bonfire's swaying glow, he laid his weight against the block-and-tackle rope while his father heaved the logs up the incline into place.

On Sunday his father said, "Take the gun, Tom, and go over this hill and keep on till you find the Willamette. See what you can see. Come back around the side of the hill and tell me which is the short way."

Within a hundred yards the cabin vanished behind the great bark-ribbed trunks of firs whose trunks were thicker through than the new cabin. They ran far to the sky and an easy cry came out of them as they swayed to the wind. Pearly shafts of light slanted down into this fragrant and still wilderness place, like the shafts of judgment light shining from heaven to earth in Redway's old geography book. Fern and hazel stood head high to him, and giant deadfalls lay with their red-brown rotted wood crumbling away.

He climbed steadily, now and then crossing short ravines in whose black marsh bottom the devil stock stiffly grew, and stung him as he passed; and down a long vista he saw a buck deer poised alertly at a pool. His gun rose, but then he heard the cold advice of his father, "Never shoot meat far from home," and he slapped his hand against the gun stalk and watched the deer go bounding into the deeper forest gloom.

A long two miles brought him to the crest of the hill, from which he saw the surface of a big river in smooth patches between the lower trees. Another half mile, very rough, brought him down to the river's margin; he turned to the right and presently the timber and the hill rolled out into the meadowlands. Directly over the river he saw a cabin in a clearing, and saw a girl at the break of the bluff, watching him. He looked at her and suffered his short shock of disappointment to find a house and people here, for he had been until this moment a lone explorer pushing through a wild and empty place.

At such a distance he would not clearly see her face; she was about his size, and she stared at him with a motionless interest. He stirred his feet in the soft earth and he raised his hand and waved it, but she continued to look at him, not answering, and in a little while he turned and followed the open meadows as they bent around the toe of the dark hill and reached home before noon.

His father said, "What did you see?"

"The river's on the other side of the hill, but it's easier to go around the hill. I saw a deer."

"That's all?"

"And a cabin across the river," said Tom. "There was a girl in the yard."

John Mercy looked to his wife. "Now," he said quietly, "there's one neighbor," and waited for her answer.

She looked at him, reluctant to be pleased. "How far away?"

Young Tom said, "More than an hour, I guess."

His mother said, "If they saw you, they'll come to visit . . . and it's a terrible camp they'll see. . . . Caroline, go scrub and change your dress. I've got to fix your hair." Suddenly she was irritably energetic, moving around to put away the scattered pans and the loose things lying under the canvas shelter.

John Mercy went toward a pile of saplings roughly cut into rafters; he cast a secret glance of benevolence at young Tom. Something had pleased him. He said, "We'll get these on in short order."

The saplings went up and crosspoles were set across them. The first row of shakes was laid when a man's strong halloo came ringing in from the meadow and a family moved through the trees, man and wife, two tall boys carrying sacks, and the girl young Tom had noticed across the river.

The man said in a great, grumbling voice, "Neighbor, by the Lord, we could of saved you sweat on that cabin if we'd known you were here. Teal's my name. Iowa."

Talk broke through this quiet like a sudden storm. The two women moved beyond the wagon, and young Tom heard their voices rush back and forth in tumbling eagerness. The men were at the cabin.

Teal said, "Boys, you're idle. This man needs shakes for his roof. Go split 'em. . . . It's a-going to rain, Mercy, and when it rains here, it's the world drowned out. The drops are big as banty eggs. They bust like ripe watermelons, they splatter, they splash. You're soaked, your shoes squash, you steam like a kettle on a fire. . . . Boys, don't stand there. Mercy and me will lay on what shakes that's cut."

The Teal girl stood in front of young Tom and stared at him with direct curiosity. She was not quite his height; she was berry brown, with small freckles on her nose, and her hair hung down behind in one single braid. Caroline cautiously moved forward and looked up to the Teal girl, and suddenly put out a hand and touched her dress. The Teal girl took Caroline's hand, but she kept her eyes on young Tom.

"I saw you," she said.

"What's your name?"

"Mary," said the Teal girl, and turned with the quickest motion and walked toward the older women.

The Teal boys worked on shakes, one splitting, one drawing the cedar panels down with the knife. The wind lifted and the roar of it was the dashing of giant cataracts all through the deep places of the forest; the men talked steadily as they worked. The smell of frying steak—brought by the Teals—was in the air to tantalize young Tom. He leaned against a tree and watched Mary Teal from the corner of his eye, then turned and walked away from the trees to the falls of the creek and squatted at the edge of the pool, his shadow sending the loafing trout into violent crisscross flight. Gray clouds ran low over the land and a deepening haze crawled forward. He hunched himself together, like a savage over a fire; he listened into the wind and waited for the scurrying shapes of the enemy to come trotting in war file out of the misty willow clumps. He sat there a long while, the day growing dull around him. The wind increased and the pool's silver surface showed the pocking of rain. His mother's voice called him back to mealtime.

He ate by the fire, listening to the voices of the older people go on and on. His mother's face was red from the heat of the fire, and her eyes were bright, and she was smiling; his father sat comfortably under the cedar tree, thawed by the company. It was suddenly half dark, the rain increasing, and the Teals rose and spoke their farewells and filed off through the trees, Mr. Teal's last cheerful call returning to them. Silence returned; loneliness deepened.

His mother said, "It was good to see people."

"They'll be fine neighbors," his father said.

His mother's face tightened. She looked over the flames and suddenly seemed to remember her fears. "Four miles away," she said, and turned to the dishes on the camp table. She grew brisk. "Tom, I want water. . . . Stack these dishes, Caroline, and come out of the rain."

John Mercy went into the darkness beyond the cabin and built his work fire; lying awake in bed, young Tom heard his father's mallet steadily splitting out shakes, and he continued to hear the sound in his sleep.

By morning a great wind cried across the world. John Mercy lighted the campfire and cooked breakfast for the women within the wagon. He laid on heavy logs for the fire's long burning and took up a piece of rope and the ax and hammer and nails. "We have got a chore to do at the river," he said to young Tom. "You pack the gun." They skirted the foot of the hill, trailing beside a creek stained muddy by the storm. The meadow turf was spongy underfoot and the southwest wind roughly shoved them forward through sheets of fat raindrops sparkling in the mealy light. When they reached the river they saw a lamp burning in the window of the Teal house, but John Mercy swung to a place where the hill's timber met the bluff of the stream.

"There will come a time," he said, "when I'll have to send you to the Teals' for help. You'll need a raft to cross."

They cut down and trimmed six saplings for a raft bed, bound them with two crosspieces nailed in. A pole, chipped flat at one end, made an oar. Then John Mercy tied the rope to the raft and towed it upstream a hundred yards beyond the Teal house. He drew it half from the water and secured the rope to an overhanging tree, and laid the oar in the brush. "You'll drift as you paddle," he said.

Homeward-bound, the wind came at them face on. Young Tom bent against it, hearing his father's half-shouted words, "It ought to be a month or more before the baby's due. But we're alone out here, and accidents come along. We've got to expect those things. No sensible man watches his feet hit ground. He looks ahead to see what kind of ground they'll hit next."

They came around a bend of the creek and heard a massive cannon crack of sound in the hills above them, and the ripping fall of a tree; its jarring collision with the earth ran out to them. They pressed on, John Mercy's pace quickening as though a new thought disturbed him. High in the air was an echo like the crying of a bird, lasting only a moment and afterward shredded apart by the storm, but it rose again, thinner and wilder, and became a woman's voice screaming.

John Mercy's body broke from its channeled steadiness and he rushed around the last bend of the hill, past the pool of the falls and into the cabin clearing. Young Tom followed, the gun across his chest. Through the trees he saw a figure by the campfire, not his mother's figure, but a dark head and a dark face standing above some kind of cloak. His father stopped at the fire before the stranger; reaching the scene, young Tom discovered that the stranger was an Indian. His mother stood back against the wagon with a butcher knife in her hand; her face shocked him, white and strange-stretched as it was.

He lifted the gun, waiting. The Indian was old and his cheeks were round holes rimmed by jawbone and temple. His eyes were sick. His hand, stretched through the blanket, was like the foot of a bird, nothing but bone and wrinkled dark flesh. He spoke something, he pointed at the food locker. For a moment—for a time-stopped space in which the acid clarity of this scene ate its way so deeply into young Tom's memory that ninety years of living neither changed nor dimmed a detail of it—he watched the latent danger rise around his father's mouth and flash his eyes; then, with complete unexpectedness, his father turned to the grub box and found half a loaf of bread. He laid it in the Indian's fingers—those fingers closing down until they almost disappeared in the bread. His father pointed at the gun in young Tom's hand and pointed back to the Indian, snapping down his thumb as though firing; he seized the Indian at the hips, lifting him like a half-emptied sack, walked a few steps and dropped him and gave him an onward push. The Indian went away without looking behind him, his shoulders bent.

His mother's voice, high-pitched and breathless, drew young Tom's attention. She was shaking, and in her eyes was a great wildness. "I don't want to be here! I didn't want to come! Mercy, you've got to take me home! I want my old house back! I want my people! I'll die here!"

John Mercy said, "Tom, take your sister for a walk."

Caroline stood in the doorway of the cabin, frightened by the scene. Young Tom went over to catch her hand. The half-covered roof kept Caroline dry, and he stood indecisively under this shelter disliking to leave it, yet compelled by his father's order.

John Mercy lifted his wife into his arms, speaking, "The creature was harmless. There are no bad Indians around here. I know the weather's poor and there's no comfort, but I'll have the roof on the cabin by tonight." He carried her into the wagon, still talking.

Young Tom heard his mother's voice rising again, and his father's patient answering. He clung to Caroline's hand and watched the rain-swept world beyond the cabin and saw no other shelter to which he might go. He was hard pressed to make up his mind, and when his father came out of the wagon, he said in self-defense, "Caroline would get awfully wet if I took her for a walk."

John Mercy said, "You did right. . . . Caroline, go keep your mother company." He looked up to the unfinished roof, he drew a hand down across his water-crusted beard, and for a moment he remained stone-still, his whole body sagged down with its accumulation of weariness. He drew a long breath and straightened. "Soon as I finish the roof, Tom, we'll line the fireplace with clay. I'll need some straw to mix with the clay. You go along the creek where the old hay's rotted down. Bring me several swatches of it."

The rain walked over the earth in constant sheets, beating down grass and weeds and running vines; the creek grew violent between its banks and the increased falls dropped roaring into its pool. Bearing his loads of dead grass to the cabin, young Tom watched his father lay the last rows of shakes on the roof and cap the ridge with boards hewn out earlier by the late firelight; afterward John Mercy, working faster against the fading day, went beside the creek to an undercut bank and shoveled out its clay soil, carrying it back to the cabin by bucket. He cooked a quick supper and returned to the cabin, mixing clay and dead grass stems, and coated the wood fireplace and its chimney with this mortar. He built a small fire, which, by drying the mud, would slowly season it to a brick-hard lining.

Throughout the night, fitfully waking, young Tom heard the dull thumping of a hammer, and twice heard his mother call out, "Mercy, come to bed!" At daybreak young Tom found a canvas door at the cabin; inside, a fire burned on the dirt hearth and a kettle steamed from the crane. The crevices between logs were mud-sealed, the table and grub box and benches had been brought in. Standing before the fire, young Tom heard the wind search the outer wall and fall away, and suddenly the warmth of the place thawed the coldness which lay beneath his skin. He heard his mother come in, and he turned to see his parents standing face to face, almost like strangers.

His mother said, "Mercy, did you sleep at all?"

His father's answer was somehow embarrassed. "I had to keep the fire alive, so the mud would dry right. Today I'll get the puncheons on the floor and we can move the beds in." In a still gentler voice, the uncertainness of apology in it, his father added, "Maybe, if you shut your eyes and think how all this will look five years from now ———"

She cut him off with the curt swing of her body, and walked to the fire. Stooping with a slowness so unlike her, she laid the Dutch oven against the flame and went to the grub box. She put her yellow mixing bowl on the table, she got her flour and her shortening and her salt. She stood a moment over the mixing bowl, not looking at John Mercy. "As long as I can do my share, I'll do it. . . . Tom, fetch me the pail of water."

He stood with his father at the break of the trees, viewing the yellow-gray turf of the meadow, and the plowed ground beyond it, and the valley floor running away to the great condensed wall of mist. He knew, from the dead gentleness of tone, that his father was very tired; it was not like him to waste time speaking of the future. "The orchard will go right in front of this spot," his father said. "That will be pretty to look at from the house. The house will stand where we're standing. These firs will go down." He was silent, drawing the future forward and finding comfort in it. "All this is free—all this land. But it's up to a man to make something out of it. So there's nothing free. There never is. We'll earn every acre we get. Don't trust that word 'free.' Don't believe it. You'll

never own anything you didn't pay for. But what you pay
for is yours. You've got it while other men wait around for
something free, and die with nothing. Now, then, we have
got to cut down some small firs, about eight inches through.
We'll split them in half for floor puncheons."

He turned, walking slower than usual; he searched the
trees, nodding at one or the other, and stopped at a thin fir
starved by the greater firs around it; its trunk ran twenty feet
without a branch. "That one," he said, and went to the cabin
wall for his ax. "Tom," he said, "I want you to go up in the
hills and see how close you can find a ledge of rock. That's
for the fireplace floor." He faced the tree, watching the wind
whip its top; he made an undercut on the side toward which
he wished the tree to fall, and squared himself away to a
steady chopping.

Young Tom passed the cabin, upward bound into the semi-
darkness of the hill; the great trees groaned in their swaying,
and their shaken branches let down ropy spirals of rain. It
was like walking into a tunnel full of sound. His overcoat
grew heavy with water, which, dripping on his trousers legs,
turned them into ice-cold bands; his shoes were mushy. Behind
him he heard the first crackling of the tree going down, and
he turned and saw his father running. The tree, caught by
the wind, was falling the wrong way. He shouted against the
wind; his father looked behind, saw the danger and jumped
aside. The tree, striking a larger fir, bounced off, and young
Tom saw its top branches whip out and strike his father to
the ground. His father shouted, buried somewhere beneath
that green covering.

His mother came crying out of the cabin. "Mercy! Mercy!"
She stumbled and caught herself, and rushed on, fighting the
branches away as she reached the tree.

When he got there, he saw his father lying with both legs
beneath the trunk. The branches, first striking, had broken the
force of the trunk's fall; and then they had shattered, to let
the trunk down upon his father, who lay on an elbow with his
lips the color of gray flour paste. Young Tom never knew
until then how piercing a gray his father's eyes were.

His mother cried, "Your legs! Oh, God, Mercy!" She bent
over him, she seized the trunk of the tree and she stiffened

under her straining. John Mercy's voice was a vast shout of warning, "Nancy, don't do that!" His arm reached out and struck her on the hip. "Let go!" She drew back and laid both arms over her stomach, a shock of pain pressing her face into its sharp angles. "Oh, Mercy," she said, "it's too late!" and stared down at him in terror.

Young Tom raced to the cabin wall, got the shovel and rushed back; a branch interfered with his digging. He found the ax, thrown ten yards away by Mercy in his flight; he returned to cut the limb away. Mercy lay still, as though he were listening. He watched his wife, and he put a hand over his eyes and seemed to be thinking; the impact of the ax on the trunk threw twinges of pain through him, but he said nothing until young Tom had finished.

"Give me the shovel," he said. "Now go get Mrs. Teal."

Young Tom stood irresolute. "You got to get out of there."

"Those legs," said John Mercy, and spoke of them as though they didn't belong to him, "are pinched. If they were broken, I'd know it . . . and they're not." He paused and a dead gray curtain of pain came down on his face; he suffered it and waited for it to pass. "Do as I tell you." Young Tom whirled and started away at a hard run, and was almost instantly checked and swung by his father's command, "You've got a long way to go, and you'll not do it starting that fast. Steady now. I've told you before . . . think ahead."

Young Tom began again, trotting out upon the meadow; he looked back and saw his father awkwardly working with the shovel, sheltered by the outstretched apron of his mother. But even before young Tom ceased to look, she dropped the apron, put both hands before her face and walked toward the wagon.

The scene frightened him, and he broke into a dead run along the margin of the creek, and began to draw deep into his lungs for wind; he ran with his fists doubled, his arms lunging back and forth across his chest. A pain caught him in the side, and he remembered his father's advice and slowed to a dog trot. He grew hot and stopped once to crawl down the bank of a creek for a drink, and was soon chilled by the wet ground against his stomach and the rain beating on his back.

After a rest of a minute he went on, stiffened by that short pause. The river willows at last broke through the rain mist forward, and the low shape of the Teal cabin. He crossed the last meadow and came to the bank; he hadn't forgotten the raft, but he wanted to save time. The wind was with him, carrying his shrill call over the water. He repeated it twice before the cabin door opened and Mrs. Teal stepped to the yard. Young Tom raised his arm, pointing behind him toward his home. Mrs. Teal waved back at him immediately and ran into the house.

Squatted on the bank, young Tom saw the three Teal men come out, lift a boat and carry it to the water; in a moment Mrs. Teal joined them, and the four came over the river. Mrs. Teal had a covered basket in her hand. She said, "Your mother, Tom?"

"My father's caught under a sapling that fell on him. That made mother sick."

Teal turned on his lank, Indian-dark sons. "Git ahead and help him."

"Oh, Lord, Lord," said Mrs. Teal. "Take the basket, Nate. We've got to go fast. It's going to be unnatural."

Young Tom started after the Teal boys, they running away with a loose and ranging ease. "No," said Teal, "you stay with us. You've had runnin' enough. The boys are a pair of hounds; let 'em go."

They went forward, Mrs. Teal now and then speaking to herself with a soft exclamation of impatience. Otherwise there was no talk. The wind was against them and the rain beat down. Young Tom opened his mouth to let the great drops loosen his dry throat, and slightly suffered the slow pace. The coming baby never entered his mind; it was of his father lying under the tree that he thought with dread, and when the creek began to bend around the toe of the hills, close by the falls, he ran ahead and reached the house.

His father had dug himself out from the trap; there was a little tunnel of earth where he had been. The two boys stood silently at the fire, and one of them motioned toward the cabin. Young Tom drew the doorway canvas back from the logs, looking in; his father had moved the bedstead from the wagon and had set it up near the cabin's fireplace. His mother was on it, groaning, and his father knelt at the bed-side and held her hands. Young Tom retreated to the fire, watching the Teals come through the trees. Mrs. Teal seized the basket from her husband and went at once into the cabin; a moment later his father came out.

John Mercy said to Teal, "It's a good thing to have neighbors. I'm sorry I can't offer you coffee at this minute." He let his chin drop and he spread his hands before the fire and gravely watched it. The sockets of his eyes seemed deep and blackened; his mouth was a line straight and narrow across his skin.

"My friend," said Teal, "the first winter's always a bad one. Don't work so hard or you'll be twenty years older by spring." He turned to the taller of his two sons. "Jack, take Mercy's gun and go fetch in a deer."

Young Tom heard his mother's sharp cry from the cabin. He moved away, he stood by the tree and stared at the trench in which his father had been, and noticed the marks scrubbed into the soft ground by his father's elbows. He walked along the tree and gave it a kick with his foot, and continued to the millpond. Here he squatted, watching the steamy rain mists pack tighter along the willows of the creek. In the distance, a mile or so, a little timbered butte stood half concealed by the fog, seeming to ride free in the low sky. He tightened his muscles, waiting for the enemy to come single file through the brush, but then he thought of the old savage, so bony and stooped and unclean, who had seized the half loaf of bread, and his picture of a row of glistening copper giants was destroyed. He heard voices by the cabin, and rose and saw Mrs. Teal by the fire. He went back.

Mrs. Teal looked at him with her kindness. "Your mother's all right, Tom. You had a brother, but he wasn't meant to stay. You understand, Tom? It's meant that way and you oughtn't sorrow."

She meant the baby boy was dead. He thought about it and waited to feel like crying, but he hadn't seen this boy and he didn't know anything about him, and didn't know what to cry for. It embarrassed him not to feel sad. He stood with his eyes on the fire.

Teal said to his other son, "That Methodist preacher is

probably down at Mission Bottom, Pete. You go home, get the horse and go for him." He walked a little distance onward, speaking in a lower tone to his son. Then the son went on, and Teal turned back to the cabin and got the saw standing by the wall and went over to the fallen log. He called to young Tom, "Now then, let's not be idle, men. Puncheons he wanted, wasn't it? We'll just get 'em ready while we wait."

A shot sounded deeper in the forest—one and no more. "There's your meat," said Teal. "You've seen the trout in the creek, ain't you? Mighty fat. Next summer there'll be quail all through those meadow thickets. What you've got to have is a horse for ridin'. Just a plain ten-dollar horse. I know where there's one."

The minister arrived around noon the next day, and out of this wet and empty land the neighbors began to come, riding or walking in from all quarters of the mist-hidden valley, destroying forever young Tom's illusion of wilderness. They came from the scattered claims along the river, from French Prairie, from the upper part of the La Creole, from strangely named creeks and valleys as far as twenty miles away; the yard was filled with men, and women worked in the cabin and at the fire outside the cabin. Young Tom stared at strange boys running through the timber, and resented their trespassing; he heard girls giggling in the shelter of the wagon. It was a big meeting. A heavy man in buckskins, light of eye and powerfully voiced, strolled through the crowd and had a word for everyone. People visited and the talk was of the days of the wagon-train crossing, of land here and land there, of politics and the Hudson's Bay Company. A group of men walked along the break of the hill until they reached a knoll a hundred yards from the cabin. He watched them digging.

In a little while they returned, bringing quietness to the people. The minister came from the cabin, bareheaded in the rain. Mr. Teal followed, carrying a small bundle wrapped within a sheet and covered by a shawl; they went on toward the grave, and young Tom, every sense sharpened, heard the knocking of a hammer and the calling of a voice. The crowd moved over and his father walked from the cabin, carrying his mother. Young Tom saw Caroline alone at the cabin's doorway, crying; he went to her and got her hand and followed his father.

A little box stood at the grave, the minister by it; he had a book in his hand which he watched while the rain dripped down his long face. Young Tom's mother was on her feet, but she wasn't crying, though all the women around her were. The minister spoke a long while, it seemed to Tom. He held Caroline's hand and grew cold, waiting for the minister's words to end. Somebody said, "Amen," and the minister began a song, all the people joining.

Looking at his feet, young Tom felt the coldness run up his legs, and his chest was heavy and he, too, cried. As soon as the song was done, his father carried his mother back to the house and the crowd returned to the fire. A woman dumped venison steaks into a big kettle on the table, and cups and plates went around and the talk grew brisker than it had been before.

Young Tom said, "Caroline, you go into the wagon." From the corners of his eyes he saw men shoveling dirt into the grave; he thought about the grave and imagined the rains filling it with water, and the shawl and the white sheet growing black in the mud. He went over to the fallen log and sat on it.

He remained there, wholly lost in the forest of his imagination while the roundabout neighbors, finished with eating and finished with visiting, started homeward through the dulling day. They went in scattered groups, as they had come, their strong calling running back and forth in the windy rain; and at last only the Teals remained. He saw Caroline and Mary Teal watching him through the front opening of the wagon. He rose and went around to the cabin, hearing the older Teals talking.

Mrs. Teal said, "I'm needed. We'll stay tonight."

Teal looked at his two tall sons. "You had best get at those puncheons. Mercy's legs will trouble him for a while. Tomorrow we are agoin' to knock down some trees for a barn lean-to."

Young Tom quietly drew back the canvas covering of the cabin's doorway. He was troubled about his mother and wanted to see her, and meant to go in. But what he saw suddenly shut him out and brought great embarrassment to him.

His father stood beside the bed, looking down, and young Tom heard him say, "I can't stay here when your heart's not in it. There is no pleasure in this work, and no point in looking ahead to what it'll be someday, if you don't feel it too. Well, you don't. We'll go home . . . in the spring when it's possible to travel. That's what you want, I clearly know."

She was pale and her eyes were stretched perfectly round; her head rolled slightly, her voice was very small. "I couldn't leave now. I've got a baby buried here. It's a mighty hard way to come to love a country . . . to lose something in it. Mercy, put a railing round that grave. I have not been of much use, I know, and it's hurt me to see you work the way you've done. It will be better when I can get up and do what I can do."

John Mercy bent down and kissed his wife, and suddenly in young Tom the embarrassment became intolerable, for this was a thing he had never seen his people do before, and a thing he was to see again only twice so long as they lived. He pulled back and let the canvas fall into place; he thought he heard his father crying. He walked by the big kettle with its remaining chunks of fried venison steak. He took one, eating it like a piece of bread. Caroline and Mary Teal were now at the back end of the wagon, looking at him.

He said, "I know a big cave up on the hill."

Mary Teal came from the wagon, Caroline following; and the three walked into the woods, into the great sea swells of sound poured out by the rolling timber crowns. Mary gave him a sharp sidewise glance and smiled, destroying the strangeness between them and giving him a mighty feeling of comfort. The long, long years were beginning for Tom Mercy, and he was to see that smile so many times again in the course of his life, to be warmed and drawn on by it, to see tears shining through it, and broken thoughts hidden by it. To the last day of his life far out in another century, that smile—real or long after remembered—was his star, but like a star, there was a greater heat within it than he was ever to feel or to know.

SENTENCE OF DEATH

By THOMAS WALSH

ITEM ONE, the grimmest and most important item, was the body of a respectable middle-aged pharmacist named Carl Sawyer. Item Two, the usual emotional item, was an attractive blond woman, apparently his widow, who was sobbing hysterically over him when Cochran and McReynolds arrived from the precinct house. Item Three—which, to Cochran and McReynolds, explained everything at first glance and completely —was a rifled cash register. Item Four, the familiar professional headache, was a store crowded with excited and talkative neighbors.

It appeared at first that every one of these people was quite willing to furnish Cochran with detailed and significant information; it developed later, when he had attended to the necessary elimination, that just four of them had actually seen anything. Mrs. Sawyer and a chance customer named Ellen Morison had witnessed the shooting; two others—a husband and wife—glimpsed a man who sprinted out of the drugstore immediately afterward, and raced away in a car which he had parked thirty or forty feet distant, in heavy shadow. This couple agreed, however, on one or two distinguishing facts about the car; and Ellen Morison, a slim and alert young girl with brown hair, intelligent dark eyes and a sensible if excited voice, described the man.

She informed Cochran that fifteen or twenty minutes ago, when she had entered the drugstore, the man had been standing in front of Mr. Sawyer. They were so close together, just a bit left of the cash register, that at first she had taken him for a friend of Mr. Sawyer, and had assumed that Mr. Sawyer was chatting with him; then the man had turned quickly, apparently in panic, looked at her quickly, fired twice at Mr. Sawyer and slapped his left hand out and down at the cash register. It was her opinion that the man was about twenty-eight years old, perhaps older; that he had blond hair, a slim build and a very sharp, narrow jaw. She seemed to be breathless and considerably upset at this time, which was quite natural, but because she remembered the right things about the man—not too many of these; just the striking and obvious details—Cochran was inclined to accept her as perhaps the most dependable witness.

The married couple, who had observed the man from the side and in motion, were the only people who had seen the car. They described it to Cochran as either a black or a dark blue sedan with a dented fender—the right rear fender. One of them thought that the man had been wearing a brown suit and brown shoes; the other, that he had on slacks and a gray sports jacket. They both declared, like Ellen Morison, that the man had been hatless. They both remembered the blond hair.

McReynolds, in the meantime, had attempted first to compose Mrs. Sawyer and then to question her. Both attempts failed. She did not appear to understand who McReynolds was or what he wanted; she would just shake her head dumbly and blindly at him, as if she were still in a condition of severe shock. Cochran left her alone. He was sure then that they wanted a man of a certain age, build and complexion; one who owned or who had access to a cheap sedan with a dented fender; who had a gun; and who, in all likelihood, had also a police record.

He and McReynolds set out to locate this man. They checked pictures and records downtown; they settled on a few possible suspects; they rounded up and detained four of these; and then, two days later, Mrs. Sawyer picked one of the four immediately and hysterically from a line-up.

The married couple supported Mrs. Sawyer's identification, even though, in Cochran's opinion, they could not be half so sure of it as they insisted they were. Ellen Morison would not corroborate. She was the only witness who had impressed Cochran to any extent, and she admitted now that the man they showed her looked something, not too much, like the man who had shot the druggist. She was not prepared to swear that he was the man . . . or that he was not. She told Cochran uncomfortably that she remembered the other man as being older and taller. This one ——

She shook her head. McReynolds became impatient with

her; Cochran, who suspected that bereaved women like Mrs. Sawyer, after and because of their bereavement, often hit out at the first convenient and likely target, reserved judgment on the identification and went out to do some routine checking.

He discovered these facts: The man Mrs. Sawyer had identified—a tough and surly young truck helper named Johnny Palica, who had a couple of minor arrests to his discredit—lived with a brother-in-law who owned a cheap black sedan. On the night in question, last Thursday, Johnny Palica had been permitted to use the sedan, which had a couple of deep scrapes on the back fender, and had kept it out from early evening until after midnight. Just driving around, he admitted uneasily to Cochran; he had his girl with him. What did anyone do when he had his girl with him? He kept to himself, didn't he? Well, then ——

The girl corroborated his story—only the girl. She was not an impressive or disinterested witness. There were still three people who identified Johnny Palica—who, indeed, were more certain of him now than they had been previously—and two of these people also identified the brother-in-law's car. There was another witness, Ellen Morison, who could not seem to make up her mind definitely about him. It was a shaky defense, very badly handled, and the jury convicted. After the conviction, which made the death sentence mandatory, Cochran began to avoid McReynolds for some reason; and then one afternoon he discovered suddenly, with a shock of acute physical discomfort, that McReynolds was beginning also to avoid him.

Each of them knew that an identification made under circumstances of great excitement and tension was not always trustworthy. And apparently each of them, because of a highly developed instinct in such matters, disliked this one. They did not discuss it with each other—it was not their province—but they did not forget about it either. Then March came, and on March fifth, at half past two in the afternoon, Cochran received a phone call which for some time, and in an uneasy and illogical manner, he had been anticipating.

"You remember the Morison girl?" McReynolds asked him, quiet enough about it—perhaps too quiet. "The one who couldn't make up her mind about this Johnny Palica?"

"Who?" Cochran said. But, of course, he remembered her immediately; he pretended not to because he did not want McReynolds to get any ideas about him. "No. I don't seem to —— Wait a minute. That one?" He rubbed his mouth carefully. "What's the matter now? What's up?"

McReynolds said stolidly, "Big news. She just told me that Palica isn't the guy. She claims she's positive. You better hustle around here, Ray. I think we're in trouble."

So Cochran got a cab for himself. He found McReynolds and Ellen Morison in an upstairs room at the precinct house, with a busy and impatient young man named Wilson who was somebody unimportant on the district attorney's staff; and he was informed by Wilson that last night, outside a tavern on Third Avenue, Miss Morison saw—or thought she saw—the man who had actually murdered Carl Sawyer. She was positive about him, Wilson added dryly, because he had turned his head and glanced at her exactly the way he had glanced at her that night in the drugstore. She did not think that he had recognized her. When she came back five or ten minutes afterward with a policeman, he was gone. A bartender in the tavern remembered him. Unfortunately, however, the bartender was unable to furnish any useful information about him. That seemed to be it, Wilson said. A long silence followed.

Cochran was waiting for McReynolds to break it; McReynolds, who looked a bit pale and haggard that afternoon, appeared to be waiting for Cochran.

At last Cochran said, "Well," uncertainly, and sat down on a corner of the desk with his hat pushed back, his lips pursed and his palms on his knees.

"Exactly," said the district attorney's man, as if Cochran had made a very shrewd and penetrating remark. "The whole thing is almost childishly simple. Last night Miss Morison happened to see someone who bore a superficial resemblance to our friend Palica. So immediately ——"

Cochran said, "We never found the gun."

"Granted. I wish we had too. But when we've been able to convince a jury without it, I don't see ——"

McReynolds said suddenly, angrily and pugnaciously, as if the words burst out of him, "Wait a minute now. Me and

Cochran are responsible for him; not you, mister. And I've kind of been sweating a little blood over it lately, if that means anything. I don't like this thing. I never did."

He went that far. Cochran—they were boosting each other along now—took his right palm from his knee, turned it over, examined it and decided to go a bit further.

Cochran said, "I've seen nervous and hysterical women like Mrs. Sawyer identify cops who were just put into a line-up to fill it out. Sure, that married couple agreed with her; witnesses like them always go along with the first person who makes up her mind. I kind of agree with Mac here. Let's talk this over."

Ellen Morison, who appeared nervous but determined, glanced at him and said quietly, "Thank you. I'm beginning to feel better. I testified at the trial that the man who shot Mr. Sawyer—the man I'm telling you I saw outside that tavern last night—seemed to be older and thinner, and a lot taller than the man you arrested. I was treated then as if I didn't know what I was talking about. I wasn't sure, or I told myself that I wasn't sure. But now I am. And now I want something done about it."

The man from the district attorney's office stopped looking annoyed and angry, and started looking concerned and worried. More discussion ensued; then it was decided that the first thing to do, if they wanted a reasonable standard of comparison, was to give Ellen Morison another and longer look at Johnny Palica. The lieutenant, who had been careful enough to dissociate himself entirely from this interview, was called in. The lieutenant phoned downtown, and then downtown made arrangements with a Captain Mooney.

At half past eight the next morning, Cochran and the girl drove up to—to that place, as Cochran had begun to think of it, very uneasily—and found Mooney waiting for them. They shook hands and conferred briefly; then Mooney glanced sidewise, without much facial expression, at Ellen Morison, and conducted them out of the visitors' room and into a corridor which had high barred windows.

They went by two men who were dressed in the uniform of prison guards; they stopped in front of a steel door which was unlocked from within, and they waited for several moments, even though they had Mooney with them, in front of another door just beyond the first, and quite as massive and powerful looking, until the one through which they had been admitted was closed and locked.

Afterward there were more doors, more prison guards, more corridors, and finally a courtyard and another and rather isolated building. When they entered that building, Cochran, who did not have to be told what it was, touched his lips in a nervous and delicate manner with his tongue. He did not look at Ellen Morison. He did not make any attempt to speak to her.

They stopped presently outside a room. It was this kind of room. It had yellow composition walls and a brown baseboard. It had a cheap oak table with a soiled blotter on it and a clean ash tray; it had two chairs, one window and one powerful ceiling lighting fixture. In this room there was a peculiar but unmistakable sort of presence waiting for Cochran. He knew why; he and McReynolds were chiefly responsible for it. He entered.

Ellen Morison, who was not to talk to Johnny Palica, but only to observe him through a grille concealed in the outside door at normal eye level, remained in the hall; but Captain Mooney entered behind Cochran, glanced at him and went out through another exit. Almost as soon as Cochran was left alone, the harsh light in the room and the intense stillness made him restless and uncomfortable. Several minutes passed; to Cochran they seemed to pass with extreme slowness. Then there were steps in the inside corridor, and Cochran jabbed his hands into his hip pockets, turned and braced himself, at least physically, for this.

Mooney came in. "All right now," Mooney said, in the simplest and most matter-of-fact tone. "In here, Johnny. You remember Ray Cochran, don't you?"

Cochran spoke the first words that came into his head. "Sure," Cochran said, his lips feeling like wet flour. "Sure, he does. . . . Come on in and sit down, fella. How've you been?"

He had intended to shake hands here, but he stopped awkwardly after starting the gesture, because Johnny Palica did not appear to recognize him. Because of that, and of what it meant, the tone which Cochran had decided to employ—

official, authoritative, but not unfriendly—became, after the first moment or two, a shabby and ridiculous pretense. There was no necessity for it. Johnny Palica was whiter, quieter and much more nervous than Cochran remembered; and as soon as he recognized Cochran, he made a desperate and pathetic attempt to ingratiate himself.

There was no more toughness or defiance in him. He was well broken. Not by Mooney, not by a couple of months' imprisonment, but by a certain idea and a certain date which Cochran and McReynolds had arranged for him. He grinned anxiously, and when it seemed that Cochran was not going to respond to the grin, he widened it in a slow, clumsy manner, with much effort.

"Fine," he said. "I'm okay, Mr. Cochran. I'm —— You got some news?"

It was the first time he had ever addressed Cochran by that title; it was a small thing, and it was intolerable. Cochran began to sweat at the same time, because he had been warned by Mooney not to excite Johnny Palica and not to tell him anything about the girl until they had one or two definite facts to go on; he muttered that there didn't seem to be anything new in this thing, not yet. Headquarters, he added, just thought Johnny Palica might want to go over his story about that night again. If he did ——

He did. He nodded violently. So Cochran put a couple of questions to him, the answers to which he and McReynolds had already checked, in so far as was humanly possible, months ago; and then Cochran pretended to listen intently to what Johnny Palica said to him, and even checked everything off, detail by detail, in a pocket notebook. "Sure, sure," Cochran muttered, even when the words had no particular application to what had preceded them. That was another thing, he'd add huskily, which he and McReynolds would check right away. They'd talk to Johnny Palica's girl, of course. And they'd go back carefully over the whole affair. They'd ——

He would have done anything, said anything, promised anything, to get out of that room quickly, to remove himself from the way in which Johnny Palica kept watching him. As if he wanted help and reassurance from somewhere, Cochran thought savagely; not as if he expected it; as if he just wanted it. And then, when Mooney concluded the interview, when Cochran picked up his coat and mumbled something hearty and cheerful and got out of there, it was worse than before. In the outside hall, Ellen Morison was waiting for him.

She was quite pale, her eyes looked extremely odd, and apparently she did not want to talk to Cochran any more than Cochran wanted to talk to her. All she did was to shake her head at him. Of course, Cochran thought, she meant that he and McReynolds had the wrong man in here. That —— He turned away from her. He did not ask himself whether she was right about Johnny Palica; before he had half completed his turn something much worse had happened to him. He felt it.

Later that afternoon, McReynolds also appeared to feel it. He did not discuss the thing logically with Cochran; he just nodded a couple of times, swallowed once, got his hat and drove over with Cochran to interview Mrs. Sawyer.

They discovered that something had happened to her, too, because she was no longer a pink and cunning little woman with demure blue eyes and fluffy gold hair. She had aged noticeably; and by gradual degrees, as Cochran talked to her, she became withdrawn, bitter, nervous and finally hysterical again.

She was still sure that it was Johnny Palica who had murdered her husband; now, Cochran reflected hopelessly, hatred and loneliness had done their usual sort of job on her. So he and McReynolds did not tackle the two supporting witnesses; that was useless unless and until they had first shaken Mrs. Sawyer. That evening McReynolds went downtown and started rechecking the files for another picture and description that might approximate Johnny Palica's; and at almost the same hour Cochran and Ellen Morison established a vigil over on Third Avenue, outside the Shamrock tavern.

They would park there, in Cochran's coupé, for five or six hours a night—the late hours—and for seven nights a week. They would stay there until half past one in the morning, with elevated trains rumbling overhead monotonously, with March wind lashing at them, and then Cochran would drive the girl home and go home himself after a cup of coffee somewhere. But he would not sleep any too well—the coffee, perhaps, or perhaps other things. He would remain restless for a while, doze again, and then rouse suddenly with the conviction in him that someone had been shouting his name just now, at an infinite distance, but quite clearly. He never managed to hear the voice—not as sound—but at the same time he recognized it, and in the end it came to have its own sort of existence for him.

He knew what it wanted from Mr. Cochran. He knew that much the first time it happened to him, and every time afterward, but he could not do anything helpful because, if there was going to be any appeal made on the basis of new evidence, he and McReynolds needed this other man. They could not find him. They could not imagine how to find him. They had twelve weeks at first, and then ten, and then eight, and then six. But nothing came up, either at headquarters or outside the Shamrock tavern.

Occasionally, after his end had dried up on him, McReynolds spent a couple of uncomfortable hours with them, but for the rest of the time Cochran and the girl had no company but themselves. At that period Cochran could have described the girl well, at least partially, although he himself did not seem to retain any personal or individual impression of her. She had dark hair, of which at times he had a vague sort of recollection, and the softness and delicacy around the mouth which had never been particularly attractive to him in other girls. He liked her all right, but he did not think about her as he had thought about one or two other girls. There was no opportunity. On those endless and monotonous evenings they rarely conversed at length because the appalling significance of their watch made ordinary conversation nearly impossible; and yet, despite that, they achieved a kind of intimacy which would have seemed very new and unusual to Cochran if he had been in any position to consider it.

Every so often, instead of just sitting there and waiting for the right man to show up, she worried him by attempting to force a resemblance between the person they wanted and some unimportant client of the Shamrock tavern. And so once, in their sixth week, he explained impersonally to her that it was rather silly to get excited about this, because the only thing they could use here was patience and more patience and again patience. You couldn't rush these things, Cochran said. You waited them out. They generally came to some sort of conclusion in the long run.

But she noticed at once that Cochran did not commit himself, here and now, as to the sort of conclusion they were going to reach outside the Shamrock tavern. She sat back in her corner of the seat and then glanced at him.

She said, "I suppose they do. Only this time"—she put her lips together for a moment—"they simply have to work out in the right way. Not that I'm discouraged about anything; I can't make myself believe for one minute that a mistake like this, a cruel and vicious mistake, is going to be—well, permitted. We'll find him. You wait and see."

"I hope we do," Cochran said. But when he looked out at Third Avenue—shabby, rain-swept, deserted, watery yellow light spilling across the black pavement in front of the tavern —he felt heavily depressed. "We've got a chance, anyway."

She said, with a confidence that surprised Cochran, "Oh, we've got more than that . . . much more. Things don't happen that way. If they did, there wouldn't be much point to the whole mess."

"Maybe there isn't," Cochran said.

"Of course that's silly," Ellen Morison said. She was very calm about it. "Or out-and-out horrible. We've just got to believe that certain things are true and important. If we don't ——"

"What things?" Cochran asked; it was the first discussion that had interested him even slightly. "You name a couple. I'd like to find out about them."

So it was that, of all subjects, they began arguing the most profound and imponderable one. They would argue it from exactly opposed viewpoints—not with the technical skill and finish of philosophers, but from each of their individual accumulations of judgment, experience and intuition. If she knew half the things he knew, Cochran would say darkly, or if she understood half the facts about the uglier side of human nature, she wouldn't talk so much about this or that being permitted or else not permitted. Things happened; that was all you could say about them.

She was earnest at first, and then irritated, and then scornful, but, of course, she never convinced Cochran. What he did admit—reluctantly and not to her—was that it might be pretty comforting to see this as Ellen Morison saw it, to believe in reasons for things, to be sure that someone, somewhere, was keeping an eye peeled in Ray Cochran's direction or Johnny Palica's.

An idea of that kind would have provided him with some useful insulation. He admitted so much, again privately; and then, little by little, and very stubbornly, he became a bit weaker in regard to his own arguments, and a bit more responsive in regard to hers. Friday night at about half past ten, he had just declared that perhaps people did achieve happier and more useful lives when they shared Ellen Morison's belief, and not his, but that didn't prove anything at all, as Cochran saw it. True was true. And if ——

A man who did not resemble Johnny Palica at all parked in front of them and went into the Shamrock tavern. Cochran glanced at him and dismissed him, but Ellen Morison froze up, made some sort of breathlessly inarticulate sound and grabbed at Cochran.

He got out of the car slowly, his heart thumping. He said, "All right. You stick here. We don't want him to know anything about you yet. I'll be back as soon as I get a better look at him." Then he walked around the front of the coupé and into the tavern . . . and went numb.

The man whom Ellen Morison had just identified for him was at least four inches taller than Johnny Palica, noticeably older, noticeably stouter; there was, apart from his blond hair, not even the slightest physical similarity between them. *What is this?* Cochran asked himself very quietly. Something broke in him. He strode back to the coupé, to that girl, but what he felt for her at this moment was a mixture of cold rage and ferocious contempt.

Did she understand, Cochran demanded thickly, what she had been doing for the last six weeks to him and McReynolds? Did she have any idea of how she had put them up on the rack, and kept them there, and twisted the wheel night after night until each of them was just about out of his head?

She looked very pale and excited, but not as if she understood what he was talking about.

"What's the matter?" she said. She was still breathless. "Why don't you —— He's the man, Cochran! I know he is! Do you think I could ever ——"

"Then where's the mistake?" Cochran almost shouted at her. He began pounding his fist, with an impression of infinite restrained force, against the roof of the car. "How did anybody ever take this guy for Palica? You kept telling us all along that they looked like each other. That's the thing we were going to spring on everybody. That's all we had."

"But he does!" She pushed her head out anxiously at him. "Of course, he's grown that mustache. That's what you ——"

Cochran spun away from her, maddened; then he got into the car blindly, closed the door, cradled his arms in front of him on the steering wheel and laid the right side of his face against them. That way he did not have to so much as look at her.

"He grew too," Cochran said. His voice hated her. "He grew four inches. Me and McReynolds were the dumbheads; all along the district attorney's office had you down for just what you were. We figured you knew what you were talking about. We were stupid enough to go through hell because somebody like you ——"

She faltered out several jerky sentences. Why was he talking like this? Hadn't they waited together for the man all these weeks? And now wasn't he in their hands?

Cochran would not answer her. The only clear idea in his mind was that if this man had looked like Johnny Palica, they might have got the witnesses to admit confusion and perhaps error. This way no one—not Mrs. Sawyer, not the married couple, not the district attorney's office—would even consider him. So ——

The girl shook him again. Then she whispered painfully, "Listen, Cochran. Will you please, please listen to me? I tell you ——"

The man came out of the Shamrock tavern, had a bit of trouble in starting his car—Cochran would scarcely have noticed him otherwise—and pulled out into Third Avenue. After a few moments, Cochran—a good, careful cop—turned on his ignition and pulled into Third Avenue after him. They drove north. By now, of course, Cochran was following him more by training and dogged instinct than because of any remaining hope in this angle. He still hated the girl; he still felt that she had first argued with him, and then convinced him, and then—most shameful of all—got him almost ready to believe Ray Cochran was something a lot more significant than an ordinary precinct detective who had been instructed to straighten something out, and who had torn himself into little pieces because he was unable to manage it. Always merry and bright, Cochran thought savagely, that was the ticket. There were reasons for everything—oh, sure! Good and logical reasons, if you were stupid enough to understand what they were. If ——

Twice she attempted to speak to him; twice Cochran would not listen to her. Then the sedan in front of him turned into a side street that seemed hazily familiar. He followed. He saw, halfway along this street, an apartment house which was also vaguely familiar to him, and then, when the sedan parked in front of it, he recognized that building with a complete and paralyzing shock.

He whispered something. He drove past the sedan, past the man who was ringing a bell in the apartment vestibule, and parked several houses away. He noticed without hate, with a complete detachment, that Ellen Morison was looking white, scared and miserable. What was the matter with her now? Cochran asked himself. What was she ——

He got her out of the car. He told her where to phone McReynolds, and what to tell him; then he moved back carefully to the sedan which he had followed up here from the Shamrock tavern. All his thoughts had become quick, sharp and decisive. His heart had begun to thump heavily again. An old car with a new paint job, Cochran saw now; no marks on it. Of course. Not so much as a scratch on the rear fender. But he and McReynolds would find the shop where that paint job had been put on, and where the right rear fender had been hammered out; and then, Cochran told himself grimly, he'd get that married couple to identify this sedan if he had to knock their heads together.

He left the sedan and secluded himself in a dim hallway

just down the street from it. The girl came back, and Cochran waved her over imperatively to him, but he did not bother with explanations because he had very little time or attention for her at that moment. He got out two cigarettes and smoked them in extraordinarily long draughts; then McReynolds and a couple of precinct men cruised past him in a department car. Cochran whistled twice. McReynolds stopped.

They discussed matters for a moment or two, Cochran explaining why he was up here, McReynolds grasping the explanation almost immediately. After that the precinct men went around to the rear entrance and to the fire escapes, and Cochran and McReynolds entered the apartment house after ringing a bell on the top floor—which was not the floor they wanted. They went up two flights, rapidly. They each took deep breaths. Then Cochran rang a bell on that landing, and after some delay the door was opened about three inches and Cochran put a palm against it, shoved and walked in.

The blond man with the dinky little mustache was in there. Cochran walked up to him, gave him a very tight, ugly smile, and hit him. Cochran hit him very hard, and for no apparent reason at all. He just felt that way. He felt fine. At the same moment, McReynolds did what he was supposed to do. McReynolds took care of Mrs. Sawyer.

Of course, after the event it was all obvious. Then Cochran told himself that he and McReynolds should have paid much more attention to the story Ellen Morison had told them. Hadn't she said that when she entered the drugstore, Mr. Sawyer and the holdup man were standing and talking together like old friends? And hadn't Mrs. Sawyer got all excited and hysterical when he and McReynolds had gone back to question her as to how sure she was about Johnny Palica? What should have been at least indicated then was that she could be making some attempt to cover up the real killer, and that, consequently, she herself might be involved in the murder.

It was also clear that Ellen Morison had walked in at just the wrong moment. Mrs. Sawyer and her masculine friend had thought up a perfectly simple and effective method through which to rid themselves of a husband who was getting along in years, and who owned a profitable business. They had attempted to arrange everything so that Mrs. Sawyer, who was supposed to be the only close witness, would describe a man to the police who did not resemble the gentleman friend in any respect; and then Ellen Morison had appeared just when the gentleman friend had nerved himself up to it, and had got himself into so much of a panic that he was unable to postpone it.

And so, on that first night, Mrs. Sawyer had pretended grief and horror, and had refused to understand McReynolds' questions, because it was necessary for her to learn as quickly as possible what Ellen Morison remembered about the man. If she had differed too much with the girl's description, which was fairly accurate, she might have started Cochran and McReynolds nosing around; and so she agreed with it, and identified Johnny Palica.

She did that to cover herself, obviously, and to keep the police busy on another angle. And then the married couple supported her identification, and Johnny Palica was unable to prove his whereabouts, and everything had begun to work out very nicely for Mrs. Sawyer and her friend. Until he had done the one thing he should never have done—until he had visited Mrs. Sawyer at home, very late at night, in the same apartment house where Cochran and McReynolds had questioned her weeks ago.

As soon as Cochran had recognized the apartment house, he had asked himself the natural question: What connection was there between this man and an attractive little woman like Mrs. Sawyer? Only one answer had seemed at all feasible. It explained immediately why Mrs. Sawyer had identified Johnny Palica, and why Ellen Morison had refused to identify him. Now Cochran was unable to understand why he had never considered that particular aspect before; and even after McReynolds and the other two men had got Mrs. Sawyer and her masculine friend—screaming at each other, blaming each other—into the department car and had started downtown with them, the whole thing continued to exasperate Cochran as the evidence of a colossal personal stupidity.

"Because in something like this we always check on the wife or husband," he insisted to Ellen Morison, who was still waiting downstairs for him. "Always! We'd have done it this time if you hadn't been there to back up her story. But when you saw the whole thing happen just in front of you —— Well, how were we going to question it? What for? It wasn't reasonable."

"But I suppose this is," Ellen Morison said. She looked very tired and miserable. "Now everything's fine. If those two make you ashamed of the whole human race, that doesn't matter at all. It's just ——" Her mouth twisted. "Get me away from here, Cochran, please. I'm scared. I don't want to hear anything else about this. All I ——"

She began shivering. Cochran soothed her. There was a perspective you attained in such matters, Cochran said; the one important thing was that you did not permit an event of this nature to throw you off balance, to make you cynical, to —— He stopped there; he remembered suddenly that not too long ago he had been arguing a similar question from another position. Ah, forget it, he thought angrily. Who understood why things like this happened the way they did? Who wanted to? He could go this far with Ellen Morison—they worked out pretty well frequently. They had worked out now, hadn't they?

It did not strike him at once that he had gone much further with her than he had ever gone with anyone else. When it did strike him, he decided that perhaps there was some sort of significance there. He got her into the car and patted her hand tentatively and murmured to her. On other nights, Cochran decided, and under different conditions, they could argue the verities, but just now he would have to be very firm and sensible about this.

He was. He started the car and got her away from there. They drove aimlessly at first, with Cochran very quiet and reassuring with her, and then he took her home and went home himself. He slept fourteen hours with nothing disturbing him, not even the garbage trucks or the morning traffic, and when he woke up at last, he discovered that he felt fine and comfortable, and that he was thinking about Ellen Morison. *Say,* Cochran thought slowly, *what is this?* But he knew. He knew almost as soon as the question completed itself.

FLASHING SPIKES

By FRANK O'ROURKE

I DON'T know what happened to most of them, and it was sheer luck that I saw Dane Bjorland playing out his long, lonesome string on a sweltering hot August afternoon in a little town. This was back in '36, long ago, but the memory returned today when I read a column about one of his former teammates. It was written by a friend of mine, a wonderful sports writer, and told how this teammate of the Dane's had been a kind but illiterate gentleman who didn't realize, even after he accepted the bribe, what he had done to his own life; and the saddest part about this is that that man was truly a gentleman and one of the greatest ballplayers who ever swung a bat. And reading his story again, after so many long years, made me think of the Dane, for he, too, was one of the greats. It sent me back nearly twelve years to a hot day in August at our county fair, with the main attraction the ball game between our town team and a crack traveling outfit.

Really to understand, you have to see the town and the fairgrounds and the crowd moving sluggishly among the exhibits of cakes and needlework and prize sows and ears of corn; and the grandstand facing the half-mile race track, with the free-act platform just across the track in front of the grandstand, and behind it, the ball diamond. To see the ball game, the dyed-in-the-wool fans crossed the track and lined up behind the restraining wires stretched along the base lines, where they could drink pop and warm beer, and yell their lungs out.

You can't know how it is to play ball on a diamond like that unless you have seen one, or, better yet, felt one under your spikes. The infield was skinned raw dirt and the outfield was mowed grass pocked with gopher holes and rough spots. They stuck two white flags on the base lines about three hundred feet down each one, and home plate was just ahead of an overhanging screen which trapped all foul balls and kept them from going back over the track into the grandstand. They ran

151

a few horse races and had the free acts, and then it was three o'clock and time for the ball game; and if you were lucky you found a place in your own dugout when you came in to hit— if the rooters from your home town hadn't already moved in and taken over. That is how it was, and still is, at those ball games.

I was playing shortstop on my town team that year. I was still in college, and considered one of the best hitters and fielders in our part of the state, with a good chance to make the grade in professional ball; and I was chock-full of the old college try and fight that made me give everything on every play with all of my two hundred pounds. Our team was composed of boys like myself, young and tough and full of vinegar. We'd licked everything in our part of the state, and after this fair game with the Carry-Carriers, the traveling outfit, we were heading for the state tournament. We knew they had a ball club made up of old pros who had slowed down too much for double-A ball or better, but who made more money with this traveling team than they could in any kind of ball from Class A down.

That was the situation on a hot August afternoon. We finished our batting practice before the Carriers came from their bus and took over the other dugout and loosened up their arms. While the crowd filtered across the race track, we sat in our dugout and watched them warm up and take their batting practice. They looked like old men to us, and maybe they were, in a sense. They only hit four apiece, mostly easy taps and bloopers onto the short grass. They finished batting in fifteen minutes and walked off the field; and we grinned knowingly at one another, and I remember how we said, "Oh, brother! Will we tie the can on these has-beens!"

We took a snappy infield workout, burning the ball around the bases, scooping up the grounders, yelping at one another and looking like a million dollars; and when we finished and their turn came, their manager, a wrinkled man in a dirty, overlarge suit, walked to the plate, and their infield trotted out and started the workout. Their manager hit easy grounders with handle hops and they fielded slowly, missing half, barely making their pegs good from base to base. They looked terrible, worse than cow-pasture ball, and the crowd behind us growled that old refrain about "What kind of punks did the fair board get to play our boys? This won't be no game. We'll beat 'em fifteen runs."

So they finished their infield practice, and while we waited for the tumblers to end their free act, and the managers conferred with the umpires, I placed the Carrier players in my mind, trying to remember how each one had hit and fielded.

Being a shortstop, I had particularly watched theirs work out at his position. He was a big, broad-shouldered man with small hips, and legs that looked fragile, but were really full of knotty muscle. He wasn't young; there was gray in his hair under the cap, and he moved with great deliberation, fielding easy ground balls and tossing them carelessly to first. But his face made me look, time after time; it was browned and seamed and filled with some old, old knowledge that, to me, was beyond anything I could understand. It was a tired and resigned look, as if he didn't care who won the game or how he played. He had a big nose and a wide mouth, and I could see the small white scars around his ears and along his jaw. His hands were big and wide, and, looking closely, I could tell that his fingers had been broken and were bent and gnarled like an old-time catcher's. I watched this big man labor through infield practice and tap four balls in hitting drill, and I told myself that I had him whipped all around the board.

We took the field and the umps called the batteries and the game started. I played a deep short, and on this fairgrounds diamond, because the infield hadn't been skinned back deep enough, I played a good eight feet on the grass. I was fast and could charge a ground ball in plenty of time, and besides, I could go either way and back for those short bloop Texas Leaguers they'd been hitting in practice. The second baseman was another boy my age—nineteen—and we knew each other completely, or so we thought, and he was playing very deep too. We had a lefty working for us, and he toed the rubber and took the sign, and we got under way.

Five minutes later I had learned the first of a great many lessons. Those old men, in their slow and seemingly bungling way, had fooled us nicely. Their lead-off man tapped at an inside ball, and it dribbled lazily toward me. I charged the ball, made a fast pickup and burned a perfect peg to first. That old man beat my throw by two feet. He wasn't so slow. So I went back to deep short again, and the second hitter did the same thing, and they had men on first and second, and that was when I slowly realized that they were playing me for a sucker. Those men could lay a ball where they wanted it, off pitching like Lefty's, who was hot stuff in our neck of the woods, but just another busher to them. And then the other shortstop came up, slouched back from the plate, and I edged up to the skinned line and told myself, *Let him lay a slow one at me.*

Lefty took the sign for his hook, and in all honesty, he did have a good curve that broke fast and cut downward with a nasty spin. This big gray-haired man didn't swing until I thought the ball was in our catcher's mitt, and then he seemed to explode that black bat, and the ball was a streaking bullet going over second, going on a line between our right and center fielders. I backed up second, and the long peg came in to Tommy, but this big man had rounded second and beat the short peg to third with a beautiful inside hook slide that showed me a quick, dust-filtered picture of him going in, legs perfect, and suddenly standing on his feet, all slouched over, dusting his pants with those big hands and staring with sleepy, half-closed eyes at our third baseman, who had missed him three feet with the tag.

We held him on third. The next two hitters flied out to short center, and the third out was a topped grounder to Lefty. I tossed my glove back on the grass and met him coming out from third. He gave me a level, unsmiling look and spoke in a soft voice that had no feeling or lift to it; it was just a voice, but somehow I remembered every word. He said, "Kinda slow infield, son," and went around me and picked up his old, dried-out, ragged glove and forgot me.

I played through three innings before I knew what he meant, and if he hadn't spoken to me again when we came to bat in the fourth, I would not have caught on. They seemed to fold up after scoring two in the first, and from then on hit fly balls and ground balls and we got them out. But we didn't score, and in the fourth I played up close and threw out two of them on those dinky ground balls. But the third man came up and swung his bat in a long end hold, and I edged toward second because I figured he'd swing late. Lefty took the signal for his fast ball, and the big man, coaching third, called in that expressionless voice, "All right, Doc!" and as Lefty delivered, the hitter shortened his hold and chopped the ball to my right, between me and our third sacker, where I should have been if I hadn't tried second-guessing. The next man flied out, and as he passed me, the big man said softly, "Your catcher crossed you up, son," and went on by with that sad, old look.

Then I understood. He was trying to help me play the game. He had stolen our catcher's signals and was giving voice relay signals to the hitters, and the hitter had taken the signal, watched me shift, and crossed me up. Then I began to understand that this big quiet man knew more baseball than I would ever learn, and I was a fool if I didn't listen to him.

I knew they were playing with us, making it a close game for the benefit of the fans, just as the Monarchs and Globe Trotters and the other fast traveling teams played when they came through our county, so that we would invite them back the following year. I caught a slow curve on the outside corner in our half of the fourth, and stretched it to a double when the ball bounced in a gopher hole on the right-field line and their fielder juggled it momentarily. I made my slide and stood up, slapping dust, and grinned at the big man.

"I caught that one," I said.

"Good hit," he said evenly. "How'd you guess it?"

"He wiggled his glove," I said. "I watched him three innings. He does when he throws that slow hook."

"Good eyes," he said, moving back to position.

I felt pretty cocky and took my lead and the pitcher turned off the rubber and grinned at me; and then the big man moved with deceptive speed, cutting in behind me, took the underhand flip from their second baseman and tagged me out by five feet.

"Watch the ball," he said tonelessly. "Don't start no jaw act when you're feeling so good."

I walked off the field without answering. My pride was hurt. I had been a sucker for the oldest gag in the game, the old hidden-ball trick. He talked to me and I forgot the ball, and their second sacker held it until I had my lead, all fat and dumb and happy, and then they lowered the boom. I was a prime hick from Podunk.

When I reached the third-base side line and tried to ignore the scorching yells from my home-town fans, I turned and looked at him. He was crouched so easily at short, not smiling, and I thought that any man who knew baseball as he did was wasting his time in the bush leagues.

The game went along smoothly, and they gave the fans double their money's worth. We scored in the sixth on a single, a sacrifice and another single by Lefty, our pitcher. By that time I had got his name from our scorebook—Bjorland—and was over my anger at being caught off second. Each time we traded positions he had something to offer me, always sober-faced, even-voiced, and as the game went on, there seemed to be something else on his face, a kind of fine-drawn fear of some old memory that threatened to come out and bother him.

We came in to hit in the last of the seventh, and while we wiped sweaty faces and sucked lemons and drank from our water bucket, and the fans talked in a loud hum all around us, I saw one of the old-time baseball fans in the county come running on his short legs. He ducked through the crowd and under the fence, and stood beside our manager, talking a blue streak, waving his short arms and glaring out at Bjorland, his face red and sweating with righteous anger. I walked over, wondering what had got his goat, and heard his words tumbling out: "—— didn't know till I went over and saw their line-up! Then I had to watch him for three innings! Sam, that's the Dane Bjorland, of the old Black Socks! I tell you, that's him!"

Then I knew. Every boy who played and loved baseball knew the Black Socks, knew how they threw the World Series a long time ago and almost ruined baseball, and were kicked out of organized ball forever. I had first read about them when I was a ten-year-old kid playing midget ball, and I knew their names by heart, and here for the first time, like an old ghost from the forgotten past, playing out his string on a dusty, bumpy small-town diamond was one of those great men, a man who led his league in fielding and hitting, a man who threw away a magnificent career for a few dollars he never received. I turned and stared at Dane Bjorland, and every man on the team heard the words passing along the fence, and turned, mouths open, to see a ghost walk.

I thought, *And he has the guts to tell me how to play baseball.*

I was young then—younger than I knew—and I had yet to read my American history and temper it with the hidden wisdom of the truth. But I was young, and I burned up. And I stared at him.

Along the fence line the murmurs began, and then someone yelled, "Start riding them! We can lick this bunch of has-beens!" Then the same voice rolled into a harsh shout "Where's your black socks, Bjorland?"

That was the beginning. I watched him when the yelling started, because there was a difference between these shouts and the ordinary razzing you hear at any ball game. This had an ugly, deep, angry tone, and he knew it. He had to, but he didn't turn that big head or make a move. He just settled back and waited for play to start.

Their manager came around the catcher and stood beside ours and I heard him say, "Took you longer to recognize him than I expected, Mr. Ronson."

Sam said, "He's not supposed to play baseball."

"Organized ball," their manager said, speaking as if he had an old and well-used speech to give. "Not bush league."

"All right!" Sam said harshly. "But you get this, buddy: I've got a bunch of fine boys on my ball team, and I don't want him talking to 'em, you hear, or even coming close to 'em."

"I understand," their manager said. "I just wanted to get it settled now."

"Yeah," Sam said nastily. "We've got three innings left, mister. Maybe we ain't got it settled."

Their manager looked at Sam for a moment and then went away.

Someone behind the wire yelled, "That's the way to tell 'em, Sam! We'll fix him!"

We didn't get a man on in the seventh, and when I ran out and passed him, he looked at me and didn't speak. But I was young and righteous, and I knew what was right and wrong.

I said, "Thanks for the advice, Bjorland."

He said, "That's all right, son."

"Yeah, thanks," I said. "I'll be damned sure I don't follow it . . . your way."

He turned and stared at me, and I saw that old pained look touch and gray his face, and for a moment I felt very small; and then someone yelled, "Don't take nothing from him, Bill! Clean his plow for him!"

I was our state's intercollegiate heavyweight champion too. And I knew it. How I knew it then! I guess he understood, for he looked at me, and then turned and went across the field to the third-base coaching box. I threw my practice pegs, and all the time I could hear them giving him unadulterated hell from that fence, a few short feet back of the coaching box. I knew that it took courage to stand out there and take it, when he could go to the dugout, but he stood there and ignored them.

Our second baseman took the peg and tossed it to me, and we ran up to the pitcher's mound for our pep talk.

Our second baseman said, "We'll get that baby, Bill. What's he trying to tell you?"

"Nothing," I said. "Now."

They scored another run in the eighth and led us three to one. We didn't score in our half, and they failed in the ninth, and we came in to do or die; and when we passed each other between innings, he didn't speak. But he looked at me. That same even, gray look. It made me boil over. I was the first hitter in the ninth, and the fans were yelling for a rally.

I went up there to hit or else, and they dusted me off. I hit the dirt and got up, moving for their pitcher, and then I knew that was childish, because I had asked for it, showing my eagerness to hit so boldly. I stepped into the box and tried to calm my nerves. I could see him at short, waiting for the pitch, big and quiet and ready. I took a strike and a ball, and then I knew what I was going to do. I hit the next pitch on the nose, a long liner into right center, and took off.

I rounded first and saw their center fielder just getting the ball, and I dug for second. He was waiting for the throw, straddling the bag and giving me plenty of room for my slide. The peg was coming in and I saw him there, so damnably cool and capable, and I went into him with my spikes high, aiming straight for his legs. I felt the spikes hit his stockings and then flesh, and I made my grab for the bag and caught it as I drove him off his feet on his side in the dust. The ball hit his glove and bounced off, and I was safe.

I jumped up and waited for him. I was ready for anything, and I could hear the crowd roar, and I knew they were all with me; it was a strange, furious feeling.

He rolled over and sat in the dust, and I saw the blood come out on his torn stockings and run down the outside. He looked up at the base umpire and said "Time," in that even voice.

Their pitcher came over, and their infield gathered around him, and he said, "Get the kit."

One of them waved at the dugout, and their manager ran out with a big first-aid kit. He rolled down his stockings and the inner sweat socks, and I looked at his legs and saw the criss-crossed, thickly laid scars and welts and bumps from a thousand spikes biting into his legs over the years, and then I was sick in my stomach. I turned away and crouched on the bag.

He sat there in the hot dust and poured the disinfectant on his legs and cleaned them, and wrapped the clean white bandages on them, and got to his feet.

Their manager said softly, "Okay, Dane?"

"Okay," he said. "Okay."

Their manager said, "Not so bad this time," and went back to the dugout.

I had to turn then, for play was starting. I saw him walk straight, but with great pain, to his position and turn, crouching down. The blood came through the bandages and caked fresh on his socks; and I looked at it and then at his face, and understood a great deal. The crowd was roaring, enjoying every bit of it, and I wondered how many times he had gone through this same inevitable sequence: starting a game and being recognized, and then waiting for the spikes at second base . . . and never backing up. Those numberless scars told how much he had ever backed up.

I looked at him and said, "Mr. Bjorland, I'm sorry."

He looked at me, and I saw something flicker behind those gray eyes—something warm and real. He said, "Why, son?"

"I ——" I said. "I don't know, Mr. Bjorland. But I am."

"Forget it, son," he said evenly. "Some things never get paid for."

Then we started play, and our second baseman singled to center and I had no time to tell him. I came home standing up, and the crowd roared at me, and I sat in the dugout and felt miserable. Everybody was yelling "Good boy, Bill!" and "That's the way to show him, Bill!" and I wanted to go home and cry.

Then that little red-faced fan who found him out came over and patted me on the back and said, "That's showing him how we feel, Bill. Just wait till the game's over. We'll show that crook how we like guys like him playing with decent boys."

I looked at him, and then I didn't dare talk. I got up and went to the water bucket and watched the game.

Their pitcher walked two men and the bases were full, with no one down, one run to tie and two to win. Our next hitter flied out to first base. I turned and watched Bjorland, and he moved to his left a little and spoke to his pitcher in that soft, low voice. I could see the blood on his stockings, bright and red, and I wondered how he could stand up. Then their pitcher delivered, and our hitter, the catcher, laid plenty of wood on the ball.

It was a white streak past their pitcher, heading for center field, a sure hit and the ball game. But he was there, waiting, all the time. He made a long dive, and the ball hit and stuck in that ragged glove, and he rolled over and trotted two steps and doubled our man off second. The game was over, ended by the finest kind of baseball, the kind you never see at the county fair or on the little-town diamonds, the kind that means the best. And then the crowd started to growl.

I have always been proud of that afternoon—at least that part of it. I ran across the infield to him and stood beside him, and he watched me quietly. I put my hand on his shoulder and grabbed his free hand and shook it.

I said, "That was a beautiful play, Mr. Bjorland. I wish you could tell me more about playing short."

They had started across the infield, all of them, and I turned sideways and looked at them; and I think my face showed how I felt. I weighed two hundred pounds, and I could fight like hell itself when riled, and my last name was Riley, and they knew me too well. They stopped and looked at us, and then broke up, and the mob became a good baseball crowd.

I dropped my hand from his shoulder, and he said, "Thanks, son."

"No," I said. "Let me thank you."

He bent over and picked up his ragged glove and rubbed his scarred, crooked nose, and then he smiled at me, and I saw the warmth and good feeling in his eyes, where it had been hidden for so long.

He said, "Son, I wouldn't be surprised if you make the big show."

I said, "If I had somebody to tell me how to play this game right, I might make it, Mr. Bjorland."

"Sometimes ——" he said thickly, "sometimes I think it'll never get paid for. Maybe it will."

That was long ago, as I said before, that hot afternoon at a county fair. It was just another ball game, you know, with some old duffers playing some kids, and winning because they were smarter. But I never forgot that ball game, and I never forgot Dane Bjorland. And today I know what he meant when he said, "Some things never get paid for." But I think he feels a little different now. If you're ever in town, come out to the stadium. They've got a pretty good shortstop playing for the Red Birds. He shifts on the pitch and plays the slow hoppers and covers the bag without fear, and he hits around .310 every year. His name is Riley, and they all say that he plays short like a ghost. Maybe he does. If that is true, he plays it like the ghost of one of the best who ever made a mistake and spent the rest of his life trying to pay for it.

THE LONESOME BEAR

By HARRISON KINNEY

UNTIL he was twelve my brother George was the unofficial leader of a gang of boys about his own age in Fairfield. Being four years younger than George, I was never included in the activities of this group, but one day I was sitting on a lower limb of an apple tree in our back yard when my brother George came up to the tree with his hands in his pockets.

"Let's start a store," he said. "Nobody will suspect anything if you're in it with me. You put up the counter and I'll try to get the stuff."

"All right," I said, climbing down from the tree.

After George had gone I erected a counter with two boxes and a board, facing our driveway.

"I had a hard time getting the stuff this time," George said when he got back. "Old Man Osgood was watching me."

He reached into his sweater and pulled out a two-pound box of chocolates, a half dozen all-day suckers, a box of marshmallows and eight chocolate bars. He arranged these on the counter.

"I'll go tell the gang to come and buy this candy from us," my brother George said.

"All right," I said.

George went away again and I was sitting on the ground, eating one of the chocolate bars, when a brown bear lumbered down through the apple orchard and came up to the candy counter, sniffing at the articles on the board.

"You'd better go away," I told the bear. "My brother George will get mad if you eat his candy."

The bear sat down and stared at the candy. After a while George and his gang came up the driveway. They stopped quite a distance from the counter when they saw the bear.

"You get away from that bear," one of the boys yelled to me. "He'll kill you with one swing of his paw."

162

"No, he won't," I said, patting the bear on the head.

"Give him some candy to eat and maybe he'll go away," another boy shouted.

So I took the wrappers off two candy bars, opened the box of marshmallows and placed them on the ground in front of the bear. The animal just sniffed at the candy, but when he found the marshmallows he slid into a crouch and began chewing them, looking at me occasionally, his head bobbing as he ate.

"I guess he just likes marshmallows," said my brother George. "We'll get him some more for you to feed him and maybe he'll go away."

"The state will pay you a twenty-five-dollar bounty for a bear," another boy said to my brother George. "They kill sheep. Why don't you keep him and get the money?"

"I guess we could keep him in the icehouse," said George.

"How are you going to get him in the icehouse?" somebody asked.

"I think he'll follow my brother in," George replied. "You lead him in the icehouse," George said to me.

"All right," I answered.

So after the bear finished eating the marshmallows he followed me into the icehouse. My brother George locked the door after us and I climbed out the small trap door in the wall. George told me not to tell anybody about the bear, for fear he would not get the money for himself. I promised I wouldn't.

My brother George promised to keep me in candy if I fed the bear. The diet was a rather irregular one, consisting largely of raw potatoes from a sack in our cellar, and meat bones I got from the butcher's store. The sawdust in the icehouse had dried into a comfortable bed for the bear. My family had had no use for the building after my father bought an electric refrigerator for our house.

After a few days the bear refused to eat anything. He would sit and make hoarse, whimpering noises in his throat.

"I think he wants some marshmallows," I told my brother George, who was standing outside the icehouse at the time.

"I'll get some," George said.

He went away and came back with a box of marshmallows,

which he passed to me through the trap door. I opened the box and the bear rooted into them, getting marshmallow on his nose and whiskers and chomping them noisily, looking at me as he ate them. When he had finished them he ate the raw potatoes and meat bones. I told George the bear was eating everything.

"We'll just give him some marshmallows once in a while," George said. "I guess he'll be all right."

The night the bear got out of the icehouse, one of my mother's aunts was visiting us. She was given my room, while a couch was set up in my parents' room for me as a temporary arrangement. During the warmer nights of midsummer we always left the doors open, inside the house, for purposes of circulation; all except my brother George's room in the attic. George walked in his sleep occasionally, so my father always locked him in at night and let him out in the morning. The trap door of the icehouse could only be secured from the inside, so George and I had propped a piece of two-by-four against it from the outside. It was always a matter of speculation as to how the bear was able to dislodge it. Everybody was asleep the night that the bear came into my father's room and tried to crowd under my couch to go to sleep. The couch had two folding sides, and the grunting animal lifted the couch at one end in his attempt to get his bulky body under it. In this manner the couch was pushed across the floor until it banged against the opposite wall. The bear snorted loudly in the darkness and lay down.

My father was a light sleeper. "Where are you, George?" he asked, sitting up in bed and thinking it was my brother George walking in his sleep.

"George isn't here," I said.

"Good Lord, son!" said my father. "Are you making all that noise?"

"No, sir," I said. "I think it's the bear."

"All right," said my father, lying down again. "Just don't wake your mother."

"No, sir," I replied.

After a few minutes my father sat up in bed again. "What did you say that noise was, son?" he asked quietly.

"I think the bear is sleeping under my bed," I said.

My father sat in the darkness for a time, thinking this over. Finally he turned on the table lamp beside his bed. This awakened my mother.

"What is it?" my mother asked with alarm. "Is it George again?"

My father got out of bed in his nightshirt without saying anything. He came over to the couch, got down on his hands and knees and looked at the bear under the couch.

"He eats marshmallows," I said.

Father got up and solemnly walked over to my mother's side of the bed. "We must all remain calm," he said. "Your aunt mustn't be upset. I don't think anybody is in immediate danger. There's a bear in our room."

My mother began weeping softly. "We'll all be torn limb from limb," she said.

"He won't hurt you," I told her.

My father asked me where the bear came from and I told him. My mother went into the next room to sleep with her aunt, and my father and I pulled the couch off the bear. The bear sat up and yawned.

"I never saw a bear like this that liked to be around people," said my father, crossing his bare feet in contemplation, and leaning against the bedpost in his nightshirt.

"I think he follows me because I feed him marshmallows," I said.

"We must always be kind to animals, son; wild or domestic," my father told me.

"Yes, sir," I said.

"His coat isn't shaggy like a wild bear's at all," said my father, looking at the bear. "I think he's tame."

"Can we keep him?" I asked.

My father didn't answer me. He wandered slowly downstairs and came back with his ukulele. He sat down in a rocking chair in his nightshirt and absently strummed some basic chords. The bear sat and listened to the music, staring at my father.

"This is a very friendly bear, son," said my father after a while. "Maybe we can keep him until his owner shows up."

"Yes, sir," I said.

The next day my father and I went across the street to the courthouse, with the bear plodding behind us.

"We'd like to get a license for a bear," my father told Miss Barnes, the clerk in the outer office.

Miss Barnes took off her glasses and looked at my father for a moment. Then she stood up quickly and looked at the bear, sitting on the floor beside me.

"What kind of a license do you want?" Miss Barnes asked slowly, still looking at the bear.

"We want him for a household pet," my father said.

"He eats marshmallows," I told Miss Barnes, patting the bear on the head.

"He does?" said Miss Barnes stupidly. "Just a moment." She got up and went into the inside office, looking cautiously at the bear over her shoulder. After a while the door of the inner office opened a crack and Mr. Gordon, the town clerk, peeked out. He finally pushed the door wide open. Three or four other people stood behind him and stared at the bear, which was sitting beside me, looking out the courthouse window.

"Do you really mean to keep this animal in your home as a pet for a seven-year-old child?" Mr. Gordon asked my father.

"He's a civilized bear," said my father, a little annoyed. "He's lots more trustworthy than some dogs in town that I know of. You can get a dog licensed. Why can't you license a bear?"

"You're setting a dangerous precedent," said Mr. Gordon. "Next, people will be wanting to license wildcats and wolves."

"He eats marshmallows," I said.

"We should not be afraid of setting precedents," said my father in the tone of voice that he used on customers at his store. "The motto for the state of Maine is 'Dirigo'; 'I direct.'"

"Oratorical rhetoric will get you nowhere," said Mr. Gordon, wiping his glasses and peering at the bear. "There are no regulations in the community, or Oswego County, governing this situation. There may be a state law which applies. I'll have to write to Augusta. In the meantime you will be solely responsible for the bear's behavior or he will have to be shot as being hazardous to the public welfare."

My father seemed annoyed as we left the courthouse. He sat down on the bottom step and the bear and I sat beside him.

"Son, a man could come up right now, as things stand, murder this bear and the state would pay him money," said my father. "By George, if Theodore Roosevelt were still in office I bet you could get a bear license."

My mother didn't care for the bear. She would never permit me to bring the bear as far as the back porch. My brother George soon lost interest in the animal, but my father usually brought marshmallows home from his general store. Sometimes my father would sit on the back-porch steps, play his ukulele and sing, while the bear sat in front of him and listened. Nothing could distract the bear's attention while my father was singing.

During the day, while my father was at work in his store and my brother George and I were at school, the bear was tethered to one of the apple trees by a long rope attached to the leather collar my father bought for him.

"We'll tie him close enough to the house so he won't get lonesome," my father told me.

The brown bear slept much of the time on the lower branches of the apple trees, or tumbled about on the ground, or ate the apples he could shake to the ground by hugging the tree trunks with his forepaws. On Mondays I would lock the bear in the icehouse, because he would ordinarily sit and watch the hired girl hang the week's laundry on the clothesline in the back yard, something which seemed to disturb her so much that she kept dropping parts of the wash on the ground.

The town's sheriff, Shirley Jones, who lived next door to us, knocked on our door one morning while we were eating breakfast. He was breathing heavily.

"Look, Stephen," he said to my father, "you've got to get rid of that bear. You don't have a license for him and I've got to insist. Do you know where that animal is right now?"

"In the icehouse," said my father, looking worried.

"He's sitting in the back seat of my car," said the sheriff. "He won't get out. He must have opened the door himself."

My father and I followed the sheriff next door. The bear had his head and forepaws protruding from a side window of the car, opposite the opened door.

"Go get the marshmallows, son," said my father quietly.

"Yes, sir," I said.

When the bear saw the marshmallows he climbed out of the sheriff's car and sniffed at the box in my hand.

"I have enough to worry about without a bear loose in town, scaring people and maybe taking a swipe at children," said the sheriff.

"He's a good bear," said my father.

"Just let him pull one funny move and I'll have him shot," said Sheriff Jones. "You'll have to get rid of him, anyway. You've heard about the bank robberies that have taken place north of here. We're expecting them to take a crack at the Farmer's Trust here in Fairfield any day now, and if I have to do any chasing of bank robbers I don't want a bear in my back seat breathing down my neck."

"We'll take him back to the woods this Saturday and lose him," said my father a little sadly.

"He'll be happier there," said my mother when we told her. She seemed cheerful about it. "It isn't really right to keep the poor animal in captivity, anyway."

When Saturday came my father hired an extra clerk for his store and got fishing rods out of the attic while I dug worms in the back yard. The brown bear made happy woofing sounds in his throat when we opened the rear door of our Essex for him.

"He likes to ride in cars, I guess," said my father, looking thoughtfully at the bear.

"He'll never be able to ride in cars if we leave him in the woods," I said.

"He won't mind," said my father. "He'll forget."

A few miles outside of town, tourists in a car with New York license plates blew their horn and started to pass us. The sound attracted the attention of the bear, who thrust his head out the left rear window just as the New York car was abreast of us. I heard a woman scream and the other car swerved off the road and shot up a grassy embankment, where it came to a stop. My father stopped the Essex and we walked back.

"Are you all right?" my father asked with some concern.

"Only a little shaken up," said the driver, a man in a white-linen suit. "That animal frightened me. For a minute I thought he was driving."

"He's a tame bear," said my father. "I hope you aren't hurt."

"He eats marshmallows," I said. "We're taking him fishing."

"I see," said the man, looking from me to my father.

They waved at us as they passed us a few minutes later. My father waved back. He always made a point of being nice to out-of-state people so that they would think well of Maine. We kept the rear windows rolled up after that.

"Next they'll be saying this poor bear is a traffic hazard," my father explained.

We left the car on a farm road and walked several miles into the forest, the bear traipsing silently behind us. He gave no obvious acknowledgment of any change in environment. We fished for trout all that day in a clear-water stream while the bear sat and watched us. At noon we ate the lunch the hired girl had put up for us and fed the bear some meat bones.

"A wild bear would crouch on the bank of that stream and knock trout out of it with his paw," said my father. "This is the most helpless animal I ever saw."

"Maybe he doesn't like fish," I said. "Maybe all he can eat now will be meat bones, potatoes and marshmallows. Maybe he'll starve out here."

"No, he won't," said my father, eating a deviled-ham sandwich and looking at the bear. "He can eat berries and nuts like other bears. Maybe he'll find a mate and learn from her."

"He likes music," I said. "He likes to hear you sing."

"The woods are full of birds that sing," said my father.

"They can't play the ukulele," I said.

"There are times when I wish you wouldn't talk to me," my father said. "I think you take after your mother at times. Please be quiet."

"Yes, sir," I said.

We fished for a while longer in the afternoon and the bear became tired of watching and wandered away into the woods.

"You mustn't feel badly about the bear, son," my father said, as we carried the fish baskets and rods back through the trees. He blew his nose in a large linen handkerchief.

"We didn't say good-by to him," I said.

"It's probably better that way," said my father. He was a theatrical man.

It was dusk when we reached the car and started for home.

Neither of us spoke for a while. When we were on the state highway the lights of a car behind us threw a silhouette of a bear's head on the inside of our windshield.

"Is the bear in the back seat, son?" my father asked quietly.

I turned and looked at the bear in the back seat. He sat with his back to us, looking out the rear window.

"I think it's the bear," I said.

My mother locked herself in her room all the next day.

"I don't know why our home has to be turned into a zoo," she told my father tearfully.

"The circus will be passing through here in a few days," my father reassured her. "They'll be glad to have a tame bear."

The bear and I waited on the back steps that evening for my father to come out and sing, but he never did.

In late June the circus was playing Millinocket on its way north and my father wired the manager that he might have the bear if he called for it. One afternoon, a few days later, a man drove up in front of our house in a coupé with a large wire cage protruding from the half-opened trunk. I brought the bear around from the icehouse. The man looked at the bear.

"I knew it was Henry," he said, nodding his head thoughtfully.

"Is that the bear's name?" I asked.

"We lost him last summer up this way," the man explained. "He must have hibernated in the woods all winter."

"He eats marshmallows," I said.

"It used to be jelly beans," the man said: "He's the most temperamental animal I ever saw. He wouldn't eat anything unless we gave him jelly beans once in a while. He has quite a sweet tooth. I wish we hadn't found him. He's such a nuisance."

He raised the gate of the cage and sprinkled a few jelly beans from his pocket on the floor of the cage.

"Let's go, Henry," he said to the bear.

The bear ambled inside the cage and began chewing the jelly beans. The man closed the gate after him.

"He likes to ride in cars," I said, looking at the bear through the wire.

"I know," the man answered. "That's all we could get him

to do, ride in the back of an old jalopy that two clowns drove around the ring. He's the most useless bear I ever saw. He wouldn't learn to ride bicycles, or roller-skate, and he ran away when we tried to teach him to dance. We were all glad."

The man sighed and got into the car.

"Thank your folks for taking care of him, kid," the man said sadly.

"Yes, sir," I said.

He drove away with the brown bear sitting in the wire cage chewing jelly beans.

It was the first year my family didn't go to see the circus when it played Presque Isle. My brother George threatened to run away from home, but my mother said she couldn't stand to look at another animal, and my father said he supposed it would make the bear unhappy if he saw us in the crowd.

"He rides in the back of an old car that two clowns drive," I told my father.

"He's probably very happy, then," said my father, patting me on the head. It was several weeks before he played his ukulele and sang on the steps of the back porch.

One morning my father was awakened by somebody throwing pebbles at his bedroom window. He got out of bed and went to the window. It was the hired girl. She told my father she didn't dare to come into the house because a bear was sitting on the front porch in front of the door. I followed my father downstairs and we looked at the bear through the curtains of the living-room windows.

"Look at the dust on his fur," said my father. "He must have walked twenty miles."

"Maybe he's mad at us for giving him to the circus," I said.

"No," my father replied. "He just got homesick for us."

I led the bear around to the icehouse and locked him in. When I got back my father was strumming on his ukulele.

"Son, Judge Holt told me he heard from Augusta that there's no legal protection for bears as pets," my father said. "I don't know what we'll do with him. We certainly can't keep him. Sheriff Jones and your mother just wouldn't stand for it."

My father went to work without telling my mother the bear was back, and it was about ten o'clock that morning when I discovered the bear had got out of the icehouse. I searched back of the orchard and finally started downtown to the store to tell my father the bear was loose in Fairfield. A block from the Farmers' Trust Building I saw the bear trudge out of an alley and climb into the front seat of a long black Pierce Arrow that was standing in front of the bank, its motor idling and the front door open. From the front seat the bear pushed himself over into the back and sat on the floor. I was looking at him through the car window when two men carrying guns and cloth sacks came running out of the bank and leaped into the car.

"The bear's in there," I told them, pointing.

The men didn't hear me, apparently. They slouched in the front seat and the car roared away just as the burglar alarm went off outside the bank. In a few minutes I saw Sheriff Jones' Reo and two cars filled with deputies race down Main Street in the direction the Pierce Arrow had taken.

My father was in the office of his store, sitting at his roller-top desk.

"The bear got in a car and the people drove away and didn't see him," I told him.

My father buried his face in his hands.

"Son," he said after a while, "this is the end. Those poor innocent people will find a bear in their car, not know he is a tame bear, go off the road and kill themselves. The bear will be shot, if he gets out alive, and I'll be put in jail."

"Sheriff Jones is chasing the bear," I said.

"You and George will have to go with your mother to live with her family," said my father absently. "You must always be good to her, son."

"Yes, sir," I said.

We drove slowly home in the Essex. He asked me not to talk to him for a while and I promised I wouldn't. A group of people were standing on the lawn in front of our house when we drove up.

"The bear is sitting in Sheriff Jones' car," I said.

"Those bank robbers didn't even get out of town," the sheriff told my father happily when we joined him. "The driver spotted that bear of yours in the rearview mirror, sitting on the back seat. They went over the edge of the culvert at the bottom of Mill Hill. Took them both without firing a shot. They're in the prison hospital."

My father sat down on the front steps to think.

"The bear likes to ride in cars," I said.

"He didn't get hurt a bit," said the sheriff. "We're going to give him part of the reward."

Several children gathered around the sheriff's car to look at the bear that had helped capture the bank robbers. The bear yawned and went to sleep on the back seat.

"He came back from the circus," I said, "but we can't keep him."

"I saw Judge Holt at the prison hospital," Sheriff Jones continued, sitting on the steps beside my father. "The judge doesn't see why the town can't give this bear a special license."

"By George!" said my father. "That's good of the judge. He's a good bear. We won't let him get loose again."

I shook the bear awake and led him back to the icehouse.

My mother was in a pleasant mood at supper that evening.

"With the two thousand dollars the sheriff is giving the bear," she said, "I think it would be a nice thing to build a comfortable enclosure for the animal in back of the orchard, with a little house for a shelter."

"We can buy him lots of marshmallows," I said.

"We might screen in the back porch too," my mother added. "I've always wanted that done."

"That might be arranged," my father said.

After supper the bear and I sat down on the steps of the back porch. After a while my father came out, carrying his ukulele. He patted the bear on the head.

"Son, tomorrow we'll get the bear a new collar with a shiny metal license tag," my father said.

"What will we do with him when winter comes?" I asked.

"He can sleep in the icehouse," said my father. "It will be dark and quiet in there. Fairfield is very proud of this bear and we must take good care of him."

"Yes, sir," I said.

Then my father began singing Oh, Dear, are You Lonesome Tonight? while the bear and I sat and listened to him. My father had a pleasant voice to listen to, and I always knew he was happy when he sang.

STRANGE WEDDING

By I. A. R. WYLIE

THIS is Camp Freilinger, Bavaria, American Zone of Occupation, Germany. Our allotted corner of the earth. Once upon a time it made the headlines. Now it is just another official headache. Otherwise we are forgotten. We tried, at first, to forget ourselves. To pretend to be dead, we found, made it easier to live. Then something happened to us. We began to dust our pasts and polish our secret treasures and to look timidly into the future. It was a very simple event. Things like that happen all the time, I suppose, in the outside world. But to us it was like the miracle of spring seen for the first time by eyes that have been blind.

There were two hundred of us. I knew our people as I know myself—Felix Rainer, elected chairman of the camp committee —like the lines of my own hand. They came to me with their grievances and their rancors, and among themselves they talked against me, hating me because I knew too much. That was the way things were among us.

I don't know why I think of Fräulein Minna first. Except for one superb moment in her life when she had slapped the face of a certain Gephardt Schlosser, captain in the SS, she had never been important. Now she was old and a nuisance. Just five feet tall, bent over and thin as a starveling sparrow, she took up too much space. So La Comtesse said, sometimes quite violently. In the summer, when the unshaded heat turned Schlafsaal B-24 into a fetid den, La Comtesse made Fräulein Minna sleep on the concrete floor—which she was glad to do, for La Comtesse was a huge, fat woman, and the bed they shared was an old Army cot that sagged in the middle. In the winter, La Comtesse treated Fräulein Minna as a hot-water bottle. She gave her orders: "Rub my feet. They are like ice blocks. Come closer. There is a draft down my spine." Sometimes she would complain so loudly that the other occupants of the Schlafsaal would first moan and mutter like an orchestra tuning up, and then burst into a regular modern

174

symphony of oaths and insults. Even the Silberbaums joined in.

"*Canaille!*" La Comtesse would hurl back at them.

La Comtesse, in fact, was French, a member of a Parisian community known as the Faubourg St. Germain. Why she did not go back to it and how she came to join the panic-stricken hordes escaping out of the Russian Zone, we didn't know. We asked no questions. We had our own secrets.

Old Jacob Silberbaum and his wife Rachel, who were privileged to share the light of the one dirty window with La Comtesse and Fräulein Minna, were quiet people. They were so quiet behind their strip of sailcloth that you would have thought they were waxen images. But sometimes when La Comtesse was more than usually vociferous, old Jacob would say one word, coldly and very clearly, "Collaborationist!"

"*Canaille!*" La Comtesse would shriek in answer.

She had brought nothing with her but a canvas bag stuffed with gaudy rags, and a small battered jewel case over whose contents she brooded secretively, and a red plush footstool. The footstool seemed to mean a great deal to her. She sat on it like a fat, elderly child on a make-believe throne. On fine days she took it outside, and sat in the sun paring her dirty nails and humming an old French song, "*Oh, Richard, oh, mon roi ——*"

La Comtesse's hair was really a yellowish gray. But she evolved a dye for it by diluting red ink which she "borrowed" from my office. The results provided a savage joke for the whole camp. Women who otherwise never exchanged a word stopped one another on the compound or whispered loudly as they waited their turn at the caldron of evil-smelling, midday soup.

"Have you seen? Just look! Pink hair . . . pink hair, actually!"

La Comtesse, carrying her tin pail as though it had been a Sèvres vase, pretended not to hear. But her bloodshot eyes shot out venom from under their hooded lids. Her fat lips pursed themselves, "*Canaille! Canaille!*"

The two windowless sections of Schlafsaal B-24 were occupied by the Silenskis, Paul Beneš and young David. The Silenskis were like lean and vicious rats which, for one reason or another, had been hunted all over Europe. They claimed to have worked with the Polish underground, but we didn't believe them. We didn't even believe that Natasha was Stanislas' wife. We suspected that Stanislas' real wife had died in the Warsaw blitz and that Natasha had used her papers to escape. Some of us suspected worse. They quarreled bitterly, but in Polish, which no one in Schlafsaal B-24 understood. German was the one language we had in common, and we spoke it like people spitting out dirt.

Paul and young David shared the fourth section of the Schlafsaal. They were both Czechs. Paul pretended to have forgotten his real name, so we called him Beneš to tease and humiliate him. He was a painter, and looked as painters are supposed to look, long-haired and wild-eyed. He hadn't any canvas, but in the gray twilight of his cubicle, with pieces of colored chalk, he drew obscene pictures on his dirty wall. The next day he would rub them off, so that he could begin all over again. When his chalks crumbled to their end, young David would wangle or steal replacements for him out of my store. For that, Beneš would weep on his shoulder in a brief gratitude.

Young David was eighteen. He had been eleven when his mother and father and fellow villagers had been routed at midnight out of their homes and machine-gunned on the square outside the church. It was a punishment for something that had happened somewhere else, no one knew what or where. David, wounded in the thigh and left for dead, had escaped. Later on, he became a German slave laborer. Though black-haired and swarthy-skinned, he was too strong and useful to be liquidated. When the Germans were defeated, he became a Russian slave laborer. He escaped again and bummed his way to Camp Freilinger. It was as though, buffeted by wild and cruel seas, he had come to rest in a backwater, its surface filmed with a gray and stagnant scum.

He limped a little from his old wound. But he was broad-shouldered and clean-limbed. His blue eyes were finely spaced under their straight black brows, and the cheeks, hollowed by chronic hunger, only added somehow to his look of untarnished youth. His generous mouth smiled easily with a warm and eager friendliness, so rare among us that we shrank from it as prisoners in a lightless cell will shrink under a burst of welcome sunshine. La Comtesse watched out for him. When he passed her, plumped on her plush stool, she would say, *"Bon jour, Monsieur David,"* with an awful playfulness. He smiled, but did not answer. He never spoke; only nodded or shook his head. Whether he had been always dumb or whether the power of speech had been broken in him, we did not know. He did not seem to know, himself.

The eight inmates of Schlafsaal B-24, like the rest of us, shared nothing with one another but the dirt. They loathed it with a bitter helplessness. Surreptitiously, at dusk, they would shuffle it under the edge of the sailcloth partition into a neighboring cubicle. But the next night it would be swept back again and there would be indignant mutterings. Co-operation would have been an acknowledgment of their common humanity. They would have had to pity one another. And pity had been drained out of them to a last drop which they hoarded jealously, almost malevolently, against some time of supreme need. Sometimes, if Fräulein Minna found the Schlafsaal empty, she would go through it with a shaggy, toothless broom which was her one domestic possession, and brush the gray accumulated filth out onto the compound. No one thanked her. But for a few days her companions acknowledged a grudging, watchful truce.

Camp Freilinger had been built before the war on a windswept plateau in the Bavarian Highlands. It was exposed to the ruthless winter storms and the unshaded heat of summer. But through the barbed, electrified wire the prisoners could look to the distant snow-capped mountains and over valleys that in springtime glowed with pale green fire.

High watchtowers guarded each corner of the compound and were linked together by the unpainted, slatternly prison huts. From them, gray-green, inhuman figures, their blank faces shadowed under steel helmets, had looked down and watched and waited. They've been gone a long time now. But we still see them.

In the center of the compound stands a red-brick, churchlike building with a high chimney for a steeple. Within are the gas chambers and the crematorium. They have been swept clean. But in the open jaws of the iron furnaces there is still dust. It seeps out from the crannies, from the black depths as from an inexhaustible source of death.

At one time the Americans had wanted to tear the place down. But we fought for it. In the daytime we passed its silence and emptiness with averted faces. At nighttime we passed it like people hunted by ghosts. But in a strange, grim way, it housed the last vestiges of our pride. It was a memorial to what we once had been.

On a fine Sunday evening the villagers, dressed in their best —the men in black broadcloth, the women in their gay, full-skirted dresses—would saunter up the hillside and stand at the abandoned gates of our camp to gape at us. Behind the barbed wire we shrank from their prying malice as from a whiplash. We were like wild animals in a cage whose doors stood open.

"Well, why don't you run?" the Germans goaded us. "You're free, aren't you?"

Some of us did run. But we always came back. I did. I bummed my way to Munich, where there is a clearinghouse for lost people. But there was no trace of Martha, my wife, and my little girl, Anna. The only home I had left was Freilinger.

Ours was one of the "bad" camps. No one could do much for us. We could not help ourselves. We had no unity of race or faith or hope. Most of us had once been decent citizens of fair cities. But the cities had become graveyards or had repudiated us. Torn from our roots, we had become flotsam that had floated into this dismal backwater. But at least we recognized one another's existence. That, in a world that had forgotten us, made Camp Freilinger seem our home. I, too, turned in my tracks.

Or a group would set out for England or America, where probably reluctant relatives stood sponsor for them. They set out timidly, for they had lost the power to hope, as they had lost faith in themselves and in human kindness. We others, left behind, watched them go in hostile, almost scornful silence.

Others came to take their place. For there was always some corner of the world where men hunted one another. They came with nothing but their lives and a few rags. The camp committees allotted them space reluctantly. For we guarded what little we had of it with a jealous passion. We hungered to be alone as we had never hungered for bread. We ate together. There was no place where we could escape one another's unwilling watchfulness. Some of us, in crazy despair, marked off squares in our cubicles, the frontiers of which our companions crossed at their peril. That's how it was with us.

Maria and her mother set out for the camp at daybreak. The train had dropped them off the night before at a wayside station. But they had been too frightened and bewildered even to try to find the road. Maria's mother was very ill. Her heart was failing her. But the peasants in their oxcarts lumbered past them unpityingly. So the sun was well up by the time they stood humbly at the gate, tags round their necks like cattle.

Fräulein Minna, shaking dust out of her old broom, saw them. La Comtesse, sunning herself on her plush footstool, looked up and snorted indignantly, *"Encore de canaille!"*

Young David stood at his favorite place close to the barbed wire, whence he could look across the valley to the distant mountains. He had watched those two toil painfully up the dusty road. Now he and Maria looked at each other as young deer coming upon each other suddenly in some wild forest glade might check in surprise and wonder, and even fear. Maria was blue-eyed like himself. But hers were a paler, gentler blue, as though tears had washed out the deeper shades, and her hair was as fair as his was dark. She looked, as he did, both younger and older than she really was.

David turned and walked away quickly. He came to me in my office and shook me by the arm. For the first time I saw him try desperately to speak, and knew that something urgent had happened . . . at least to him.

The two newcomers, it seemed, had escaped from the Russian Zone, where they had been condemned to slave labor. Maria's father had had ideas of freedom, for which he had died, and Maria and her mother could not betray his faith. They had said brave things which it was not wise to say. So, by a miracle, they had escaped into the American Zone, where no one knew what to do with them except hustle them on from one place to another.

We didn't know what to do with them either. We had no space for them. I called a committee meeting. But all of us were sullen and determined. What little we had we kept. So there was nothing for it but the old crematorium. It was clean, anyway. An old Nazi sign still hung over the doorway:

IN THE INTERESTS OF CLEANLINESS, REMEMBER TO WASH YOUR HANDS BEFORE YOU LEAVE THIS PLACE.

It was one of our bitter jokes.

I found some spare bedding for the two women and helped Maria lay it out in a far corner. But the furnaces were there. Even I, who am tough and hardened, felt their oppressive shadow on me. Their mouths, half choked with dust, gaped like the mouths of starved and savage beasts.

At supper, Maria stood in line with the others, carrying her own and her mother's food in a pail, for her mother was too ill to stand. The narrow shed that we called ironically the "dining room" was thick with the smell of greasy soup, unwashed bodies and the pungent odor of resentment and despair. David stood behind Maria, waiting his turn at the steaming caldron. The light through the open door fell on her hair that was the color of pale sunlight and neatly drawn to the nape of her thin young neck. He stared down at it so that he forgot to move, and someone behind him pushed roughly. In the scuffle he fell against Maria, and her soup spilled out and over her poor dress. There was just so much soup for everyone, and Paul, who was cook for the day, grinned maliciously. She went on out of the doors with her own half-empty pail.

David followed her. He touched her shoulder and smiled, and filled her pail from his own. Words formed themselves in his throat. But there was still a barrier past which they could not break.

"*Danke*," she whispered. "*Danke*."

And they looked at each other fleetingly for the second time.

The windows in the crematorium were small and high-pitched, so that night came to them early. Maria sat on her thin, dirty mattress with her back to the wall and her arms locked tightly about her knees to stop their trembling. There was no sound but that of her mother's hard-drawn, uneven breath. As the light faded, the white notice board over the door stood out more starkly: IN THE INTERESTS OF CLEANLI-

NESS —— Then that, too, faded. The great furnaces merged with the shadows. Now that she could not see them, they became more terrible. They were alive. They were crawling closer on their black bellies. She could feel their hot, hungry breath on her face. Horror and evil crowded down on her. In spite of dank, chill air, the sweat ran down her body. She tried to say "Our Father ——" But her Father was in heaven. And she and her dying mother were in this dreadful place alone.

Fräulein Minna, lying on the concrete floor—for La Comtesse was having one of her restless nights—heard that first scream. It was like a knife wound in the night silence. The second scream tore the wound wide open. The whole camp heard it and sat up shivering with remembered terror. It was as though each one of us had screamed. But we stayed where we were. We cowered down in our individual safety. *It is not my turn . . . yet* was our one thought.

"Canaille," La Comtesse muttered.

But David got up, pulling on his ragged trousers.

"Keep still, imbecile!" Paul cursed at him.

The two Silenskis screeched, "Shut the door, can't you?" for the faint breath of fresh air infuriated them.

David raced out into the night and across the compound. He knew whence the screams had come. The door of the crematorium had been torn open and someone fell against him and clung to him. He held her close against his own hard-beating heart.

She gasped, "I saw them! I saw their wicked faces! They were coming for me, just as they came for my father! They were going to push me in . . . alive!"

He ran his hand over her hair as, long ago, he had run his hand over his mother's hair, wondering at its silky loveliness. And suddenly he heard his own voice, harsh and rusty with disuse, "Don't be afraid, little one. Don't be afraid."

He carried her back to her bed, feeling his way along the wall, and set her down. Her mother whispered, "Take care of her," and then grew quiet, as though overtaken at last by deep and merciful sleep. All that night David stayed with Maria, holding her in his arms until she relaxed and her breathing became as quiet as that of an exhausted child.

When morning filtered through the dirty windows, he looked across at the calm gray face of the older woman. He had seen death so often that it seemed as commonplace as life. It did not trouble him. But his aching arm drew the girl closer to him. When she woke, he hid her face against his naked breast, soothing her, murmuring his pity in his own tongue, which had come back to him.

We died easily at Camp Freilinger. Our people dropped life with a sort of contemptuous indifference, as they would have dropped a dirty rag. It was the custom to roll the bodies in a cloth and carry them in a pushcart to the potter's field outside the camp. There was always quarreling as to who should dig the graves. For we hated work as we hated our bitter idleness.

But for some reason or other, Maria's mother was a special case. Perhaps because she was a newcomer, we felt reluctant stirrings of hospitality. Or it might have been because David had gathered up some old planks and built a coffin and covered it with a flag which the UNRRA people had left behind them. It was an American flag, and looked almost gay in our drab midst. It seemed to challenge us. There was even competition as to who should be the pallbearers. The whole camp walked behind them, even La Comtesse, who wore some of her jewels for the occasion . . . very cheap stuff, Natasha remarked maliciously. Even the gold was false. But the diamonds of La Comtesse's necklace sparkled in the sunlight like real stones.

"One must do one's best to observe the decencies," she said soberly. "One must, at least, respect the dead."

She waddled haughtily at the head of the procession just behind Rabbi Wiseman, who was to say a few words by the graveside. Maria and her mother were not of his faith, but that was of no matter.

"We commend this, our sister, to Thy loving pity, O God," the rabbi intoned solemnly.

We didn't believe in God. Not any more. But we looked shyly at the pale, quiet girl and said, "Amen" and bowed our heads. David helped fill in the grave. He had gone into the fields outside the camp and gathered an armful of wild flowers, which he laid gently on the raw earth.

That night Maria slept alone in her corner of the cremato-rium. For some reason or other, she seemed to have lost all terror of the place. Perhaps she was just too brokenhearted. But on my last inspection round I recognized a sentinel shadow against the wall near to the door. I should have ordered it to quarters. Instead I said, "Good night, David," and his unac-customed voice answered, "Good night" with a tranquil firm-ness.

They love each other, Fräulein Minna whispered to herself. She even ventured to tell La Comtesse, "They love each other, those two."

And La Comtesse, very surprisingly, began to talk about love. She herself, it seemed, had been loved so much so often that her memories were confused. But there was a boy whom she recalled clearly—her first love. "He was good, that one—a fine fellow."

The Silberbaums and even the Silenskis, nagging one an-other behind their sailcloth partition, grew quiet, listening. But Minna had traveled far back into the past, so that La Comtesse's voice reached her only as a meaningless rumble. She had been young too. She had worn golden pigtails with blue bows on either shoulder. Someone had said, "How pretty you are, Minna!" Someone had kissed her.

We didn't welcome this stranger—this young love in the midst of our bleak loneliness. Old wounds ached. The dust of our dead stirred in their graves. We men watched resentfully how David straightened his broad shoulders, brushed his thick, unruly hair smooth and swung across the compound whistling like a young blackbird who has just learned to whistle. The women saw how Maria's sad face grew bright and sweet at sight of him, and snickered sardonically among themselves. At dusk the two of them stood together by the barbed wire, like children gazing into a show window full of miraculous toys and wonderful things to eat. The world beyond the dreaming valleys and stern mountains wasn't really hostile. It waited for them.

They came to me at last, hand in hand, grave but confident. My so-called office is no more than an old cell that I share with the rabbi, but those two didn't see its gray forlornness any more than they realized that they themselves were shabby and poor and homeless. Their forthright eyes looked through me into an enchanted country.

"We want to be married," David said in German—but now it was not an ugly language—"so that we can be together always."

I thought of Martha, my wife, and how much good marriage had done for us. I didn't try to swallow my bitterness.

"If you want to make fools of yourselves and more trouble for us," I said, "I can't stop you. Don't you know you're free?"

So there was to be a wedding at Camp Freilinger. Our first. It presented a problem that, hardened to problems as I was, I couldn't solve. When I tried to think it out I grew angry and cursed those two for stirring me up, throwing me from my stride, my acquired calm and indifference.

I called a committee meeting. We sat at the long trestle table in our so-called dining room. The air was rancid with the odor of rotten food and unwashed bodies. But the door stood open and a breath of spring crept in shyly. It carried the warm sweetness of the fields and of fruit trees laden with a late, rich flowering.

I looked down that double row of colorless, hard-set faces. I thought, cynically, that I knew their thoughts. There was nothing I could beg from them. Each one of them clung to his rags and tatters, his miserable, castoff remnant of identity, with the ferocious tenacity of a starved animal. I rubbed my hand over the stubble on my unshaven chin, and, for no reason at all, thought of Martha and of how sad and disappointed she would be if, by a miracle, she walked in through the open door. She had always been so absurdly proud of me. I'd have to pull myself together. Even if she was dead and would never know, I couldn't fail her. It was an irrational thought, having no connection whatever with what I had to say.

"It's a lot of damned foolishness," I growled.

"You can't stop people from being foolish," Paul said. "You can't stop life going on. The Germans tried it. But life's more bullheaded even than they are. You may not believe it"—he gave us a malicious grin—"but even we are still alive . . . after a fashion."

I scowled at him. "All right. Life goes on. Fools go on. But what are we going to do with them?" I found myself stammering. "They've got to be together somewhere."

"There's always the crematorium," someone said, and laughed.

Rabbi Wiseman spoke up sharply. Patches of indignant color showed on his high cheekbones. "It's impossible," he said, "indecent."

As though we cared for decency.

"My husband, the count," La Comtesse began unexpectedly, "was a romantic. All poets love Italy, even if they are good Frenchmen. I remember his saying to my father—I wasn't meant to hear him, but I had crept downstairs to listen to those two—'A woman should wake that first morning with the sun of Italy in her eyes.' So we went to Florence. The Arno flowed under our window. Sometimes at night I hear it ——"

I wondered for a moment if she had exchanged some of her precious jewels with the hostess of the village inn for a bottle of *Schnaps*. Her fat face had a vague, blurred look—almost as though the fat were melting. From underneath its concealing layers someone began to emerge whom we had never known.

"I could move out," Paul said. "Our little Maria can take my place and I can take hers." He snickered. "I'm not afraid of ghosts."

We looked away from him, away from one another. Our averted eyes saw the squalid cubicle and the dirty dividing curtain that would not shield those two. We could see them cowering together, their love naked to that prying greedy silence. The women stared down at their clenched hands, and their knuckles were white under the strain. Their gray faces were flushed faintly with shame and anger.

Then it was Fräulein Minna's turn. She, who had always been so timid and so quiet, spoke with a resolution that made me understand how once she had been able to exchange freedom for a proud, indignant gesture.

"We've lost everything," she said, "our homes, our people, ourselves, our faith and hope and kindness—all the things that made us what we really were. There's nothing left of us that matters. But David and Maria will go away one day. They're young. The world has forgotten us, but it'll want them. Perhaps they'll go to England or America, where they will live as we were meant to live. They must take with them what we once had; we must see to it that they do, as though they were ourselves, our children." She looked from one to another of us, pleading for us to understand that she was struggling with a thought too big for her. "So, after all, we shall go on."

La Comtesse must have been busy with some secret thought of her own. She clapped her plump, soiled-looking hands. "Of course," she said, "we must give them a wonderful wedding present."

The rabbi married them, not according to his own ritual, but according to a very simple faith. "In the name of the one God I pronounce these two man and wife," he said. He blessed them and wrote their names and the date in the old Hebrew Testament that he had carried against his heart through the bitter years of persecution.

It was a calm, lovely summer's day. The camp cook had made some rough sandwiches for the youngsters, and they set out together for the valley. A day alone. That was to be their honeymoon. A group of villagers who had watched the ceremony from the gates laughed at the shabby pair who walked bravely past them, hand in hand.

"*Canaille!*" La Comtesse shouted furiously.

Fortunately, the Germans didn't understand. But they jeered at the ugly, angry old woman, and someone threw a stone at her.

I knew something of that day, because afterward they told me. It was strange that at first they were not lovers, but just lost children who had found their way home to childhood. They ran together down the meadows to the brook that threads itself through the narrow valley. They took off their poor broken shoes and paddled in the sparkling, dancing water and splashed each other. With his hands, David tried to catch a trout drowsing among the reeds and Maria laughed at him. But when, eventually, he did catch a small, unwary fish, she was respectful, as a wife should be. They threw the fish back and with smiling eyes watched it scud thankfully out of sight. For that day they did not want anything to die because of them.

At midday they came to rest under a willow tree and ate their sandwiches. Now they did not talk much and their laughter was stilled. They were not children any more. In those short hours they had grown to maturity, and the shadow of their sad love was over them. David laid his head in Maria's lap and looked up at the sky, fretted by the branches of the tree, and then into the blue of Maria's eyes bent down on him with anxious tenderness. He took her hand and kissed it gently. The coming night and the ugliness that waited for them had begun to gnaw at their poor happiness.

"Are you afraid, Maria?"

"A little."

"Of me?"

"Oh, no, not of you . . . ever." She began to cry softly, helplessly. "If we could only run away . . . hide somewhere where no one would ever find us."

But there was no place where they could hide. The boy sat up and drew her into his arms and comforted her as he had done that first night. It was strange that those two who had known little of life but harshness and cruelty should have known so well, so tenderly how to protect their love, even from themselves.

It was quiet and dark at the camp gates. The usual evening stragglers had disappeared. Only in the window of Schlafsaal B-24, a light showed like a friendly eye watching out for them. David held Maria's hand.

"Perhaps we shall have to wait a long time," he said gently. "But one day we shall be alone."

"We can wait," she answered. "We love each other."

The door opened smoothly under his reluctant pressure. They couldn't believe at first. The dirty dividing curtains had gone. It was a real whole room, swept and garnished. Two beds, spread with clean sheets, stood primly side by side. There was an old rug on the scrubbed floors, flowers in a vase on the table under the curtained window. Two chairs. A rocker. A toothless broom. A dresser set out with all the bits and pieces we had got together—chipped cups and saucers, plates, a frying pan, a battered saucepan—our last possessions that we had clung to so bitterly. Where Paul had scrawled his hating, hateful pictures was written WELCOME HOME, and the painter had drawn a lovely landscape in gay colored chalks and signed it boldly, proudly with his real name. And by the rusty pot stove stood La Comtesse's red plush footstool.

David closed the door gently and gathered his young wife to his heart.

La Comtesse and Fräulein Minna, the Silberbaums, the two sleek rats, Stanislas and Natasha, and Paul slept in their corners of the crematorium. Now they had nothing left . . . not even the rags of their privacy. But in this dark and dreadful place hope set down its roots and the black engines of death gave up their ghosts.

"If your feet are cold, Comtesse," Fräulein Minna whispered, "I could warm them for you."

"Sleep, little Minna," La Comtesse told her, smiling to herself. "And you must call me 'Mitzi.' That was what my friends called me when I was young and beautiful."

ALEXANDER BOTTS
VS. THE INCOME TAX

By WILLIAM HAZLETT UPSON

EARTHWORM TRACTOR COMPANY
EARTHWORM CITY, ILLINOIS
INTERDEPARTMENTAL COMMUNICATION

To: GILBERT HENDERSON, *President*
         EARTHWORM TRACTOR COMPANY
         EARTHWORM CITY, ILLINOIS

From: ALEXANDER BOTTS,
         Earthworm Sales Manager
         SCHROEDER HOTEL
         MILWAUKEE, WISCONSIN

Date: Tuesday evening, September 9, 1947

I NEED fifty thousand dollars right away. The circumstances are as follows: This afternoon I happened to be in Milwaukee with a few hours to spare. I called on my old friend, Mr. Stephen Phillips, of the Phillips Precision Laboratories. As you probably know, Mr. Phillips is the engineering genius who does the very delicate and highly important final processing on the injection-valve assemblies for our Diesel engines.

"I just dropped in to find out how you're getting along," I said. "At the factory I have heard disturbing reports. They say you are behind in your shipments. You're not slipping, are you?"

"Worse than that. I'm sunk." He pointed to his desk. It was covered with papers. The papers were covered with figures. Everything in general seemed covered with confusion—especially Mr. Phillips. His elderly intellectual face had a wild look. "It's the income tax," he said.

"This is September," I remarked soothingly. "You don't have to worry about your income tax until March."

"That's what you think," he said, "but wait till I tell you about it."

"I'm listening."

"A couple of weeks ago a man came in from the office of the Collector of Internal Revenue or some such thing. Now, I have nothing against this man personally. Doubtless he is one of God's creatures. Probably he means well. But what he had to say does not make sense."

"What did he say?"

Mr. Phillips shuffled the papers around and finally pulled out one on which he had written some notes. "According to the collector's office, I am always making mistakes. On my 1944 Federal-income-tax return they say I figured the depreciation on my laboratory fixtures here at two per cent per annum."

"Is that wrong?" I asked.

"Apparently so, because on my 1943 return, which seems to be dated March 15, 1944, I figured the depreciation at three per cent. They want me to explain this discrepancy. But how can I explain what I did so long ago that I can't remember why I did it?"

"You could invent an explanation."

"And three years from now I would have to explain that. They also claim that my method of computing the depreciation on the laboratory instruments does not conform to the provisions of Section One Hundred and Fourteen of the Internal Revenue Code and Bulletin F of the Bureau of Internal Revenue. All right, here is Bulletin F—ninety-three pages of words that don't mean anything."

"They must mean something," I said.

"Well, on the first page they try to explain what they are talking about, as follows: 'Information and statistical data relating to the determination of deductions for depreciation and obsolescence, from which tax payers and their counsel may obtain the best available indication of bureau practice and the trend and tendency of official opinion in the administration of pertinent provisions of the Internal Revenue Code and corresponding or similar provisions of prior Revenue Acts.' I suppose you understand all that, Mr. Botts?"

"Well ——" I began.

"Neither do I," said Mr. Phillips. "And that is not all. I employ six men here in the laboratory. And the Internal Revenue man claims"—he picked up another piece of paper—

"that in the second quarter of nineteen-forty-six I sent in twenty cents less than the pay-roll deductions for the same period for the withholding tax on these six employees. Besides which, there was another man that came in last week and began talking about the state income tax."

"You mean the state of Wisconsin?"

"Yes." Mr. Phillips picked up another piece of paper. "It seems that on the nineteen-forty-six Wisconsin return I was all wrong in figuring the surtax, which, as defined here, should be 'equal to the normal tax after credit for exemptions, less thirty-seven dollars and fifty cents, divided by six.'"

"How is that again?"

Mr. Phillips read it over, "'The surtax should be equal to the normal tax after credit for exemptions, less thirty-seven dollars and fifty cents, divided by six.' And here is another. The Federal man says one of my employees got divorced last year, and I was supposed to deduct more money from his pay on the withholding tax, but I didn't do it because he never told me he was divorced, and I never asked him, and why should I be supposed to pry into his private affairs, anyway?"

"Wait a minute," I interrupted.

Mr. Phillips continued, "And here is still another. Besides withholding money for the withholding tax, I am supposed to withhold additional money for another tax which is not the withholding tax. This other tax is the Social Security tax, and they claim that I have made several mistakes in several different years in adding up the amounts that I should have withheld. I tell you, Mr. Botts, it's too much figuring for anybody but an expert."

"You're an engineer, Mr. Phillips. You ought to be good at mathematics."

"I am," said Mr. Phillips. "I have no trouble at all with the logical structural mathematics of engineering. Nobody loves more than I do the beauties of geometry and calculus. But this tax business is different—all this donkey work adding and subtracting and trying to interpret idiotic statements like 'the surtax equals the normal tax after credit for exemptions, less thirty-seven dollars and fifty cents, divided by six.'"

"Mr. Phillips," I said, "I am beginning to apprehend the basis of your difficulties. Quite obviously you have the type of engineering mind which is characterized by what psychologists would call a high degree of structural visualization. You are, therefore, an expert in geometry and all related forms of spatial mathematics. But your accounting aptitude—your ability to handle figures rapidly and accurately—is probably as low as my own. In this I sympathize with you.

"I, too, am hopelessly inaccurate with figures. It may interest you to know that the Earthworm Auditing Department has pronounced my expense accounts the most hopeless mess they have ever encountered."

"You mean you have trouble with figures too?" asked Mr. Phillips.

"No," I said, "because I refuse to let them bother me. I hold myself above such foolishness. Anybody who can add and subtract with speed and precision I consider as belonging to a lower order of animal life. I refuse to waste my high-powered mind on what you so aptly term mere donkey work. I, therefore, leave the figuring to the meticulous and dried-up little clerks and bookkeepers who take pleasure in that sort of stuff. And I would advise you to do the same. Hire a smart girl. Let her handle the paper work."

"Oh, no," said Mr. Phillips, "I couldn't do that. I am the head of this business. If there is any mistake in this stuff I am the one that would go to jail."

"What about that schoolteacher daughter of yours? Couldn't you trust her with your accounts?"

"I wouldn't insult Martha by asking her to waste her time on this nonsense. Besides, she has her teaching job."

"Then you'll have to get somebody else. You must learn to delegate authority."

"Absolutely not. My laboratory is known all over the country for its accuracy. I have built up this reputation by attending to everything myself."

"You have six men working for you, haven't you?"

"Yes, but after they have finished, I check everything personally. As long as I am running this business, nothing will go out of here—whether it is tractor parts or tax returns—without my personal approval."

This statement left me a bit nonplused. Being a keen judge of men, I recognized that Mr. Phillips is one of those extremely subjective or introverted geniuses who are temperamentally unable to trust anybody else to handle anything for which they feel responsible. Such people, even though they may be highly intelligent and talented, are usually so stubborn that it is almost impossible to influence them. However, I had to say something.

"Other people have tax problems," I began.

"I don't care about other people. I am worried about myself. This tax business is getting to be more than I can stand. I spend half my time figuring taxes and earning the money to pay them."

"Oh, come now, Mr. Phillips," I said; "you are exaggerating."

"I am not. In the first place, the United States Government grabs about twenty-five per cent of my profits for my personal income tax. That means I work three months out of every year for the Government."

"Which leaves you nine months to work for yourself, doesn't it?"

"It does not," said Mr. Phillips bitterly. "The Wisconsin state income tax takes three or four per cent. That is another week and a half or two weeks. The local real-estate taxes that are hidden in my rent on this laboratory take another couple of weeks."

"Which leaves you eight months," I said.

"Certainly not," he said. "A lot of what most people call the high cost of living is really hidden taxes. I have been looking it up." Again he referred to some notes. "I find I am paying taxes every time I light a match, smoke a cigarette, take a drink, play a game of cards, go to a movie, to a show or to a ball game, every time I take a trip on a train, plane or bus, send a telegram or talk over the telephone."

"Are there really taxes on all those things?" I asked.

"Sure, and the Federal Government also collects taxes from me if I buy an automobile or if I buy automobile parts, gasoline, tires, a radio ——"

"The way you tell it," I interrupted, "it sounds incredible."

"It is incredible. And in addition to all the time I put in earning the money to pay taxes, I have to put in a whole lot more time working for the Government as a bookkeeper and a tax collector."

"You mean you have a job with the Bureau of Internal Revenue?"

"Certainly. The Government hands me the job—at a salary of nothing a week I am forced to act as tax collector for my six employees. And it is a lot of work."

"How do you mean?"

"As I was trying to tell you before, the Government makes me responsible for seeing that they fill out statements regarding their dependents. Then I have to figure the amount of their tax and collect it out of their wages. The final result of the whole thing is that in each year I work just about six months for the Government and six months for myself. No wonder folks are turning communist."

"You aren't thinking of joining the Communist Party yourself, are you?"

"That would be even worse than what we've got," he said. "But what we've got is so bad that I have just about reached the end of my endurance. The Government makes it so hard for me to stay in business that I have decided to quit."

"You can't quit," I said; "you're too important. Don't you realize that the expert work you do here contributes thousands of tons to the annual food supply of the world?"

"If my job is so important, why doesn't the Government let me work at it? If they would let me spend even three quarters of my time at the work I can do best, I could carry on the research that is necessary to keep this business progressing the way it should. As it is, it is no longer possible for me to do this job right. So I have decided not to do it at all."

"But there must be some way to handle this," I said. "Couldn't you turn over the business management of your laboratory to some big company like Earthworm?"

"That's exactly what I have decided to do."

"You mean you want to sell your business to us and let us hire you, so you can carry on as an employee?"

"Oh, no, Mr. Botts. I am sixty years old—too old to learn new tricks. I have been my own boss for forty years. It's too late for me to start taking orders from somebody else. I am going to sell the business to the Behemoth Tractor Company and retire."

At these words I almost fell out of the chair on which I

had been sitting. "What? You are going to sell out to our competitors, the Behemoth Company? How did you ever get mixed up with those crooks?"

"A very polite representative of the Behemoth Company called on me last week," said Mr. Phillips. "He said he had heard I planned to retire. He offered fifty thousand dollars for my business."

"The dirty skunk! What's his idea?"

"He thinks that if he buys my tools and apparatus, and hires my six skilled workmen, he can get as fine a finish on the Behemoth injection valves as you have been getting on Earthworm injection valves."

"What did you tell him?"

"I said I would think it over. He said he would be back some day this week. When he comes, I will tell him I have decided to accept his offer."

"That would be a major disaster," I said. "Besides, what would you do with the fifty thousand dollars?"

"I have a friend in Chicago who is a broker. He says he can buy me some municipal bonds, which are as nearly tax-free as anything you can get in this degenerate age. They would pay me about a thousand dollars a year. I can live on that, plus a little income I get from other sources. As soon as I finish this donkey work on my back taxes, I'll be free!"

"If the Earthworm Company offered you fifty thousand dollars and agreed to carry on the business and keep your six workmen on the pay roll, would you accept?"

"Yes."

"Sold!" I said.

I jerked out my checkbook—which happened to be on my personal account at the Earthworm City National Bank—and rapidly wrote him a check for fifty thousand. I told him we would take possession of his laboratory within a few days. And before he could change his mind I hurried back here to the hotel.

Thus, through my decisive action, the Behemoth threat has been removed. And it may not even be necessary for us to take over the Phillips Laboratory. I am still hoping I can figure some way to adjust Mr. Phillips' tax difficulties so he will continue his essential work.

In the meantime, Henderson, there is no need for you to worry and no need for you to interfere. All I need from the Earthworm Company is fifty thousand dollars. It is absolutely necessary that you deposit this sum in my account. Otherwise, when the check gets back to the bank, my account will be overdrawn exactly $49,943.29.

Most sincerely,
ALEXANDER BOTTS.

TELEGRAM
EARTHWORM CITY, ILLINOIS,
WEDNESDAY, SEPTEMBER 10, 1947.

ALEXANDER BOTTS, SALES MANAGER,
EARTHWORM TRACTOR COMPANY,
SCHROEDER HOTEL, MILWAUKEE, WIS.

I CANNOT AUTHORIZE PURCHASE OF PHILLIPS LABORATORY UNLESS THE DEAL IS APPROVED BY OUR PRODUCTION DEPARTMENT, A REPRESENTATIVE OF WHICH WILL GO TO MILWAUKEE NEXT WEEK TO INVESTIGATE THE SITUATION. IN THE MEANTIME PLEASE HOLD IN ABEYANCE THE WHOLE PROJECT, AND ASK MR. PHILLIPS NOT TO PRESENT CHECK FOR PAYMENT UNTIL SUCH TIME AS THE TRANSACTION MAY BE FINALIZED.

GILBERT HENDERSON.

EARTHWORM TRACTOR COMPANY
EARTHWORM CITY, ILLINOIS
Interdepartmental Communication

To: GILBERT HENDERSON
         EARTHWORM CITY, ILLINOIS

From: ALEXANDER BOTTS
         MILWAUKEE, WISCONSIN

Date: Wednesday evening, September 10, 1947

I have just returned to the hotel after a very busy day. I find your astonishing telegram awaiting me. How can I "hold in abeyance" a deal which was closed yesterday? How can I ask Mr. Phillips not to present that check when he has left town and taken the check with him?

Please put that fifty thousand in my account at once. Furthermore, I want you to put in an additional ten thousand which I am turning over as a gift from the Earthworm Tractor Company to a girls' school here in Milwaukee. In order that you may realize how important it is for you to get the grand total of sixty thousand into my account before these checks get back to Earthworm City I will give you a full account of the remarkable progress I have been making today.

Early this morning I decided to consult Miss Martha Phillips, the intelligent and competent daughter of Mr. Stephen Phillips. I found her in the western suburbs of the city in a plain brick building which houses the Laura E. Perkins Female Seminary.

I told her very frankly of my talk with her father. I explained how I had been forced to buy his business to save it from the wolves of the Behemoth Tractor Company. And I then appealed to her sense of filial devotion.

"Can't you do something," I pleaded, "to save your father from this strange tax phobia?"

"I have asked him to let me handle his accounts," she said, "but he won't do it. He says it would interfere with my work here—which he thinks is important."

"Is it?"

"Well . . . no."

"Tell me about it."

As she started her story, it sounded not only unimportant but dull. As she went on, however, I realized that the situation was fraught with sensational and staggering potentialities.

"Last June," she said, "when I graduated from college, I signed a contract as principal of this institution. It sounded like an important position. But now I find the trustees have mismanaged the school, and the work they have been trying to do seems to be getting out of date."

"What sort of work?"

"The original endowment, set up years ago by an old lady called Laura E. Perkins, provides free instruction for the poor in useful arts and trades. But the endowment has largely disappeared through poor investments. The quality of teaching has gone down. The enrollment has declined. And this fall there is not a single application for admission."

"What are you going to do?"

"The trustees and I have been considering various plans. The charter is broad. We could take in boys as well as girls. We could teach almost anything. But the trustees are getting so tired and disgusted with the enterprise that they are about ready to liquidate the whole thing."

"Are there any assets? Is there any income?"

"The school owns this building. In recent years about the only income has been money received from the sale of garments produced in the sewing classes."

"And a good share of this income goes to pay taxes?"

"Oh, no. Schools are tax exempt."

"No income taxes? No real-estate taxes?"

"Certainly not. But that doesn't help any, because there isn't enough income in the first place."

"This is getting fantastic," I said. "You have complete freedom from taxes. But it does you no good because you have no income. Your father has a nice income. But it does him no good because he is sunk by taxes. If we could only combine ——"

Suddenly I leaped from my chair. "Silence!" I shouted. "I am going into conference with myself." I started pacing the floor in a state of intense mental concentration. Inside my brain, various fragments of thought which had never before been associated began coming together in small groups. These, in turn, began to form larger groups. Finally all the separate elements united into a single idea with a snap that I could almost feel against the inside of my skull.

"Martha," I said, "you can now relax. All your difficulties are over. All your father's difficulties are over."

"I don't understand."

"I have evolved a perfect plan of action. Like all perfect plans, it is childishly simple. I am going to amalgamate the Phillips Precision Laboratories with the Laura E. Perkins Female Seminary. I am going to move all the machinery over here . . . this afternoon, if possible. In the meantime, you are going to call a meeting of your board of trustees."

"What for?"

"So they can elect a new board and resign."

"Suppose they refuse?"

"You told me they are tired and disgusted. You said they

want to liquidate this whole thing. Incidentally, how many trustees does your charter require?"

"Not less than three. Not more than seven."

"Okay. Write this down: The new trustees will be yourself and I and a man called Gilbert Henderson."

"Who is he?"

"Just a dummy to fill out the number. You and I will run the place."

"But what are we going to do?"

"We're going to continue as a trade school . . . with one small difference. Instead of teaching dressmaking and supporting the school by selling dresses, we're going to teach the final processing of injection valves, and support the school on the proceeds of that."

"But, Mr. Botts, who would do the teaching?"

"You would, Martha."

"And who would be the students?"

"Those six skilled workmen from your father's laboratory."

"How could I teach them anything about processing injection valves?"

"What difference would that make?"

"But it wouldn't be a school unless people were learning something."

"Don't be absurd, Martha. I have a nephew who spent four years at the most expensive preparatory school in Massachusetts and learned absolutely nothing."

"But if these six men didn't learn anything, what would be the idea of having them here?"

"They would process the valves. The Earthworm Company would pay for them. The school would receive the money and pay the workmen. They would get the same pay as before, but it would be in the form of scholarships, instead of taxable wages."

"But it would still be a business, not a school."

"Martha," I said, "for a college graduate you are unusually obtuse. Have you never heard of semantics? Don't you know that in dealing with the law, the important thing is not what you do, but what you call it?"

"Just the same, I don't see how you can call it a school if it's really a business."

"It's done all the time, Martha. Agricultural colleges run farms and dairies; they produce and sell farm products, milk, cream, butter and cheese. Much of the work is done by students who are working on scholarships. Many colleges make fabulous profits on amusement enterprises known as football games. The performers are paid through scholarships. But it is all done in the name of education."

"You really think we could?"

"I know it. And everybody will benefit. A combined school and laboratory will be free from all income and real-estate taxes. You, Martha, will have a tax-free teaching fellowship. The six workmen will have tax-free scholarships. The Earthworm Company will have a sure supply of injection valves. And, after we get going, we will try to talk your father into emerging from his retirement and taking a position with us.

Martha began to warm up. "It sounds good," she said, "but how are we going to pay our running expenses until the money starts coming in from the Earthworm Company?"

"That's easy. The Earthworm Company will be delighted to make a small donation to the school."

In an offhand way I wrote and passed over a check for ten thousand dollars. As I had hoped and expected, this gesture completely won the young lady's co-operation. She promised to call the board of trustees together at once and do everything she could to put through my magnificent project.

I then rushed over to the laboratory, where I learned that Mr. Phillips had left for Chicago. The six workmen said they would be willing to continue work at the new location in the Perkins School. They looked a bit puzzled when I explained their new status as students. However, they had no objections, provided the pay and the working conditions remained the same. With their help, I was able to contact a trucking company and move the apparatus and machinery to the school.

By the time this job was completed it was five P.M. Martha Phillips reported to me that the school trustees had carried out all my requests. Just as we had expected, they were delighted to desert what they thought was a sinking ship and to see the responsibility turned over to what they regarded as a new bunch of suckers.

I told the six workmen we would start operations first thing tomorrow morning, and I came back to the hotel with the proud consciousness that I had put in as fruitful and productive a day as any in my career.

The only flaw in an otherwise perfect picture is your failure, Henderson, to provide the fifty thousand dollars which I requested yesterday. However, now that I have explained all the advantages of what I am doing, I am sure that you will come through with the money at once—and this time be sure to make it sixty thousand dollars. Remember, I am counting on you.

Yours,
—ALEXANDER BOTTS.

TELEGRAM
THURSDAY, SEPTEMBER 11, 1947.

ALEXANDER BOTTS,
SCHROEDER HOTEL,
MILWAUKEE, WISCONSIN.

CANCEL DEAL WITH PHILLIPS AND ALSO WITH SCHOOL. I AM NOT DEPOSITING THE REQUESTED FUNDS IN YOUR ACCOUNT. TO DO SO WOULD BE AIDING AND ABETTING A TAX-EVASION SCHEME WHICH, IF PERSISTED IN, MIGHT EVENTUALLY RESULT IN YOUR LANDING IN JAIL.

GILBERT HENDERSON.

EARTHWORM TRACTOR COMPANY
EARTHWORM CITY, ILLINOIS
Interdepartmental Communication

To: GILBERT HENDERSON
EARTHWORM CITY, ILLINOIS

From: ALEXANDER BOTTS
MILWAUKEE, WISCONSIN

Date: Thursday evening,
September 11, 1947

I am sorry to tell you that your attempt to keep me out of jail by withholding the sixty thousand dollars which I requested has had the actual result of landing me in jail much quicker than I had suspected would be possible. You may also be interested to know that your delay has permitted the situation to develop to a point where it is now too late for the money to do any good—as you will realize when I give an account of the day's events.

This morning, being wearied by yesterday's activities, I slept until almost noon, and was finally awakened when my hotel room was rudely invaded by a bunch of cops and a lawyer with a lot of legal papers. In answer to my violent protests, the lawyer—a most obnoxious person—explained that I was under arrest. I was accused of a long list of crimes and misdemeanors, including fraud, larceny and issuing a worthless check. At first I could not understand why anyone should bring any such obviously false charges against me. But the lawyer's remarks soon revealed the false reasoning behind his actions.

Apparently Mr. Phillips had visited his broker friend in Chicago yesterday afternoon, handed him my check and asked him to convert it into bonds. The overcautious broker had telephoned the Earthworm City National Bank. When he learned that my fifty-thousand-dollar check was drawn against an account with a balance of $56.71, he promptly returned the check to Mr. Phillips with the totally unwarranted statement that I was obviously a crook.

Poor old Mr. Phillips, somewhat puzzled, returned to Milwaukee last night. This morning he visited his laboratory. The machinery was gone. There was no one around who could tell him where it had been taken. Thoroughly bewildered, he sought out a lawyer. And in his inexperience he made an unfortunate mistake. Instead of a reputable attorney who would have attempted to smooth things down, he happened upon one of the ambulance-chasing types who started stirring up as much trouble as possible with the obvious purpose of increasing his fee. His first act, as I have explained, was to get a warrant and have me arrested. When I explained that nobody could blame me because the Earthworm Company had failed to cover my check, he replied with an attempted wisecrack, "Tell that to the judge." He also told me that I might get off a little easier if I would tell him where I had hidden the machinery. He said that Mr. Phillips wanted to sell it to the Behemoth company. To this, I replied with my usual sparkling wit, "Oh, yeah?"

By this time I was dressed and the cops marched me off to

the hoosegow. I then called the Earthworm Tractor Company's legal representative here in Milwaukee. I asked him to come down in a hurry and bail me out. Before he had time to arrive, however, Mr. Stephen Phillips came in to see me. He wanted to give me his version of what had been going on.

He said, "It didn't take me long to find out where you took the machinery. I called up one of my workmen. His wife answered the telephone. She told me that he was at my daughter's school, and that the machinery was there too. So the Behemoth man was kind enough to take me over there in his big truck."

"Why a big truck?" I asked.

"To move the machinery."

"Stop!" I cried. "I can't stand it!"

"You mean you don't want me to tell you what happened?"

"No."

"But you really ought to hear about it, Mr. Botts. When I reached the school, my daughter told me all about the incredible scheme that you two had cooked up. It gave me a good deal of a shock."

"Don't blame her," I said; "the idea was mine."

"But she has been putting it into effect. And she tells me she has carried your strange ideas even further."

"How?" I demanded suspiciously.

"Martha is very clever at bookkeeping," said Mr. Phillips. "She has figured that your new setup will save so much on taxes that she can reduce prices to the Earthworm Tractor Company, raise everybody's pay and still have a lot more than she had expected for research and development. It's wonderful."

"I thought you said all this was a shock to you?"

"It is. What shocks me is the realization that I have been dragging along through years of tax misery, and I never thought of this glorious remedy myself. However, I am accepting a teaching fellowship which will pay me a little more than my previous profits and will permit me to run the business the way I want to. Of course—on account of indirect taxes—I'll still be working about three months out of each year for the Government. But I can now put in three quarters of my time on the work that I do best."

"What about the Behemoth man?" I asked. "What about that check I gave you? What about that check I gave your daughter?"

"Take it easy," said Mr. Phillips. "I have sent the Behemoth man home. And I have decided I would not want to use your check—even if it were good—to buy any of these supposedly tax-free bonds. Now that you have saved my business, I don't need any investments. To show my gratitude, I have torn up the check you gave me. And Martha has torn up the one you gave her."

"Thank you," I said. "But don't forget I am still in jail."

"I'm sorry!" exclaimed Mr. Phillips. "I will tell my lawyer to drop all charges and get you out as quick as possible."

Before long I was free again. And I am happy to report that I am preparing to leave Milwaukee in a warm glow of satisfaction induced by my success in rescuing Mr. Phillips from the slavery of the tax collector, and setting him up in a position where he can work happily and successfully for the benefit of himself, his daughter, his employees and the Earthworm Tractor Company.

And even this is not all. I am hurrying back to Earthworm City, where I want you to call a special meeting of our board of directors to transform the entire Earthworm Tractor Company into a tax-free educational institution. It will be necessary to convert the common stock into bonds which will pay a sliding scale of interest rather than dividends. The stockholders and the present directors will become trustees. Executives like you and me will be given tax-free teaching fellowships. Other employees will be paid through tax-free scholarships. The entire institution will be free from corporation income taxes. The plant will be free from local real-estate taxes. And all of us— like Mr. Phillips—will be free to put in at least three quarters of our time on the work that we do the best—the production and distribution of the superior tractors which are so desperately needed to increase the food supply of a hungry world.

Yours with three rahs and a sis-boom-bah for the new Earthworm Institute of Technology.

ALEXANDER BOTTS,
Present Sales Manager, Future Fellow in the Department of Sales Psychology.

SCANDALOUS CONDUCT

By ROBERT CARSON

THAT summer the worst was over. The gross sales of Flannery Brothers Department Stores—downtown Los Angeles, new branches in Beverly Hills and Pasadena—were up forty-seven per cent, and the net, which made even the brothers happy, they kept to themselves. There was every indication that nothing could stop the rising graph on T. J. Flannery's wall. Congratulations were in order to the young president, Ashley House, but no one could bring himself to the point of uttering them. Ashley happened to be the plague of retail merchandising.

Finally T. J. Flannery got up his nerve, hired a huge supper room in a Hollywood hotel, engaged two orchestras, invited the complete staffs of all the stores and prominent figures from the Chamber of Commerce, and put on his black tie. B. R. Flannery, the brother who operated from the New York end, flew in for the party. The younger Flannerys assembled. Before coming west to grow up with the country, ancestors of the family had long lived in the north of Ireland, where they had worn orange rosettes on St. Patrick's Day and had their hands out against all men. A close-knit clan, they were easily distinguishable by their red hair, hot blue eyes and emotional instability. It was said that they never failed a friend or missed pasting an enemy, and that no determined character worked for them very long.

The celebration of Ashley House's third anniversary with the stores went off quite well. There were cocktails, four kinds of wine, champagne, indestructible squab chickens, peach Melba, and a brandy the hotel had been trying to get rid of for years. The mayor and others spoke.

Then T. J. rose. "Ladies and gentlemen and fellow workers," he said. "You've heard much in praise of Mr. House. I want to give you the straight dope. Four years ago our store seemed to be getting old-fashioned and on the downgrade. We hired Ashley House on a three-year contract, hoping he could straighten us out. Well, you know what's happened. He has persuaded us to spend a great deal on branches and in renovating our main store. A lot of times we haven't agreed with him, and there have been arguments. But I'll have to admit Ashley has been right. Ashley is always right." T. J. seemed to choke on his next words. "We all ought to be very grateful to Ashley, folks."

The applause was light.

B. R. stood up. "I have little to add to my brother's words," he said, "except to agree with them. Negotiations are now in progress on a new contract for Ashley." B. R. appeared to fight off a faint attack of nausea. "We hope to have our president with us for many years more."

The applause was lighter still. T. J. asked Ashley if he didn't want to say a few words to the loyal and efficient employees who had done so much to carry out his program. Ashley confronted the loyal, efficient and hostile people. He was a tall, pale, close-cropped young man in an elderly, skimpy English dinner jacket and saw-tooth collar. His cold gray eyes raked the assemblage. He had a harsh, incisive voice, and he obviously didn't care whether they liked him or not.

"Business is business," Ashley stated, "and friendship is friendship. I have never believed in mixing the two except in special circumstances, and I feel no urge to begin tonight. The advance of Flannery Brothers Department Stores results solely from the application of modern merchandising methods and new efficiency in sales and services. I see no reason for you or anyone else to be grateful for my efforts and success—I have been well paid for both. On the other hand, I cannot think I owe you any thanks for performing your duties well— that is what you are paid for. Mr. B. R. Flannery has kindly said that a new contract is being prepared for me, but I don't want too great a confidence placed in that. As you probably know, not a single high executive has ever lasted more than three years with this organization. Besides that, the new terms I am going to demand will undoubtedly cause both of the Flannery brothers to reach for more of this horrible brandy on the table. Perhaps I won't be with you to celebrate another anniversary. Thank you."

Great applause greeted his last words. Grim persons actually broke into smiles and gazed at the crimson-faced Flannery brothers. The orchestra broke into For He's a Jolly Good Fellow, and a few outsiders and politicians sang it to Ashley. There was not a wet eye in the house.

"Ashley," T. J. said, and leaned over to the president. "Ashley, exactly what are your terms?"

"I have a lawyer," Ashley said. "He'll call on your lawyer, T. J., and discuss them."

T. J. leaned back to B. R. and reported. B. R. cussed softly.

Pretty soon the more elderly salespeople went home to get off their feet. The younger set stayed on and danced. Though he was bored and deep in an idea for building a super service station on each one of Flannery parking lots, thus getting the customers going and coming, Ashley felt he could not leave the party given in his honor. Wandering around the edges of the floor, he encountered Mrs. Martin. She was the tall, slim, gray-haired and diplomatic head of the personnel department, and his only confidant.

"I see you didn't bring a girl tonight," Mrs. Martin remarked.

"No," Ashley said. "I'd have had to talk to her, and I happen to be deep in service stations."

"Sometimes," Mrs. Martin said, "I think maybe you ought to go in for service, Ashley. They could put you up on the hoist and grease your manner. It's uncompromising."

"If I'm right, I'm right. I ask no favors."

"Would you like a girl to dance with?"

"Thank you, no."

"You should dance with some of the employees. Female, that is. It'd look nice."

"I don't want to dance with any of the employees," Ashley said, "female or male. The pay increases and the bonuses we have paid are much more impressive than any silly attentions I could pay to the help."

"How right you are, Ashley," Mrs. Martin said. "Girls want pay increases, not attentions. Ignore them completely. What do you care if you're alone in the world?"

Frowning slightly, Ashley moved on. Presently he was approached by a small girl in a strapless green gown, who greeted him cordially. She had hot blue eyes and red hair and a lovely Hibernian countenance, and he didn't recall having previously seen her. Certainly he would have remembered if he had, since her gown was not only strapless but nearly dressless, and left a great deal to base recognition upon.

"You're the president, aren't you?" she said. "Mr. Ashley. The guy who made the speech."

"Mr. House," Ashley said. "Yes. Mr. Ashley House. . . . I'm sorry, but I don't dance."

"Who asked you, Icehouse?"

"Ah . . . no one." Ashley twitched. " 'Icehouse'?"

"That's what they call you at the store. I just remembered."

"Are you an employee?"

"Would I be cooling my heels at this Indian burial ground tonight if I weren't?"

"I take it," Ashley said coldly, "that you don't enjoy the party."

"You couldn't have taken it more correctly," the girl said, "nor in a quicker gulp. This is the dullest joint, populated by the dullest people, that I have come across in twenty years."

"Twenty years being your age?"

"You have taken it right again, Icehouse."

"I prefer not to be called by that name."

"Icehouse, that's too bad."

Ashley lifted his eyebrows. "I meant to my face. After all, I am head of Flannery Brothers, and you are an employee."

"Let me ask you something, Ashhouse," the girl said, and was obviously cheered and pleased. "How could I best offend you? Give me a hint. Shall I go on calling you by your nickname or would it be more expeditious to throw a glass of water in your face?"

"I never lose my temper, if that's what you're getting at. But if you wish to be fired ——"

"That's what I'm getting at, Icehouse."

"Your name, please?" Ashley said.

"Molly Smith."

He made a note of it. "I'll see what I can do, Miss Smith."

"Alas," Molly said, and sighed. "This is all in vain. You can't do a thing. Not even if you inflate your windbag to the bursting point."

"I can try!"

"You'd better go in the lounge and put the stuffing back in your shirt, Icehouse."

"Miss Smith," Ashley said. "I'm quite impervious to your insults." He managed to smile, by dint of great effort, and tossed aside the note he had made. "Doubtless when you are sober you'll regret this conversation."

"I am quite sober, Ashley," Molly said, and turned a vivid shade of crimson. "Furthermore, I am not so calm as you. I ask you to put up your dukes, because I'm going to knock your block off for that last remark!"

A young man hastened over and grabbed Miss Smith. He said humbly that he was Edwards, from Household Appliances, and tried to dance off with the other employee.

"Unhand me," Molly said. "Let me go. I'm going to kill that Harvard man!"

Still struggling, she was borne away by the youth from Household Appliances. Ashley mopped his brow and decided to go home. For a time he could give no further thought to the service stations—all his mind could handle was the mad, red-haired, unclothed girl. He guessed she was from Ladies-Ready-to-Wear, probably the Teen-Agers Shop, or possibly the Hosiery Section. Or the Liquor Department in the Beverly Hills store; you couldn't rule that out. Despite what he'd said, he was angry. But he could not fire a poor girl who would be shattered in the morning at the thought of what she'd done.

Ashley's office at the main store was run in an atmosphere of quiet, murderous, glacially cold and broad-accented high tension. Department heads wishing they had pistols, machetes or vials of acid consumed the whole next morning of the president. When he finally had a moment to let down, on the brink of the lunch hour, his secretary brought in a load of papers for him to sign. She was a beautiful, blue-eyed blonde in a dressmaker's suit, named Donna Morrison—Ashley liked decorative, smart office girls. They also had to have iron digestive systems; Donna had lasted two years, but the two previous secretaries had retired to live on crackers and milk and their memories.

"I saw you at the party last night, Mr. House," Donna said. "That—that was a lovely speech you made."

"You should have come over and said 'hello,'" Ashley said. . . . "Look at this letter. Isn't that an erasure?"

"Yes, sir, but it's just one word. Unless you hold it up to the light, it doesn't ——"

"You know I never permit errors in my correspondence. And I don't want any excuses, either. Do this over."

"Yes, sir."

There was a long silence while Ashley House wrote "Ashley House" many times.

"I had a new dress on last night," Donna said. "Very décolleté."

"I met a girl in practically ——" Ashley frowned. "Never mind."

"Mr. Partridge from Credit took me. But I found him dull. I can't seem to get interested in any men since ——"

"Did you buy your dress here?"

"Ah . . . no," Donna said. "No, sir. I got it from Mode o' Moment because the blue just matched my ——"

"That's loyalty for you," Ashley said. "We sell the best merchandise in town beyond any question of doubt, and yet our employees are willing to forgo their discounts and trade elsewhere. Why can't people ever see beyond their noses?"

"That's what I keep asking myself," Donna said. . . . "Is that all, Mr. House?"

"That's all," Ashley said.

On his way to the executives' dining room, he prowled briefly through the store. These frequent trips and his remarks to the careless and unwary were already a matter of legend. It had got so everybody working in the store was on his toes and pitching, even the union stewards. Today he selected the Luggage Department for a visit.

Beside a pile of suitably priced, attractively arranged overnight cases Ashley found Molly Smith. She was in a dress of somber hue that the management preferred, but it was much too tight, and on one wrist was a bracelet of emeralds that would have given any customer an inferiority complex. In addition, she was leaning on the display, smoking a cigarette and meditatively contemplating her nail polish.

"Ah," Ashley said. "We meet again, Miss Smith!"

"Oh, hello, Icehouse," Molly said. "Looking for a bag?"

"Not precisely, Miss Smith," Ashley said.

"If you don't see anything you want here," Molly said, "why don't you try some of the models we have in our exclusive Promenade Shop? There are some real bags slinking around up there, reputedly selected by the pasty-faced head of this store. Former sweeties of his, I presume."

Ashley placed a hand upon an overnight case and steadied himself. "Miss Smith, you are trying to exhaust my patience, aren't you?"

She smiled in a pleasant manner. "No, not really, Icehouse. I suppose if I goaded you to apoplexy and you dropped dead, it would benefit a lot of people."

"Miss Smith, you are smoking a cigarette!"

"I just finished my lunch!"

"Employees are not permitted to smoke, except in designated rooms, and never on duty. Besides, your dress is too tight."

"Too tight, Icey?"

"Uh . . . much too snug," Ashley said. "It exhibits a—a —— Furthermore, Miss Smith, that stupendous emerald bracelet violates a rule ——"

"Please, Ashley," Molly said. "This bores me. Run along and peddle your camisoles and New Looks."

"I demand that you leave the floor!" Ashley said loudly, scaring the head of the Luggage Department. "At once! Otherwise I will take immediate action, Miss Smith!"

"With pleasure," Molly said cheerily. "Why don't you come with me? There is a corridor behind this department perfectly suitable for mortal combat. Whilst you slip out of your coat, I will gird up my ——"

"Miss Smith, this is my last warning!"

"Be fair," Molly urged. "Give me a chance at you. I'll beat your brains out."

Ashley raised a trembling hand to his throat and tugged at his tie, which seemed to be tightening on him. "M-may I have your sales number, Miss Smith?"

"Just a minute; I'll look in my book. . . . Let's see . . . I'm Convict Four-oh-two-seven, doing a life term."

"Thank you, Miss Smith," Ashley said, keeping his voice

steady. "I suggest you make immediate inquiries regarding other employment."

"Poor old Icehouse," Molly said. "Living in that dream world ——"

During the elevator ride upstairs, Ashley stopped shaking. He told himself the whole thing was ridiculous, particularly his reaction to it. The unfortunate gorgeous girl simply needed a long rest and a psychiatrist. It was merely another experience in the employee-employer relations of modern merchandising.

Nevertheless, he sat silent and glowering during his lunch. The Flannery brothers were there, and they were also silent and glowering. No executives ever took long for a meal in Ashley's presence, especially when he was in a bad humor, and soon the room was empty, aside from the Flannerys.

"Ashley," T. J. said, "your lawyer talked to our lawyer. I have never heard such absurd and ridiculous demands in my whole life."

"I have exactly calculated my worth to you so far," Ashley replied, "together with my probable worth to you for another five years. I included with those figures a mathematical forecast of business for that period, taking into consideration every possible contingency. You cannot lose by my proposals, if you consider them on an unemotional and scientific basis. . . . Didn't my lawyer show your lawyer the calculations?"

"Yes, he did," T. J. said, "and you're right, Ashley. But ——"

"Personally," B. R. said, "I would take Ashley and ——"

"B. R., I beg you to remain calm," T. J. said.

"I am calm," B. R. said. "I'm only speaking from cold, murderous rage."

"There is no possibility of our accepting your terms, Ashley," T. J. said.

"Very well," Ashley said. "Thank you for your courtesy, gentlemen."

"Courtesy?" B. R. said. "Listen, all I ask is to be alone with him for five minutes ——"

"Take it easy, B. R.," T. J. said. "This is business . . . and we're getting it." He fought down plain revulsion. "Ashley, don't regard this decision as final."

"Very well," Ashley said. "I'm quite happy to give you a few more days."

"He's quite happy!" B. R. said. "Why, I'll ——"

"B. R.!" T. J. said.

On the way downstairs, Ashley visited Mrs. Martin's office. He asked for the employment card on No. 4027, a Molly Smith. An odd expression disrupted the usual urbanity of Mrs. Martin. She waited while Ashley checked the card.

"Ah, yes," he said. "Employed two weeks. From New York. Former nightclub singer and dancer. Two years at Wellesley. . . . Was Miss Smith given our customary employee-indoctrination course?"

"Well," Mrs. Martin said, "sort of."

"What do you mean, 'sort of'?"

"Yes . . . she was."

"You must mean sort of, judging by her conduct." Ashley laid his palms on Mrs. Martin's desk for emphasis. "Mrs. Martin, I have an amazing story to tell you."

"I have an amazing one to tell you first," Mrs. Martin said hastily. "Ashley, you're overdoing this efficiency and hard-driving stuff. You're forgetting you live and work among ordinary human beings with ordinary human emotions. You've got to slow up and soften a little, if only on grounds of simple decency."

"I don't understand," Ashley said.

"Ashley," Mrs. Martin said, "the other day a girl came in here—a lovely girl—one of your employees. She sat down with me and cried like a baby. Do you know why? Because she's in love with you, hopelessly in love, and to her you're positively inhuman. The poor child's heart is breaking. Are you willing to go on crushing everything in your path, Ashley, for the sake of Flannery Brothers?"

"No," Ashley said, and stared at Mrs. Martin. "No, I'm not. . . . This is a great shock to me, Mrs. Martin. A lovely girl, eh? In love with me?"

"Head over heels."

"Who is she?"

"I can't tell you that. She swore me to secrecy. But she's probably not the only one."

"My goodness!" Ashley said. "In love with me . . . pining away! I'll be darned!"

"Think it over, Ashley," Mrs. Martin said. "Slow down. Don't spurn the faithful, unrequited heart. . . . In the meantime, what can I do for you on Number Four-oh-two-seven?"

"Uh . . . nothing," Ashley said. "Forget it."

He went reflectively back to his office and sat heavily at his desk. Suddenly the two queer episodes with the shapely redhead were clear. The desperate girl was mad about him, and she had risked everything in order to attract his attention—even her livelihood. She was willing to endure possible poverty and disgrace rather than continue to be ignored by him. Greater love had no woman in the entire store. It made him feel funny to have an adoring girl after him. His ambition, of course, had always been to be respected. Still, respect was different from reckless passion. He was a delicately balanced precision machine, and the information Mrs. Martin had given him appeared to pour sand in the works; he felt dizzy and couldn't think of anything else for a while. Somebody loved Icehouse.

Donna came in with a reminder of a conference at two o'clock. Looking up, Ashley smiled at her in gentle melancholy. The girl gave a nasty start of surprise.

"Well, well," he said. "Miss Morrison. Donna." He glanced at a calendar and sighed. "I note it is nearly September, and yet my mood coincides more with the vernal equinox than with the autumnal equinox."

"Huh?" Donna said. "It does? Yes, sir."

"Donna, do you feel my manner is too severe with my business associates? Am I giving rise to unnecessary heartache and mental perturbation by an unfortunate coldness of temperament? You can be frank."

"Oh, no. I think you're wonderful—your manner, I mean, Mr. House. I—I ——"

"Yes?" Ashley smiled again, and Donna grew pale.

"I never saw your teeth before," she said. "They're nice. . . . Uh . . . no, everything's fine, Mr. House. I wouldn't have you changed for a million dollars. Except ——"

"Thank you," Ashley said. "I wonder if you'd mind going down to the florist's shop and selecting a little red flower for my buttonhole? Don't forget my employee's discount."

He was gentle and considerate at the conference, arousing deep suspicions among his associates. At four, still oddly bemused, he dropped in on the Luggage Department again. No. 4027 wasn't there. Somebody thought she had been transferred to Parcels. Descending to the basement, Ashley eventually found the strawberry blonde wrestling with medium-sized bundles. She gladly paused in her work, took a cigarette from her purse, struck a match on a No Smoking sign, and gazed at him sardonically.

"Icehouse," she said, "don't your duties keep you on your feet too much? A man your age should rest and ——"

"I am age thirty-three," Ashley said.

"That seems old to me," Molly said. "Well, what can I do for you, Stuffy? Mrs. Martin put me down here because she thought I was attracting your attention."

"You are, Miss Smith. Your campaign has worked."

"What?"

"Mrs. Martin did not betray your confidence, but I understand everything and am sympathetic. You can relax, Miss Smith."

"I can, eh?"

"Yes," Ashley said in a kindly fashion. "I am not entirely heartless, my dear. What are you doing tonight?"

"Nothing that would interest you, brother."

"Perhaps I am doing something that would interest you. In fact, I'm sure it would. Will you dine with me and attend a lecture?"

Molly evidently fought for control and won by a hair. When she was calm once more and had stopped choking on her cigarette, she said, "So that's the way it's going to be, huh? A fight to the finish."

"It's the least I can do, under the circumstances."

"Yeah, I guess it is."

"Shall I pick you up at the employees' entrance at six-ten?" Ashley asked.

"At six," Molly said, "because I always quit a little early. . . . I accept your challenge, Ashley."

"Invitation," Ashley said.

"Invitation," Molly said.

He took her to an excellent downtown restaurant, and they chatted warily until the salad course. Then a peculiar incident took place.

"I saw your emotions when I asked you to go out tonight," Ashley remarked. "Bless your heart, Molly, your joy and surprise touched me."

She dropped a whole leaf of romaine. Her eyes widened amazingly.

"I am happy," Ashley continued, "to be able to afford you happiness. Though our relationship can lead to nothing serious, of course, I am delighted to offer you my platonic friendship. One day the right man will come along and you'll forget me."

"I must confess," Molly said, "that you are a faster man with a dead-pan rib than one would ever suspect from your dead pan. I'm getting a grudging admiration for you. I asked for it, and I got it . . . but don't make me choke on this lettuce."

Full of dinner, they went on to an auditorium, where a brilliant, unintelligible Government economist spoke at length on the world economic situation. Molly listened incredulously for ten minutes, gazed narrowly at Ashley, muttered, "Your round, Ashley," put her head on his shoulder and slept throughout the remainder of the talk.

Waking the child at last, Ashley took her to a drugstore for ice cream. Sitting on a stool eating a fudge sundae with chopped nuts, whipped cream and maraschino cherry seemed to do something to him, and he told her the story of his life. It developed that he was the eldest of five children, his father had been a ne'er-do-well, and he had resolved never to walk in his old man's footsteps. His ambition had perhaps made a machine of him, but he had at least educated himself and graduated with honors from the Harvard Business School, as well as providing for his mother and the schooling of the other children in his family. The rest was history, first in retail merchandising in Chicago, and now here in Los Angeles with Flannery Brothers. Molly didn't bother to stifle a yawn.

"That's a real dull story you have there, Icey," she said. "Even more sleep provoking than the one the guy had in the auditorium. You are a hard-working, honest, uninteresting man, and I sincerely wish I could wish you well . . . which I can't. Take me back to the Flannery-employee parking lot."

Ashley saw her to her car through the darkness of the lot. Her car was an enormous, brand-new, terribly expensive cabriolet, but he didn't notice it. His mind was on other things. The way of a man with a maid had him tied in knots.

"You poor little kid," he said. "This unimportant episode is the height of your dreams, isn't it? Tell me, are you disillusioned?"

"No," Molly said, "I have a little nausea, but it isn't important."

Moved by compassion, good will, confusion and certain urges detailed statistically in the Kinsey Report, Ashley took her in his arms and kissed her on the mouth. Intended originally as a brotherly peck, the kiss became a full-length feature and was almost held over for a second big week. Molly made only a token resistance. They were both shaken by the incident.

"Had I wished, Ashley," Molly said, "I could have applied a jujitsu hold I know when you attempted to embrace me, tossed you backwards over my head and broken both your wrists."

"Didn't you?" Ashley said. "I feel as if ——"

"No, I didn't," Molly said, "and it's too late now. . . . Well, good night. Stay as sour as you are, Icehouse."

"Don't thank me," Ashley said. "I'm genuinely glad that I could bring a ray of sunshine into your life."

That night he dreamed he was in the middle of the vernal equinox, dancing on a field of flowers and singing something by Jerome Kern. The following day his lawyer telephoned to say that, after preliminaries involving taking the Lord's name in vain, Flannery Brothers had agreed to all his terms. Ashley exhibited his teeth repeatedly to Donna, and the girl got a hunted look. Finally he wasn't even satisfied with that.

"Ah, Miss Morrison," he said. "Donna. Were you out with your one and only last night? Did he steal a kiss? How are things in—uh—Gloccamorra?"

"Lousy, Mr. House," Donna said. "I stayed home and read a book. I've got the blues." Tears came in her eyes. "You act so funny, Mr. House. Is something the matter? It makes my stomach hurt."

"Nonsense, Donna," Ashley said. "Everything is splendid . . . splendid. Drink a glass of bicarbonate of soda. Get it from our Drug Department."

Throwing caution to the winds during the afternoon, he went down to Parcels. Molly wasn't around, and a timid employee stated reluctantly that he believed the kid had been moved up to the Promenade Shop. Ashley hastened to the elevators and soon discovered his admirer parading in front of a group of women customers in some of Flannery Brothers underwear. Putting a trembling hand upon her arm, he led her to a dressing room.

"No, no," he said. "This can't go on. I won't have you—Miss Smith, who is responsible for this?"

"Mrs. Martin, I guess. She heard of your visit to Parcels yesterday."

"She is guilty of a grave mistake. I won't have you up here in Underwear."

"It is dangerous, Ashley," Molly said. "Suppose somebody hollered. 'Take it off'? I probably would. You know, I worked in a night club where a girl used to come out and ——"

"Please," Ashley said. "I'd rather not hear. Molly, I am willing to contribute again to your happiness. Where would you like to go tonight?"

"Some place you ain't."

"Poor child. You needn't keep up that pose. I can promise you nothing except that I will stay with you until you are cured of this unhappy infatuation."

Molly stared at him. "Oh? The joke is still on, huh? Okay. Let's meet in some neutral saloon at eight o'clock. How about the Medici Club on Sunset Boulevard?"

"With pleasure, my dear," Ashley said. "Now go put your clothes on."

They met at the appointed hour, and dined and danced amidst tobacco smoke and the blaring of music. Molly put her head on Ashley's shoulder again, and he found he didn't miss the economics a bit. As they had a last turn around the floor at two o'clock in the morning, he requested the gorgeous eccentric to tell him about herself.

"I'm a kind of an incognito ticket-of-leave woman from New York," Molly said, among other things. "They're trying to rehabilitate me by putting me in that fun-house you run downtown. I was bored by school after a couple of years, so I started singing and working in night-club choruses. My people went nuts. Of course, they won out. And here I am."

"Here with me," Ashley said. "I've never heard a more fascinating story. . . . When did love first come to you, Molly?"

"When I was eight," Molly said. "I was going to Miss Birdwell's school in New York, and there was a little boy of ten who ——"

"Never mind," Ashley said. "We will discuss that another time."

They parted on the Medici Club parking lot. Ashley took Molly in his arms and kissed her. Some time was consumed by that. There was no display of jujitsu. Both suffered shock afterward. Ashley's remarks, when he recovered his breath, were a profound surprise to both of them.

"I am ready to reciprocate your tender feelings," he said. "I love you, Molly. Will you become my wife?"

"Ashley," Molly said, "you have done me a great honor. I scarcely know what to say. I ——" She gave a convulsive leap. "Wait a minute, you pasty-faced bum! Which is this—revenge or to make sure your new contract is signed?"

"What?"

"Don't try to tell me you haven't found out that I'm B. R.'s daughter!"

"But I haven't, Molly! I thought you were in love with me. Mrs. Martin said ——"

"Oh, that's your secretary. Everybody in the store knows about that."

"Then you weren't trying to attract my attention by ——"

"I was trying to insult you, so I'd get fired and thrown out of the store."

"Ah," Ashley said, and suddenly became the president of Flannery Brothers. "I see. . . . Miss Smith—Miss Flannery—I regret having taken up your time while under a misapprehension. Accept my apologies. I bid you good night."

"Good night, Icehouse," Molly said, and nearly ran into the parking attendant as she drove away.

That night Ashley dreamed that he was run over by a Flannery Brothers truck filled with household furnishings.

In the morning he found Donna in tears as he came to work. Though he was as cold and dead inside as one of the refrigerators on display on the eighth floor, pity moved him. He gently lifted the charming blonde to her feet.

"I have learned your story, Miss Morrison," he said, "and I understand and sympathize. Old Icehouse's heart is broken too."

"Oh, Mr. House!" Donna said brokenly. "I—I just can't ——"

"You poor little kid," Ashley said.

He bent and kissed her tear-stained cheek. The door opened. Tottering a little, Molly studied the embrace. Then she burst into tears, slapped Ashley's face and departed.

"This is the end," Ashley said. "Miss Morrison, there is nothing left for any of us in this retail triangle. Shall we go out tonight, think not of the morrow, and get drunk?"

"Now you'd take me out, wouldn't you?" Donna said. "Now that you've lost the boss' daughter! Well, I don't play second fiddle, you pasty-faced bum!"

Fresh tears coming, she paused only to slap Ashley's face, and left the office. He sank into a chair and put his red face in his hands. The telephone rang and he answered it. The Flannery brothers wanted him.

He was scarcely across the hall and in T. J.'s office before both of them jumped on him.

"You're through!" T. J. shouted. "Fired! Sacked! The deal is off! Get out of our store!"

"You red-faced bum!" B. R. said. "Leading my daughter on. Trying to become a Flannery!"

"Turning this place into a love nest," T. J. said. "Kissing Molly, kissing your secretary. You dry-goods Casanova!"

"You're right, gentlemen," Ashley said, "and I'm wrong. Good day to both of you."

He returned to his outer office, a beaten man. Mrs. Martin was there.

"You'll need a new secretary, Ashley," she said. "Donna has quit. She says her stomach is gone."

"I will have no further need of a secretary," Ashley said. "My suggestion is that you start checking around for a new president."

"I'll get you a homely one," Mrs. Martin said. "Miss Flannery is in the inner office. My suggestion is that you interview her. I've straightened her out on a number of points."

"Oh, my goodness!" Ashley said.

He rushed inside. The former 4027 was beaming. He gazed at her weakly.

"Icehouse," she said, "I feel that I have acted hastily after talking with Mrs. Martin. I have decided to reconsider your parking-lot offer."

"Circumstances beyond my control," Ashley said, "force me to withdraw from the deal. I will not marry into the Flannery tribe in order to secure a lucrative contract, though personally I regard you with great esteem. Furthermore ——"

"Pardon me," Molly said. "I'll put this on a business basis, Ashley. Everybody hates you except me, as you know. Well, if you marry the boss' daughter and become head of the firm, it'll make you popular. People won't dislike you for your efficiency and brains; they'll say you got ahead the regular, human way. Don't you want to be loved?"

"Yes, I do," Ashley said. "Very much. You've sold me."

He took her in his arms. It was the story of the parking lots all over again.

Molly grew flushed and breathless. "Uh . . . can't we keep this on a business basis?" she said.

"Ever since I saw you in our underwear," Ashley said, "it has not been on a business basis."

SUICIDE FLIGHT

By WALT GROVE

Wilson had breakfast that morning alone with his wife before their child was awake. It was early and they ate at the table in the kitchen. Wilson was freshly shaved and he was wearing a clean white shirt. Helen had on a dressing gown and her face was still soft from sleep. She was a tall, quiet girl, and she was always kind to their child, but she worried about Wilson a good deal.

During the past year Helen had worried almost constantly. The year before that it had not been so bad because he had been testing internal-combustion-powered aircraft. But when he had switched to the jets Helen had begun to worry a great deal. And now, with the new stepped-up production schedule at the factory, she had it very bad. The night before, they had gone to sleep without ever settling an argument about his quitting.

Helen was not eating, she was having only a cup of coffee for breakfast. After a long period of silence, she said suddenly, "Jack, I'm serious."

"Let's not start it again, Helen."

"See?" she said. "You won't even ——"

"Look," he said, "I'll explain it once more. Now try to understand. It's just a job. And there is a certain amount of danger. But it is a known thing and I can compute it like gasoline consumption."

"Oh, you're just talking!" she said.

"Well, I'm trying to tell you," Wilson said.

"I don't want to hear any more talk."

"Okay," he said. "Okay, then."

Helen turned her face away and said, her voice slightly thick, "Jack . . . please quit."

"No, Helen. I won't."

"Jack, please don't go today. Just call ——"

"Listen," he said, his face hard, "you've got to stop this . . . this nagging. You nag at me all the time."

"All I want ——"

"Helen, I know what you want. And I know what you need. And to get you what you need I have to have money. Well, they're paying me big money now and ——"

"Oh, Jack!"

"That's right," he said. "It's hard. Well, it's a hard racket and a hard world. But I'm going to beat it. I know I can. I'm a smart boy and as long as they pay big dough, then I work for them."

"But we have so much money now ——"

"No," he said. "We don't have enough yet."

She folded her arms on the table and put her head on them. She wasn't crying, she was only very tired. Wilson began stroking her hair with his hand.

"Baby," Wilson said. "Poor baby."

"If you got killed, Jack, I couldn't live."

"Hush, honey," Wilson said, still stroking her hair. "No one'll get hurt. Not me, anyway. And they'll pay me lots of big dough and we'll get rich and then we'll go away somewhere and buy us a little hick airport and a bunch of small planes and teach kids to fly. How about that?"

It was an old joke and he always ended the argument with it, but this time she did not smile and say jeeringly, "Yes, I can see you flying a small plane." Instead, she kept her head on her arms and sighed.

Wilson patted her shoulder, put his arm around her and kissed her cheek. Then he put on a leather jacket and walked out the kitchen door and unlocked the big garage door, got into his coupé, and backed it out. He stopped it just outside the garage and lit a cigar. When he looked up, Helen was standing in the kitchen door and she called, "What time will you be home tonight?"

Wilson called back, "Six okay?"

When she nodded he put the coupé in gear and backed the rest of the way out of the drive, turned, and drove away.

When Wilson came to the factory he stopped at the gate and showed his identification to the guard, then drove the coupé down to the hangar line and parked it. He got out, the cigar clenched between his teeth, and went inside one of the hangars. There was a small locker room inside, and Wilson went in there first, but none of the other test pilots was there.

He glanced through the connecting door into the chief's office. Turner wasn't there yet. Wilson went into the office and looked at the blackboard. On it was a list of aircraft to be tested and the kind of tests to be performed. When he heard the door open behind him, he glanced over his shoulder and saw Turner and, behind Turner, a short, red-faced little man in an Army uniform, Colonel Fogerty.

"Morning, Wilson," the colonel said. "Looking over the list, eh?"

"That's right," Wilson said.

He was not fond of Colonel Fogerty, who had been sent by the Army to expedite the delivery of certain special aircraft. He knew that the colonel was in too great a hurry and if the colonel kept yapping about rushing this job or that, then pretty soon the boys would start flying them into the ground.

"Why weren't you bowling with us last night, Jack?" Turner said, as he went behind his desk and sat down, wiping his forehead with the flat of his hand.

"Helen and I went to the movies," he said.

"The agenda for the day," the colonel said. He was standing in front of the blackboard, and he let out a little cry of delight. "Oh, that XF-Eleven has come off the line. It's ready to be tested. Turner, let's get one of your boys right on that. Washington is all excited about its potentialities."

"I'm hot," Turner said. "I don't see how a man can sweat as much as I do. I even sweat in the winter. You don't sweat a lot, do you, Jack?"

"Not a lot," Wilson said. He sat down, and he was watching the colonel. He knew that the colonel was excited about that XF11, and that meant money, and he could feel something inside himself quicken and tighten.

"What're you doing today, Jack?" Turner asked.

"Nothing," Wilson said.

"You can get started on the XF-Eleven then."

Wilson had seen the XF11 when it had come off the line late the afternoon of the day before. He knew what it was, but he wanted the money. He said, "You mean that single jet fighter that looks like a coal truck, don't you?"

"Well, it's a little heavy," Turner said.

"A little?" Wilson said. "Why, it must weigh thirty thousand pounds."

"Sh-h-h!" the colonel hissed. "Not so loud!"

"You talk like you don't like it," Turner said. He wiped his face with a handkerchief.

"Look," Wilson said, "I'm no kid. I've been around in this business. Don't think you can suck me in on this and make me like it."

"Don't get so huffy," Turner said. "You act like I was trying to pull a fast one. I'm not. You'll get the usual fifteen hundred bonus for this—if you get all the tests completed within the minimum time."

Wilson shook his head and stood up. "Well, it was nice working for you, Turner. I'll see you around."

"Now, wait a minute."

"No," Wilson said. "Not in that. Not for fifteen hundred. Fly it yourself. Or let the colonel."

"See here, Turner," the colonel said. "Don't take any nonsense from this fellow. I can get you a pilot, just like that. And it won't cost you a cent."

Wilson laughed. "Where, colonel?"

"The Air Force is full of splendid young officers who do not hesitate to do their duty," the colonel said.

Turner mopped his face with his handkerchief. "Sit down, Jack. Let's talk this over."

"All right," Wilson said.

"Well, as you know, it's heavy," Turner said. "It's the heaviest fighter we've built yet. It's powered by a single jet turbine. We hope to get more range out of it than the usual couple of hours. And on this one we're not going to use kerosene. But high-octane gasoline."

"And you ask me to risk my neck for fifteen hundred," Wilson said. "Chief, I'm no fool."

"How much?" Turner said.

"Thirty-five hundred," Wilson said, and because Turner said nothing, he added, "above taxes."

"We have thousands of splendid young officers, willing and eager to sacrifice ——" the colonel began.

"Oh, can it, will you, colonel?" Turner said. "You want this thing tested, not flown in the ground. That's what we're trying to do for you. Fulfill our contract." He turned back to Wilson. "I'll see what the front office says, Jack. But it'll have to be on the condition that you complete the tests without accident to the aircraft."

Wilson hesitated only a moment. "No. That's out. You've got to give me the dough if I crack it up or not. I've got to protect my wife and kid."

"Well, I'll see," Turner said.

Wilson got up and walked to the door that opened into the locker room. "When you find out, let me know," he said. He went into the locker room and closed the door behind him.

He went to the window and looked out. An aircraft was being pulled out of a hangar by a tractor, and he saw that it was the XF11. There was a small crowd watching. It was built very close to the ground and it was very heavy looking. Its wings were stubs far back of the bubble on the fuselage that was the pilot's canopy. The tail was high, built that way so it would be clear of the blast coming out of the tail pipe. The air intake scoops that fed air to the turbine were in the wings, inboard next to the fuselage. Wilson saw that two fat auxiliary wing tanks had been fastened to the wing tips already.

Turner opened the door. "Okay, Jack. You win."

"Let's put it in writing," Wilson said.

"What the hell, Jack, don't you trust me?"

"Sure. But I got to look out for myself."

"Well, you look over the flight data then while I get someone to draw up a contract."

"Sure." Wilson took the bound notebook from Turner and sat down on a bench. The XF11 had been flown a few times before, but not since the new experimental gasoline-burning turbine had been put in it. Very carefully he went over the flight reports and plans and estimates for the aircraft, checking to see how it had been put together and what the estimated speeds and strains and stresses were. All that was theoretical, of course, and what the aircraft would do and could withstand would not be known until he tested it.

About thirty minutes later Turner came in with two legal-sized pages and handed them to Wilson, who read them through, slowly.

"Oh, come on, come on," Turner said.

"You and the colonel," Wilson said. "How come you aren't in the Army anyway, chief? You're an eager boy."

"Go to hell," Turner said.

Wilson laughed and took Turner's fountain pen and signed the contract. "There you go."

"No," Turner said. "There you go."

"I guess that's right," Wilson said.

He went to his locker and got a pair of glare glasses and went through the hangar and outside to the apron and across it to the XF11. That was all he was thinking about now, there wasn't another thought in his mind.

A mechanic named McClarney was sitting on the concrete in the shadow of the aircraft, and another man was in the cockpit. When Wilson got closer he saw that it was a test pilot named Johnson. He said in a hard voice, "Get the hell out of my airplane, Johnson."

Johnson got out of the cockpit, and jumped down from the wing. "Think you can fly it?"

"McClarney, is she ready to go?" Wilson asked.

"Sure," the mechanic said.

"Want to ride in my lap?"

"Hell, no."

Wilson walked around the wing to the front of the fuselage and put his feet in the steps and climbed into the cockpit. He had the engineering data with him and he sat there checking the position of the controls and the instruments on the panel until he had the feel of it and knew exactly where everything was. Then he got out.

Johnson was still standing there, watching him. "I know you're a smart boy, but you'd better be damn smart this time. You'd better not make a mistake."

"You talk like an old woman," Wilson said. "I've flown these things before."

"You've never flown one like that before. Look at it. It's heavier than hell. If anything goes wrong with that turbine you won't even have time to spit."

"What's the matter with you?" Wilson said.

"I wouldn't test this thing for all the money in the world," Johnson said.

"Well, that's where you and I differ," Wilson said. "I would. And I am. I'm getting mine."

"Yeah, in the neck." Johnson walked off.

"He's a sorehead," Wilson told McClarney. "Just a sorehead."

"Sure," the mechanic said.

But Wilson knew exactly what the other test pilot had meant. Jets were much more simple in many ways than the old internal-combustion engines. But in other ways they were not. The rotary compressor wheel, for instance, had to be balanced perfectly. And the bearing-lubricating system could not fail, for if a bearing overheated and did not function, then the compressor wheel, turning over at something like 18,000 r.p.m., would literally disintegrate—taking half the aircraft and the pilot with it. As long as everything worked, then everything was fine.

Wilson said to McClarney, "Well, get the starter truck out here. I'll taxi her before I take her up."

Wilson went back to the locker room and got his chute and his aluminum-backed data pad, which he strapped to his thigh. He put on a long-visored cap and went back to the aircraft. The starter truck was there and he climbed into the cockpit.

McClarney was looking up at him blankly.

Wilson set the brakes. "Contact."

"Contact."

The electric starter motor whined and Wilson opened the throttle and the jet turned over. Its exhaust made a whistling noise like a peanut vender's stand.

Wilson called the tower and asked permission to taxi. The tower gave him an okay, and he waved McClarney aside and took off the brakes and the XF11 moved like a truck across the apron to the runway. Wilson taxied it up and down, and it did not taxi well; but then, no jet ever did. On the ground they were like fish out of the sea. All Wilson had hoped to do was to get some feeling for the aircraft, but as he turned it back on the apron and cut the switch, he feared that he had not.

He dropped to the ground and told McClarney, "You better get the gas truck out here again so the weight'll check exactly on take-off." Then he went into the hangar and into Turner's office and sat on the edge of the desk.

"Okay, chief," he said. "I'm ready."

"Try a preliminary speed test first," Turner said.

"You don't waste a minute, do you?" Wilson said. "I'll be three hundred feet off the ground and if anything goes wrong I won't have a chance."

"You're getting paid," Turner said.

"Okay," Wilson said. "I'll fly you a speed test."

He went outside. The gas truck was just pulling away and the starter truck was there, waiting, and he got into the cockpit and started the turbine. He rolled the canopy closed and switched on his radio and asked the tower for clearance to take off. The tower told him to taxi to the south end of the north-south runway.

He taxied the XF11 down the runway and turned it and sat, waiting. The sky was very blue and clear. Then the tower came in with, "You're clear for take-off, XF-Eleven."

Wilson almost locked his brakes and cracked the throttle not quite too full, and then released the brakes and gave it full throttle and the XF11 began going down the runway very sluggishly. Jets were always slow on take-off, and they required a long stretch of runway. Wilson dropped the flaps halfway and waited for the small feeling of lifting that would tell him he was airborne, but it did not come, and he began to sweat. The XF11 had not been off the ground since the new experimental gasoline-burning turbine had been put in it.

Then the continuous reaction of the turbine began to function more efficiently, and the ship lifted. He climbed two thousand feet in a matter of seconds, cut out of the traffic pattern and headed southwest. At four thousand feet he passed over the field and glanced down at it. He held the ship level and wrote on his data pad: "Airborne at 1102, take-off normal."

He looked then at his instrument panel to check his gauges. His speed was about four hundred miles an hour and the turbine was making 18,000 r.p.m. The oil pressure on the main bearing was 700 pounds per square inch and the temperature was 400° F. The tail-pipe temperature was 1600° F. As he glanced at each gauge he noted the information on the data pad strapped to his leg, and when he glanced back at the tail-pipe temperature to check his figures he saw that it had dropped to 1400° F.

Something was wrong, the tail pipe should have been hotter than that. But he did not stop to wonder why. He said into his mike, "XF-Eleven to tower."

"Come in, XF-Eleven."

"XF-Eleven requesting immediate clearance to land. Emergency. Repeat. Emergency."

"You're clear to land, XF-Eleven."

Wilson was scared, he was sweating, and he cut the throttle and began losing altitude. At three thousand he turned back to the field and at two thousand he cut into the traffic pattern. He kept waiting for the thing to fly apart under him. His shirt was stuck to his sides with sweat and he kept glancing at the instrument panel. The tail-pipe temperature remained at 1400° F. and everything else was normal. But in his mind he could see something going wrong with the turbine, and the compressor wheel sheering off, taking half the fuselage and him with it. When the wheels touched the ground he let out a long breath and cut the turbine. He braked the ship to a stop and sat there until the tractor came out and towed the ship to the hangar.

He saw Turner and Colonel Fogerty standing on the apron, but he had to sit there and tug the release handle for a few seconds before he could roll the canopy back and clamber down.

"What's up?" Turner said.

"Anything seriously wrong?" the colonel asked.

"Tail-pipe temp's low," Wilson said, still breathing hard. "It dropped a couple hundred degrees."

"How low?" Turner asked.

"Down to fourteen hundred."

"Oh, that's all right," Colonel Fogerty said, grinning with relief. "That's not too low. Hop back in, my boy, and take her up again."

"Hop back in yourself, you louse," Wilson told the colonel.

"Now, Jack," Turner said, "that's no way to talk."

"Well, shut him up then," Wilson said. He was still sweating and he said, "You can cook your goose up there damn fast, and I thought mine was. Have you got a cigarette?"

"Here," Turner struck a match. "Now, let's look at this calmly. A two-hundred-degree drop in the tail-pipe temp doesn't mean much. You're just all wound up. This job has got you scared, that's all. Now how about flying it?"

Wilson told him where he could go.

"You can't talk to me like that," Turner said, his face getting red.

"I'll talk to you any way I like," Wilson told him, throwing down his cigarette. "All you do all day long is sit around in your office. Now go get me my mechanic."

"You can't order me around," Turner said.

Wilson stepped up to him and said, "Go get me my mechanic, Turner," and Turner backed away and turned and went hurriedly into the hangar.

Wilson sat down on the concrete in the shade of the wing. He felt a little sick, now that he was down. McClarney came walking across the apron.

"What's up?" he said.

Wilson told him.

McClarney walked into the hangar and came out with a couple of mechanics wheeling a stand. They put the stand beside the XF11 and got up on it and took off a section of skin on the side so they could get to the turbine.

Wilson sat there until McClarney called, "I found it."

He got up then and climbed up on the stand and saw that McClarney was holding something in his hand.

"Fuel-metering jet," McClarney said. "You weren't getting all the fuel in one burner that you should've. That's why the temp was low. Must be dirt or something in this one. I can put in a new one in about thirty minutes."

"Okay," Wilson said. "I'll be getting coffee."

He took off his chute and left it in the cockpit and went and had two cups of coffee and lit his second cigar of the day. He still had most of it left to smoke when he went back to the XF11. It was ready. He snubbed the fire off his cigar and kept the butt clenched between his teeth as he climbed in.

He took the ship up the second time, climbing very rapidly. At five thousand, crossing the field, he looked at his instruments and saw that they were all registering normally. The sun was brilliant and the sky quite blue, and, below, the earth had a perfect, clean, geometric appearance that he was never aware of on the ground.

He flew south, going about four hundred miles an hour. The aircraft did not handle badly in the air for all its weight. But let that power plant shut off, Wilson thought, and this thing would glide like a rock. He went about forty miles south until he saw the two pylons, striped red and white, that marked the measured-mile course over which he would have to fly to have the speed of the ship clocked exactly.

There was an electric eye shooting out a beam in each pylon and as the aircraft broke the first one a clock would begin and as it broke the second the clock would stop. Each pylon was three hundred feet high, and that was all the altitude Wilson would have. The two pylons themselves were in a clear stretch of ground, but the approach and the ground on either side of them were covered with trees.

As Wilson pulled away he saw the crash truck parked beneath the base of one pylon. Flying away so that he could turn and come into the course, he began to lose altitude. He had no direct communication with the men inside the pylons, he had to talk to the tower, and the tower talked to the pylons over a telephone.

"XF-Eleven to tower. Standing by for speed test."

"Stand by, XF-Eleven."

Wilson glanced at his gauges, being careful to check the oil-pressure and temperature gauges. They remained at seven hundred and three hundred as though they were glued there. He was feeling all right now, and telling himself that this was the easiest money he had ever made.

"XF-Eleven, you are clear for speed test."

"XF-Eleven at two thousand feet turning south into course."

He turned the aircraft south and went down to three hundred feet and leveled off. He was doing over four hundred miles an hour now and up ahead he could see the first pylon. He was right down on the deck and he could not take time to look at his instruments but when he was only about ten miles from the first pylon he glanced briefly at the panel. It was only for a second, but as he glanced he saw the oil-pressure gauge drop from about six hundred and thirty pounds per square inch to five hundred. The oil-temp gauge went down to two hundred degrees and the r.p.m.'s fell off to 15,000.

His heart almost stopped beating. With one hand Wilson cut the switch and with the other he pulled the nose up. He was waiting, with his stomach coming up in his throat, for the compressor wheel to fly off, and the thing to explode, but it did not. And he felt the ship climb as high as momentum would take it and he could feel it beginning to stall, and he leveled off. He was only at eight thousand feet.

He had gone about half the distance to the first pylon. On the other side of it was a clear space. Everywhere else there were trees. *I'm getting out of here*, he thought, and he tugged on the canopy release handle. The canopy didn't budge. It was stuck. He tugged harder and he was beginning to sweat. He couldn't get the canopy open, he would have to stick with it and land it. Somehow he would have to stretch his glide to cover the remaining five miles.

As he pushed the nose down to gather speed he said into his mike, "XF-Eleven to tower. Emergency landing. Engine gone," and then with the increased speed he leveled off and held it there as long as he could. The tower was yammering in his ear, "XF-Eleven. XF-Eleven. Can you make it? Can you make it?"

The ship began to wobble violently then and he had to dip the nose down and sacrifice more of his precious altitude for speed, and his mouth and throat were dry, and he was breathing hard. He leveled the ship off again and he was only two hundred feet from the ground. He became aware of the tower in his earphones, "Crash truck standing by," and he tore the earphones off, and the ship was beginning to stall out again and he had to dip the nose down once more.

The pylon was still too far away, he was down to a hundred feet now, and he was afraid that he could never make it. He tried again to roll the canopy back. The trees beneath him were rushing past, the pylon looming up, and the wings were tilting and falling away and the ship was going down like a rock, much too fast, and he hauled the stick back and came in with his wheels up.

He heard the tail rip through the trees and the way ahead of him was clear, and then he hit, flat, and the ship plowed forward until one wing dug in, and it ground-looped. The force slammed Wilson's face and head and shoulder into the instrument panel. For a second he was out, but the pain was so strong that he pushed himself back with his good arm and tried to stand up.

He felt the heat of the fire then, and saw the smoke—when he had hit, the gas tank had apparently sprung open and the high-octane gasoline had leaked back to the heated jet engine. Wilson began fumbling irrationally with the catch on his safety belt, but he could not get it undone. The fire was getting much hotter and he was trapped and he knew that it would explode any second and he suddenly stopped fumbling with the catch and began to pound on the canopy and scream for help. It was then that the two men in asbestos suits climbed up on the wing and forced the canopy back and got him out.

The next day, when he finally came out of the ether, he was very sick. The nurse told him that he could only hold the water in his mouth, then spit it out, but he swallowed it, and then he began to retch and for a while he thought he would never stop. When the nurse had quieted him down she told him that he could see his wife, but only for a minute.

Helen came in and sat beside his bed, dropping her purse on the floor, and held his bandaged left hand. "Oh, Jack," she said, and then she began to cry uncontrollably.

"It's all right," Wilson said. He could not speak very loud. "It's all right, Helen. You mustn't cry." But he could not get her to stop, and finally he tried to joke. "Look, Helen. I'm alive. And I came awfully close to getting killed. What more do you want for your nickel?"

She put her head down on the bed and Wilson patted her shoulder with his left hand and said, "It was a dirty job, Helen, but I held out for a lot of money. Now we got a lot of money and we can quit and go buy that hick airport and some little planes and ——"

She raised her head, and her face was wet and she said, "How can you joke about it now? How ——"

"That's no joke," Wilson said. He was very tired and sick; he felt as if he could sleep for a million years. "I mean it this time, Helen. I'm through."

She smiled at him then and she tried to joke a little too. "Don't—don't you ever dare do this again."

And just before Wilson went to sleep he said, his voice a whisper, "Oh, I won't . . . I promise."

SURPRISE PARTY

By NORMAN KATKOV

Y̲ou understand, this is my story I want to tell. Understand, please, that I'm talking about what happened to me in the weeks before December 18, 1928, when I was in the sixth grade at Linden School, Livingston Avenue and Delos Street, St. Paul, Minnesota.

Listen now. I was ten years old and we lived then on Clinton Avenue, which ran parallel to Livingston, two blocks east. There was Clinton, then Robert Street, the shopping block, then Livingston. From north to south there were Colorado, Delos and Isabel streets. This was my world then, you understand: my house, the school, the playground across the street from the school, the grocer, the drugstore, the movies, all on Robert Street, and the fruit store owned by the Italian. This was my world, my orbit.

Not much of a world, was it? Just those city blocks. My younger brother, whom I pulled around in a coaster wagon twenty years ago, could have flown over it in 1945 and erased it with one bomb. Not his bomb load, you understand, but one bomb.

Still, I know of no ordained geographical limit for tragedy. Nor is there a chronological basis for grief. We can get it at any age, can we not?

I remember it as well now, in this winter of 1948, as when it happened. I remember shining the Sam Browne belt each night rubbing the badge with my ma's silver polish. I remember the discarded Al Smith buttons we wore; they were blue and white. I didn't remember the Italian's name, though. We always called him "the Italian," and when I began to think of telling the story, I called my ma in St. Paul and she remembered.

"Ma," I said, after the hello's and how-are-you's. "Ma, you remember when we lived on Clinton Avenue?"

"Yes, Joe. Of course."

"You remember the fruit store on Robert Street? An Italian ran it, and we called him 'the Italian.'"

"Yes, Joe, yes. Why, Joe?"

"What was his name, ma? Do you remember his name?" I asked.

"His name? His name? Yes. His first name was George. George—George—George Paradino."

Paradino. Sure, the Italian. George Paradino. Sure.

"Joe? Joe, why?" she asked again.

"You remember the year I was a school cop and I had the second grade to take care of? You remember what happened, ma. You remember."

"I'll never forget, son," she said.

"Well, I want to tell it. I want to write it now."

"Yes, Joe," and her voice was soft. "Yes, Joe," and her voice was gentle. "Yes, tell it, Joe."

You see, she was in on it with me too. Right from the start, although it was my idea. You see, now, at thirty, I remember it all as though it were happening to me now, today.

Understand, at thirty I don't want to tell you about Santa Claus. Not about Santa Claus, nor about miracles, nor about angels, nor about —— Well, listen now.

The second-grade kids were my responsibility that term. I met them at Robert Street every morning, took them across with the metal sign we carried, and took them back at lunch. I crossed the street with them four times each day.

You see, I'd been made a school cop just before Thanksgiving, when Johnny Albertanti moved up on Hamline Avenue. His family moved and he changed school, so there was this extra belt and badge. I remember the day Miss Thompson, our principal, called me in, and she said, "Joe, would you like to be a school policeman?"

"I think so." Holy smokes! A cop! Holy kopoly, a cop!

"You think so?"

"I mean, I'd like to, I guess."

"You guess?"

"Well, cripes!"

"Cripes?"

"Gee, Miss Thompson," I said. I remember looking out of the window behind her, reading the sign, RIVERVIEW COM-

MERCIAL CLUB; reading the letters slowly to myself, pronouncing each letter, trying somehow to get my stomach together and my throat clear and my lips wet so I could say what I wanted to say.

"Gee, Miss Thompson!" A badge! And the belt! Holy smokes, wearing the belt all the time! Cripes, the belt!

She laughed then, at last. Smiled at me and laughed, put her arm on my shoulder and led me to the outer office, to her secretary's desk. There lay the belt and there, propped against a thin glass vase, No. 869—I'll never forget the number—was the badge. There was my badge.

"You'll have the second grade, Joe," she told me, "and at noon hour you are to report to Frank Kazaley, who will instruct you in procedure."

"Yes, ma'am." He didn't have to instruct me. Every day, crossing the street with the other kids, it was I who always stood in the center, arm high with the metal sign, the cars stopped on each side.

"All right, Joe."

"Yes, ma'am." Instruct me!

"All right, Joe."

"All right, ma'am."

"You may go, Joe."

"Yes, ma'am." You understand, I couldn't move. Eight cops and three hundred kids, and me one of the eight.

"Joseph, will you get back to your class?"

"Yes, ma'am."

She saw it then. She saw it on me, I guess. She smiled; she picked up the belt and came toward me, slipping it over my shoulder, and then she pinned the badge on the belt. Was ever brave warrior knighted by so gracious a queen? Was ever subject so completely the slave of his sovereign, and can I tell you, even now, how I felt that day?

I had won sprint races in St. Paul playground track meets. I had been to summer camp, and my uncle had taken me up in an airplane, an open biplane. He had bought me skates, and Tom Mix had autographed his picture for me, right there on St. Peter Street at the door of the Orpheum. But the belt! The belt and the badge!

So I was a cop. I was a good cop, and I wanted to be the

best cop, and I guess maybe I was. The week before Thanksgiving everybody in our room chipped in and Miss Morgan, our teacher—she was young and red-haired and had a boy friend; he was gym teacher at Clinton Junior High—Miss Morgan bought a present for each of us, and cakes and apples and small colored cookies. We had a party after two o'clock; we skipped music and math that day. Our room was about the happiest in the school that day, I guess. Maybe the happiest in the city.

I told ma all about what happened in Miss Thompson's office that night at home. I told her about my idea that night. We'd been the only room to have a party, and I said I wanted to have a party for my wards, for the second grade. I remember I was sitting in the kitchen watching her iron, a glass of milk beside me, and my homework and a book of Ralph Henry Barbour's. I wore the belt, and the badge was propped up against the milk.

"I'll give the party, ma."

"You, Joe?" She dipped her hand into the glass on the ironing board and sprinkled water on a shirt of mine.

"I can do it, ma. I can do it."

"You are not the teacher, Joe." She was always patient with me, listening always and talking everything out with me.

"Well, ma, listen." I sat beside the kitchen radiator. "Listen, ma; when Miss Morgan told us about the Thanksgiving party, she said we'd all pitch in and she got everything for us. Well"—I spread my arms wide and the milk sloshed over—"well, I'll do the same thing. I'll get money from my kids and hold it, and then, the last day of school before Christmas vacation—well, I'll buy them things and it'll be a surprise. Nobody will know and the teacher will be surprised."

I could see me then, sitting there by the radiator and drinking the milk, up in Miss Thompson's office. I could see me there with the belt and the badge, Miss Morgan being called up and the second-grade teacher, Miss Le Tourneau, she having come to tell Miss Thompson about it, all three of them there. I could see myself standing before them, and Miss Thompson telling Miss Morgan the whole story, and Miss Morgan taking me to our room and telling my class the story. I could see me then taking the second graders across

Robert Street that afternoon, and next year—cripes, next year maybe captain. I'd be captain! Captain of all the cops and march in the school-cop parade holding the Linden School flag.

"Holy kopoly, ma!" I was filled with the thought of this great adventure. "Holy kopoly! Cripes, ma! Don't you think so, ma?"

She set the iron on end and came toward the table. She turned then, I remember. I remember all this, you see. She turned and went back to the ironing board, pulled the cord from the socket and then came to the table.

I had my scratch pad before me, and a pencil, and I pulled a chair for her over next to me. "See, ma," I said, "I've got thirty kids; there are thirty kids in class. I know that. I've got their roster here," and I reached behind the Sam Browne belt and unbuttoned my shirt pocket, got the mimeographed roster out for her. "Well, there are thirty of them," I said, "and what I'll do, I'll take two cents a day, and five days a week . . . and how many weeks until the eighteenth, ma? Do you know, ma?" I got up and went to the grocer's calendar hanging high on the wall above the telephone on the kitchen-cabinet shelf. I stood on a chair and counted the days, and there were twenty, all right.

I figured it out there on the scratch pad, and it was twelve dollars. Cripes, what I could buy with twelve dollars. I thought then of a baseball glove or bat for each boy and a doll for each girl, and then ma said, "You, Joe."

"Me?"

"Yes, son, you have to pitch in too."

"Me?"

She nodded, her eyes soft as only her eyes could be—the brownest, softest, most gentle, kindest eyes I've ever known. "You're not only the manager, Joe," she warned. "You can't be just the treasurer. You must also pitch in."

"Okay, then. Swell. I'll put in two cents a day."

"A nickel, Joe," she smiled at me.

"A nickel?"

"You are in the sixth grade, Joe, and they in the second."

"But a nickel!"

"Your allowance is larger."

"Allowance. I haven't got any allowance. Cripes, we can't

afford allowances, ma. Gee, ma, you're trying to spoil it for me."

She never became angry with me. She reached into her apron pocket then and got her coin purse. She opened it there on the table and she found a quarter, and she said: "Here, Joe; this is for the first week. Here is your pitch-in for the first week, and Monday you begin your pitch-in from the second grade." Maybe she didn't speak grammatically, my ma, but she was some ma. Take my word for it, friends, she was some ma, all right.

That night in bed I went over it and over it and over it. I was so pleased with myself that night and all day Saturday and all day Sunday. Sunday night I could barely sleep. I was reading in bed and my ma came in with some apples. She sat on my bed and we ate the apples, and then she took the book. She said to go to sleep, but I'll tell you now, it must have been near dawn when I stopped thinking of my plan.

I was on Robert Street at seven-thirty. I was supposed to be there at eight, but I came at seven-thirty and I told the kids to meet me at lunchtime. As I took each group across the street, I told them there'd be a meeting of the second grade at lunch hour behind the Delos Street precinct station.

I remember now how enchanted they were with the idea. At noon I showed them the quarter and said this was my first week's contribution. I put it in my cap, holding the cap before me, and then each of them, the girls pulling at the knots in their handkerchiefs, the boys taking off their mitts, their money in the thumb of the mitt, each put his or her pennies in the cap.

I hadn't thought it would work out so easy, and I ran home with the money, down the middle of Delos Street, running stiff-legged, so as not to jostle the coins. I counted them while I ate. There was eighty-five cents, all right—sixty from them and my quarter. I had to eat quick and get back to the corner, so I gave the money to ma.

I was full of my secret that afternoon, but had made the second graders promise they would not tell; each of them nodding solemnly at me, lips tight.

That day after school, after we'd got all our classes across the intersection, there was a cop meeting in Miss Thompson's office. She talked about our deportment. Our deportment must always be the best, she said, in school and during noon hour, and even after school. Even on the playground or even at the movies or if we were downtown with our mas, we had to behave like leaders, because we were leaders, she said. Then she made hot chocolate for us on the electric plate she had, and afterward, between the eight of us, four on each side, we walked with her to Robert Street, eight of us across Robert Street, holding up traffic while Miss Thompson crossed. She bowed to us when she had crossed the street, and I hurried home to tell ma.

That night after supper, when the dishes were finished, ma gave me an empty tea can. She bought tea in red, maybe six-inch-high, tin cans, and this was to be my bank. I got a slit in the top with a chisel and hammer, and then ma wrapped it—the can—in red and blue crepe paper she had up on the shelf in the closet. She taped it up all pretty, and I dropped the coins in one by one. I took the tin bank to bed with me, and I lay there shaking it quietly, I thought, until I dropped off to sleep.

That first Saturday, after a week of collections, ma took me downtown to the dentist. Afterward, still feeling the drill in my mouth, we walked to Seventh Street and the department stores. I guess that in my head I bought everything I saw that day. The windows were full of toys. I'd never been touched one way or the other by these displays, because always, without ma telling me, I knew how meager our Christmas would be. I don't even remember my father; he died when my brother Phil was born, and I guess we were pretty poor.

I sure got crazy that day, though. Cripes, I wanted to get everything for those kids, and ma took me from one store to the next, and never said a word, never put the damper on my talk. I did it myself, coming home on the South St. Paul trolley. My teeth had stopped aching then, and I said, "I can't buy that stuff for the kids, ma."

"No, son."

"Gee, I must be nuts thinking of that stuff."

"One day, Joe."

"Yeah? When?" We were crossing the bridge, and I watched a barge coming down the Mississippi, and I was the captain taking her down through St. Louis and into New Orleans and out into the Gulf of Mexico. "When, ma?"

"When you have your children, son; your own children."

"Yeah. Well, we'll have to think of something to buy those kids." I felt very old.

"You'll buy good things for them," she said.

That tin box got pretty full by the last week. There were mostly pennies and nickels, you see, and it got pretty heavy. During the day ma kept it in her kitchen cabinet, but at night, after supper, I'd keep it on the kitchen table next to me, holding it with my hand while I read or did my homework.

The last week the kids were on me all the time, and I had to bring some of them home with me after school to show them the box. Thinking of it now—how those six-year-olds kept their secret, not even telling their parents; never knowing, really, whether there would be a party, but, having promised, keeping their promises—thinking of it, I wonder at the trust of the very young—the simple, complete faith in whatever is told them.

Wednesday night ma and I talked about the presents, and she got it. She said what to buy, finally. I could get a huge fruit basket from the Italian. He'd fix me a beautiful basket, she said, and I could carry that into the second-grade room, bring it right in there and put it on Miss Le Tourneau's desk, and there would be the surprise. She said the Italian would wrap portions for everyone, and all of it under cellophane paper.

I got the tin box and, after the dishes, I walked to the Italian's. Do I remember him? I can tell you now how he looked—a thin, short man, always with a two-day growth of beard, and always with a white apron, and his shop the cleanest, the freshest-smelling place in all the world. He was alone in the shop when I came in, and he said, "What do I do for you, little mister?"

"I want a basket," I said. "A fruit basket."

"Sure, then. Absolute. How much money for the basket, little mister?"

I walked to the side, to a wrapping board slung beneath the orange racks, and I set the tin box down. I didn't let him help me, but worked it open myself, tearing the tape and the crepe paper, and finally pulling the lid back. He was a wise man, I guess, for I remember he let me count it all, waiting while I sorted pennies—hundreds of pennies—and nickels and dimes and ma's quarters. I counted it once and it was $11.70, and then I counted it again. He counted it the third time, and I told him there'd be $1.30 more. I told him I had some more money coming, but with the secretiveness of youth would not divulge my plot. I couldn't, you see, for I would then betray my kids and myself.

"You buy this all for the school?" he asked, looking at the belt.

So I nodded yes. I could not tell, and there was the admiration in his face, the warm glow in his eyes at this youngster who bought such a present with his money. Of course I was guilty, taking the credit this way, but I was ten. I was ten years old, you understand.

He took my hand and he showed me what there would be in the basket. He showed me tangerines and he showed me huge, thick-skinned oranges. He showed me the beautiful, baseball-sized Jonathan apples and pomegranates, nectarines from Florida, bananas and those yellow, soft, juicy oranges. He showed me walnuts and hazel nuts, Brazils, cashews. He showed me tiny, bright-colored boxes of animal crackers, and he showed me candy canes.

"Oh-ho!" he said. "What a basket I make for you, little mister," and he showed me the basket, bushel-sized, the woven strips green and red and blue and pink. "Oh-ho!" said the Italian. "I make you prettiest basket in St. Paul, you bet."

Thursday after school I collected four cents from each kid while they besieged me with questions. I must tell them now, they pleaded, but I'd kept the secret for so long and so well that now I could only pledge them to continue waiting.

There behind the station house I outlined my plans, all of them gathered about me while I spoke. The next morning in their room they were not to answer the roll call. They were all to sit straight, hands clasped on the desks, and when Miss Le Tourneau started the roll, they were to be silent. They were to wait, did they understand?

I would get them all across Robert Street, and then I'd go for the present. I'd have the present in my room, and after my roll call, then Miss Morgan would excuse me and I'd bring the present down to their room. Far from being angry, Miss Le Tourneau would be the happiest teacher in the school.

They were fascinated by the cabal. I remember their eyes alive, and each looking from one to the other, delighted with the intrigue. My heart pounded with the telling of it and I felt then as though I were leading a revolution, as though here, with my army, I, the general, planned a swift, bloodless coup.

That night I brought the Italian the rest of the money, and then, while I watched, he began preparing the basket. He gave me a tangerine, and I stripped it clean, eating a section at a time, feeling the tang of it and the juice of it far back in my throat.

He was a surgeon now, the Italian, and this his operating room. The basket was set on a long sheet of cellophane there on his table in the back room. He wrapped small balls of fruit—apples, tangerines and oranges—then a candy cane, a box of animal crackers, and on top of each a container of peppermint. He wrapped thirty of them, and I told him about the teacher, and he wrapped a special bag for her. I stayed until the basket was ready, until he had brought the cellophane up and around the basket, the bags within lying alongside giant oranges and grapefruit. I stayed until he had tied it all with a red silk ribbon. I told him then that I'd come for it the next morning, and he gave me another tangerine.

"You are a fine boy, little mister," he said.

"Thank you."

"By golly, not many boys think to bring such a presents for school friends. For teacher."

"Thank you," I said again.

"If I have a boy 'stead of four girls, like I have, then I sure wish boy to be like you, little mister," he said.

"Thank you. I better be going home," I said.

"Oh-ho," he laughed. "Momma waits now, eh?"

Of that night I can't remember anything now. I can't remember whether I slept or talked with my ma first or whether I had milk before bed. I can't remember any of it, but of the activity the next morning, of the affair then, I can recall everything, and I can yet, even as I write now, feel the trembling in my stomach, the dry throat, the cold hand at my heart. I've remembered that morning always at Christmas, and now it becomes difficult to move the pen across paper.

All right, then. I went first to the Italian's who had the basket on a small wagon. He told me I could take the wagon and return it at lunch hour.

To the kids who crowded around me there at the intersection I repeated my instructions, pledging them to silence when the roll was called. I hurried them across quickly, and then ran down the block to the Italian's. You remember that my world was bounded on the south by Isabel Street. I walked around Isabel, behind the school, and then, leaving the wagon, came in by a narrow door used by the janitors. The basket was awfully heavy. I remember now pausing at the foot of the stairs and again at the top of the first flight.

I got the basket into my room, set it on my desk, pushed my way through the kids who gathered around the basket, and hurried down the hall, down the stairs to the first floor and the second grade. They were all at their desks, and I stood a moment inside the door, forefinger at my lips, until I heard the teachers talking in the distance and scurried to the water fountain to pretend I was drinking.

There I waited until Miss Le Tourneau had passed, until she had entered the room, and then, unmindful of the bell, tiptoed to the door and looked in. She was at her desk, arranging her books, smiling at the class. They, the little, obedient soldiers, sat with hands clasped, unsmiling and waiting.

So the end was near, the weeks of waiting finished, the surprise at hand. I was ten, remember, but I took the first four steps in one leap, and then, holding to the railing, flew up the two flights, down the hall and into my room for the basket. Miss Morgan would excuse me; I knew she'd excuse me.

She was pleased. She smiled at me as I entered, turning her head from the kids gathered around the basket as she watched them digging into it. "Joe"—she smiled and she beckoned to me with her hand—"Joe, this is wonderful and thoughtful of you."

But I couldn't move, you see. I stood just inside the door, motionless, and I couldn't move. The cellophane had been ripped off the basket, scattered about the floor. The oranges, the grapefruit, the lovely, lovely, individual packages that the

Italian had wrapped were now in the hands of my class. Of course, the kids here had thought it was their present and had torn the cellophane immediately.

"Joe," she said, "how nice of you, and sweet. A Christmas surprise," she said.

The kids didn't even turn. They were too busy digging into the basket. I saw the cellophane scattered over the floor, and now I wanted only to get away, to run to my mother, to get to the closet there in the front hall of our house and pull the door behind me and lie forever in the dark and never be discovered. They'd come for my belt and badge, and I'd never be a school cop again.

And those kids. I could feel the tears coming, and I could only look at Miss Morgan, seeing her red hair in the sunlight. Those kids! Sitting there and not answering the roll and waiting for me! Holy smokes, those kids!

I ran. I turned and ran from the room, leaving my cap in the cloakroom, thinking, as I ran, that my ma could come back for it. I'd never return to this school; I couldn't.

Down the stairs, down the hall, panting now, my breath coming short, and I remember kind of groaning in sorrow and self-pity as I ran. I can remember my life broken, my world shattered, the years to come shadowed always by this horrible, horrible thing that had happened to me. Those kids and their two pennies every day. This had happened because there were thirteen dollars, because I hadn't been honest with the Italian, let him think it was all my party, and then I began to sob. I sobbed then, but it wasn't until I stood outside their door, standing on tiptoe and looking in through the round window, seeing Miss Le Tourneau standing before her desk, the kids white and frightened, but still silent, waiting now for their leader and general, it wasn't until then that the tears came. I should have gone in, right? Entered and told Miss Le Tourneau, right? But I was ten, and I'd been betrayed, you see, and now I could only move away from the door, unable to check the tears, moving blindly for the outside door and my ma and the closet.

I didn't see them—neither Miss Thompson nor the Italian—but I heard them behind me. "Joe," she said. "Oh, Joe, wait," she said, and I moved faster then, wanting to get to the front doors before she could stop me.

"Him," I heard the Italian say. "Is him, tha's little mister, sure. . . . Hey, boy," he said. "Hey, boy," he said, and now I thought that I had done something wrong to him, too, that he had come for me. I walked faster, head down and then he had my arm, turning me so that Miss Thompson saw I was weeping, and he saw it and became silent. He squatted like a baseball catcher, the apron trailing on the floor, and he took my arms.

"Wha's matter you, boy?" he asked. He looked up at Miss Thompson. "Wha's matter here, Miss Thompson?" he asked, and then she knelt.

"I'm so proud of you, son," she said. "Mr. Par—Par ——"

"Paradino, Miss Thompson. Me, Paradino. George Paradino."

"Mr. Paradino came to tell me of your wonderful gift," she said, and I looked from one to the other, the tears gone now, and sick with the knowledge of how it might have been.

"The basket, Joe," she said. "Mr. Paradino was so impressed with your gesture that he brought a basket, too, and told me about what you had done."

"Sure," the Italian said. "Absolute," he said. "You do him, little mister. You do him, so I do him. Me, citizen, George Paradino," he said, and smiled at me.

So I've told you of no miracle and I've offered no proof of Santa Claus nor shown signs of angels. Thus it happened in 1928. Miss Thompson listened as I blurted out the story, and the Italian, George Paradino, carried his basket into the second grade, I following, and then Miss Thompson.

That afternoon they had their party and we had ours upstairs, and Miss Thompson came to both. It was all right then, you see, and Miss Le Tourneau came up and shook my hand, and Miss Morgan was proud of me, she said.

Later, after I'd got the second graders across Robert Street, standing there with the other cops, we saw Miss Thompson, and we all ran forward to meet her and take her across. But she took my arm and she smiled at me. She smiled then, all right, and her face was warm and friendly, all right.

"Thank you, boys," she said to the others, and then to me: "Will you escort me," she asked, smiling still, "little mister?" she said.

LITTLE MISS NOBODY

By PATTERSON McNUTT

E DIDN'T know it at the time, but when Dave Sturgeon
and I were digging for a story gimmick on a Larry
Danforth picture we were really cooking up one of those
Hollywood wars. Those battles in the picture business are
always strictly from Hatfield and McCoy, and by the time we
washed up this Danforth thing we were all tangled up in one
of those screwy knife-throwing acts.

Dave is an old-timer in Hollywood, and when I was writing
shooting script for him on the Danforth picture he was a hot-
shot director who was really doing all right for himself on the
Superba Pictures lot. Al Spengler was running the studio, and
whenever Dave wanted to go places where it might be very
nice to be, Al would never slow him up with too many questions about how he was going to get there. He'd figure that
a director like Dave would probably know his way around,
and right away he'd just give him the green light.

Both Dave and Al were show-business gamblers who were
strictly high players. Any time they got together on a picture
they were always shooting for nothing but a smasheroo. It was
a nice setup all the way around, and if it hadn't been for a
couple of nickel-nursing dopes by the names of Ben Brockman
and George Bledsoe there wouldn't have been any war. Bledsoe
was a New York banker and chairman of Superba's board of
directors, and while Spengler was making the top pictures at
Superba, Brockman was producing all the B pictures for the
studio. These pictures are those quickie cheeseolas you will
always find on the second half of a double-feature bill, but
Brockman always turned 'em out for nickels and dimes, and
Bledsoe practically wanted to get married with the guy. It
was when they ganged up on Spengler that those knives I was
talking about really got a workout.

A Danforth picture was a gravy assignment. Once a week
Larry was crooning those torch numbers on the radio, and
whenever he turned his trick tonsils loose in a picture, the

bobby-soxers would practically break down the doors to get in. But Dave went looking for trouble when he asked Al Spengler for a green light on Molly Dugan. When Dave first met up with Molly, she was only six years old, and except for a few people in Hollywood, nobody had ever even heard of her. With the customers at this time Molly was strictly little Miss Nobody.

Dave met up with Molly after we had lunch off the lot one day with Danforth, while we were all trying to come up with some kind of gimmick which would at least give us a start on a story for Larry. When we were finished with lunch we were still fresh out of this gimmick, but when we went back to the studio, the thing practically jumped up in our laps. We were on our way through the front gate when we noticed that there was quite a little crowd of extra people just outside the gate. They were bunched up in a circle, and they were clapping their hands and stamping their feet as if they were keeping time to some kind of music.

"What gives?" Dave asked the cop at the gate.

"There's a terrific kid in there," the cop told him. "You'd oughta get a load of her, Mr. Sturgeon."

"A show-business kid?" Dave shuddered a little. "Not me, brother. They've all got mothers."

Maybe this cop should have been an agent. He grabbed Dave by the arm, wouldn't let him through the gate.

"Wait a minute, Mr. Sturgeon," the cop said. "This kid's different."

"No mother?" Dave asked him.

"But smart," the cop said. "This kid's really been handled right, Mr. Sturgeon. No cute stuff that gags you, and she won't knock you down with that brass either. I've got money says the kid doesn't even know she's good."

"That I gotta see," Dave said.

Larry and I couldn't believe it either, and when Dave moved in on this crowd of extras we joined up with him. It was the usual picture mob you will always see around the front gate at Superba when the sound stages break for lunch—Indians and cowboys from some Western set, dress extras working a night-club number, some bridesmaids from a big church scene and a couple of pirates and a beachcomber doing one of those

South Sea island things. Most of them had worked with Dave in other pictures, and when we moved in, they opened up for us.

"Here's your chance, Molly!" one of them yelled. "Now you can do your stuff for a big shot!"

"Give with that Annie Laurie number, Molly!" another one called out. "Swing it for him, honey!"

Molly was a chunky little kid, and the first time Dave got a look at her she was dolled up in kilts and a pair of tap shoes. She had a nice thick mop of curls, and there was something about the look of her eyes that gave you a quick jolt. They were such solemn eyes, as if they were haunted by the memory of a time when Molly had been badly hurt.

The cop on the gate was right about Molly. She didn't have any tricks. When Dave squatted down alongside of her, she was just Molly, and Dave could take it or leave it. One of the reasons Dave was a top-drawer director was that he was both smart and sensitive in the way he handled people, and with Molly you could tell he'd really made up his mind quick.

"I just came in, honey," Dave said to her. "But the way I heard it, you can sing a song called Annie Laurie. Is that right?"

"Yes, sir," Molly said. "I can sing Annie Laurie."

"Would you sing it for me?" Dave asked her.

"I will dance it for you too," Molly said.

Molly didn't have any help with that Annie Laurie number. She had no make-up, no lights, no music, no set back of her. But what Molly did have is that thing you can't ever tag in show business. She had that thing that grabs at your heart; that thing that made you watch everything she did as if you were a little bit hypnotized.

The first time around, Molly sang the number almost straight. There was just enough burr in her accent to give you at least a small whiff of the bluebells and the heather. But the real build-up of the number was when she did a swing version of the old tune, and practically knocked herself out with a tap routine. When she went into her dance, her stubby little legs were really flying, her curls were all over her face and she was blowing like a little porpoise.

"Thank you." Dave squatted down again with Molly when she'd finished the number. "Thank you very much."

"You're welcome," Molly said.

"What's your name?" Dave asked her.

"Molly," she said. "Molly Dugan."

"Well, now, that's a mighty pretty name," Dave told her. "My name is Dave. Dave Sturgeon."

"That's a pretty name too," Molly said.

Dave now discovered that Molly could also get laughs, and nice laughs at that. When those extras were quiet again, he asked her the sixty-four-dollar question. When she didn't even go cute on this one, Molly was practically Dave's dream girl.

"Maybe you might sing a song for me someday in a picture," Dave told her. "Would you like to be in a picture with me, Molly?"

Molly just looked at Dave for a second with those big wide eyes. His question seemed to puzzle her a little.

"I guess so," she said. "My mom could tell you."

Molly was doing all right for herself. She'd already vamped an ace director, and now she added a No. 1 box-office star to her string.

"She can be in a picture with me, Dave," Larry Danforth said. "With the right kind of song numbers, I'll go out there in front of those cameras with Molly any day of the week. And I guarantee we'll murder 'em."

You could hear those extras gasp. It was as though they were all holding their breath for Molly. Larry was really going places fast with the kid, but all of a sudden Dave flagged him down.

"Take it easy, honey," he warned Larry. "We just had a look at something, but how do you know we can find a spot for it? Why make this racket any tougher for the kid than it already is?"

Now Dave spoke again with Molly.

"Maybe I'd better have a talk with your mom, honey," he told her. "Where is she?"

"Over there." Molly pointed across the street. "Come on. I will show you my mom."

Molly's mother was sitting on a bench in front of a little

lunchroom joint which is just across the street from the front gate at Superba. She was a pretty woman, dressed in a pleated gray skirt with a light-blue sweater and scarf to match. You'd guess her age at about twenty-five. When we all showed up with Molly, she stood up to meet us, and you didn't need more than a quick once-over to realize where Molly got that solemn look in her eyes. Sometime—and it was a good gamble it hadn't happened so long ago—Molly's mother had been hurt pretty badly herself.

She was proud of Molly, but immediately defensive. She couldn't wait to explain both the cause and the purpose of Molly's sidewalk routine. She told us that they'd come from the East, that they'd been in Hollywood for only a month. Kids on the make for a shot at pictures are a dime a dozen in Hollywood, and they hadn't been able to get even close to a casting office. Ditto for the agents. After she'd knocked on all the doors in town, and they wouldn't open up for her, Molly's mother got the idea that Molly herself might kick those doors open with a dance routine. Maybe, if every day Molly would just do her stuff on the sidewalk in front of one of the big studios, they might attract the attention of a passing big shot.

Dave was the big shot they'd been looking for, and there wasn't any doubt that Molly had clicked with him. But Dave is always a smart showman, and he was still playing it cagey.

"I won't promise a thing, Mrs. Dugan," he did give just a little, "but there's at least a chance anyway that those doors might swing open for you. I will guarantee you this much: If I ever have a spot for Molly, I'll see she gets a shot at it."

Molly's mother could hardly talk. She just looked at Dave and swallowed hard. "Oh," she did manage a whisper. "Oh, dear."

"If I should have a spot, we'll want to make a test," Dave told her. "Where can we get in touch with you?"

"We haven't got a place to stay yet," she said. "A permanent place, I mean. We've been living in auto courts, and every few days we have to move. But you can always reach me where I work."

"Oh?" Dave said. "Where's that?"

"It's a drive-in at Beverly and La Brea," she said. "I'm behind the counter there every night from six to two. I took a night job, so that during the day I could be with Molly at the studios."

When she told us that one, something happened with Larry Danforth. He went overboard. He lifted Molly off the sidewalk and cradled her on his arm. When she was comfortable, he asked her if she could keep a little secret with him.

"I guess so," Molly said. "What kind of a secret?"

"It's a special kind of a secret," Larry said. "You can tell your mom, but nobody else."

Molly liked this. She smiled at Larry. "All right," she said. "What is the secret?"

Larry didn't try to whisper it into her ear. We could all hear it.

"You're due for the jack pot, honey," Larry said. "You and your mom both. I can feel it. Maybe that won't seem like much of a secret to you, Molly, but I've got a hunch your mom might get quite a bang out of it."

The build-up was still too fast for Dave. He didn't like any part of it, and when we were in his office in the studio, he put Larry on the pan again.

"That kid and her mother are nice people, Larry," he said. "Why take a chance on breaking their hearts?"

"I know what kind of people they are," Larry said. "They're my kind of people, Dave. When I was a kid back in New York, maybe only a couple of years older than Molly is right now, I was making my first dough out of show business. Every night I was hustling the sidewalks around Broadway, singing and hoofing for the intermission crowds at the theaters. The nickels and dimes I took home were plenty important, but I still can't forget the nights when a nickel's worth of hope would have meant more to my mother than a dollar bill. The build-up with Molly and her mother was strong on purpose, Dave. The way they were looking at us, I had a hunch they could use some hope. I had a hunch they could use it right now, and plenty of it."

After you've been around show business for a while, you never pay too much attention when an actor blows his topper, the way Larry was doing with Dave. Selling emotion is an actor's business, and if you're not careful, they can make you

buy anything. If they're good at it, they always sell themselves first, and whenever that happens they're really peddling
gospel. Larry was plenty good, but Dave was smart enough to
be skeptical.

"Maybe I'd better pin you down," he said to Larry. "You
told Molly and her mother they were due for the jack pot.
There's only one way that could happen right away, Larry.
Molly would have to have a top part in a picture with you.
You know that, don't you? The kid's got stuff, but nobody else
in town has bought it yet."

"Okay," Larry said. "What's wrong with that?"

"Maybe a lot," Dave told him. "The sure-fire box-office setup with you is one of those boy-meets-girl routines, with a
torchy dame like Dottie Lawton handing you plenty of that
gimme-gimme in the big song numbers. If you were in a boy-
meets-Molly Dugan story, the bobby-soxers might decide to
stay home for a change. You might be talking yourself into
a flopperoo, Larry."

"Could be," Larry admitted. "But I'd still like to take a
chance."

Dave still couldn't quite believe it. He gave Larry one more
test.

"Maybe you'd like to make it official," he said. "Are you
telling me you want us to dream up a story so this kid can be
your next leading lady?"

Larry laid it right on the line. "I wish I was running the
studio," he said. "I'd make that an order."

All of a sudden, Dave was sold. He was sold up to here.

"Who wants to bet on sure things?" he grinned at Larry.
"It's when you're cashing those long shots that you really
get a charge out of this screwy business."

Now Dave turned to me. He was really beginning to get
hopped up over the idea of giving Molly her big break.

"You know something?" he said. "We might make this
one just for fun. Be nice, huh?"

Molly's test was nothing but a breeze. She clicked on film,
just as she had out on that sidewalk the first time we saw
her at the front gate. And it was Molly's mother who gave us
the story gimmick we were looking for. Dave and I were both
nuts about that wistful thing Molly had in her eyes, and we

figured if we could handle it right, she might break your heart with that look. It was her mother who told me where that look came from.

Molly's father was a small-time hoofer. He was nuts about the kid, and practically from the time she could walk, he was teaching her those dance routines. Three months before Molly showed up in Hollywood she was trouping with her father and mother in one of those honky-tonk carnival outfits. There was a night when the troupe was moving during a bad storm, and one of the carnival trucks went over the side of a mountain.

Molly's father was killed. They buried him in a little town in Virginia and stayed on with the carnival till the end of the summer season. Molly's mother was working in the cook tent and helping out with wardrobe, but all they were getting was coffee-and-cake money, and when they started for Hollywood at the end of the season, they had to hitchhike.

It was a natural for a picture setup almost the way she told it to me. There were both color and heartbreak in the carnival thing, and we knew there'd be good pictorial stuff and a chance for off-beat musical numbers when we were shooting the hitchhiking sequences. We picked up Larry in one of the auto camps, made him a one-time hot-shot crooner with a big band who was on the skids because he couldn't handle the bottle. When they first got together, Molly was on the way up, Larry was on the way down. Regeneration for Larry because of Molly and her mother. Triumph at the finish for all of them. It wasn't a yarn that would win any Academy Awards, but there was some heart in the thing, and it was loose enough so we could always find room for the musical numbers that would really sell the picture.

Al Spengler was a pushover for Molly's test.

"She's nice," he told Dave, after they'd looked at the test in Al's projection room. "Maybe she's better than nice. That we'll know when an audience tells us. While we are waiting for Mr. and Mrs. Public to make up their minds, maybe the little girl would be happy with seventy-five bucks a week. The day she starts work on the picture, we will sign up a long-term contract. When the picture's released, if she is then maybe sensational, like you think, every week we will pay her so much money she will have to stand up on a chair to see over it."

It was a square shake, and Dave knew there wouldn't be any argument with Molly's mother. He asked Al if he wanted us to tell him our story. Spengler laughed at him.

"Story headaches you are welcome to," he said. "I've already got all the headaches I can use, just running the joint. All I'm asking is you will make me a good picture. If you are smart enough maybe, and we are both of us lucky, we will even have a good picture which will also make money. If we are neither one of us lucky, Dave, we should both of us be looking around right away for some other kind of a business."

Two months after Spengler gave us the green light on Molly, we were all set with a finished shooting script. Spengler had given us the top song-writing team on the lot, and we were nuts about the words and music they'd turned in. We were all getting a wallop out of the idea of putting Molly across, and it was as Dave said it would be. We really were doing this one for fun. We were practically ready for those cameras to roll, and nobody had had a headache yet.

And then, boom! The roof fell in! All of a sudden we had a brand-new Mr. Big at Superba, and right away we were all of us up to here with those headaches. Our new Mr. Big was nobody else than George Bledsoe's nickel-nursing pal, Ben Brockman.

"Switcheroo at Superba!" Variety spread the news with its usual show-business lingo. "A's for Brockman, B's for Spengler!"

That knife-throwing act was really on the bill again, and both sides were playing for keeps. Brockman had just come back from New York. While he was East he'd snuggled up to George Bledsoe and all the other bankers who were handling Superba's stock. He'd been making those B pictures plenty cheap, and he sold the bankers on the idea that he could make the big A productions for a lot less money than Al Spengler was spending on our top pictures.

It all added up to bad news for Molly. No long shots for Brockman. He was strictly a sure-thing player, and he didn't want any part of Molly. Our picture for Molly and Larry went out the window quick, and when that happened, those knives really started to fly. Both Dave and Larry said if they couldn't do the picture with Molly, they'd take a suspension. Brockman gave it to them. But quick. It was costing Dave three grand a week while he was in the doghouse, and any time Larry couldn't make a picture he was out a hundred and fifty thousand. The rent they were paying was plenty high, but both Dave and Larry said they'd never come out of that doghouse on their hands and knees.

If it hadn't been for Al Spengler, they might be in there yet. Al was really an old-timer in Hollywood. He was around when a custard pie and a baggy-pants cop were the biggest things in pictures, and he knew all about those throat-cutting routines. Whenever anybody started tossing those knives, Al was a handy man to have on your side. It was about a week after Dave and Larry went on the suspended list when Al asked them both to drop into his office.

Dave showed up ahead of Larry, and he was a little surprised to find Al looking very cheerful. There'd been some talk around the studio that Spengler might resign before he ever actually made one of those dopey B pictures, but when Dave walked in on him, Al didn't seem to have a care in the world. When Dave sat down at his desk, Al handed him a copy of one of the trade papers. He asked Dave to look at a gossip item he'd marked with a pencil.

"Maybe you will know if this means anything," Al said. "If it does mean something, it might be good news for both of us. Also it might be bad news for a certain party whose name I will not mention, but whose initials are Ben Brockman."

The item was brief. Also, after the publicity we'd had about Molly's discovery, it was very much to the point.

"What radio and picture crooner is drinking plenty of coffee these nights at what Beverly Boulevard drive-in?" the thing read. "And is it just the coffee he's putting away that's giving him those dizzy spells in the daytime?"

Dave looked up at Al.

"It's on the level," he told him. "They're really overboard for each other. Or at least they were, before the picture was called off. What happens now I wouldn't know about."

Now Spengler was really beaming.

"On what happens now I got a terrific hunch," he said. "On our side, Dave, we got love. How could we lose?"

It was a cinch that Al was working on some kind of a hot angle, but Dave couldn't figure it. When Larry showed up, Al mapped it out for both of them.

"I would like to do Brockman quite a little favor," he said. "Maybe you boys could help me."

"Quit kidding, Al," Dave said. "What's on your mind?"

"On account of the big story charge on the picture you cooked up for Larry and Molly," Al said, "Brockman is beefing like he was spending his own money. Including the music, this story is already costing the studio a hundred and ten thousand bucks. Brockman is now screaming his lungs out about this dough, and he's telling me it is only fair I should be willing to take this script and make it now as a B picture. You will understand that when Brockman is asking me to be fair, he is only hoping I will maybe be a sucker and let myself get stuck with this script."

Larry was touchy about that script. Now he burned a little with Al.

"Nobody's a sucker who does that one," he said. "That's a good script, Al."

"Maybe I should explain you something," Al said. "With me it is a terrific script. A couple of the songs, the way you and Molly could sing them together, should be on the Hit Parade. But now I am making the B product for the studio I am allowed to spend no more than four hundred thousand dollars on any one picture. If I would start with a charge of a hundred and ten thousand dollars for my story, I would have to make the picture only with Molly and a lot of other actors nobody ever heard of either. Also the director I could afford would be strictly a cluck. So what happens? But nobody buys a ticket, the picture shows a terrific loss, and then those bankers would be telling me I couldn't even make B pictures any more. So, when that happens, maybe you think Brockman would be crying his eyes out."

"He's right, Larry," Dave said. "With her first picture Molly's got to be teamed up with a box-office name."

"That part I am now coming to," Al said. "While you are on suspension, Larry, you are not getting a nickel from the studio?"

"No," Larry said.

"Also you can't take money for making a picture anywhere else?" Al asked him.

"That's right," Larry agreed.

Al turned to Dave. "It is also the same with you, Dave?" he asked.

"You know it is," Dave said. "Brockman's got us both hooked. So what about it?"

"So maybe we all give up too easy, Dave," Al told him. "Maybe, if we would always just keep right on being smart, nobody would ever stay hooked very long. If we are smart enough, it might even be somebody else who would be hooked."

Now Al played his trump card. It was a big ace.

"Now I will tell you something about your contracts which maybe you wouldn't know about," he said. "Not even away back in the fine print is there anything in your contracts which says that either one of you couldn't make a picture for nothing. Are you maybe beginning to catch on a little?"

Dave was looking at Al as if he were hypnotized. Just for a second or two he couldn't even talk, but when he found some words again, he was really making plans.

"You're right, Al," he said. "We do give up too easy. But I'm getting smart enough again to buy this one. Why, the thing's perfect. We still give Molly her crack at a big break, and if we come up with a real clickeroo, we'll make a Grade-A chump out of Brockman. While we're doing it, on account of Larry and I are both on suspension anyway, it isn't costing either one of us a nickel. After we wind this one up for free, we tell Brockman we're ready to go to work again, and right away he's got to let us out of the doghouse. When we come out of there, we're handing him the biggest horselaugh in town. . . . How's about it, Larry? Have we got a deal?"

"Don't be a dope." Larry now had a grin on his pan from here to there. "All I'm worried about is that Brockman might still be able to find some way so he could even stop this one."

"Don't worry," Al told him. "The way it is now around here, Brockman is doing the A pictures and I'm doing the B's. Just how I am making these B pictures, as long as I am never spending more than four hundred thousand dollars, is strictly my business. Even those dopey bankers wouldn't argue about that."

"Wait a minute, Al." Dave was suddenly alarmed. "How's about those bankers, honey? This thing is perfect for me and Larry, but maybe you're leading with your chin. Maybe back in New York they won't like it so well if you make a chump out of their new Mr. Big."

"With you, Dave," Al said, "I will make a little deal. You worry about the picture, I will worry about bankers. Already I am cooking up an angle which could maybe be dynamite with those bankers."

"Yeah?" Dave grinned at Al. "Such as what, honey?"

"No questions, Dave," Al said. "This angle I am speaking about I am keeping strictly to myself."

There's one thing about show business that always gives me a special jolt. It's the fastest crap game in the world. Any time you roll 'em out there in show business, you're always shooting for seven, eleven or snake eyes. Whenever you ask Mr. and Mrs. Public to tell you what you've got, they never keep you waiting. They tell you quick, and their answer is never qualified. With Mr. and Mrs. Public it's either thumbs up or thumbs down.

They told us quick about Molly. We previewed the picture in Santa Barbara, and Mr. and Mrs. Public told us what we had with their laughter and their tears. They told us some more when they filled the shadowy theater with that special and electric excitement which always attends the birth of a new star. The comments of the preview cards only added to the jubilant tale of Molly's triumph. We were told again when the preview was finished, and Molly came into the theater lobby with her mother and Larry Danforth. The police had to be called to clear a path to Larry's car. Molly Dugan, in only a little more than an hour, had become a celebrity.

The day after the preview, Al Spengler's office was littered with the evidence of Molly's success. An office couch was stacked high with bundles of enthusiastic preview cards, and the glowing notices in the trade papers were spread face up on Al's desk. I stopped in to see him around noon. Dave and Larry were there ahead of me, and we spent a pleasant half hour handing one another bows. Our mutual-admiration society was presently broken up by the summons of a phone on Spengler's desk. When Al answered the call, he suddenly stiffened a little, as if this was a message he had anticipated and for which he was especially prepared. He listened attentively for a moment, and then he spoke warmly to the mouthpiece of the phone.

"Why, sure, George," he said. "Be glad to see both of you. Only the way it is today, George, I'm a very busy man just taking those bows. Maybe you could see me in my office, huh? . . . Okay, George. Right away."

Al hung up the phone. He looked at us with a grin of pure contentment.

"When Brockman goes to New York he snuggles up with bankers," he said. "Now the bankers are coming to Hollywood, and they're snuggling up with me. My way I think I like best."

"What gives?" Dave asked him.

"Right away we're having company," Al explained. "And big shots, no less. Maybe you wouldn't believe it, but George Bledsoe and Ben Brockman are both on their way over here right now. Only B pictures I'm producing, but all of a sudden the chairman of our board of directors and the head of the studio are both dying unless they can talk to me right away. I can't understand it."

"Neither can I." Dave was grinning at Al. "But if I know anything about this screwy business, I'd say you've got a knife up your sleeve right now that's about this long. Do you mind if we stick around and watch you use it?"

"Do I mind!" Al's chuckle was gleeful. "Look, Dave. Like everybody else in pictures, I've got plenty of ham in me. With Brockman and Bledsoe I am playing my big scene. Should I be a dope and chase away my audience?"

Al gave his big scene a good build-up. When Bledsoe and Brockman arrived, there was a hearty exchange of greetings, and boisterous laughter followed the most feeble witticisms. A half hour was used up with idle gossip of mutual friends in New York, but while the talk went on there was a mounting tension in the room. It was Spengler who presently decided that the mood of their banter had properly prepared the way for the special scene he wanted to play with his antagonists.

"Maybe we should all quit stalling?" He was abruptly blunt. "Maybe we should all lay it on the line, huh?"

"Perhaps that would be best," Bledsoe cautiously agreed.

"Okay," Al said. "The way it is now, Molly Dugan is worth at least one million dollars a year to any studio in town. When I was making the A pictures here, I signed up Molly to a studio contract. To begin with, she was getting only seventy-five bucks a week, but when Brockman moved into the A spot here, Molly was fired."

Brockman reddened, glanced nervously at Bledsoe.

"I've explained to George how that happened," Brockman said. "A mistake was made by the legal department. They were supposed to take up her option, but instead ——"

"So for lawyers around here we've got dopes," Spengler conceded the point. "Is that any reason I should be a dope myself? On account of once in a while anyway I am at least a little bit smart about my own business, Molly Dugan is now under personal contract to me. She is under contract to me for the next seven years, and we are both of us sitting pretty. This afternoon I could take her out to Warner Brothers, and just to start with, they would give her at least twenty-five hundred bucks a week."

"Now wait a minute, Al," Bledsoe protested. "That wouldn't be fair. You must admit that Superba should have first chance at the little girl's contract."

"Did I say no?" Al demanded. "But with Superba there would be some special conditions. Maybe you and Brockman wouldn't like them so much, George?"

"We're listening," Bledsoe said. "What conditions?"

"Twenty-five hundred a week for Molly," Al said. "What she gets after the first year we will worry about later. Superba will also pay Larry Danforth and Dave Sturgeon their regular wages for the picture with Molly they just did for free."

"We can make a deal," Brockman said. "I'll okay that."

Brockman was really leading with his chin. Maybe he was a little too anxious.

"The way it is now, Ben, we will make a deal when I say we do," Al said. "And only when I say so. We will make a deal when George tells me that you are again producing the B pictures around here, and I am once more making the A pictures.

Only this time my deal will be fixed up so that once in a while anyway I can turn my back and not worry about getting my ribs carved up while I'm not looking. Okay, George?"

Al had aces wired. Bledsoe knew it, but for an instant he hesitated. Brockman, watching Bledsoe, paled a little. Abruptly he knew that he was licked.

"One million dollars a year," Al seemed to be tasting the phrase. "And from here to Warner Brothers it's only a half-hour trip. Make up your mind, George."

Bledsoe wasn't a bad sport. When he threw in his hand he even managed a rueful chuckle. "Okay, Al," he said. "You win."

Maybe actors have elephant blood in their veins. The beating that Brockman was taking was plenty brutal, but Larry Danforth still wasn't satisfied. When he came back from his honeymoon in Mexico with Molly's mother, he brought Brockman a present. It was a little clay figure of a donkey. He sent it to Brockman's office with a short note.

"Herewith an Oscar of sorts," the note read. "With love and kisses, to the Keeper of the B's."

HOLIDAY OF A STAR

By PHYLLIS DUGANNE

I T was somewhere between five and six o'clock when William Ellery Sheridan made a right turn into the driveway of Australian Pines Inn. Palms, as well as pines, edged the winding white-sand road, and when the inn itself appeared, oleander and hibiscus bloomed brightly against its white cement walls. He cut his engine and heard the sound of surf rolling in on the beach, saw the water of the Gulf of Mexico, turquoise and jade, streaked with the rose and lavender of the sunset.

He ambled across cement flagstones to the entrance of the patio, a tall slim man, not shabby, but careless in his dress, not fashionable, yet not without distinction.

"Good evening," said a masculine voice, and William Ellery started slightly at the suddenness and noiselessness of the gentleman's materialization from nowhere. He was a tweedy gentleman, with a white mustache, a shock of white hair, and a pipe held casually in one hand.

"Good evening," said William Ellery. "Have you any rooms?"

The gentleman smiled without warmth. "For yourself?"

William Ellery nodded, and then blinked his blue eyes. An extremely pretty young woman, clad in what at first looked like an arrangement of the Sunday Times, but which on second glance proved to be a dinner dress made of white silk imprinted with news columns of type in a most confusing manner, had tiptoed behind the tweedy gentleman and was standing still, a finger to her red lips, her large and lovely brown eyes inspecting William Ellery with interest.

"Did someone send you here?" the gentleman inquired. His smile, which rearranged only his mouth without reference to his other features, remained fixed. "I am Mr. Lamb, the proprietor," he added.

"My name is Sheridan," said William Ellery. "No one sent me here." He repeated, "Have you any rooms?"

Mr. Lamb's eyes looked up at the sky for a brief instant, and behind him the young woman thrust out her lower lip and placed one finger mysteriously beside her pretty nose. William Ellery wondered abruptly if inn was a euphemism for sanitarium.

"We ordinarily do not take guests who arrive unrecommended," explained Mr. Lamb. "How did you happen to come here?"

William Ellery Sheridan was tired. He had been tired and cold when he started driving, and now he was tired and hot. "I left Ohio the day before yesterday," he said. "I am an astronomer. By the process of keeping my right foot on the accelerator of my car, I arrived in whatever town I just came through some fifteen minutes ago. Wishing to be close to a beach, I steered in a westerly direction, crossing a bridge to what I assume is a key. Observing your sign, I assumed that inn meant a place to stay, and turned into your driveway. I have been vaccinated against smallpox, have all my own teeth, and no bad habits, with the possible exception of astronomy."

Behind Mr. Lamb, the literately costumed young woman clapped her hands together noiselessly, and looked pleased.

Mr. Lamb murmured, "Ah," and added, "How long do you expect to remain in Florida, Mr. Sheridan?"

"Until I'm rested," said William Ellery. "Two weeks, three weeks, how do I know?"

Mr. Lamb cleared his throat. "I believe," he said, like a profession of faith. "If you will come with me."

The room was cool, attractively furnished and quiet. A boy in a white jacket brought William Ellery's bags, and William Ellery got into bathing trunks and pointed his nose toward the Gulf of Mexico.

"Just as I thought!" announced a feminine voice, as he turned the corner of the patio. Her lovely brown eyes glowed. "A man," she added admiringly. "D'you mind if I come along and watch you?"

"Why, no," he said.

"You can't possibly imagine what you mean to me," she confided, breathlessly trying to keep pace with him. "I've been here twenty-two days, which leaves sixty-eight more to go, and you're the first male under fifty these young eyes have rested on."

Twenty-two, sixty-eight, fifty, thought William Ellery. It sounded like a football signal. "Sixty-eight to go?" he inquired.

"Residence," she said. "Ninety days to get a divorce."

They had reached the beach and she sat down on the white sand and gazed up at him. "You certainly add that something that's been lacking," she said. "Go on in. The water's fine."

William Ellery grinned, and went on in, holding his shoulders a bit straighter than usual. The water was fine, and he dived through a wave and rolled over on his back, floating like a sleepy dolphin. Gulls flashed white against the lavender sky, and he relaxed and forgot about the young woman watching him, until he came out.

"You'll really never know!" she told him. "Just to see a male body that isn't racked by rheumatism or arched by arthritis or lumped by lumbago ——" She smiled delightedly. "I could go on with that forever. My name's Victoria Goodwin—Mrs. Goodwin for sixty-eight more days. Most people call me Vicky. What do they call you?"

Most people called him Professor Sheridan, he admitted.

"No," she said. "We have three retired presidents here—of companies, not the White House—and a professor is not the touch. I shall call you Bill. You're not very tanned, are you, Bill?"

William Ellery looked down at his white chest and flat white stomach. "People in my profession don't tan a great deal," he told her. "Especially in the winter in Ohio."

"You're an astronomer, aren't you? Don't think I was eavesdropping, but I chanced to overhear you telling Lambkin."

"That's right," said William Ellery.

"You teach people about the stars?"

"No," he corrected her. "I find out about the stars."

She beamed. "That's cute," she announced. "You teach the teachers, huh? We have a star here. Beryl Hilton." William Ellery registered nothing. "She's taking a rest from Hollywood. And boy, is this the place to take it!" She trotted along at his side, like a puppy. "There she is, now!" she exclaimed, as they went through an arched opening, dripping with bougainvillaea. "Beryl, look! A man!"

William Ellery Sheridan had not seen many movies in his adult life, and none of the ones he had seen prepared him for

Beryl Hilton. She was small and beautiful, and William Ellery was reminded of a Tanagra figurine. Against an amber-colored cotton evening dress, her neck and arms were the color of cocoa; she had been born a blonde, and Hollywood had merely gilded the lilies of her compact well-shaped head. Her eyes were cool like moonlight, huge and gray, and as they saw Vicky and William Ellery, they shimmered like moonlit water.

"So he is," said Beryl Hilton, and her voice sent ripples down his bare spine. It was a warm voice, deeper and more resonant than seemed possible from such a slender throat.

"His name is Bill," Vicky continued. "He knows all about the stars, Beryl. You know, the ones in the sky."

"I've heard about them," said Beryl, smiling. She was holding out a small firm brown hand. "Hello, Bill."

He undoubtedly said hello. He even mumbled other words, but William Ellery Sheridan did not remember what, when he reached his room. Nothing, in his scientist's life, had prepared him for Beryl Hilton. He dressed in a daze. For the first time since an interval in his teens, he had difficulty in deciding which necktie to wear. He had difficulty in combing down his reddish-brown hair, which he realized needed cutting. He wondered why he had never paid more attention to his wardrobe.

Vicky and Beryl were eating fruit cup when he entered the dining room. White heads stirred like cotton clusters in a breeze, as a waitress led him to a table. He ate methodically, without interest, finishing some time before Beryl and Vicky, so he had a second cup of coffee and made it last until they rose and went out to the patio. He followed hastily, and more white heads moved like pale moons against the cloudy dark shadows of lounge chairs.

"Here I am, Bill," called Vicky's voice from a dim corner. "Were you looking for me?"

He was looking for Beryl Hilton, but she had disappeared. He sat down beside Vicky.

"This is always the saddest hour of the day for me," she told him cheerfully. "Waking up is the other one. I just can't get used to not seeing Hank—he's my husband. After dinner really gets me down. Another day gone forever, another lonely night."

William Ellery could not think of a proper comment.

"I don't suppose you'd like to go to a movie or the dog races or anything, would you, Bill?" she asked wistfully. "Maybe Beryl would come along too."

Beryl did not come along. They took Vicky's car, which she insisted on his driving.

William Ellery was somewhat astonished by his first double-feature entertainment from Hollywood. Afterwards, when Vicky had skillfully maneuvered him to a night club, he asked her what sort of plays Miss Hilton appeared in.

"Oh, romantic, you know," said Vicky. "Love, passion, sometimes renunciation, though she's still a bit young for that. Hank thinks she's the most glamorous woman on the screen. She's little, but what curves! Genuine, too; I've seen her bare."

William Ellery blinked.

He did not know how to dance, so they watched others, and Vicky told him what a marvelous dancer Hank was. When they drove up to Australian Pines, the hotel was dark. A dim lantern swung in the patio, making stealthy shadows. Vicky put a finger to her lips.

"I always feel like I was back in boarding school sneaking in after hours," she whispered. She held out her hand. "Thank you, Bill, it's been simply marvelous. You don't mind if I don't kiss you, do you? I'm not going to kiss anyone until after my divorce."

"That's quite all right," said William Ellery.

The next morning when he entered the dining room, Vicky was having breakfast alone.

"Why don't you sit with me?" she suggested. "Eating by myself almost kills me, and Beryl never comes down for breakfast." The waitress moved his place, and she added, "I do like to watch a man eat!"

When they had finished, the waitress said, "Will Mr. Sheridan have lunch with you and Miss Hilton?"

"Will you?" cried Vicky eagerly. "All your meals, Bill!"

"You don't think that Miss Hilton ——" he began.

"Oh, she'll be delighted!" Vicky interrupted him. "It isn't as if you were a movie fan or a wolf or anything objectionable. I mean your being an astronomer makes it okay, don't you think?"

William Ellery was grateful for his chosen profession, though somewhat bewildered by its new implication.

Vicky was going into town to the hairdresser's, and William Ellery got into his bathing trunks and strolled down to the beach. It had not occurred to him that Beryl Hilton would be there, and he trembled with surprise when he saw her Tanagra body in a white silk bathing suit as graceful as an ancient Greek tunic and, in fact, adapted from one. She was walking slowly just out of reach of the ruffled waves, and every few feet she leaned over to pick something up, graceful and measured as a classical dancer. He moved toward her as though pulled by a wire.

"Hello!" she said. "Aren't these beautiful?" Against her palm, tiny sea shells were like a raja's jewels, pink and purple and yellow, striped and plaided. "This is rather a rare one. An alphabet cone." The curve of her cheek as she looked at it was exquisite.

"I see," said William Ellery. They walked on, side by side, and he stooped. "This is nice," he offered.

She smiled. "It's a perfect one too! A king's crown." Her small hand was already full.

"Shall I carry them for you?" he offered. Her hand, gritty with sand, brushed his as she poured the coquinas into his cupped palm. When both their hands were filled, they turned and walked back to where she had left her white beach robe and absurdly small white sandals. More shells were piled on a rose-colored towel.

"Are you an authority on shells, Miss Hilton?" he asked.

Her eyes crinkled. "Well, I know more about them than some people," she answered. "I bought a book. For sixty cents." She set several small tawny shells in a row. "These are cat's-paws," she told him. "They're my favorites. They're so subtle. They look—oh, Mayan or Etruscan or Egyptian."

"So do cats," said William Ellery.

She looked up at him swiftly, through her golden lashes. "Do you like cats?" she demanded.

"I have five," he answered.

Her sandy hand slipped into his. "Shake," she said. "Anyone who likes cats and stars is all right with me."

They shook hands. "Do you like stars too?" he asked.

Like her voice, her laughter was deeper than one would expect from so small a body. "The celestial ones," she said.

It was almost noon when Vicky joined them, her dark hair curled and glossy. She was wearing a scarlet bathing suit, and a scarlet cap dangled from her freshly manicured fingers. She dropped to the sand beside them and lay on her stomach, her chin in her hands.

"Lambkin's uncrating a couple more antiques," she announced gloomily. "Male and female. They must be over ninety."

Beryl smiled at her. "Poor Vicky."

"Why did you pick this hotel?" asked William Ellery. "There must be gayer places in Florida."

"My pappy picked it," she said. "A girl getting a divorce needs a respectable background. Anyway, I don't feel like being gay."

William Ellery said, "Why are you getting a divorce?"

Vicky's underlip pushed out, and Beryl murmured lightly, "You're a direct type, professor."

He looked at her inquiringly. He had few purely social contacts in his life; in the world of science, one not only asked about but one investigated the things which aroused one's interest.

"Because my husband is a stinker," said Vicky flatly. She sat up and pulled the scarlet bathing cap over her curls and ran down the beach into the water.

"That," said Beryl, "is a very unhappy little girl, professor. She worries me."

"You mean she doesn't want this divorce?" he asked. Beryl nodded, and he said, "Then why is she getting it?"

She smiled. "Oh, professor," she said softly. "How simple your starry world must be!"

"Simple!" he echoed.

Her golden head nodded. "You've never been married, I gather."

"No," he said. "Have you?"

"Twice," she answered.

He glared at her, and sudden laughter poured from her and floated on the wind up the white beach.

Vicky returned, dark lashes wet and pointed, slim legs dripping. "Maybe Hank isn't really a stinker," she addressed William Ellery. "But he wants to marry someone else."

"Oh," said William Ellery. "Do you think he'll be happier with this other person?"

"No!" said Vicky. "She's a mess. He'll find out!"

"Why do you let him, then?" asked William Ellery. "It doesn't make sense."

"Of course it doesn't!" agreed Vicky. "That's what's burning me up! But good gracious!" She stared at him. "Don't you know anything about sex?"

Beryl sneezed, and sat up, wiping sand from her face. "You asked for it, professor," she told him sweetly.

Vicky was regarding him with somber brown eyes. "Even if you've never been married, you must have had some sex life," she said.

"That," retorted William Ellery stiffly, "is my affair."

William Ellery glared as both his companions burst into gales of laughter. "It must be lunchtime," Beryl said contritely.

Twice, their luncheon was interrupted by long-distance calls for Beryl. Mr. Lamb himself announced the first one, solemnly, almost reverently. Hollywood was calling Miss Hilton. The second, too, was from Hollywood, and Beryl's face was stony when she returned.

"Let's go out to dinner tonight," she suggested. "I'm depressed." She looked at William Ellery. "Now that we have a man, let's make the most of him. Let's go to the Tampico."

"He can't dance," said Vicky.

"He can learn," said Beryl.

William Ellery had never before escorted two ladies, or even one, to a place like the Tampico. He had never escorted a movie star anywhere. He was both amazed and interested by the evening. Beryl Hilton disposed of two reporters and several autograph collectors easily and charmingly. She produced a dancing partner for Vicky like a rabbit from a hat, and surveyed William Ellery amusedly.

"May I have this dance, professor?" she asked him.

He grinned. "You're asking for it, now, Miss Hilton," he warned her.

In his extreme youth, he had attended Mrs. Gardner's Dancing Class for Children. William Ellery rose and made a stiffly formal bow, as Mrs. Gardner had taught him, and put his arm around Beryl's waist. The music swelled, horns carrying the melody, drums pulsing the beat, and suddenly he realized that he was willing to learn anything which kept Beryl Hilton in his arms.

"You know, you're not bad," she murmured, her golden hair brushing his mouth as she looked up at him. Her hands, like the hands of an experienced rider on an uncertain horse, guided him and gave him confidence.

"I like it," he said.

Vicky was not at their table when they returned. Beryl's eyes swept the room and she said, "Oh, there she is."

William Ellery followed her gaze to where Vicky sat with a group of noisy young people. The orchestra swept into a rumba, and they watched the dancers, Vicky flushed and laughing, a little disheveled, as she danced.

"I'm no authority on these matters," said William Ellery, "but don't you think Vicky has had enough to drink?"

Beryl smiled. "How much is enough, professor?" she asked, rather dryly. "She's still conscious."

He frowned. "I think we should take her home."

Beryl's gray eyes were amused. "You're very sweet, you know," she told him.

"You're worried about her, yourself," he said.

She shrugged. "Of course I am. And I'm sorry for her. But what can anyone do? She's grown up."

They watched Vicky return to the table, watched her drink a highball quickly, like a thirsty child.

"Who are those people, anyway?" he asked.

"Just people," said Beryl. "Extras, in pictures. If it weren't them, it would be others." She looked at him curiously. "You don't believe that anyone can really help anyone else, do you?"

"I never thought about it," said William Ellery. He thought about it. "Yes, I do," he answered.

Vicky was dancing again, and he reached out and caught

her dress as she whirled past. "We're going, after this dance," he told her.

She nodded, smiling, and when the dance was ended, she slipped into her chair.

"Maybe I won't go with you two," she said. "They want me to go on to another place with them."

Beryl's eyes were intent on William Ellery's face.

"I think you'd better come with us," he told her.

Vicky giggled. "You sound like my pappy, Bill." The young man with whom she had been dancing approached, carrying a drink. "Is that mine?" asked Vicky, reaching for it.

"No, it isn't," said William Ellery. He took the glass and set it firmly at the farther end of the table.

"Hey, what's the idea?" demanded the young man belligerently.

"Mrs. Goodwin is leaving with us," said William Ellery.

Vicky giggled again. "Why don't you fight about it?" she suggested. "I love to see men fight."

Beryl Hilton was smiling, sitting silent and remote, with the air of a spectator at a play.

"I hardly think it's necessary," said William Ellery. "But if the young man insists ——" He started to rise.

The young man did not insist. He muttered, "Okay, okay," and retreated.

William Ellery paid the check and escorted Beryl and Vicky to the car. As he opened the door, Beryl's hand touched his shoulder. He looked down at her inquiringly, and she rose on tiptoes and kissed him.

Somehow, he drove the car. Beryl disappeared with Vicky, and he went to his room and got into bed. For a serious scientist who had never considered marriage, William Ellery Sheridan accepted the idea with remarkable rapidity. Lying awake, listening to the wind in the pines and the surf on the shore, he thought about Beryl Hilton and did not see how he could endure life without her. He realized that there might be obstacles to overcome. He realized that he knew nothing about the world in which she lived, little about her, except that she was beautiful and companionable and that he would like to see her every day. He waited a week, before he asked her.

"Why, Bill!" she said. She leaned back on her elbows on the sand, her face upturned, her eyes shining. "I'm very flattered."

"Well, will you?" he demanded.

There was tenderness in her eyes, as well as amusement. "I'm afraid it wouldn't work," she answered. "I'm not easy to live with—as my other husbands often informed me. And our interests are really quite different."

"How do you know?" he asked.

She laughed, but softly, almost breathlessly.

"We're both adults," he told her. "There's no reason why we shouldn't go on with our careers after we're married."

"I said you were sweet, and you are," she murmured. Her face remained upturned. "Would you like to kiss me?" she asked.

"I'd like to marry you," he said, not moving.

The corners of her eyes crinkled, and her mouth quivered. "You mean I can't interest you in a kiss?" In spite of its lightness, there was surprise in her voice.

"I don't believe so," said William Ellery.

Any critic who thought that Beryl Hilton was getting a trifle old for ingénue roles would have reversed judgment had he seen her then. Her eyes widened and her lips parted, and remained parted, as she watched William Ellery stride down the beach.

William Ellery walked for several miles without picking up, or even seeing, a single sea shell. He had proposed marriage and been refused, but he had no intention of accepting the refusal. Beryl Hilton's implication had been that they were light-years apart, and light-years were William Ellery's business. He smiled to himself, as he thought further that stars were his business too.

At dinner Vicky announced, "Sixty more days to go. Two solid months. Beryl, if you go away I shall die."

William Ellery looked quickly at Beryl. If she went away he would follow her—to Hollywood, high water or hell. "Are you going away?" he demanded.

She shrugged, and her white gown slipped from one cocoa-colored shoulder. "I've overstayed my parole, already," she answered. "I'm scheduled to start a new picture next week."

Her eyes dropped, and she examined a spot on the tablecloth intently.

Vicky was staring out the window at the night, her eyes brooding, her mouth unhappy.

"It is my impression," stated William Ellery, "that both you ladies need a change of scene. What about the Tampico?"

Vicky's face brightened, but Beryl's remained unreadable.

"You two go," she said. "I have to write some letters."

He tried to meet her eyes, but she avoided looking at him. Hoist with his own petard, he thought, and took Vicky to the Tampico.

"Tell me about this husband of yours," he suggested, after they had danced together rather unsuccessfully.

He listened at length while Vicky told him about Hank, and the repulsive female wolf who had ensnared him.

"Are you sure he wants to marry her?" he asked.

Vicky's lips trembled. "I'm not sure of anything," she said. "But I remember what I said to Hank. He'll never forgive me, never! I was awful, Bill!"

"H'm," said William Ellery. "You couldn't—reconsider?"

Her cheeks flamed. "I'd die first! I wish I were dead!"

William Ellery changed the subject. He felt, too, that he had earned the right to discuss the subject closest to his own heart.

"Tell me about Beryl," he said.

Vicky had to remain at Australian Pines. William Ellery had to remain so long as Beryl was there. And Beryl stayed on, day after quiet day, collecting shells, lying on the sand, ignoring phone calls.

"Do you like being a movie star?" William Ellery asked her.

Vicky had gone again to the hairdresser, and they were alone on the beach.

Beryl patted the sand beside her firmly. "Do I like being a woman?" she countered. "I am a movie star."

"That's no answer," he said.

She sat up, wrapping brown arms around brown knees, her eyes meeting his. "Maybe it's the only answer," she said. Her voice was deeper than usual, rough with excitement and intensity. "Maybe I can't escape the one any more than I can escape the other, Bill. Maybe I have to go on and on until I'm playing mother parts and finally grand old ladies!"

He smiled. "Mother parts," he said. "Ever considered one without a camera?"

Her eyes were angry. "Have you ever considered giving up astronomy?" she demanded.

"No," he answered. "What are you so angry about, Beryl?"

"I'm not angry," she said furiously.

"Did I ever tell you that I'm a fairly rich man?" he asked.

Her small jaw set, and her eyes became explosive. "If we're discussing our financial status, I have enough money saved ——"

She stopped short, because he was laughing at her. She unwrapped her arms and stood up, scattering sand, and ran down into the water.

Vicky's sixty days to go became fifty days. William Ellery Sheridan had been at Australia Pines for three weeks, and Beryl Hilton for a month.

"Now they're really building a fire under me," Beryl told William Ellery and Vicky, when she returned to the dinner table from another long-distance call. "They're sending down a runner to smoke me out." Her eyes were defiant, and a little alarmed.

"A runner?" William Ellery inquired.

"Publicity man. Trouble shooter. Bring 'em back alive." The defiance conquered the alarm in her eyes. "I have a right to take a month off, if I want to! Two months, if I want!"

He put his hand over hers. "Or a lifetime," he said.

Vicky was staring at them. "Well, am I dumb!" she exclaimed.

Beryl's face crimsoned as she withdrew her hand. Her director would have shouted for color cameras had he witnessed her blush.

"I never even suspected!" declared Vicky.

Beryl's lips parted, and closed. Even an experienced actress could not explain away that blush.

"Live and learn!" said Vicky. Her brown eyes were wide. "You must have been wanting to put me in a sack and drown me! Little Vicky, the demon chaperon! Little Vicky, tagging along ——"

"Don't be silly," said Beryl sharply.

"Silly!" Vicky echoed, her voice rising so that white heads turned toward their table. "I was born silly, I guess."

Beryl said gently, "Pipe down, honey. You're all wrong."

"All wrong," agreed Vicky. "You never said a truer word."

Beryl pushed back her chair and took hold of Vicky's shoulder. "Come on, honey."

William Ellery Sheridan watched, and everyone else in the dining room watched, as the two women went out. Beryl had not returned when he finished his dinner. He sat down in a corner of the patio, to wait, and suddenly she slipped into the chair beside him.

"That poor kid," she said. She laughed without amusement. "Well, the first divorce is the hardest."

"Look," said William Ellery. "Let's us get out of here."

Beryl looked up, at the white heads like tired moons against the chair backs in the shadows of the patio. "All right," she agreed.

They took the path to the shore, and walked up the beach in the starlight. Beryl was silent, and William Ellery did not attempt to break her silence. They walked for a mile or more with no sound but the pounding surf and the rusty squeak of their footsteps upon the hard-packed sand.

"Who's this character who thinks he's going to take you back to Hollywood?" he asked at last.

Her voice sounded tired. "Just another yes man. His name is Alan Miller."

He put his hand on her shoulder and turned her about. "Do you know what you want, Beryl?"

"Does anyone?" she asked him.

"I do," he said. "Apparently Vicky does."

"Vicky," said Beryl. Suddenly her fingers were gripping his arm. "I want to go back, Bill."

"What's the matter?" he asked.

She was running. "Nothing, I hope," she answered. "I just— oh, it's just a notion, I'm sure."

"What is?" he demanded.

"Vicky. She was pretty hysterical when I left her. I didn't think. I handed her some sleeping tablets, a whole bottleful. I ought to have my head examined."

"You don't think ——" began William Ellery.

"Yes, I do," said Beryl.

The moons had set, in the patio. Australian Pines was dark, except for the one swinging lantern, making silent shadows on the flagstones. William Ellery followed Beryl to Vicky's room. Vicky was lying on her back in her bed. She wore peppermint-striped pajamas, and to William Ellery she looked like a sleeping schoolgirl.

Beryl took hold of her shoulders and shook her. She said, "Wake up, Vicky!" in a fierce whisper. Then she slapped her face, hard. "Help me sit her up," she ordered.

Vicky was like a limp rag doll, unjointed, inanimate.

"Go and wake up Lamb," said Beryl. "Tell him to get some black coffee and a bottle of brandy here, quick." She let Vicky drop back on the bed and went into the bathroom. William Ellery heard water running as he hurried across the patio.

Mr. Lamb was horrified, but quick. He appeared in his bathrobe, bearing a brandy bottle and a steaming coffeepot, his brown eyes stricken.

"Shouldn't I call a doctor?" he asked in a hoarse whisper. "Dear me, Miss Hilton, what possessed Mrs. Goodwin?"

Beryl was pouring coffee between Vicky's lips. "Give me the brandy," she ordered. "You hold up her head, Bill."

Mr. Lamb said, "This is dreadful. Nothing like this has ever happened at Australian Pines. A death here would give the place such a bad name."

Vicky choked as the brandy went down her throat. She raised a limp rag doll's arm and brushed her hand across her forehead. Her eyes opened. "Wha's matter?" she asked.

"Okay," said Beryl crisply. "You two get her on her feet and walk her."

More coffee, more brandy, more steps up and down the small room. "I'm tired," said Vicky fretfully. "What are you ——" Her voice died. "Oh," she said. Her eyes were reproachful. "Why didn't you leave me alone?" she demanded. "Why did you have to interfere?"

Beryl nodded her golden head. "You two boys run along," she said. "I can take over from here."

In the patio Mr. Lamb said, in a whisper, "I am certainly

grateful to Miss Hilton. I presume life in Hollywood prepares one for such emergencies."

William Ellery Sheridan looked at Mr. Lamb without seeing him.

"I have to make a long-distance call," he said.

It took only fifteen minutes to locate Mr. Henry Goodwin, in New York. Mr. Goodwin's voice had a note of eagerness when he said, "Hello," after the mechanical voice of the operator had informed him that Florida was calling.

William Ellery had not known that he was excited. He heard, with detached surprise, his own voice open the conversation. "Listen, you damned young idiot," it said.

Hank Goodwin listened. He listened until William Ellery paused for breath. "Who the hell are you?" he asked then.

"I am an old astronomer," said William Ellery angrily. "It doesn't matter who I am. Are you getting a night plane out of New York or aren't you?"

"I am getting a night plane," said Hank.

William Ellery hung up the receiver. He turned, and Beryl Hilton was standing just outside the office, staring at him.

"And as for you," said William Ellery. "As for you ——"

"Oh, Bill!" said Beryl Hilton, when she was able to speak.

The orchestra at the Tampico was playing a rumba. William Ellery had ordered champagne. Hank and Vicky sat close together on the green banquette, watching the Cuban waiter fill their glasses.

"Beryl!" exclaimed a voice, and they all looked up.

"Oh, hello, Alan," said Beryl calmly. "Sit down. What a nose for news you boys do have." She introduced him to the others. "Mr. and Mrs. Goodwin and Professor Sheridan." The Cuban waiter brought another glass, and Beryl watched him pour the wine. "I'm about to propose a toast," she said. She stood up, her amber lace evening dress shimmering in the soft light, the topaz earrings and chain of topaz about her brown throat burning bright. "To Vicky and Hank—happy marriage forever." William Ellery had risen, and Alan Miller got to his feet. "And the same—for the identical period—to Bill and me." Her eyes glinted toward Alan, and returned to rest on William Ellery's face.

Alan Miller choked. "Listen, you can't do this to me!" he protested when he stopped choking. "Beryl, who is this guy and are you serious?"

"I'm serious," said Beryl, "and he's an astronomer."

"An astron ——" Alan's voice cracked. He snapped his fingers, a light of fanaticism or genius burning in his eyes. "Beryl, I love you, baby! An astronomer! Sheridan, I love you too! It's a natural!"

"That's what I thought, myself," said William Ellery.

Alan ignored him. "Get this," he addressed the table. "Dear heaven, I couldn't have done it better out of my own massive brain! The Astronomer and the Star!" Both his hands were out, fingers clicking like two pairs of castanets. "Can't you see it? The star, the darling of Hollywood, sweetheart of the nation, on vacation in some palm-fringed exotic dream-set. The astronomer—better make him the unworldly, absent-minded type professor ——" *Click* went the fingers of his right hand. "He loves her, but she realizes the unsuitability of their union, despite the promptings of her own heart. Obstacle!" The left hand went *click*. Alan Miller paused for breath.

Across the table, Beryl's fingers snapped, like a revolver shot. "Obstacle!" she said. "Danger. Threatened tragedy." *Click!* "Who comes to the rescue? Who solves the problem, proves himself a man of action, a man obviously able to take care of our heroine for the rest of her happy life?"

"The astronomer!" cried Alan and Vicky and Hank, in one breath.

Beryl stood up, her gray eyes shining, her glass raised. "Ladies and gentlemen, I give you the astronomer!" she said. "At least, I give him to you for the time it takes to drink this. After that, he's all mine!"

HORNBLOWER AND THE MAN WHO FELT QUEER

By C. S. FORESTER

THIS time the wolf was prowling round outside the sheepfold. H.M. frigate Indefatigable had chased the French corvette Papillon into the mouth of the Gironde, and was seeking a way of attacking her where she lay anchored in the stream under the protection of the batteries at the mouth. Captain Pellew took his ship into shoal water as far as he dared, until, in fact, the batteries fired warning shots to make him keep his distance, and he stared long and keenly through his glass at the corvette. Then he shut his telescope and turned on his heel to give the order that worked the Indefatigable away from the dangerous lee shore—out of sight of land, in fact.

His departure might lull the French into a sense of security which, he hoped, would prove unjustified. For he had no intention of leaving them undisturbed. If the corvette could be captured or sunk, not only would she be unavailable for raids on British commerce but also the French would be forced to increase their coastal defenses at this point and lessen the effort that could be put out elsewhere. War is a matter of savage blow and counterblow, and even a forty-gun frigate could strike shrewd blows if shrewdly handled.

Midshipman Hornblower was walking the lee side of the quarter-deck, as became his lowly station as the junior officer of the watch, in the afternoon, when Midshipman Kennedy approached him. Kennedy took off his hat with a flourish and bowed low, as his dancing master had once taught him, left foot advanced, hat down by the right knee. Hornblower entered into the spirit of the game, laid his hat against his stomach and bent himself in the middle three times in quick succession. Thanks to his physical awkwardness, he could parody ceremonial solemnity almost without trying.

"Most grave and reverend signior," said Kennedy, "I bear the compliments of Captain Sir Ed'ard Pellew, who humbly solicits Your Gravity's attendance at dinner at eight bells in the afternoon watch."

"My respects to Sir Edward," replied Hornblower, bowing to his knees at the mention of the name, "and I shall condescend to make a brief appearance."

"I am sure the captain will be both relieved and delighted," said Kennedy. "I will convey him my felicitations along with your most flattering acceptance."

Both hats flourished with even greater elaboration than before, but at that moment both young men noticed Mr. Bolton, the officer of the watch, looking at them from the windward side, and they hurriedly put their hats on and assumed attitudes more consonant with the dignity of officers holding their warrants from King George.

"What's in the captain's mind?" asked Hornblower.

Kennedy laid one finger alongside his nose. "If I knew that, I should rate a couple of epaulets," he said. "Something's brewing, and I suppose one of these days we shall know what it is. Until then, all that we little victims can do is to play, unconscious of our doom. Meanwhile, be careful not to let the ship fall overboard."

There was no sign of anything brewing while dinner was being eaten in the great cabin of the Indefatigable. Pellew was a courtly host at the head of the table. Conversation flowed freely and along indifferent channels among the senior officers present—the two lieutenants, Eccles and Chadd, and the sailing master, Soames. Hornblower and the other junior officer—Mallory, a midshipman of more than two years' seniority—kept silent, as midshipmen should, thereby being able to devote their undivided attention to the food, so vastly superior to what was served in the midshipmen's berth.

"A glass of wine with you, Mr. Hornblower," said Pellew, raising his glass.

Hornblower tried to bow gracefully in his seat while raising his glass. He sipped cautiously, for he had early found that he had a weak head and he disliked feeling drunk.

The table was cleared and there was a brief moment of expectancy as the company awaited Pellew's next move.

"Now, Mr. Soames," said Pellew, "let us have that chart."

It was a map of the mouth of the Gironde with the soundings; somebody had penciled in the positions of the shore batteries.

"The Papillon," said Sir Edward—he did not condescend to pronounce it French-fashion—"lies just here. Mr. Soames took the bearings." He indicated a penciled cross on the chart, far up the channel.

"You gentlemen," went on Pellew, "are going in with the boats to fetch her out."

So that was it. A cutting-out expedition.

"Mr. Eccles will be in general command. I will ask him to tell you his plan."

The gray-haired first lieutenant with the surprisingly young blue eyes looked round at the others.

"I shall have the launch," he said, "and Mr. Soames the cutter. Mr. Chadd and Mr. Mallory will command the first and second gigs. And Mr. Hornblower will command the jolly boat. Each of the boats except Mr. Hornblower's will have a junior officer second in command."

That would not be necessary for the jolly boat with its crew of seven. The launch and cutter would carry from thirty to forty men each, and the gigs twenty each; it was a large force that was being dispatched—nearly half the ship's company.

"She's a ship of war," explained Eccles, reading their thoughts. "No merchantman. Ten guns a side, and full of men."

Nearer two hundred men than a hundred, certainly—plentiful opposition for a hundred and twenty British seamen.

"But we will be attacking her by night and taking her by surprise," said Eccles, reading their thoughts again.

"Surprise," put in Pellew, "is more than half the battle, as you know, gentlemen. . . . Please pardon the interruption, Mr. Eccles."

"At the moment," went on Eccles, "we are out of sight of land. We are about to stand in again. We have never hung about this part of the coast, and the Frogs'll think we've gone for good. We'll make the land after nightfall, stand in as far as possible, and then the boats will go in. High water tomorrow morning is at four-fifty; dawn is at five-thirty. The attack will be delivered at four-thirty, so that the watch below will have had time to get to sleep. The launch will attack on the starboard quarter, and the cutter on the larboard quarter. Mr. Mallory's gig will attack on the larboard bow, and Mr. Chadd's on the starboard bow. Mr. Chadd will be responsible for cutting the corvette's cable as soon as he has mastered the forecastle and the other boats' crews have at least reached the quarter-deck."

Eccles looked round at the three other commanders of the large boats, and they nodded understanding. Then he went on, "Mr. Hornblower with the jolly boat will wait until the attack has gained a foothold on the deck. He will then board at the main chains, either to starboard or larboard, as he sees fit, and he will at once ascend the main rigging, paying no attention to whatever fighting is going on on deck. He will see to it that the main topsail is loosed, and he will sheet it home on receipt of further orders. I, myself, or Mr. Soames in the event of my being killed or wounded, will send two hands to the wheel and will attend to steering the corvette as soon as she is under way. The tide will take us out, and the Indefatigable will be awaiting us just out of gunshot from the shore batteries."

"Any comments, gentlemen?" asked Pellew.

That was the moment when Hornblower should have spoken up—the only moment when he could. Eccles' orders had set in motion sick feelings of apprehension in his stomach. Hornblower was no maintopman, and Hornblower knew it. He hated heights, and he hated going aloft. He knew he had none of the monkeylike agility and self-confidence of the good seaman. He was unsure of himself aloft in the dark even in the Indefatigable, and he was utterly appalled at the thought of going aloft in an entirely strange ship and finding his way amid strange rigging. He felt himself quite unfitted for the duty assigned to him, and he should have raised a protest at once, on account of his unfitness. But he let the opportunity pass, for he was overcome by the matter-of-fact way in which the other officers accepted the plan. He looked round at the unmoved faces; nobody was paying any attention to him, and he jibbed at making himself conspicuous. He swallowed; he even got as far as opening his mouth, but still no one looked at him and his protest died.

"Very well, then, gentlemen," said Pellew. . . . "I think you had better go into the details, Mr. Eccles."

Then it was too late. Eccles, with the chart before him, was pointing out the course to be taken through the shoals and mudbanks of the Gironde, and expatiating on the position of the shore batteries and on the influence of the lighthouse of Cordouan upon the distance to which the Indefatigable could approach in daylight. Hornblower listened, trying to concentrate despite his apprehensions.

Eccles finished his remarks and Pellew closed the meeting, "Since you all know your duties, gentlemen, I think you should start your preparations. The sun is about to set and you will find you have plenty to do."

The boats' crews had to be told off; it was necessary to see that the men were armed and that the boats were provisioned in case of emergency. Every man had to be instructed in the duties expected of him. And Hornblower had to rehearse himself in ascending the main shrouds and laying out along the main-topsail yard. He did it twice, forcing himself to make the difficult climb up the futtock shrouds, which, projecting outward from the mainmast, made it necessary to climb several feet while hanging back downward, locking fingers and toes into the ratlines.

He could just manage it, moving slowly and carefully, although clumsily. He stood on the foot rope and worked his way out to the yardarm—the foot rope was attached along the yard so as to hang nearly four feet below it. The principle was to set his feet on the rope with his arms over the yard, then, holding the yard in his armpits, to shuffle sideways along the foot rope to cast off the gaskets and loosen the sail.

Twice Hornblower made the whole journey, battling with the disquiet of his stomach at the thought of the hundred-foot drop below him. Finally, gulping with nervousness, he transferred his grip to the brace and forced himself to slide down it to the deck—that would be his best route when the time came to sheet the topsail home. It was a long, perilous descent; Hornblower told himself—as indeed he had said to himself when he had first seen men go aloft—that similar feats in a circus at home would be received with "Oh's" and "Ah's" of appreciation.

He was by no means satisfied with himself even when he reached the deck, and at the back of his mind was a vivid picture of his missing his hold, when the time came for him to repeat the performance in the Papillon, and falling headlong to the deck—a second or two of frightful fear while rushing through the air, and then a shattering crash. And the success of the attack hinged on him as much as on anyone—if the topsail were not promptly set to give the corvette steerageway, she would run aground on one of the shoals in the river mouth, to be ignominiously recaptured, and half the crew of the Indefatigable would be dead or prisoners.

In the waist, the jolly boat's crew was formed up for his inspection. He saw to it that the oars were properly muffled, that each man had pistol and cutlass, and made sure that every pistol was at half cock, so that there was no fear of a premature shot giving warning of the attack. He allocated duties to each man in the loosing of the topsail, laying stress on the possibility that casualties might necessitate unrehearsed changes in the scheme.

"I will mount the rigging first," said Hornblower.

That had to be the case. He had to lead—it was expected of him. More than that; if he had given any other order, it would have excited comment . . . and contempt.

"Jackson," went on Hornblower, addressing the coxswain, "you will quit the boat last and take command if I fall."

"Aye, aye, sir."

It was usual to use the poetic expression "fall" for "die," and it was only after Hornblower had uttered the word that he thought about its horrible real meaning in the present circumstances.

"Is that all understood?" asked Hornblower harshly; it was his mental stress that made his voice grate so.

Everyone nodded except one man. "Begging your pardon, sir," said Hales, the young man who pulled stroke oar, "I'm feeling a bit queerlike."

Hales was a lightly built young fellow of swarthy countenance. He put his hand to his forehead with a vague gesture as he spoke.

"You're not the only one to feel queer," snapped Hornblower.

The other men chuckled. The thought of running the gant-let of the shore batteries, of boarding an armed corvette in the teeth of opposition might well raise apprehension in the breast of any of them. Most of the men detailed for the expedi-tion must have felt qualms to some extent.

"I don't mean that, sir," said Hales indignantly. "'Course I don't."

But Hornblower and the others paid him no attention.

"You just keep your mouth shut," growled Jackson.

There could be nothing but contempt for a man who an-nounced himself sick after being told off on a dangerous duty. Hornblower felt sympathy as well as contempt. He him-self had been too much of a coward even to give voice to his apprehensions—too much afraid of what people would say about him.

"Dismiss," said Hornblower. "I'll pass the word for all of you when you are wanted."

There were some hours yet to wait while the Indefatigable crept inshore, with the lead going steadily and Pellew himself attending to the course of the frigate. Hornblower, despite his nervousness and his miserable apprehensions, yet found time to appreciate the superb seamanship displayed as Pellew brought the big frigate in through these tricky waters on that dark night. His interest was so caught by the procedure that the little tremblings which had been assailing him ceased to manifest themselves; Hornblower was of the type that would continue to observe and to learn on his deathbed.

By the time the Indefatigable had reached the point off the mouth of the river where it was desirable to launch the boats, Hornblower had learned a good deal about the practical ap-plication of the principles of coastwise navigation and a good deal about the organization of a cutting-out expedition, and by self-analysis he had learned even more about the psychology of a raiding party before a raid.

He had mastered himself, to all outside appearance, by the time he went down into the jolly boat as she heaved on the inky-black water, and he gave the command to shove off in a quiet, steady voice. Hornblower took the tiller—the feel of that solid bar of wood was reassuring, and it was old habit now to sit in the stern sheets with hand and elbow upon it—

and the men began to pull slowly after the dark shapes of the four big boats. There was plenty of time, and the flowing tide would take them up the estuary. That was just as well, for on one side of them lay the batteries of St. Dyé, and inside the estuary on the other side was the fortress of Blaye; forty big guns trained to sweep the channel, and none of the five boats could withstand a single shot from one of them.

He kept his eyes attentively on the cutter ahead of him. Soames had the dreadful responsibility of taking the boats up the channel, while all he had to do was to follow in her wake—all, except to loose that main topsail. Hornblower found himself shivering again.

Hales, the man who had said he felt queer, was pulling stroke oar; Hornblower could just see his dark form moving rhythmically back and forward at each slow stroke. After a single glance, Hornblower paid him no more attention, and was staring after the cutter when a sudden commotion brought his mind back into the boat. Someone had missed his stroke; someone had thrown all six oars into confusion as a result.

"Mind what you're doing, blast you, Hales," whispered Jackson, the coxswain, with desperate urgency.

For answer there was a sudden cry from Hales, loud, but fortunately not too loud, and Hales pitched forward against Hornblower's and Jackson's legs, kicking and writhing.

"The swine's having a fit," growled Jackson.

The kicking and writhing went on. Across the water through the darkness came a sharp, scornful whisper. "Mr. Hornblower," said the voice—it was Eccles putting a word of exasperation into his sotto voce question, "cannot you keep your men quiet?"

Eccles had brought the launch round almost alongside the jolly boat to say this to him, and the desperate need for silence was dramatically demonstrated by the absence of any of the usual blasphemy. Hornblower opened his mouth to make an explanation, but he fortunately realized that raiders in open boats did not make explanations when under the guns of the fortress of Blaye.

"Aye, aye, sir," was all he whispered back and the launch continued on its mission of shepherding the flotilla in the tracks of the cutter.

"Take his oar, Jackson," he whispered furiously to the coxswain, and he stooped and with his own hands dragged the writhing figure toward him and out of Jackson's way.

"You might try pouring water on 'im, sir," suggested Jackson hoarsely as he moved to the after thwart. "There's the bailer 'andy."

Sea water was the seaman's cure for every ill, his panacea. But Hornblower let the sick man lie. His struggles were coming to an end, and Hornblower wished to make no noise with the bailer. The lives of more than a hundred men depended on silence. Now that they were well into the actual estuary they were within easy reach of cannon shot from the shore, and a single cannon shot would rouse the crew of the Papillon, ready to man the bulwarks to beat off the attack, ready to drop cannon balls into the boats alongside, ready to shatter approaching boats with a tempest of grape.

Silently the boats glided up the estuary; Soames in the cutter was setting a slow pace, with only an occasional stroke at the oars to maintain steerageway. Presumably he knew very well what he was doing; the channel he had selected was an obscure one between mudbanks, impracticable for anything except small boats, and he had a twenty-foot pole with him with which to take the soundings—quicker and much more silent than using the lead. Minutes were passing fast, and yet the night was still utterly dark, with no hint of approaching dawn. Strain his eyes as he would, Hornblower could not be sure that he could see the flat shores on either side of him. It would call for sharp eyes on the land to detect the little boats being carried up by the tide.

Hales at his feet stirred and then stirred again. His hand, feeling around in the darkness, found Hornblower's ankle and apparently examined it with curiosity. He muttered something, the words dragging out into a moan.

"Shut up," whispered Hornblower, trying, like the saint of old, to make a tongue of his whole body, so that he might express the urgency of the occasion without making a sound audible at any distance. Hales set his elbow on Hornblower's knee and levered himself up into a sitting position, and then levered himself farther until he was standing, swaying with bent knees and supporting himself against Hornblower.

"Sit down, damn you," whispered Hornblower, shaking with fury and anxiety.

"Where's Mary?" asked Hales in a conversational tone.

"Shut up!"

"Mary!" said Hales, lurching against him. "Mary!"

Each successive word was louder. Hornblower felt instinctively that Hales would soon be speaking in a loud voice, that he might even soon be shouting. Old recollections of conversations with his doctor further stirred at the back of his mind; he remembered that persons emerging from epileptic fits were not responsible for their actions, and might be, and often were, dangerous.

"Mary!" said Hales again.

Victory and the lives of a hundred men depended on silencing Hales, and silencing him instantly. Hornblower thought of the pistol in his belt, and of using the butt, but there was another weapon more conveniently to his hand. He unshipped the tiller, a three-foot bar of solid oak, and he swung it with all the venom and fury of despair. The tiller crashed down on Hales' head, and Hales, an unuttered word cut short in his throat, fell silent in the bottom of the boat.

There was no sound from the boat's crew, save for something like a sigh from Jackson, whether approving or disapproving, Hornblower neither knew nor cared. He had done his duty, and he was certain of it. He had struck down a helpless idiot, most probably he had killed him, but the surprise upon which the success of the expedition depended had not been imperiled. He reshipped the tiller and resumed the silent task of keeping in the wake of the gigs.

Far away ahead—in the darkness it was impossible to estimate the distance—there was a nucleus of greater darkness, close on the surface of the black water. It might be the corvette. A dozen more silent strokes, and Hornblower was sure of it. Soames had done a magnificent job of pilotage, leading the boats straight to that objective. The cutter and launch were diverging now from the two gigs. The four boats were separating in readiness to launch their simultaneous converging attack.

"Easy," whispered Hornblower, and the jolly boat's crew ceased to pull.

Hornblower had his orders. He had to wait until the attack had gained a foothold on the deck. His hand clenched convulsively on the tiller; the excitement of dealing with Hales had driven the thought of having to ascend strange rigging in the darkness clear out of his head, and now it recurred with redoubled urgency. Hornblower was afraid.

Although he could see the corvette, the boats had vanished from his sight, had passed out of his field of vision. The corvette rode to her anchor, her spars just visible against the night sky—that was where he had to climb! She seemed to tower up hugely. Close by the corvette he saw a splash in the dark water—the boats were closing in fast and someone's stroke had been a little careless. At that same moment came a shout from the corvette's deck, and when the shout was repeated, it was echoed a hundredfold from the boats rushing alongside. The yelling was lusty and prolonged, of set purpose. A sleeping enemy would be bewildered by the din, and the progress of the shouting would tell each boat's crew of the extent of the success of the others. The British seamen were yelling like madmen. A flash and a bang from the corvette's deck told of the firing of the first shot; soon pistols were popping and muskets banging from several points of the deck.

"Give way!" said Hornblower. He uttered the order as if it had been torn from him by the rack.

The jolly boat moved forward while Hornblower fought down his feelings and tried to make out what was going on on board. He could see no reason for choosing one side of the corvette in preference to the other, and the larboard side was the nearer, and so he steered the boat to the larboard main chains. So interested was he in what he was doing that he remembered only in the nick of time to give the order, "In oars." He put the tiller over and the boat swirled round and the bowman hooked on.

From the deck just above came a noise exactly like a tinker hammering on a cooking pot; Hornblower noted the curious noise as he stood up in the stern sheets. He felt the cutlass at his side and the pistol in his belt, and then he sprang for the chains. With a mad leap he reached them and hauled himself up. The shrouds came into his hands, his feet found the ratlines beneath them, and he began to climb. As his head cleared the bulwark and he could see the deck, the flash of a pistol shot illuminated the scene momentarily, fixing the struggle on the deck in a static moment, like a picture. Before and below him a British seaman was fighting a furious cutlass duel with a French officer, and he realized with vague astonishment that the kettle-mending noise he had heard was the sound of cutlass against cutlass—that clash of steel against steel that poets wrote about. So much for romance.

The realization carried him far up the shrouds. At his elbow he felt the futtock shrouds, and he transferred himself to them, hanging back downward with his toes hooked into the ratlines and his hands clinging like death. That lasted for only two or three desperate seconds, and then he hauled himself onto the topmast shrouds and began the final ascent, his lungs bursting with the effort. Here was the topsail yard, and Hornblower flung himself across it and felt with his feet for the foot rope. Merciful God! There was no foot rope—his feet searching in the darkness met only unresisting air. A hundred feet above the deck he hung, squirming and kicking like a baby held up at arm's length in his father's hands. There was no foot rope; it may have been with this very situation in mind that the Frenchmen had removed it. There was no footrope, so that he could not make his way out to the yardarm. Yet the gaskets must be cast off and the sail loosed—everything depended on that. Hornblower had seen daredevil seamen run out along the yards, standing upright, as though walking a tightrope. That was the only way to reach the yardarm now.

For a moment he could not breathe as his weak flesh revolted against the thought of walking along that yard above the black abyss. This was fear, the fear that stripped a man of his manhood, turning his bowels to water and his limbs to paper. Yet his furiously active mind continued to work. He had been resolute enough in dealing with Hales. Where he personally was not involved he had been brave enough; he had not hesitated to strike down the wretched epileptic with all the strength of his arm. That was the poor sort of courage he was capable of displaying. In the simple vulgar matter of physical bravery he was utterly wanting. This was cowardice, the sort of thing that men spoke about behind their hands to other men. He could not bear the thought of that in himself;

it was worse—awful though the alternative might be—than the thought of falling through the night to the deck. With a gasp, he brought his knee up onto the yard, heaving himself up until he stood upright. He felt the rounded, canvas-covered timber under his feet, and his instincts told him not to dally there for a moment.

"Come on, men!" he yelled, and he dashed out along the yard.

It was twenty feet to the yardarm, and he covered the distance in a few frantic strides. Utterly reckless by now, he put his hands down on the yard, clasped it and laid his body across it again, his hands seeking the gaskets. A thump on the yard told him that Oldroyd, who had been detailed to come after him, had followed him out along the yard—he had six feet less to go. There could be no doubt that the other members of the jolly boat's crew were on the yard, and that Clough had led the way to the starboard yardarm. It was obvious from the rapidity with which the sail came loose. Here was the brace beside him. Without any thought of danger now, for he was delirious with excitement and triumph, he grasped it with both hands and jerked himself off the yard. His waving legs found the rope and twined about it, and he let himself slide down it.

Fool that he was! Would he never learn sense and prudence? Would he never remember that vigilance and precaution must never be relaxed? He had allowed himself to slide so fast that the rope seared his hands, and when he tried to tighten his grip so as to slow down his progress, it caused him such agony that he had to relax it again and slide on down with the rope stripping the skin from his hands as though peeling off a glove. His feet reached the deck and he momentarily forgot the pain as he looked round him.

There was the faintest gray light beginning to show now, and there was no sound of battle. It had been a well-worked surprise—a hundred men flung suddenly on the deck of the corvette had swept away the anchor watch and mastered the vessel in a single rush before the watch below could come up to offer any resistance.

Chadd's stentorian voice came pealing from the forecastle, "Cable's cut, sir!"

Then Eccles bellowed from aft, "Mr. Hornblower!"

"Sir!" yelled Hornblower.

"Sheet that topsail home!"

A rush of men came to help—not only his own boat's crew but every man of initiative and spirit. Halyards, sheets and braces; the sail was trimmed round and was drawing full in the light southerly air, and the Papillon swung round to go down with the first of the ebb. Dawn was coming up fast, with a trifle of mist on the surface of the water.

Over the starboard quarter came a sullen, bellowing roar, and then the misty air was torn by a series of infernal screams, supernaturally loud. The first cannon balls Hornblower had ever heard were passing him by.

"Mr. Chadd! Set the headsails! Loose the fore-tops'l! Get aloft, some of you, and set the mizzen tops'l."

From the port bow came another salvo—Blaye was firing at them from one side, St. Dyé from the other, now that they could guess what had happened on board the Papillon. But the corvette was moving fast with wind and tide, and it would be no easy matter to cripple her in the half-light. It had been a very near-run thing; a few seconds' delay could have been fatal. Only one shot from the next salvo passed within hearing, and its passage was marked by a loud snap overhead.

"Mr. Mallory, get that forestay spliced!"

"Aye, aye, sir!"

It was light enough to look round the deck now; he could see Eccles at the break of the poop, directing the handling of the corvette, and Soames beside the wheel, conning her down the channel. Two groups of red-coated marines, with bayonets fixed, stood guard over the hatchways. There were four or five men lying on the deck in curiously abandoned attitudes. Dead men; Hornblower could look at them with the callousness of youth. But there was a wounded man, too, crouched groaning over his shattered thigh. Hornblower could not look at him as disinterestedly, and he was glad, maybe only for his own sake, when at that moment a seaman asked for and received permission from Mallory to leave his duties and attend to him.

"Stand by to go about!" shouted Eccles from the poop; the corvette had reached the tip of the middle-ground shoal and was about to make the turn that would carry her into the open sea.

The men came running to the braces, and Hornblower tailed on along with them. But the first contact with the harsh rope gave him such pain that he almost cried out. His hands were like raw meat, and fresh-killed at that, for blood was running from them. Now that his attention was called to them, they smarted unbearably.

The headsail sheets came over, and the corvette went handily about.

"There's the old Indy!" shouted somebody.

The Indefatigable was plainly visible now, lying to just out of shot from the shore batteries, ready to rendezvous with her prize. Somebody cheered, and the cheering was taken up by everyone, even while the last shots from St. Dyé, fired at extreme range, pitched sullenly into the water alongside. Hornblower had gingerly extracted his handkerchief from his pocket and was trying to wrap it round his hand.

"Can I help you with that, sir?" asked Jackson. Jackson shook his head as he looked at the raw surface. "You was careless, sir. You ought to 'a' gone down 'and over 'and," he said, when Hornblower explained to him how the injury had been caused. "Very careless, you was, beggin' your pardon for saying so, sir. But you young gennelmen often is. You don't 'ave no thought for your necks nor your 'ides, sir."

Hornblower looked up at the main-topsail yard high above his head, and remembered how he had walked along that slender stick of timber out to the yardarm in the dark. At the recollection of it, even here with the solid deck under his feet, he shuddered a little.

"Sorry, sir. Didn't mean to 'urt you," said Jackson, tying the knot. "There, that's done, as good as I can do it, sir."

"Thank you, Jackson," said Hornblower.

"We got to report the jolly boat as lost, sir," went on Jackson.

"Lost?"

"She ain't towing alongside, sir. You see, we didn't leave no boat keeper in 'er. Wells, 'e was to be boat keeper, you remember, sir. But I sent 'im up the rigging a'ead o' me, seeing that 'Ales couldn't go. We wasn't too many for the job. So the jolly boat must 'a' come adrift, sir, when the ship went about."

"What about Hales, then?" asked Hornblower.

" 'E was still in the boat, sir."

Hornblower looked back up the estuary of the Gironde. Somewhere up there the jolly boat was drifting about, and lying in it was Hales, probably dead, possibly alive. In either case, the French would find him surely enough, but a cold wave of regret extinguished the warm feeling of triumph in Hornblower's bosom when he thought about Hales back there. If it had not been for Hales, he would never have nerved himself—so, at least, he thought—to run out to the main-topsail yardarm; he would at this moment be ruined and branded as a coward instead of basking in the satisfaction of having capably done his duty.

Jackson saw the bleak look in his face. "Don't you take on so, sir," he said. "They won't 'old the loss of the jolly boat agin you, not the captain and Mr. Eccles, they won't."

"I wasn't thinking about the jolly boat," said Hornblower. "I was thinking about Hales."

"Oh, 'im?" said Jackson. "Don't you fret about 'im, sir. 'E wouldn't never 'ave made no seaman, not no'ow."

BRANDY FOR THE PARSON

By GEOFFREY HOUSEHOLD

Y PARTNER, Tony, says that only an Englishman could be as crazy as this. He is English himself, but it pleases him to be amused by the simple reactions of his own countrymen. Of course, I am not a good citizen—I don't like being a good citizen—but because, strictly speaking, I swindle my country, it doesn't mean that I am prepared to see her landed in international trouble when I could get her out. That is why Petronilla and I must convince the suspicious that the British Imperial Andean Exploration Society never existed at all.

In the second year of the war I transferred to Commandos, and was appointed skipper of a native schooner operating in the Aegean. They gave me only a six months' course in navigation, but never once did I scrape the bottom. So I took to the sea for a hobby, and when I was demobilized and had married Petronilla, I bought from the army the ketch Antigua for us to live in.

On the Disposal Board which sold the army craft there were two chaps who wanted their girl friends shipped to England from occupied territory, so I got the Antigua cheap. They wrote off her Diesel as seized up—which it wasn't—and saw no reason to mention to busy inspectors that her missing spars and sails had been properly laid up and cared for during the war.

I sent for a couple of hard cases from my old crew, and we all went to work on the Antigua. Then we sailed away on our maiden voyage, brought home the Disposal Board poppets and landed them on the Essex marshes without bothering the immigration authorities at all. The job was so easy that it gave us ideas for our future. The Antigua would provide a living as well as living quarters.

We fell in with Tony when he was exploring the commercial possibilities of a deserted wharf up Restronguet Creek. He had been in the navy as a port-control officer. He never went farther to sea than two miles from his office, but he had learned all there was to know about the habits and routine of coast guards, Customs Department and port police. So a firm of importers gave him a swell civilian job. They weren't anxious to fill out forms in quadruplicate for everything they wanted to import, and Tony was just the man for them.

Petronilla, who is a fine judge of character, said he was sour but sound, and we agreed to work for him. It was easy. He gave us our orders and organized the discharge. All we had to do was to turn up on a dark night at the right place on the right tide.

The bottom was knocked out of the business when our politicians withdrew the basic petrol ration. From then on the police had the right to stop any truck anywhere, and check its reason for being on the road. Night traffic was as likely as not to be questioned and examined. Tony's importers decided the risk had become too great for a respectable firm.

Tony knew too much for the directors to be impolite, so they didn't exactly fire him; they gave him a gratuity and told him that his department was closed for reorganization. He came down to spend Christmas with us. I didn't want to say where we were. Let's call it the Coombe River. And when I talk of the ketch Antigua, owned by Bill and Petronilla Rancy, you mustn't expect to find just those names in Lloyd's Register.

Coombe River was as warm in the winter sunshine as the Mediterranean. We lay in deep water, close to the shore. Up the valley you could see a bare hill and the telegraph posts at the side of the main road to the east which marched along the high ground, clear of interruption by all the little fingers of the sea pointing and twisting inland. Within two miles of us there wasn't anything you could call a road—just paths through the woods, and muddy farm tracks.

Over the Christmas week we did ourselves pretty well. Petronilla used to be a high-class accountant. What with our moves from port to port, our ration books and temporary ration cards, she could get food offices, butchers and grocers so hopelessly muddled that we were always allowed to buy twice as much grub as we were entitled to.

Well, of course one can live amply on double rations, and

Petronilla and I and George and Henry—my ex-Commando crew—were feeling poetical after lunch. Petronilla sat at the top of the companion, so that only her ankles kept us company. And very good company they were. "I'd like to get on a horse and ride for miles and miles," she murmured. "Far away from crowded roads and the stink of petrol and prying eyes."

"That's the stuff!" George growled admiringly.

"You mentioned horses," I encouraged her.

"Riding up from the sea," she said, "with the wind blowing through my hair and a keg of brandy across the horse's saddle ——"

"You'd break his back, Petronilla," Tony remarked.

"That's just the trouble," she answered. "I've no experience."

I began to follow her inspiration as closely as if it had been my own. Her thoughts had started—I knew it—from a little footpath that came down through the woods to the foreshore, and had wandered on over the high turf, mile after mile, to the east among the rabbits and the sheep.

"In old days," I said, "smugglers used a string of pack horses."

"What weight can a pack horse carry?" she asked immediately, taking out a pencil.

There Henry chipped in. You could forget for hours that Henry was on board at all, for he never opened his mouth unless he had a simple fact to tell.

"Two 'undred pounds," Henry answered.

Then I remembered that when he had been drafted to my unit, with a crime sheet as long as your arm, he had some inarticulate story about not liking mechanical transport and being used to horses in India. As soon as I discovered that whatever was made of metal just depressed his spirits, he gave me no trouble at all; as for sail, he learned all we could teach him in a week.

When Tony returned to London, he called on his firm of importers. They would not finance us or organize us, but they did say that any brandy of reasonable quality which we delivered to a warehouse in the suburbs would be paid for at three to four pounds a liter.

Petronilla worked it out. Five ponies could carry five hundred liters. After deducting cost of brandy, gear, packsaddles and ponies, there would be a profit of a thousand pounds on the first trip and a lot more on subsequent trips. She called it amortization of transport, but that's what she meant.

Our creek near the Coombe River was perfect. We could come up with any night tide, discharge the cargo, and at dawn be on a yacht-club mooring in the main channel, all clear and ready for Customs. While Tony was away, we rehearsed the drill. We found that at half water the Antigua could anchor within fifty feet of the shore, and that we didn't need a boat. We could lower the barrels overboard and drag them ashore on a line.

Organization on land was much more tricky. When we had our first full-dress conference with Tony, the whole beautiful dream began to fade away.

"We'll have to give it up," I said at last. "There hasn't been a string of pack horses seen in England in living memory. How are we going to explain them? Circus horses?"

Tony suddenly looked up with a flashing grin on his tired naval face. "The British Imperial Andean Exploration Society exercising its ponies," he said.

It was one of those irresponsible suggestions that knock you cold. When we came round, Petronilla and I began to point out the difficulties.

"Nonsense, children!" Tony interrupted. "Don't you see that it puts the whole world with us from the start? All the countryside delighted! Cops benevolent! Farmers helpful! And the dear old ladies running out of their gardens with the last of the week's sugar ration for the sweet ponies!"

"But suppose people start writing letters to the Imperial whatever-it-is?" Petronilla asked.

"Let 'em. Who expects a reply from a public body in less than three months? And I'll find a safe address just so that the letters won't be returned."

Well, we decided that the plan was worth a trial. We bought five Exmoor ponies, and my old friends who sold me the Antigua put me in touch with another Disposal Board, which handled packsaddles and harness, and of course had no market for them. Lovely stuff it was, and dirt cheap. It did you good just to stroke the leather. Then we found accommodation for Tony and Henry and the ponies at a remote Devon farm, where they could all get used to each other and to the pack-saddles. Tony was right. Nobody questioned our story of the British Imperial Andean Exploration Society exercising the pack ponies for its forthcoming expedition.

Petronilla and George and I ran down to the Loire for freight. That sounds like a simple statement, but I wouldn't like any of my readers who have a bit of capital lying idle to think that smuggling is easy. Buying is as risky as selling, for Customs informants are everywhere, and well paid. So don't take it for granted that you won't be caught just because you step ashore with a wooden leg full of wrist watches. The chances are that the Customs know who supplied them and how much he charged; and when they start to search, you'll be lucky if your wooden leg is the only one to be sawed in half.

That's by the way. I just want to point out that you must be sure of your supplier. Ours was an old-fashioned wine shipper with long experience and a reliable staff. His customers paid in pound notes, and anything they wanted for their little ships was brought quietly alongside as extra water in casks. He was expensive, of course, but quality and discretion were guaranteed.

There is also the sea to be considered. To sail round Ushant in February and into the bay is no pleasure trip. We should never have tried it so early in the season if we hadn't been short of funds after fixing up the society and the ponies. The Antigua can ride any sea like a duck, but she made fifty miles of westing, hove to on a sea anchor. You can imagine the discomfort.

Our passage home, running before half a gale from the southwest, was too damn quick. I couldn't carry less canvas with safety, and Lord knows we had little enough! We were just four days from the Loire to the Coombe River, and we never touched the engine once till we were nosing round the woods into our own creek.

I had wired Tony to expect us in anything from five to eight days—a period when there was no moon and the night tide would serve. He was to camp on the high ground and watch the estuary every night for the yellow flash of our signal. That four-day passage, however, was the devil; there was a horrid risk that the expedition would not have arrived

or that they would not be looking out for us. I had to take
it. The only alternative was to heave to off the Devon coast,
and probably be reported as in difficulties or acting suspiciously.

Henry saved us. Plodding down to the west into the teeth of
that wind which howled across the downs, he had been thinking of the Antigua. For two days, according to Tony, the only
remark he made was to state as a fact that the missus wouldn't
let her jibe. She didn't, or I should not be here now. Henry
silently bullied them into forcing the pace, and the first thing
he did when they reached the last camp was to have a look
at the creek. He had not been up under the telegraph posts for
more than half an hour when he saw our flash and answered.

The tide had turned. It was touch and go whether we could
run the cargo ashore in time to get out of the creek into the
main channel. An hour after the signal, we heard the ponies
rustling down over the dead leaves on the hillside. We were
ready for them, barrels in the water and lines ashore. It was
half tide, and the weeds were showing on the banks. We just
had a moment for a word with Tony, and then Petronilla and
I took the Antigua out into the main channel in the dark, leaving George behind with the praam.

That was a nightmare, if you like. At this stage of the ebb,
the twisting channel was never more than fifty feet across,
and the last thing we wanted was to be found high and dry
on the mud in the morning. In the third bend the propeller
was fouled by weeds, and the tide swept us out stern foremost
while we kept steerageway on her with the jib. It was a wonderful piece of navigation, but in our trade, artistry of that
sort is out of place. Everything should go like clockwork.
George joined us just before dawn. He had had to come out at
the bottom of the tide, walking down the bed of the channel
on his hind legs and pushing the praam in front of him.

In the morning, after we had checked in and dropped our
cards on the yacht club, we left George on board and started
out to join the British Imperial Andean Exploration Society. It
took us most of the day to catch up with them. They were ten
miles from the coast. They couldn't go farther because the
ponies had had no rest the previous night, but when you are
inland in Southern England, the sea has no longer any effect

at all on the lives and thoughts of the local inhabitants. The villager will suspect eccentric strangers of coming 200 miles from London, but never of coming 10 miles from the sea.

The camp was in a dry, sheltered valley, under the lee of a clump of thorns. There was a fire going, and Henry was grilling rabbits. Two green pup tents were pitched and the ponies, all in neat little blankets, were picketed and munching happily. Again I had to admit that Tony was right. That camp could no more be suspected of smuggling than could the Archbishop of Canterbury. We belonged, obviously, to the world of Church and State.

Church, I know, seems farfetched, but wherever you find a sort of naval-and-military-club atmosphere, there's a chaplain just around the corner. And just as I was thinking out what I meant, and Petronilla was gnawing the last of the rabbit bones, up the hill came the rector and his wife. They had heard all about the society, though Tony swore he had only seen a shepherd and only said good evening to him. I hadn't even seen a barn or building till the rector appeared. Then I spotted the top of a Norman church tower sticking up above a clump of trees in the vale.

They were as charming as could be, and wanted to know if there was anything they could do for us. Tony kept them amused with stories of the navy in Valparaiso—which he must have heard in the port-control mess—and Petronilla had the effrontery to ask for a bath. She went off down the hill with the rector and his wife, and the last I heard of her she was promising to lecture to the Women's Institute on the objects of the expedition.

She came back in the dark, full of tea, with the salt washed out of her hair. The camp equipment was sketchy—for it had to be kept light—but when we had crawled into the second tent, we found our night's rest luxurious. Our sleeping bag was cozy; the ground was dry and stayed parallel to the horizon; and we didn't have to turn out every four hours to relieve the wheel. Tony complained that the cold at the top of the Andes couldn't possibly be worse than that of an English spring, but even he got a kick out of the open-air life.

It was a convincing expedition when we had loaded up the ponies in the morning. Ground sheets, blankets and tents were neatly folded and hanging down on each side of the ponies to hide the barrels. Here and there Henry slung some odd frying pans and junk, in order that the packs should not look too tidy. He and Tony seemed to have no difficulty in walking twenty-five miles a day. Petronilla and I, who prefer anything but our feet to move us, marched along with them till eleven. That became the routine. We walked just as long as we enjoyed it, and then took a train or bus to some point within easy reach of their next stop.

All went smoothly till we were tramping over the bare downs between Blandford and Salisbury. It was a morning when the wind and rain swept across the grass, and the air was dull gray, like an elephant's back.

A chap came bowling out of the low clouds, driving a tractor as if it were his personal tank, and drew up alongside as we plodded through the driving damp. He was all muffled up in leather, wool and mackintosh, and showed nothing but a lock of lank, dark hair flopping over one amused dark eye.

"Dirty weather," he said, clearing a space in his wrappings to talk through. "Are you going far?"

"Camping under Clearbury Ring," Tony answered.

"The glass is still falling. And, if you like," he offered, "I've plenty of room for you and the ponies."

We didn't much care for close inspection, but it was hard to refuse; and, with the weather as it was, we didn't want to refuse.

"Are you doing this for pleasure?" he asked. "Pilgrimage to Walsingham or something?"

"Well, as a matter of fact," I replied, "as a matter of fact, we are just hardening the ponies of the British Imperial Andean Exploration Society."

Tony congratulated me afterward. He said I had the proper apologetic tone of an Englishman who is caught doing something out of the ordinary.

"This will harden 'em all right," the man agreed. "Well, come along and get dry. My name is Redworth, and my farm is down in the dip there."

And he charged off in his tractor as if he had just got the order to get into position, hull down on the ridge.

We struck across a long slope of plowland, and turned into

the yard of an old, gray-stone manor. Redworth showed us a fine barn, and told us to do what we liked with it. The barn might have been made for us. There was ample light, but when the high doors were shut, farm hands couldn't see inside.

Henry stayed on guard over the barrels, and again our excuse that he would not be separated from his animals sounded pretty feeble, though it happened to be true. The rest of us trooped into the farmhouse for lunch. Redworth did us well, with a prewar hospitality. When the port had circulated, he remarked, "I was born in La Paz."

"How romantic!" said Petronilla, who had been cooing at him for some time. "Where is it?"

"In Bolivia. On top of the Andes."

"Our experience," I said quickly—"Petronilla's and mine, I mean—has been wholly in Central Asia."

"But your exploration society?" he asked. "I suppose it's all planned by experts on the Andes?"

Tony immediately began to throw around the names of patrons and financiers, keeping carefully off geography. The trouble was that we had thought of everything except looking up some patter on the Andes.

"You're going to the Montaña, of course?" Redworth insisted.

He said it as if there were no other possible territory for exploration, so we agreed.

"With those ponies?"

"They have been specially selected by the Royal College of Veterinary Surgeons for high-altitude work," said Tony impressively.

"Then they certainly won't live long in the Montaña. And why do your people go to the expense of shipping ponies, when you could get mules on the spot? Don't think me rude," he added, "but I know the country."

I won't spin out the agony. Even when Petronilla pretended her garter had broken, she couldn't head him off. Redworth found out just how much we knew about the Andes, and kept circulating bottles.

"Now, look here, boys and girls," he said at last. "I'm only a farmer, but I've knocked around the world a bit. What's the racket? And let me say that whatever it is, I think you're sports."

Petronilla is a clever girl. She stopped Tony just as he had started on a marvelous story about selling pack ponies for mountain guns in Palestine.

"Tell him the truth," she said. "He's going to laugh."

Tony and I looked foolish, so she didn't wait. She told him the whole venture right from the beginning, and it didn't lose in the telling. When she dealt with our February voyages to and from the Loire, I felt like Sir Francis Drake.

"And you're going to give this stuff to some black marketeer at three quid a liter, when he'll sell it at seven?" he asked. "What you poor fish need is a marketing board. . . . Now, Rancy, is this stuff drinkable?"

"If it's the same as we tasted in the shipper's office," I said, "it's good, and we'll get four pounds easy."

"If it's the same as you tasted!" Redworth exclaimed. "Do you chaps trust the first fellow who comes along?"

"Any complaints?" Petronilla asked.

Well, that made him chuckle. Then we went out and prized Henry off the barrels, where he was sitting as obstinately as a broody hen, and tapped one.

"I imagine," said Redworth, running the brandy over his palate, "that this is what you tasted."

He drew himself another, and lectured us on the decay of country life. You were not allowed petrol, he said, to visit your neighbors, and when you broke the law and did visit them, there was little or nothing to drink. We revived, he told us eloquently, the glories of the past, when every country gentleman defied the government and filled his cellars and dressed his wife off the backs of the pack horses.

We had another all round; then Redworth asked, "Can I have the rest of that puncheon at five pounds a liter?"

"Six," said Tony.

"I'll make it five ten," he offered, "and we'll talk business for future shipments. Why should those spivs in London have all the good stuff while we have to put up with government port in the country? I'm going to form a syndicate."

Redworth thought that his local market could consume the product of two more trips; and two more were certainly all we dared undertake. People would begin to wonder why the society's ponies needed so much practice.

As for our march to the London suburb, he suggested that we should call it off then and there.

"Send your barrels up by rail," he proposed, "two by two from different stations. Stencil your preposterous society's name all over them, and mark them SPOILED STORES FOR ANALYSIS. The only risk is that one of them might be holed, and that's very unlikely if you put them on a passenger train yourselves."

We took his advice, and sent the nine remaining barrels by four different routes. Tony's firm of importers disliked sending their plain van all round London to pick up the cargo, and I gather they approached the barrels pretty cautiously, but they collected them, and they paid out at three ten.

The next trip was uneventful. The Antigua had a fine run out, with a change of wind just when we wanted it, and there was calm all over the Atlantic on the way back. That came a bit heavy on the Diesel fuel, but we didn't worry. We had earned, so Petronilla said, twelve hundred pounds clear profit on the first trip, and—with a guaranteed market at five pounds the liter—we stood to make two thousand on this. The cross-country march was a picnic. We kept clear of Redworth's farm, to avoid any connection between him and us, and off-loaded in a remote barn belonging to one of the syndicate, where we rebuilt a potato clamp over the top of the barrels. They were ten-liter puncheons this time, to make distribution easier.

Redworth met us at the barn, and paid in pound notes on the spot. He said that half a dozen country houses were taking the stuff, and that two barrels—just to keep up the tradition—were going to the cathedral close. The next cargo, he told us, had been largely ordered by the lawyers and land agents, and he had a request for a small lot of the finest Armagnac obtainable at almost any price we liked to ask.

He was a queer fellow, Redworth. Tony says I am wrong, but I swear he never took a penny profit, and Petronilla agrees with me. He was a passionate country lover, and he was determined to take some of the melancholy out of country life. And then, of course, if you have been born in a Latin civiliza-

tion, you have no patience with governments which put puni-
tive taxes on the juice of the grape.

Tony was all against running a third cargo into the Coombe
River. Petronilla and I, who had less respect for the Customs,
disagreed. We insisted that the first trip did not count, for the
ponies, owing to the luck of our quick passage and Henry's
eye for weather, had come and gone in the dark, and had never
been seen near the coast at all. The Antigua was not suspected.
The yacht club had even invited us to serve on the regatta
committee.

Down in the Loire we had no trouble, and loaded up some
first-class expensive wallop for those lawyers and land agents.
We lost the jib, and very nearly me, off the Lizard, but George
fished me out as I came roaring along the lee quarter on top
of a sea. Meanwhile Tony was having one scare after another.

On the second trip he had, of course, called on the local
landowner and obtained his permission to exercise the society's
ponies on his hillsides. The steep wooded slopes, he said, were
just the practice ground we needed to test the ponies for the
Montaña. We knew all about the Montaña now from
Redworth.

That second cargo had been landed in heavy rain, and the
path through the woods, which at first had been hard, was
thoroughly churned up. Tony thought it wise to find out what
the owner thought before he committed himself to those woods
for a third time.

He left Henry and the ponies a day's march away, and went
to pay a call at the big house in the most correct naval manner. The landowner was cordial as could be, but much too
curious; he was puzzled by the hoofmarks.

"I see you give your ponies more weight coming uphill," he
said. "What do you load them with?"

"Water," Tony replied. "We pack it in skins, to find out what
weight they can carry on any angle of slope. Every detail is
scientifically checked."

The man was not in the least suspicious, but it was certain
that the whole district would know that the society had taken
its pack ponies down to the water, and certain that the Customs
would wonder why. In the country an exciting visitor such as

the British Imperial Andean Exploration Society is a heaven-sent topic for conversation.

When the local sergeant of police deliberately came up to the camp for a longish chat, Tony told him plenty about weights and angles, and added that this was the last journey before the expedition embarked for South America and that the ponies were moving back toward London the next day. The sergeant went away happy, but the game was up.

Tony had to work fast, for we were due in a couple of days. The first, immediate essential was to send Henry and the ponies twenty miles to the east, and that he did. He said good-by to the landowner and other casual friends around the Coombe River, and thanked them for their help and courtesy. In our experience there's no man or woman in England—especially if not asked for a subscription—who isn't thrilled to help explorers.

For us in the Antigua it was always nervous work creeping upriver in the dark, for we couldn't tell what might have happened while we were away. We were ready for any disaster. So it was not altogether a surprise when we nearly ran down Tony in a hired dinghy as we were about to change course into the creek. He had been out there for two nights pretending to fish.

We took him aboard and he gave us the news. If the ponies again left tracks down to the shore, he explained, on the very night of the Antigua's arrival, someone was sure to notice the coincidence, and the police would have every excuse to call at the camp and search the packs.

"It has cost us three hundred quid," he said, "but I think we'll get away with the cargo. Can you take the Antigua along-side the road, Bill?"

"What do you think she is?" I snapped. "A buffalo?"

Knowing Tony's nautical proficiency as I did, it wouldn't have surprised me if he had proposed to tie up the Antigua in a car park. I misjudged him. He had a really promising plan. He explained with some warmth that at the entrance to the next blasted creek a bend in the road came down to within a hundred feet of high-water mark.

We dived into the saloon to look at the chart. There was a mile of mud between us and the road, and it was doubtful if there would be enough water for the Antigua to get close in-shore. The tide was making, however, and would float us off again if we went aground. So the gamble was good.

"Run up as close as you can," Tony said. "Then I'll row ashore. I've a bicycle hidden under the hedge, and in about an hour I'll bring the transport."

We waited long enough for him to be well on his way, and then began to close in to the shore on the top of the tide. There was little traffic on that road after midnight. George paddled ahead in the praam, taking soundings. Once across the mud, he found a steep-to beach of broken shale. I went ashore and looked at the afternoon's high-tide mark. I reckoned that I could risk shoving the Antigua's bows into the land, foot by foot, until she touched, especially if we piled all the cargo forward, ready to be lowered overboard.

We could hear Tony's transport half a mile away. When it arrived—a great black bulk against the sky, looking unneces-sarily large—I touched the beach. As soon as the barrels were overboard, the bows rose clear, and Petronilla, who was stand-ing by the engines, went astern and anchored.

Of all the things! That transport was an enormous caravan, marked MacGinnis' Mammoth Fair, towed by a Diesel trac-tion engine. The three of us and MacGinnis had the stuff in-side, where the swing boats were carried, in less than a quarter of an hour. Tony told us where to find his camp, and they rumbled off into the night.

We were all safe on our moorings in the morning, and the Customs turned us inside out. I don't blame them. They had, thank the Lord, no reason to connect us with the ponies, but it was the third time that we had come into the river after dark. They searched even the fuel tanks and the mattresses, and when we complained of the damage, they merely told us in a nasty way that it would teach us to arrive during daylight in the future.

They found nothing. There wasn't even a smell except Pe-tronilla's perfume—bought in England, of course. She broke a bottle accidentally, in case the barrels of brandy had left a faint memory behind them, and then painted herself up to look like a girl who had to have her particular Fleurs de Castor Oil even on the high seas.

We remained in the Antigua for twenty-four hours, putting things to rights, and then joined the society's camp. We found Tony asleep. He had had four nights without shutting an eye, and only catnaps in the day. When he woke up, he filled in the gaps of his story that he hadn't had time to tell.

After sending Henry and the ponies farther inland, he had a tough day in the local market town looking for transport. One truck driver, when asked if he would like to earn a hundred quid, had simply walked off. Another, in charge of a furniture van, had said he wouldn't risk any monkey business for less than five hundred. It was only when Tony was bicycling out of town, convinced that we should have to throw the cargo overboard, that he had seen the three caravans of swings and dodge'em cars belonging to MacGinnis' Mammoth Fair. It wasn't very mammoth, and he guessed that MacGinnis might be glad of some spare cash while wintering on the south coast. MacGinnis turned out to be a sport. Most show people are. He stood out for three hundred quid when he heard what the job was, but he did it.

They drove inland with the cargo, and at first light had a desperate half hour, beating about for a place near the roadside where the load could be safely dumped. At last they turned into a gravel drive which led to some important house and was bordered by a neglected shrubbery of laurels and rhododendrons. They shoved the barrels into the bushes, and prayed that the gardener wouldn't choose that day to start pruning or sweeping up the leaves. The next night Tony and Henry picked up the load with the ponies and returned to camp.

For this last journey we chose a new route, well to the north of our usual track, through the deep lanes and meadows of the Somerset border. Some of our camps were not so lonely as we should have liked; on the other hand, the curiosity we aroused was all fresh and innocent—until, that is, we fell in with the press.

We never had any trouble with reporters. They don't look for stories on top of the downs; but in the vale, passing close to one bustling little market town after another, we were news. On the night before we reached the sheep and the short turf and safety, we had a call from an enterprising lad who worked for the local paper.

Tony filled him up with pink gin and Redworth's yarns of the Andes. In three more days we intended to sell the ponies and disappear into the mass of respectable citizens, so it didn't much matter what he said about the British Imperial Andean Exploration Society. The only information Tony would not give him was the personnel of the expedition. He threw out broad hints that the object of the society was to look for a special uranium in the Montaña, that we were prominent scientists and that on no account should our names be mentioned.

The newsman ate that up. He was enormously impressed by the trust we had placed in him. He asked if he might take a photograph of the string of ponies when we climbed up to the downs at dawn. We said that we should be delighted, so long as he didn't mind our hats being pulled well down over our faces.

He took his shots of us, and we went on our way, striking southeast along the edge of Salisbury Plain, then over Cranborne Chase and home like the swallows—which were just arriving—to that lonely barn and the potato clamps. Tony remained on the spot to collect from Redworth, and Petronilla, Henry and I took the ponies down to Dorchester market. At our last camp we made a bonfire of the pack saddles, and that, we thought, was the last of the British Imperial Andean Exploration Society.

Tony joined us in Dorchester with the cash. Our total profit for the three trips—after Petronilla had conscientiously deducted repairs to the Antigua and yearly depreciation—was nearer six thousand than five thousand. The ponies were in fine condition; on them, too, we made a profit. We handed the proceeds to Henry as a special bonus.

We were feeling on top of the world, and telephoned Redworth that we would all like to come over and say good-by. He was in a dither. What with Bolivian excitement and English reticence, he was so obscure that I could get no sense out of him. At last he said, "Haven't you read The Times?" and hung up.

I hadn't. I grabbed a copy off the table in the hotel lounge and had a look. You know those gorgeous photographs on the back page of The Times. English countryside. Fields of wild daffodils. Flights of geese on the marshes. Old cider presses under snow. And so on. This was one of the finest they ever printed. You looked up to the crest of the downs, and thorn and grass were bending before the wind, and there on the sky line was the string of ponies, beautifully spaced, moving together, looking like a frieze modeled against the racing clouds. Underneath was the caption: THE RETURN OF THE PACK HORSE. THE BRITISH IMPERIAL ANDEAN EXPLORATION SOCIETY EXERCISING ITS PONIES.

We hired a car, and within twenty minutes we were out of that hotel and on our way down to the Coombe River. After that publicity, and a fake address for the society, and no answer to any of the letters addressed to it, the cops were sure to make some inquiries. So we all sailed over to Ireland, where our faces weren't known. By the grace of God, there was nothing whatever to link the Antigua with the society and its ponies!

When we had settled down comfortably in a sheltered little anchorage on the Galway coast, I sent Redworth an unsigned picture post card with our address. In a few weeks he wrote us a most discreet letter, just giving the local news as if it had nothing at all to do with us.

He said that he and a dozen other farmers had been bothered by the police about a certain British Imperial Andean Exploration Society, and that none of them knew why. The society had seemed to them quite genuine.

"I have been making a few inquiries on my own," he went on, "and it seems that our poor old country is being shot at again. I cannot imagine what on earth induced this society to call itself Imperial. I hear that there have been strong protests from every single South American republic that owns a bit of the Andes, and that when the Foreign Office swears there isn't and never was such a society, it simply makes things worse, for there's a wild rumor going the round of the embassies that we're after uranium deposits. It looks as if they might hold up our meat shipments, and there's not a thing that anybody can do about it."

But that is where he was wrong. I could write this story. And I have.